THE
WAY
AHEAD

— Book 3 —

THE
WAY
AHEAD

— Book 3 —

Kaleb England
aka NorskDaedalus

Podium

To my beta readers
Roland Hansson, Aelia Aeldyne, Pel-Mel, Magma,
Pastafarian, Heavenly Daoist, and w1k3d

Cover design by Podium Publishing

ISBN: 978-1-0394-1603-1

Published in 2022 by Podium Publishing, ULC
www.podiumaudio.com

THE
WAY
AHEAD

— Book 3 —

CHAPTER 1

Settling Off

"So. I just want to be very clear about this." Edwin suspiciously eyed his companion. "You're *sure* that this won't hurt, won't permanently fuse us together into some kind of abomination, won't create an utterly unbreakable bond between us, won't corrupt me into something else, won't turn me into your eternal servant—"

"Yes! *Blight*, Edwin, why are you so worried? You're usually so much more willing to go along with this sort of thing," Inion cut him off with a cocky grin, her dark green hair drifting around her head as though she were floating underwater.

Edwin rolled his eyes. "Well, *usually* I'm not about to allow a *literal fey*—who, I will remind you, are infamous for trying to trick foolish mortals into silly contracts—to perform a binding ritual to attach herself to my *physical body*. I'm *still* skeptical about that deal we made about letting you watch me in exchange for general help, and this is *way* more . . . intimate."

"Oh come on, Edwin. It's not a binding ritual, it's a magical ritual meant to transfer my binding point from the spring to the fey-primed Skill that manifests in and across your body."

"That explanation literally included both the words *ritual* and *binding* in it."

"Did it? Hmm. Well, *that's* on your language for not having adequate vocabulary, then."

"We don't . . ." He sighed. "Never mind."

It may not have made Edwin feel any better, but he was already sitting half reclined in Inion's pond, Fey's Caress at full bore turning his skin and hair to water, while the fey was flitting around, arranging floating plants in an approximate circle around him. "And you're *absolutely certain* this won't have any negative consequences for me in the long run?"

No matter how many times he'd done it, Edwin wasn't sure if he'd ever get used to being able to see his muscles exposed through his "skin." His Anatomy Skill *loved* it, naturally—in the week it had taken to get him prepared for this, it had already passed level 20, higher than even Flying had reached and he used that almost *constantly*. Because of course he would.

"Yes! Now, calm down or something might *actually* go wrong."

"You're not doing a very good job of reassuring me, you know."

"Oh, you'll be *fine*. It's only for a few hours anyway."

The idea was "simple," apparently. While Inion was bound to her spring and thus sharply limited in power anywhere else, she could change the exact target for her binding relatively easily if it wasn't a "major" change—namely, something of the same type of material and in close proximity. With a newly acquired Skill that allowed him to change the composition of his skin in a very feylike manner, Edwin could sit in her pond and be about as "minor" of a change as possible. Theoretically. Assuming nothing went wrong.

Of course, even a complete success still meant that he'd have a real-life fey *literally* bound to him, physically as well as contractually, which Edwin still wasn't sure how to process. Still, once they left the Verdant, and the magic-disrupting barrier that surrounded it, Inion planned to bind to a river, possibly even the Rhothos itself, and leave Edwin once again to his own skin.

He'd even required an oath as binding as he could sufficiently wrangle that Inion would not harm him in any way during the transfer, and that she would leave him as soon as she could, making all reasonable effort to ensure that "as soon as she could" came around *quickly*. Edwin was almost positive he'd messed up somehow, though. Maybe-sorta friend or not, Inion was *not* human and it was a constant struggle to remind himself of that, despite how critical it was that he did.

Even so, he was nervous. Inion may have been his only, or at least the closest, thing to a friend he had in this new world and even seemed to genuinely care about his well-being, *and* she was magically obligated to not harm him, but none of those precluded *accidents*.

He screwed his eyes shut as Inion sang a melodious song with neither lyric nor rhyme, keeping them closed as tightly as possible until the itching in his watery skin and the sound around him faded away. He peeked out with a single eye. ". . . Did it work?" he hazarded.

"Ya! You're good!" Inion cheerfully exclaimed, pulling him from the water.

Edwin breathed a sigh of relief as Fey's Caress faded away upon his exit from the pond, returning his skin to its normal, solid and opaque state. He could feel . . . power coursing through him, magical strength flowing through his limbs and torso in a new way that was both disquieting and reassuring at the same time.

Congratulations! For willingly serving as a Bind for an ancient fey, you have unlocked the Fey Supplicant Path!
Congratulations! For fusing yourself with an ancient fey, you have unlocked the Feykind Path!
Level Up!
Fey's Caress Level 16→28

He mentioned how he felt to Inion as he dressed, and she nodded thoughtfully. "That . . . that *sounds* about right? I know there are some fey—we call them fairies—who choose to bind themselves closely to mortals. Those they tie themselves to tend to get some interesting abilities. I've heard of eternal youth, the ability to fly, some transformations, that sort of thing. I doubt you'll really get *too* much that way, 'cause you're not a true Bind and it won't last for very long, but it's not impossible, either. Just part of the magic involved—I become more like *you*, you become more like *me*."

Edwin nodded. Sounded rather fun, all told, and trying to call up his mana was *significantly* easier than it had been previously. At the mention of flight, he took to the air, reveling in the comparative river of mana he was able to call upon, letting him rise some two meters into the air, a good four times higher than his normal limit. "Pity!" he called back down. "I could get used to this."

"Oh? You *want* me to keep you as a Bind?"

"Uh . . ."

"Kidding!"

Edwin breathed a faint sigh of relief as he returned to the ground and gathered his travel possessions together. He also swept through Obairlann one last time, just to ensure he hadn't left anything behind. It wouldn't be the last time he ever came to the little home he'd made for himself deep within the magical Verdant, but it would be the last time for quite a while. He was in a contemplative mood, he mused, running his hand along the living wood frame of the place he'd lived in and trained at for the past year.

It had been a bit of a chore to fully pack up *everything* he could use, including harvesting what crops were ready from his garden, but he'd eventually managed it. He had tried to stack Improbable Arsenal containers endlessly, to see if he could fit everything he had into his pocket, but it unfortunately didn't work.

Whenever he put one container affected by Improbable Arsenal inside of another, only the one farthest inside actually benefited from the Skill. The outer container's increased volume shrank by the exact amount of additional space within the subcontainer. Also, he found that for whatever reason, using Improbable Arsenal on his Apparatus containers, while still functional, was less effective than on more "real" objects, not that it mattered all that much in the end, thanks to the stacking issues.

However, instead of being able to load up on everything he could want, Edwin had to be somewhat pickier with what he'd take with him. Fortunately, he still managed to get most of what was actually *important* packed away, though the result was a bag nearly as big as he was between both the basic backpack and all the stuff and improvised bags strapped onto it.

He was having to leave pretty much all his pottery behind, but with his new Sapper's Apparatus Skill, that wasn't too great a loss. After all, he didn't really have a use for most of his simple clay labware and only really needed to bring materials and potions with him.

Speaking of materials, Edwin had two notable absences from his basic supply for being an Alchemist-*Errant*. Namely, actual explosives and smoke bombs. Sure, the former he could *mimic* through careful use of Firestarting, only made easier with Basic Thermokinesis, but it was still far from reliable. All he *really* had in the direct offense sense was his alchemist's fire, the not-really-a Molotov cocktail he'd devised from firevine. Anything more than that had no assurance it would actually *work*, as his explosive grenades required him to Infuse them while mid-flight, a tactic he had firmly abandoned after many frustrated months of getting it to work even twice in a row, let alone a majority of the time.

No, he needed genuine bombs, preferably ones he could detonate with his Skills but that didn't *require* them to work. If he couldn't get it to reliably work in practice, no way was he ever going to try to do so in actual life-or-death combat. And without grenades, he really didn't have much in the way of true force projection. Hmm. Perhaps he *should* have taken an explosives-related Path, though he wasn't sure what he would have been willing to give away for it.

He almost wished he was back at Clan Blackstone, ironically. Sure, they had enslaved him for a month trying to get him to make cement, insulted and threatened him regularly, and held him a prisoner underground against his will, but they *had* provided him with the materials he needed to make explosives. His homemade kiln, even post-rebuild—*especially* post-rebuild, he just hadn't put the same amount of work into it as its predecessor—simply couldn't get hot enough to turn limestone into lime, which was what he used for all his gear back then. The few times he *had* tried, the bricks had crumbled and given out, breaking under the extreme temperatures well before the limestone he'd collected could react properly.

Thinking back on his escape, it was honestly a *miracle* he hadn't blown himself up while trying to escape. Though, with the benefit of hindsight, Packing likely helped reduce the chance of his "will explode if shaken too hard" arsenal going up in flames. He'd probably gotten much closer to death with that whole escapade than even he had realized at the time, and far closer than he wanted to be in the future.

But that tied back into his other desire of making smoke bombs. What better way to help ensure his safety than to obscure everything that was going on? If he could make it an aerosol dispenser, he might have a decent way to disperse sleeping gas, but more pertinent to the concept itself, he would lose pretty much any straight-up fight he found himself in against a competent foe. His "fight" with the bugbear assassin sent after him by the Blackstones was proof enough of that.

So, the obvious solution was to just never put himself in a straight-up fight. He'd need to obscure what was going on, blanket the battlefield with explosives, and run away. Not necessarily in that order, either, but misdirection would have to be a major tool of his going forward.

Even though his bag felt as light as a feather, compared to the sorts of weights he lifted when training his Skills, it still was about as big as *he* was, once he had everything factored in. Well, nobody could deny that he didn't look like an alchemist if nothing else. Not with the glowing potions tied like Christmas lights ringing his pack. It was kind of nice, in a way.

All of his actually valuable things were in the very bottom of his bag, inside a sealed Apparatus box, and his coin pouch was locked in a similar construction that utilized the way Improbable Arsenal worked—namely, that it didn't expand the opening—to be outright impossible to remove while the Apparatus was active. Dismissing his own conjurations was merely the work of tapping it while activating the Skill again, but breaking them was significantly harder and certainly not subtle.

Edwin had no doubt that there were pickpocketing Skills that could bypass all his precautions, but he had no way to prevent them totally, just make it harder for them. Hopefully they'd be rare, anyway, what with the way the Empire had their Skill Management system set up. It mostly raised the question of how the Phantom Pickpocket Tara apprehended in his first visit to Vinstead got his Class, but perhaps he was just an Outlaw. There had to be a few within the city itself, especially if they were focused on stealth, right? Something to ask while he was in Vinstead.

"Ready?" he asked Inion, shouldering his pack and hefting his walking stick.

"I've been here *so* long, it's strange to leave."

Edwin nodded sympathetically. "I know what you mean, and it's only been a year for me. We'll be back here eventually; I want to harvest that hispera when it reaches maturity in two years if nothing else."

"Always the alchemy with you, isn't it?" she asked, and Edwin took a moment to parse her tone. She didn't sound mad, that much was a relief. Rather, it *seemed* like she was genuinely asking.

He gave a curt shrug. "It's who I want to be. Interacting with people may be a lost cause, but I at least have some hope of figuring out how my chemicals and potions work."

"Who you want to be, eh?" she prodded. Huh. Inion wasn't normally quite this inquisitive about Edwin's personal thoughts. Perhaps moving out got her sentimental?

"Well, I *am* a scientist. Sure, we settle into the role of peeling back the mysteries of the universe—which is amazing and rewarding in its own right—but we don't get *into* science without some part deep down that wants to be a mad scientist, doing all sorts of things that just flatly contradict everything we know about creation. Freeze rays, teleportation, time travel, interdimensional portals, warp drives, lightsabers . . . That's the sort of thing that drives us, on a deep and fundamental level. Because we *want* them to be true, and now I find myself in a world where all that stuff might actually *be* possible?" He shook his head as they drifted along the riverbank. "It's like if I had been told I was going to wizard academy when I was ten, but better because I know how to scientifically test stuff. Everything I thought I knew is vastly incomplete."

"Wizard academy, eh? But you aren't trying to be a mage?"

Edwin shrugged. "I have *no* basis for how to be a decent mage; you've admitted yourself you don't know how to teach me anything." Inion reluctantly nodded. "But science? I can do that. Besides, my mana manipulation is pitiful. Sure, I want to improve it in time, but I already have a solid base for Alchemy, why would I not use that? It doesn't matter if it takes me ten minutes to charge up a dagger with mana if there's no time pressure for it. Doing most of my magic stuff beforehand means I can neatly bypass past-Edwin's mistakes. One day, maybe I'll try to figure out magic without the science, but the science will do nicely until then."

Inion hemmed in agreement as they flew forward.

"You know, I'm kind of nervous this time," Edwin admitted, faced with what he knew to be an invisible wall that kept all the crazy magical stuff—like fey—inside the Verdant.

"Why? Last time you didn't even *notice* it," Inion countered as she toed the line demarcating the forest from the rest of Rhothos.

"Sure . . . but last time I wasn't half fey."

"You're not *half* fey. You're . . . fey-adjacent."

"Still not sure how much of an impact that has, though."

Edwin vaguely mumbled some kind of agreement and brought his hand up toward where the barrier apparently was . . . and felt no resistance.

"Huh. Guess it still doesn't affect me," he noted, uneventfully stepping out of the forest. "You having trouble there?" he asked Inion, who was slowly struggling against the fierce "wind" keeping her penned inside.

"I . . . can . . . *got it*!" She stumbled forward as she pushed through the resistance, recovering her balance before she fell in the dirt, fortunately without needing Edwin's help; if he had tried, who knew how his backpack would react, and he did *not* want to have to repack it all. "It was easier that time," she remarked, brushing imaginary dirt from her arms.

"Glad you have it so easy," Edwin wryly replied. "I'd hate to see you have to work."

Inion stuck her tongue out at him as they floated to the road, and Edwin drew his tone into a more serious one, checking in on his friend, "But you're feeling all right? No water deprivation or sensation of slowly dying?"

She shook her head. "Nope. It feels more like I'm in Obairlann, other than the lower magic out here."

Edwin frowned, trying to sense the mana in their surroundings. It did feel rather anemic and was only made more obvious by directing his Perception toward the task. Using Ritual Intuition, too, there was little of the feel of nature he had come to associate with his surroundings. Instead, it felt more like a faint breeze tapping at the edge of his senses. There was still a hint of life and nature, but it felt like sprawling grasslands rather than the greenhouse-like sensation within the Verdant. "Huh. I think I can feel what you mean."

As they reached the road, Edwin sank back to the ground, taking the strain off Flight.

Level Up!
Flight Level 18→21
Ritual Intuition Level 14→16

Fast leveling or no, the Skill still had a strain on him that was just *tiring*. Granted, he could *probably* keep it up for most of the day thanks to his Stamina and Mana, but doing so would be like if he spent the entire day hiking pre-System. Meanwhile, walking essentially didn't tire him in the slightest. He had plenty of time to level Flight, after all.

He wasn't planning to try and reach Tier 3 until his Alchemy was at least level 120 and he got the Alchemy Specialist Path. By then, Flight and what it evolved into would have had more than enough time to hit level 60, he was sure. He'd make sure to use it as much as possible to help speed it along, but he wasn't pushing himself that fast anymore.

Besides, he could use the Skill's existence as a Path lightning rod to give him security when completing Attribute-granting Paths, giving him another shot to unlock them before he went for the full Tier 3 jump.

Edwin felt much more confident now in his ability to take care of himself. Not only did he have an actual defensive Skill—two if he counted Fey's Caress—but he had Health, First Aid in the 80s, and a whole suite of health potions. He could take a few bumps, even if he couldn't return the favor.

"So how does it work, when you bind to something like the Rhothos? How does it compare to your pond?" he asked Inion as they walked down the road.

"I'll be stronger once I'm bonded to it than with my pond, but it'll also be less localized. Basically, I get more freedom and more power!"

Edwin raised an eyebrow. "Then why weren't you bonded to it before, if it's so much better?"

"Eh"—she waved her hand dismissively—"Aenliss had bonded to its spring so she had a strong claim to it. With whatever is keeping the Verdant separate, though, the main river'll be unclaimed, just for me!"

"What if another naiad is already bonded to it, though?"

"No big deal. The river is big enough to support loads of fey as proper river spirits. It'll just mean the power is divided up some. Still great for me, and still with loads of mobility."

"So again . . . why didn't you do this earlier?"

"Because I had people visiting me, that's why. I enjoyed having my own little cult who came and asked me for wisdom and stuff. I was a big deal back when, I'll have you know!"

"Sure you were," Edwin replied, placating her in a manner he knew would irk her pride, speeding up as he did so.

"I was! Oh, come on. Don't be like that. Edwin! Edwiiiinnnnn!"

Longstrider helped hasten their journey significantly, not that Edwin really anticipated anything else, and the pair found themselves at the bank of the Rhothos by noon. The flooding wasn't as extreme as the last time they had come through, and was even lower than the first time Edwin had come through, but the river was still far larger than anything Edwin had ever seen on Earth, to the point where he couldn't even see the far bank.

Fortunately, there were still plenty of quiet places where the current wasn't as strong, curling into eddies along the bank, forming semi-stagnant pools of water perfect for their purposes.

Before Inion began the ritual, the two of them worked to create a circular hole that would serve as the "circle" for the magic. Inion didn't know much about the basics of what she was doing, just following her instincts and what she had been taught, sort of like how most people could ride a bike, but fewer knew how to *build* one, and possibly knew *why* they worked. Last Edwin had heard, at least, it was still at least marginally debated. Something about knowing the forces involved, but not how they combined?

Anyway. Once the hole was dug, it was a relatively simple matter for Inion to weave some nearby rhoreed into further circles and glyphs for the magic and set them floating around him. As she began the ritual, Edwin sank into Fey's Caress, turning even more of himself than before to water. Huh. Was that what the inside of his bones looked like? Interesting. And those must be his arteries—wow, it was strange to see blood just vanish and reappear elsewhere as the veins switched in and out of being transformed into water.

If he twisted his head—yep, his heart too. Man, he'd have to be *careful* to never turn into wind at this level of the Skill—he'd literally flay himself alive. He kind of wished he had a mirror of some sort, that he could see what his skull looked like. Had his eyes turned to water as well? What was he seeing through? Could he see his brain?

Ooh. Would he be able to evolve or develop this Skill to transform *other* things? It would be an absolutely *phenomenal* Skill for doctors and surgeons: be able to just peek below the skin and into the body's makeup with no harm, no fancy equipment.

"—*done* now, you know. You don't *have* to keep lying there."

Inion's voice broke him out of his thoughts. "Really? That was fast. Everything went that smoothly?"

"Ha! It took me an *hour* to get everything ready because it all went so badly. You were just floating there checking yourself out, didn't even react when I pulled the bond away."

"An hour? No way." Inion just nodded. "Seriously?"

"Ya! Haven't seen you that focused in all the time I've known ya."

Edwin sheepishly withdrew from the water, the transformation fading away as he did so, leaving him slightly damp as the last bit of water clung to his recently re-formed and magically dead skin. He wasn't as cold as he expected, and he directed a bit of Basic Thermokinesis along the surface of his skin to encourage further evaporation while he got dressed.

Level Up!
Adaptive Defense 11→12
Anatomy Level 23→26
Basic Thermokinesis 13→14
Fey's Caress Level 28→35

Adaptive Defense? That was . . . ah, that was probably why he didn't feel cold, wasn't it? It had adapted to help keep him warm? He suspected as much; nice to see it not exactly *confirmed*, but at least lend a bit more evidence to his hypothesis. He didn't feel as bad as he'd expected, with some echos of the power he'd felt when bound to Inion still lingering.

"How does it feel?" Edwin asked, getting dressed as he watched Inion splash around in the river with all the acrobatics of a dolphin and the enthusiasm of an eight-year-old.

"Great! So free, so much space! There's *nobody* else in this river, and it's *amazing!*" she sang out.

Edwin chuckled as his friend played around in the water while he geared up. Fortunately, it didn't end up being *too* complicated, he just needed to be careful to not overbalance when picking up his backpack and slipping it on. Once he was done, he called out, "Okay! We don't have all day!"

"Five more minutes!"

Edwin sighed and conjured himself some solid spheres to practice juggling. It had been a while, but he picked it back up within just a few minutes, and even after Inion finally emerged from the water—soaking wet, naturally—she just floated around watching him for a minute. Eventually, Edwin dismissed the constructs, the blue crystal disintegrating into drifting motes of light, and they set off once more.

Level Up!
Longstrider 18→19

It wasn't quite nighttime yet when they arrived at the Curicnan shrine they'd slept in on their last visit to Vinstead, but it was close enough that they decided to stop anyway. Edwin reclined on his bunk, luxuriating in the feeling of being on a *mattress* instead of in a hammock, and Inion sat at the foot of his bed while they chatted.

"So what exactly *are* you planning now? You've always just said you want to travel, but *where* and *why*? Also, why head to *Vinstead?*"

Edwin shrugged. "Honestly . . . I don't know. I want to get more Alchemy stuff, but I don't really know where I *can* find that sort of thing. I'm hopeful I might be able to find out where it's usually grown and head in that direction, maybe see if I can't be useful in some capacity either here or there.

"As for why Vinstead? Well, I do still have the commitment that comes with being an Adventurer to talk about what Skills and Paths I get." He forestalled Inion's interjection with a raised hand. "I'm allowed to keep some secrets, so whatever you're about to say I shouldn't share, I won't."

Inion frowned. "No, that's not it. Explaining your Paths wouldn't require telling any of my secrets. I was just surprised that you were so open about being an Outsider, you know, what with not wanting to tell *me*, but that's the secret, isn't it?"

Edwin nodded. "Yeah, pretty much. Anyway, I want to keep my end of the bargain, and I want to take a healing course to get properly licensed for using medical Skills, so I don't get arrested or killed for trying to bandage a cut. Plus, a cart of some kind would be rather nice, so I don't have to haul around my every worldly possession on my back. Other than that . . . just a few odds and ends, I suppose, and Vinstead is the primary place I know to get that sort of thing. I'd prefer to not stay that long, but I don't think it'll be possible to avoid Sash . . . Shash . . . the governor forever, may as well get it over with, you know?"

She shrugged. "If you say so."

Edwin mirrored the gesture. "So yeah. It's the closest thing I have on Joriah to a home city and I want to get my bearings, possibly pick up some miscellaneous supplies and Skills, and figure out where I'm going from there."

He fell into silence for a little while, trying to persuade himself that he really *did* know what he wanted and wasn't just wandering . . . well, for the sake of wandering. That's what people who didn't know what they wanted in life did, and he was better than that! He was only out here because he *wanted* to see the world and expand his knowledge! It wasn't at all because he just needed to get *out* of Obairlann before it started feeling claustrophobic, before the loneliness set in too quickly. . . .

And he most *certainly* wasn't wandering in the hopes that he might be able to find people who liked him, then moving on before they could get sick of him.

He breathed out and closed his eyes. Nothing good would come out of that line of thinking. Not tonight, at least.

"G'night, Inion."

"Good night, Edwin."

Watchful Rest made sleeping interesting. Some tiny part of Edwin stayed awake throughout the night, letting him know as the air cooled overnight, when the wind picked up outside, whipping around their little shelter. Then, when the first birds began their morning symphony and the sun began to rise.

Because he wasn't *actually* awake, though, he only got vague impressions, and he wasn't sure if he genuinely experienced all that in real time or just had it all shoved into his memories upon waking up. There was no conscious thought, at least not yet. It also meant he didn't get any System notifications until after he was actually awake.

Level Up!
Watchful Rest 8→9

Magical sleep or no, Edwin was still bleary-eyed when he dragged himself out of bed, extricating himself around Inion, who had lain down next to him at . . . some point. Clearly, Watchful Rest still had a ways to go before he could actually feel safe at night in unknown territory if it missed her joining him at some point.

Interestingly, it almost looked like Inion was *asleep*, which was certainly an unusual development. He gently prodded her, and her eyes fluttered open, "Whazza. . . . Oh, hi, Edwin." She yawned, sitting up and stretching provocatively.

Edwin rolled his eyes and turned away. Once upon a time, he would have been flustered, but it was hard to not be inured to the fey's antics after a year of living in close proximity.

"Get up and get dressed. I'd like to make it to Vinstead before noon."

There was a bit of good-natured grumbling as Inion got ready, and Edwin took the time to have some breakfast; he was *trying* to develop good eating habits, but the food he had tasted like cardboard. Ugh.

He'd need to figure out some trick for living with Arcadian Elixir, wouldn't he?

He wasn't an *idiot*; he figured out what the Skill was doing to him within the first day of having it. Anything he had made since his tier-up had tasted *sublime*, whereas anything he'd made before then, including most of his travel food, tasted bland and flavorless by comparison.

Even turning off the Skill—which was *surprisingly* difficult, it kept trying to spring back up and if it did so, whatever he was making would be enhanced by it—didn't help, because he'd already *tried* food made with the Skill, so turning it off didn't do anything to help with the fundamental problem.

Fey food was a well-worn staple of fantasy, and considering the unusual degree to which Joriah liked to cleave to that standard, it wasn't a surprise that a feylike Skill pertaining to food would mean he'd get a similar effect of his own. At least he wasn't dependent on an outside source for it, so *he* could enjoy the fruits of his labor.

The primary question he was left with was whether or not the Skill actively made other things he tasted *worse*, or if what he ate with the Skill really *was* that delicious and filling, as it would impact how moral it would be for him to make other people food. Maybe both? In any case, he should default to caution until he knew better. He *absolutely* didn't want to deal with the ramifications of making a bunch of people addicted to, well, him.

In the meantime, he was stuck eating cardboard. As the Skill would only level *up*—and at level 8 the same food made with the Skill was easily twice as good if not *more* than made without it—he should make sure that he got rid of all his old food before it started tasting even *worse*. There had to be some way to cheat this, he was sure. Maybe he could make a spice mix, then apply that to food he didn't make? Even if he only tasted the spice, it might be enough to get him through this. Something to try once he got to Vinstead, perhaps. He could probably dry some of his herbs and make them into a spice.

Somewhere in the distance, a hawk cried out. Edwin narrowed his eyes looking for it and spotted a bird diving toward the Rhothos. It snagged some prey from the river and took off, flying a short distance before settling on the ground and starting to eat its meal.

Edwin blinked and came back to himself. It must have been half a mile away, but he could still see the scene in startling clarity. "Perception and Seeing is weird."

Inion nodded in vague agreement, and Edwin let his mind wander once more as they carried on with their walk.

Level Up!
Longstrider 19→20

Getting into the city was relatively uneventful, especially without Inion there to cause problems. She was splashing around in the Rhothos, and Edwin would see about meeting up with her as soon as it was practical, which they both knew may be a while. Meanwhile, he just handed his Adventurer's license to the guards—different ones than last time—answered a few questions about what he was bringing in, and that was it.

He took a bit of a winding route to the garrison, which was *absolutely* intentional and not at all because he got turned around at one point, and entered through the massive front gates under the watchful eye of Xares, before taking some increasingly familiar stairs to Rizzali's office. Best to get it out of the way early, and if history was anything to go off, Tara might track him down while he was there and spare him the effort of finding *her*.

Rizzali's office was no different from the last time Edwin was here. Piles of paper buried the solitary desk against the leftmost wall, and a wooden chair stood facing the wooden construction. The far side of the room had no wall, instead opening into the grand space above the central foyer, giving Edwin a clear view of Xares's shoulder. The gnome's head was initially only visible as a shock of blue hair amid a sea of off-white, but when Edwin stepped through the doorway, it snapped up to assess him.

"Edwin! My friend! Back at last! Delightful new Class you have there, you simply *must* enlighten me. Sit, sit!"

Edwin smiled as he set his bag down and pulled up the chair.

Study Skills

"Well, you're braver than I, that's certain," Rizzali noted, reclining in his seat as he made the last few notes on his stack of papers. "Taking two Paths pertaining to the fey?" He shook his head, whistling softly. "This is what sets the successful Adventurers apart from the failures, I do suppose.

"Although I must say, your Skill Researcher Path . . . it seems quite promising. It is quite worthy of a special note, and it seems as though it were relatively simple to earn? If the information you provided is actionable, we may seek you out for a commendation of some sort."

Edwin nodded and had a thought strike him. "Oh yeah," he spoke up. "I was wondering about something. How many Adventurers *are* there, anyway?"

"Well, that's a tricky question, young man." The gnome set his papers off to the side as he finished writing on them, and Edwin caught the brief flash of a Skill illuminating them as he did so. "As the individual identity of Outlaws is rarely accounted—how does one tally the absence of something? However, it is estimated that some half of all Outlaws in Rhothos are Adventurers, a number which I can only commend Lady Tara for, as said count is largely from her work."

"I thought she hated Adventurers?" Edwin cut in, his brow furrowed.

"Lady Tara is an exemplary Enforcer and doesn't allow her personal feelings to interfere with the duties of her office. The benefit of Adventurers for the grander society is not found in their futile efforts to do the work of the guards, but in their sacrifice providing new information for the Registrars that we might always determine greater Skills and Paths for future generations."

"What prevents someone from just lying?"

"We have our ways," the Registrar replied with a smirk. "And as all Skills have weaknesses, I shall not reveal what it is to you lest you determine how to circumvent it."

"*That's* what you get from knowing Adventurers' complete Classes, isn't it?" Edwin realized. "So you can try to figure out what their pressure points are."

"Their what?"

"Their, uh . . . weak points. The places where you can leverage just a bit of strength to cripple a powerful Skill."

Rizzali nodded in understanding and winked at him. Yeah, that checked out, and Edwin probably could have figured it out himself if he had put more than two minutes of thought into the matter at some point, but he had never really bothered.

"What about my unknown Skills, then? If you don't know them . . ."

The gnome dismissed the concern with a sweeping hand. "I needn't know the specifics of your Skills that allow you to . . . Take notes, yes?" Edwin nodded. "And an Efficient Space variant, and while such being at Tier 2 is *exceptionally* rare, it is something only a mage can take advantage of and thus not useful to us."

". . . Fair enough," Edwin conceded.

"In addition, Tara vouched for you personally, which is *far* from typical, I assure you. Speaking of, did you have any questions for me in my capacity as Skill adviser?"

"Yeah, actually," Edwin recalled, "I had a few. What's the Skill set for normal alchemists like? I'm curious how mine compares."

Rizzali's eyes briefly flashed with a Skill and he rifled through a stack of papers, consulting one near the bottom. He muttered something and tossed it to the side, then hopped off his high chair and started ransacking some unseen drawers in his desk. Just as Edwin began to zone out and start meddling with Almanac, Rizzali jumped up clutching a paper.

"Aha! Here it is. I knew I still had the basics stashed somewhere. Let's see . . ." he muttered, scanning over the page, eyes aglow with some ability. "Process, Herbalism, Mixing, Measure, Reading, and Writing!"

"No Alchemy?"

"If you had found a way to directly obtain Alchemy as a basic Skill, young man, you'd be the hero of Panastalis! But no. The Potioneer Path upgrades Eating to Potion-Making, and taking the Alchemist Path once more brings the Skill to proper Alchemy by the third tier."

"So late?"

"My dear friend, the third tier is usually considered a mark of adulthood! You truly were secluded in your youth, were you not?"

That was . . . true enough, so Edwin vaguely nodded in agreement.

"What else? I may have exactly *none* of those Skills, but it's still interesting to learn about what they have to work with."

In response, the gnome just handed the paper to Edwin. It took a moment for Polyglot to help him adjust to the written language, and a bit longer to parse the lingo being used, but he got there in the end. Hmm . . . Let's just copy this down into the Almanac while we're here. . . .

Edwin ignored the conjecture and hypotheses scribbled all over the page, as well as what the Class name should be at each step of the way, focusing instead on the bare essentials, but even that provided a wealth of new information.

Walking through Sentry: Standing, through Sentry again: Sentry's Vigilance, through Marathon Reader: Project Focus

Seeing through Artist: Colorimetry, through Nighttime Hunter: Thermal Vision

Language through Chanter: Chanting, through Astrologer: Timing

Identify, Beginner: Common Knowledge, Alchemist: Alchemist's Insight

Status, Novice: Status Log, Expert: Detailed Record

Herbalism, Medic: Poultice, Potioneer: Potency

Reading + Scholar: Book Smarts + Mental Memorialist: Mental Notebook

Writing + Scribe: Transcribing + Marksman: Steady Hand
Mixing + Cook: Emulsify + Blacksmith: Alloy
Measure + Merchant: Precision Measurement + Alchemist: Allocate
Process + Alchemist: Induce Reaction + Batch Alchemist: Speed Reaction + Practiced Alchemist: Potent Reaction
Eating + Potioneer: Potion-Making + Alchemist: Alchemy

"I expected more uses of the Alchemist Path, I'll admit."

"That's the common mistake! Utilizing only a single Path can result in your Skills merging with one another in function, reducing the spectrum of distinct abilities you can call upon. Whereas with our expertise, it is possible to gain a vast array of utility Skills! After all, the Alchemist Path would never grant the capabilities of Sentry's Vigilance!"

Edwin furrowed his brow. "Oh yeah, what *does* that do? What's up with the Sentry Paths in general, actually?"

Rizzali nodded, and Edwin noticed a faint flash of Skill light around his ears as he answered, "'Tis a common upgrade for many tedious jobs. Standing does exactly as it suggests and enables its users to stay motionless for exceptional lengths of time. Sentry's Vigilance chases off weariness and sleep while standing. Together, they enable alchemists to brew potions that take hours or even days of continuous attention."

"Huh." Okay, he had to admit, that was pretty neat. Edwin made a quick note in the Almanac about their functions. "I see how that'd be useful. I would have never thought of that on my own."

A beaming smile spread across the gnome's face. "That is what we provide! And why I am always oh so very sad when a promising individual breaks free from the Management because they feel as though they know better than millennia of accumulated knowledge."

Edwin nodded. "Makes sense, I suppose. Man, I really wish I had you when I first—" He caught himself just in time. "Actually, nope, can't say that. I wish I had you as an adviser a few years ago. Out of curiosity," he added, "what *does* Walking give if evolved using Alchemist?"

"Walking and Alchemist . . ." Rizzali looked into the air and tapped his desk. "Ah! Alchemical Stamina, which improves the efficiency of stamina-restoring alchemical potions. Not terribly useful, you understand?"

Edwin nodded. "Wow. You guys really have a lot cataloged, don't you?"

The gnome spread his (tiny) arms at the piles of paper around the room. "These are my most common references, and you can see how many I have called upon in the previous two seasons alone."

"So I was wondering what a lot of those Skills did? It's not on the paper? Can you help fill me in on that sort of thing?" Edwin asked.

"But of course! As it is directly related to your profession, I can answer any questions you may have about the Skills! Unfortunately, I am not cleared to discuss further Skills that you do not possess. If you desire such, Xarenia and its Grand Library has the records you would seek and is open for all scholars."

"Wait, why?"

"Imperial policy. I believe the reasoning I was given was ensuring that such information does not fall into too many hands."

"How does going to the library help with that, though?"

"How many blue-feathered youths would be liable to make the journey and then go diving off trying to determine their own Classes? With a single location, it aids in increasing the barrier for such individuals."

"Fair enough, but it still doesn't seem like that would be enough for the people living near it?"

"Young man, would you like to hear what I have to say or not?"

"Right, right. Sorry."

The gnome cleared his throat and began, a Skill soothing his throat as he spoke. Edwin, for his part, scrambled to get it all written in the Almanac as the Registrar provided his explanation.

Standing: Reduces strain when standing. By the time it hits level 60, can be done indefinitely and even when sleeping

Sentry's Vigilance: Pushes off need for sleep while standing, with the maximum length increasing with level

Project Focus: Aids with attention span when focusing on a single task

Colorimetry: Improves color perception—apparently useful in some potions

Thermal Vision: Allows for estimation of temperature with a glance; something about Detailed Record?

Chanting: Reduces vocal strain and improves rhythm, useful for potions that require actions repeated on a tempo

Timing: Accurate estimation of time passed; apparently useful with Detailed Record

Alchemist's Insight: Learn quality and effects of ingredients/potions (Man, that sounds useful.)

Status Log: Look back on previous System notifications

Detailed Record: System records all uses of Skills. Such as the exact temperature of an object measured with Thermal Vision, or time passed with Timing. (Oooh. That's *cool.*)

Herbalism: Aids in the growing and harvesting of herbs—more specific than Gardening, usually only T2 or above

Poultice: Make medical potions with improved quality, power, and proficiency

Potency: All potions made are more potent

Reading: Read faster

Book Smarts: Recall information from books, and where to find information in a read book easier.

Mental Notebook: Store memories and notes in a mental book with perfect recall

Writing: Speed of writing is improved

Transcribing: Ability to copy a text precisely greatly improved

Steady Hand: Improves hand-eye coordination and reduces hand shakiness

Mixing: Mixed ingredients are mixed more completely; also includes what is being mixed in Detailed Record

Emulsify: Incompatible elements are more easily mixed

Alloy: Mixed ingredients become permanently mixed

Measurement: Similar to Numeracy, but based around counting and quantities, allows Detailed Record to access the information

Precision Measurement: Increased precision of measurement, improving Detailed Record precision

Allocate: Dole out precise amounts of substances (exactly 1 ~~gram~~ grain of water, etc)

Process: Following a formula or recipe has improved accuracy and is Recorded

Induce Reaction: A Catalyst Skill, makes components that might not react to do so

Speed Reaction: Speed up a targeted reaction

Potent Reaction: The results of anything made that has a reaction involved have the end product be stronger

Potion-Making: Improved proficiency and potency with potions

"That's a lot of potency improvements." Edwin whistled as Rizzali finished and took a sip of water from a goblet retrieved from his desk somewhere.

"Indeed. Their quality is unmatched," the gnome agreed.

"I wasn't expecting Detailed Record to be so impressive, either. How'd that combination show up?"

"Such is the might of the Empire's knowledge. It was originally found by a warrior who had little use for its endless tales of how her strikes landed true or missed. However, such information was capitalized upon by my predecessors, who swiftly determined which Classes could benefit from said information more than other possible Status upgrades."

"So how do you know that what you have is the best possible Skill evolution?"

"*The* best? Alas, we usually fall short of such a prestigious standard, as the truly fantastic Skills require accomplishments that are simply impractical to be obtained by many, be it on account of time, lethality, or unknown factors.

"However, all we have determined is still more than satisfactory, and even beyond the third tier we are capable of providing a stunning amount of guidance. In time, we can hopefully determine in totality which Skills are optimal within the fourth tier and so ensure that none waste their precious Skills on failed Paths."

"I . . . guess that makes sense? Also, that reminds me of what I was going to ask a while ago. Adventurers? How many are there, that they can keep expanding what you know?"

"Ah, well as I said, half of Rhothos's Outlaws had been registered as Adventurers, and while I am not the only Registrar in the province, far from it, I am rather commonly consulted among your kind. I have . . . oh, perhaps two or three dozen whom I see regularly?"

"That's it?" It seemed . . . low. There had to be hundreds of thousands of people at least living in Vinstead alone, and only a few dozen Adventurers in total?

Rizzali nodded sadly. "Alas, on account of them frequently ignoring the quality advice dispensed by my peers and I, it is quite common for Outlaws and Adventurers to gain Skills they are ill-suited for, and when combined with a hazardous lifestyle, very, very few survive long. I have met and registered hundreds of Adventurers, yet only the truly exemplary survive. Sadly, those few inspire the hotheaded youths who think that being an Adventurer means *they* will be exemplary and so seek to reject their citizenship. Those poor, poor fools. If I could strengthen the Management, I would. But alas, only the Emperor knows what is required to obtain or strengthen it."

Ouch. That had to sting. It sounded like Rizzali had had something personal happen, but Edwin didn't pry. It wasn't his place. He tried steering the conversation to something less tragic.

"Do you have any advice for my Flight Skill? You must have seen something like it before, as you work with avior?"

"I have seen the *Flying* Skill, yes. *Flight*, however, particularly magical, is utterly outside of my experience. Mages are truly, truly rare. Even here, where plant mages are so common, that is still mere dozens out of thousands of citizens. With such few numbers, we are mostly blind to their grand potential, and so we find that their abilities are squandered. Such individuals have their own Registrar whom they tend to visit, and I know not their stratagems."

"Huh. So not many people can use magic, then?"

Rizzali shook his head. "With precious few exceptions, no. Those who can are greatly valued by all of Rhothos for their grand nature-related spells, but every single individual is unique and irreplaceable, making it problematic when one does pass on, no matter how rare such an occurrence may be."

"Wait, they don't die much? Why's that?"

"One of their Skills, I do believe. This is once again *far* out of my specialty, but one of the few established Path guides aids them in upgrading Eating all the way to Boundless Verdancy, a Tier 6 Immortality Skill."

"An Immortality Skill? That's a category?"

"Any Skill that adds more to your life span than it takes to level it is considered such. Immortality itself is perhaps the most well known of such, as it adds one year to your life span every level, and levels once a year."

"That seems . . ."

"Less than ideal, yes. Even when the Skill is upgraded, all too often it does not become an Immortality Skill of its own, but rather something which bestows some benefit based on age. Losing immortality after decades of use . . . it is rarely pleasant, and a pitfall we have steered many away from. Unaging, Eternal Youth, Incorruptible, and Living Legend are all generally considered superior, as they do not require one to never tier up again to continue being immortal."

"How do you get *those*?"

"That is restricted information."

Edwin tried to control himself, but failed quite quickly. "Restricted? *Restricted?* You know how to make people immortal and you're withholding the information? You're almost *literally killing* people by not giving them the tools you *have* that would save them."

Rizzali held up a hand to calm Edwin, and he reluctantly complied.

"It is restricted because the Skills and Paths required to get said Skills are nonreplicable by the general populace. Incorruptible requires no less than two uses of the Unkillable Path, among other hazardous Paths and Skills, which I believe you have experience with? Yes. To obtain that Path, one must survive a situation that would ordinarily kill them save for extraordinary circumstances. While there have been attempts to determine a systematic and relatively safe way to obtain Unkillable, the high life cost has forestalled significant progress from being made. Is it immoral to pursue an avenue of immortality at the cost of so many lives? And what if an Outlaw were to obtain the secrets to the Skill? There is one Immortality Skill which has been found that requires the regular consumption of, and bathing in, the blood of children. Would you like such knowledge to be publicly known, Edwin?"

He closed his mouth, slightly mollified but still indignant. "Well . . . no, but maybe? But also, shouldn't you be pursuing that sort of thing really heavily? You're still kind of condemning people to death through inaction."

The gnome inclined his head in agreement. "I will not dispute that such Skills are tremendously beneficial for the common folk, and that is why we are attempting to replicate them reliably. In the meantime, I have faith in my superiors and colleagues that they are upholding their duties to the best of their ability. That they have not yet found a way for all to benefit from an Immortality Skill speaks to the difficulty of the problem at hand, not their motives."

I don't have faith. Not concerning their motives on Immortality. They've got to just be controlling it for themselves. Edwin didn't voice his thoughts, nodding in agreement instead.

"I . . . see, I suppose."

Rizzali grinned at him. "You may not believe me, but I do have faith in the Empire. We've done many great works these past centuries."

"I suppose I'll have to take your word for it. Though with your Management Skills and the like, how are there any criminals? I mean other than Outlaws." Edwin preempted the obvious case by saying, "Surely there are more lawbreakers than those who would wholly revoke association with the Empire?"

"An excellent and frequently asked question. The simple fact of the matter is that there are those who would seek to improve their capabilities outside of the System. Pickpockets learn to choose their targets from those without Perception or a Vigilance Skill and cut purses, thieves use the Running Skill for ill gain, and so forth. Such petty criminals are scarcely much threat to any but the naive and unaware. It is with Outlaws where such crime becomes problematic, for reasons I am certain you can grasp. They make for the most legendary of burglars, able to pull coin from a sealed pouch and leaving the owner none the wiser."

It wasn't a *perfect* explanation, but it did explain enough to set Edwin at ease that his coins likely weren't to be stolen from where he kept them by some stupid undetectable pickpocketing Skill.

He sat silent for a moment before speaking up again, "Thank you for your time. I'll be honest; I kind of expected Tara to have come and snatched me away at this point, so I don't really have a plan for what I should do now. Do you have any input on that matter?"

The gnome stroked his chin. "Yes, I suppose Lady Tara is off on some mission or other at the moment, which would forestall her normal greeting of you. What is your remaining purpose in Vinstead?"

Edwin shrugged. "Not entirely sure, to be honest. I want to get a healer's license, but I don't really know how to go about doing so."

"I see. I do not know the process there, though I presume that it likely involves speaking with the Senior Physician."

"Do you know where I . . ."

"No."

Edwin sighed. Of course it wouldn't be that easy. "Well, do you at least know where I can start?"

Rizzali shook his head again, and Edwin had to suppress his reactions. Fortunately, while he hadn't needed to control his emotions that much in the past year, being around Inion who didn't care what he was actually like, he still had the required Skills to hold back a rant or at least some rather rude exclamations.

"Fine. Do you at least know where I might be able to find an inn for the time while I'm staying in the city? Or know who I can ask?"

"Hmm. Yes, I suppose so. Two of the better establishments of which I am aware would be the Golden Grain, not far from here, and the Black Wheat near the outskirts of the city."

"The outskirts?" Edwin asked, surprised.

"Popular among merchants, I believe," he clarified. "Nearer that end of the city."

Edwin nodded in understanding. Okay, that made enough sense.

"How about getting a friend into the city? I don't think she'd want to be an Adventurer, but she did want to see the city. Last time we were here, though, the guards wouldn't let her in."

"I am once again unable to aid you with that, I am afraid. The governor or Lady Tara would be the ones who might know the proper procedures for foreign guests to enter."

"I see. Well, I suppose I'll take my leave then. Thanks for all the information." Edwin bowed out, hefting his bag. He looked out at the massive central foyer, dozens of feet below, and had a thought cross his mind. On a whim, Edwin stepped off the stone platform that held Rizzali's office, tying his Flight tether to the wall.

Even though he had to stay within about a foot of the side, Edwin couldn't help but feel satisfied as he drifted to the ground. Even still, the sight of hundreds of avior flocking up and down the garrison's spire still inspired a pang of jealousy in Edwin, and he vowed to figure out how to fly freely at some point.

Level Up!
Flight Level 21→22

Edwin contentedly flopped onto his bed, his bag sitting in the corner of the room. The mattress wasn't the softest he'd ever slept on, but it was comparable to the sort he encountered in the Curicnan shrines he usually spent the night on and thus felt like a cloud at the moment.

He was so socially drained, he just wanted to lie here for the rest of the night. He'd found the Golden Grain without too many difficulties, albeit with a few wrong turns that had lengthened the trip considerably, but between his talking with Rizzali and the loud bottom floor of his inn, to say nothing of the crowds of people he'd had to navigate on his way to his temporary home, Edwin was exhausted. Even if he hadn't had to individually interact with them, that many people still wore him out by sheer proximity, and as it turned out, being almost completely alone for a full year didn't help in that regard.

In the end, he'd worked out a decent deal with the innkeeper—a Feather of Wealth, a Class name that tickled Memory, though he couldn't remember why—paying one ager (silver) per four nights, with an up-front cost of two ager, giving him just a week before he'd need to pay more. He wouldn't be refunded any if he left early, which he felt was a decent compromise from the initial offer of one ager for three days, one ager up-front and with refunds.

His room was one of a dozen like it on the second of three floors, a solid not-maple door set into nedar (not-cedar) walls and floors, which gave the entire building a vague, pleasantly woody scent. It was also much cleaner and neater than he had anticipated, with all the woodwork interlocking so perfectly he couldn't even tell where one board ended and the other began.

His door was kept shut by a brass lock and a key, which also opened the chest set at the foot of his bed. The key itself was of an unusual construction, a double-sided shape that reminded Edwin of a battleaxe, only connected to the primary keyshaft at the end. There were terms for all those words, he knew, but for all that Memory was tickling him, he couldn't remember *what* those terms were. Ah well, they'd probably come to him eventually if it ever mattered.

A single window was set into the top of the stone wall opposite the door, and peering through it (using the ceiling as a tether for Flight so he could keep lying down) showed Edwin a lovely view of the back of the inn, a winding alley filled with junk. Well, at least the room smelled nice and cut off almost all noise from the outside—at least one of those effects originated from a Skill embedded in the walls, and Edwin presumed it was the sound-blocking one. Handy.

His Skillful Assessment also informed him that the room was expanded through Efficient Space, a gentle "tug" of light pulling the walls away from him. It looked distinct yet similar to his own Improbable Arsenal, which took the form of a grid of scaffolding whose dimensions didn't line up properly if studied. It had given him a headache last time he studied it too closely, so he similarly didn't peer too heavily at Efficient Space's structure, either.

Level Up!
Skillful Assessment Level 15→16

A faint murmur of the conversation downstairs, which probably translated to a burst of uproarious laughter, reminded Edwin he wasn't alone. It prompted him to drift out of bed to the door, locking it. As he clicked it shut, a Skill took hold, briefly washing out from the lock and across the entire door and wall. Interesting.

While he was up, he figured he ought to unpack slightly and transferred a lot of his loose possessions, such as the potions and tools tied to the outside of his bag, into the provided chest. It, too, was enlarged through Efficient Space, though not to the same extent as his room, and so accepted everything he had with ease.

Edwin chuckled as he realized one of his exterior potions was missing. It must have either dropped off at some point, or more likely was swiped by some enterprising thief hoping it was really valuable.

Well, the joke was on them. It was just a glowleaf indicator potion stored in an Apparatus bottle. If Edwin was able to remotely dismiss his creations, he would have done so just then, but he sadly didn't have that ability . . . yet.

Oh, that reminded him. He conjured an Apparatus construct within the keyway for his room lock, fixing it in place so it'd have to be broken if anyone wanted to try and get in. He, naturally, could remove it with a mere touch.

Hmm.

He also transferred most of his valuables from his backpack into the chest. If he were to be in a city with pickpockets, he probably shouldn't keep it all directly on him, now should he? They might not be directly supernatural for the most part, but it only took one. Granted, inside the chest might not be the optimal location, either, so Edwin also split off some of his coins into a few nooks and crannies in his room, creating Apparatus containers to hold them in place and leaving Almanac notes as to where they all were. Perfect.

Level Up!
Sapper's Apparatus Level 26→27

Did he have anything else he needed to do? Hmm. Inion knew it might be a day or two before he was able to get her into the city, so no rush there. Tara was apparently out of town on a mission and who knows when she'd be back. He should try and get a cart of some form to carry his stuff around in, and get ingredients for cooking. Possibly a proper cauldron, too. Or maybe he could use Apparatus for a cauldron? Or would it shatter like glass? He'd need to give it a try. Oh, what about—

Edwin's stomach rumbled, and he groaned. Ugh. Why did his body need to be so needy? He could go literal months without food and be all right, yet he still got hungry three times per day. He could ignore it and it'd go away soon enough, just like he had at lunch, but he *was* trying to develop better habits, so . . .

Edwin pulled himself out of bed, double-checked he had his coin pouch and that it was secured to his belt by Apparatus and let himself out, locking the door behind him and replacing his block in the key-way. He would have used multiple separate Apparatus conjurations, but standing awkwardly in the hallway for a single minute was long enough.

Venturing back downstairs brought the noise back into full bore. It was midafternoon, so the room was relatively empty, but the handful of individuals carousing amid the tables were loud enough for a large room. If he looked really hard, he could even see the hints of passive Skills at work. Shouting or something similar, if he were to guess, and the workers must not have been able to turn it off.

He sighed. Best he get this over with.

Pulling himself a chair at the bar, he ordered dinner from the inn-keeper with his last few ves—he'd need to get some change at some point. The avior passed the message along to the back, and within a few minutes, a wooden bowl of some kind of stew made its way back to him alongside a wooden tankard of water and a small loaf of bread. The wood just felt *weird* on his lips, so Edwin spent a couple minutes creating himself a proper glass and a spoon, an action that he realized postcompletion drew way more attention from the innkeeper than he would have liked.

Fortunately, the avior didn't ask about what he was doing, and Edwin gulped down his water in peace.

Level Up!
Fresh Air Level 7→8

. . . Well, *that* was unexpected. He thought it only applied to breath-ing, but did it also purify water he drank? Or maybe it was from breath-ing normally, and it leveling right as he took a drink of water was just a coincidence?

Whatever. Time to "enjoy" a bit of food. He really needed to figure out how to . . .

Huh.

It actually tasted good! Better than what he could make, even! It made sense that there would be cooks that made really good food thanks to Skills, and they'd certainly be higher-level than his Elixir.

That meant he could actually enjoy food that other people made! This was fantastic!

Edwin nearly scarfed it all down in less than a minute before he caught himself and made himself actually *enjoy* what he was eating. He was about halfway through savoring his meal when the door slammed open, drawing his attention to the far wall.

Three armed guards stepped through the *very* open door, and the din of the room fell silent as the avior among them—a Senior Sky-guard—stepped forward, eyes locked on Edwin. "You are the Adventurer Edwin," they commanded. "Come with us. Governor Shash'falara demands your presence."

Edwin sighed. *Guess I should have eaten quickly after all.*

CHAPTER 3

Meet and Greet

The soldiers stood straight, staring expectantly at Edwin. He sighed and downed the remainder of his soup in a single gulp, dismissing his Apparatus utensils as he stood up. As an experiment, he enabled Flight to suspend him just a hair above the floor. He might as well use the time *somewhat* productively, as he didn't really expect this meeting to go all that great. Best-case scenario, he'd be bored out of his mind.

"Fine, fine. I'm coming. Don't get too excited."

As he approached, the guards shuffled . . . not nervously, but expectantly, and he approached the avior who had addressed him, doing his best to not look down at the shorter individual. "Well? Lead on."

Apparently the Senior Skyguard hadn't been expecting that, as they—Edwin still wasn't sure how to tell the gender of the avian humanoids most of the time—started slightly before nodding. "Correct. Follow us. She awaits your presence."

Some spell seemed to break as they began to file out of the inn, allowing conversation to start up again at full volume after it had been dispelled, which Edwin mentally tuned out as they ventured down the streets. If movies had taught him anything, he ought to try and strike up a conversation with the guards as they walked, so he could build up a rapport with them and potentially have some allies in case this went badly.

However, *personal* experience told him there was no faster way to make someone not like him than to talk to them, so it probably wasn't a great idea for him to try and copy that tactic. He could put on a bit of a show to make himself seem decent, sure, but . . . he also just didn't feel like talking. So he instead simply allowed himself to be led by his flanking guards, the avior before him and the two humans behind. There weren't too many gawkers as they passed, which Edwin appreciated, and the few who did pay attention to them only spared a scant handful of glances at most.

Once the "getting lost" part involved in getting from the garrison to the Golden Grain was removed, it was actually a pretty short walk between them. He couldn't help but feel unusually intimidated as they passed under the outstretched wing and scepter of Emperor Xares's massive statue, leading Edwin to a section of the building he hadn't yet explored or even looked at in all that much detail despite it objectively being the most ostentatious part he'd yet seen.

Massive marble pillars flanked an arched room as it seemingly stretched on to infinity. Some few hundred feet past the demarcation of this section's beginning, a dais rose from the smooth stone floor, a single block of stone melded into the floor, intricately worked with all manner of naturalistic engravings, some of which even moved. There were swaying stalks of wheat, a glimmering blue vein of stone that seemed to flow like a river, and much like the Blackstone carvings he'd seen so long ago, there seemed to be an almost fractal nature to it all, with details recursively spiraling to and beyond the detail he was physically capable of seeing from this distance.

Atop the dais there was, unsurprisingly, a throne of sorts. From what Edwin could tell, it, too, was a part of the same massive stone block that made up the dais and even part of the floor. Upon it sat an imperial-looking avior with jet-black feathers and an almost corvidlike beak, instead of the hawklike ones he normally saw. She was busy speaking to someone, but Edwin noticed a Skill that interfered with his efforts to tell what was being said or to whom.

Interesting.

In any case, it was only a few short minutes before the audience before him came to its conclusion, and he was prodded to approach the throne. His feet fell silent against the stone floor, their force precluded by his Flight as he ventured forth, but he still felt every eye in the infinite-looking hall turn to face him. Though by modern standards the crowd may not have been enormous, there were still dozens upon dozens of individuals present.

Edwin felt small. Oh so very small. It was even worse than his last presentation, because this time he didn't have a topic he knew intimately that he could "prattle on" about. He'd never thought he'd *miss* the ability to annoy people by talking about things they didn't follow, but Joriah was full of surprises.

Unpleasant memories aside, he didn't want to screw this up. Should he bow? He should probably bow, but that felt so very awkward, and what if he wasn't supposed to? Hmm. Instead, he settled for something between a deep nod and a shallow bow, inclining his head and shoulders in respect before he straightened up, squaring his shoulders and looking up at the looming Canny Ruler of the Fields, trying to look her straight in the eye.

Or should you *avoid* doing that with royalty? Ah, whatever. He would do his best and try to not get executed for doing something really minor and really stupid, but without knowing the customs. . . . Dang it, he should have asked his escort about what he was supposed to do. Who knew that avoiding being social at all costs might *actually* have costs associated with it? Truly, a shocking and wholly unforeseen development.

Well . . . He'd just try to be as polite as he knew how to from back on Earth. He'd always been able to put on a good *enough* of a show, after all. It was how he fooled some people into thinking they'd like him!

He was . . . fairly certain the governor was supposed to say the first thing, though he couldn't really explain *why* he felt that way, so he just stayed silent while the avior assessed him in his position beneath her throne. Do not speak until spoken to, or something? Edwin had the feeling that stepping out of line would not be healthy for him, and that meant playing it as safe as humanly—er, *outsiderly* possible.

There were a whole host of Skills at play, permeating the air with so much noise Edwin could barely parse any of it, even directing the totality of his Perception to the task . . . which was probably a bad idea, in case the governor decided to speak. He reluctantly disabled the Skill, making a mental note to return here to help level it in the future.

Level Up!
Skillful Assessment Level 16→19

Yeah. He *really* needed to return at some point. Also, he needed to disable his System notifications. It wouldn't do to have *another* thing distracting him during this.

Edwin shifted slightly, his hand itching to fidget with something, but he squashed the urge before he could do something so rude. Still, with the System, he never really *didn't* have something to keep him occupied, be it working on his Almanac or Visualizing and Prototyping various objects.

So far, he could make two objects or one fairly complicated one, even if he couldn't make anything more complicated than a rigid body yet; he could make a two-link chain, but not a rope. He felt pretty confident that in time stuff like flex and tensile strength would eventually start being included in the simulations, an occasion that he eagerly awaited.

Edwin flicked Perception and prodded his Memory to ensure he hadn't missed the governor saying something—he hadn't—and while he tried to stay focused and at attention, he settled for leaving a sliver of attention on hand to make sure he didn't miss anything while his mind wandered elsewhere. Honestly, what was taking so long? *Were* they waiting for him to make the first statement or something?

The governor didn't look impatient, so . . . probably not? She was still studying him like he was a particularly shiny piece of bread. Well, when she wanted to talk, he'd be here. He wasn't going to be tricked into doing something stupid and rude.

Prototyping seemed like it ought to have been superabusable, but the only information he was able to get was how whatever he Visualized physically interacted with its surroundings, and even then the objects reminded him of basic video game graphics. He could Visualize a mirror, but it wouldn't automatically show anything he didn't actively imagine in its reflection. He could Prototype a massive ear trumpet, but it wouldn't make sounds any louder.

He could also Prototype with his eyes closed, in which case his simulations would play out in an empty, featureless plane instead of the . . .

"Do you know why you are here today, Adventurer?"

Oh hey! The governor was talking to him. How long had it been? Unfortunately, Numeracy didn't tell him how much time passed unless he actively focused on it, so it didn't have an answer for him. This time.

Edwin quickly routed all his Perception to listening and watching the ruler. "I cannot say that I do, no," he tried to answer with his best "I'm competent and nice" voice.

"Disappointing," she sneered. "Though not unexpected. And you would disrespect me in this manner? You will address me properly!"

Well, this was off to a *phenomenal* start, and Edwin bit back a sarcastic comeback. No, no agitating the governor. He was better than that. "Apologies . . . ma'am?" he tried. "I do not—"

"Do you not know the proper manners of redress? You truly are a pathetic little thing, aren't you?" she cut him off before he could finish. "Address me by my full title or not at all!"

"Do you wish for me to address you as Governor Shash'falara . . . Governor Shash'falara?" Edwin's mouth wrestled with the tongue twister of a name, but if he could struggle through S'fashkchlil properly, he could manage this. Seriously, was it some kind of rule that people in power had to have obscenely overcomplicated names? Well, no. Xares was a simple enough name. Weird. Everyone *else* had normal names. Maybe it was a modern trend of royalty or something?

At least she hadn't complained this time about his address, which he took as confirmation that he must have been doing *something* right, and so he continued, "To answer your initial question, I would presume it has something to do with finding out what Tara and her superiors find so interesting about me . . . Governor Shash'falara."

"You disrespect Enforcer Lisana as well? Have you no shame after she took such pity on you?"

Edwin raised an eyebrow. "Are you . . . are you *trying* to antagonize me? Governor Shash'falara," he hastily added, before quietly cursing himself. He had *not* meant to say that, it had just slipped out. Could he blame a Skill effect for that? He'd blame it on a Skill.

"Answer the question. *That* is your role here!"

Edwin wrestled his annoyance back in place, trying to get this debacle back on track before it could devolve further, though it did still seep through slightly in his response. "My apologies, Governor Shash'falara. *Tara* has never once voiced a complaint about my manner of address with her, nor is her interest in me on account of pity. I am a person of interest for her, and her superiors trust her judgment. I would advise you to do so as well. Assuming, naturally, such an action pleases you, Governor Shash'flara."

Edwin winced as his tongue tripped over the name. Gah, he messed it up that time. Ah well, can't get them all.

The avior's beady eyes stared down Edwin, who returned the gaze unblinkingly. There was some emotion behind the motion, but Edwin had no clue what it *was*. Hopefully not anger?

"Yes, well, we've all seen the level of competence we can expect from her and her associates on firm display today. Regardless, your assumption is unusually well placed for an *Adventurer*, so please do enlighten the court as to what makes you so *special*."

"I have been advised by . . . Tara that the story should not be shared widely. Declaring my history in public is momentously against that advice, and so I would like to decline. Governor Shash'falara," he again hastily added.

"You would defy me?" Her voice rose, and Edwin felt his resolve crumble . . . hang on a moment. He flicked on Skillful Assessment and noticed a sort of radiating presence from the governor, waves of some kind seeking and attempting to intimidate him. Knowing it was indeed a Skill effect made it marginally easier to deal with, but just barely. Honestly, the sheer pressure *without* Skills, from a person of authority, would have likely been enough to make Edwin give way.

Nearly made him give way.

All but made him give way.

"All right, all right!" Edwin gave way. "I'll tell you! Just . . . could I have some level of privacy? You won't want this story shared around your entire court any more than I do."

"No. Now speak."

Edwin struggled more against the command, doing his best to push through it. He had managed to beat the dwarven compulsion, what made this different?

The mental strain pushed, and Edwin pushed back.

I will not tell everyone what my story is. That is nothing but asking for trouble and will swiftly torpedo any remaining hopes I have of remaining free and at least marginally anonymous. I will not. Give. Way. I can do this.

Edwin gritted his teeth, opening his eyes and staring down the governor. "I don't owe you answers," he ground out.

The avior laughed. "Petty boy. You owe me *everything*. This is my land, you are a guest here, and you *will* answer my question."

The intensity of the Skill was increasing, and there seemed to be an additional effect being mixed in there, but Edwin just stared it down. He felt the overwhelming urge to speak, tell his past, but he resisted it. It was just like social pressure, or like his emotions. As he stood his ground, it slowly became slightly easier and easier to resist, and he clamped his mouth closed before he could say anything he would regret. It didn't *matter*, and so it could be ignored.

His rational mind refused. His emotional mind refused, albeit under protest. His conscious mind cooperated and refused as well.

No.

No.

He would not give up, he would not give way. His past was *his* business alone. He had spent the last *year* growing stronger, enduring so much training with Inion, practicing his Skill so he'd never be in this position again. He would not be pushed around by the petty tyrants of the System. A bit of anger snuck out of its box and into his glare, and he stood in silent defiance of the mental force crashing into him.

He didn't need to *beat* it, no more than a pebble needed to "beat" the ocean. He just needed to withstand the force, to not get lost in it or let it overwhelm him, and withstanding it became easier with every passing moment. His emotions ran free, helping him beat back the foreign invaders into his mind.

He was the only one to wreck his mind with unwarranted social pressure, darn it!

It must have looked rather amusing to the bystanders. The two of them just stood (or sat, in the governor's case) in silence, staring at each other.

Neither would give up.

Neither would give in.

Anger burned back the pressure to comply. Edwin's emotional control shoved the desire to be nice in a box. The box was tossed out the back. He wasn't winning. He *was* withstanding. And he could keep withstanding for as . . .

"Speak."

Then it tripled down. A new compulsion started. It joined the previous ones, forcing him to say something. Anything.

Anything? He could work with that. A defiant, malicious grin crept across his face. "No."

The pressure was gone. The governor wasn't amused. She glared imperiously. "I command *you*, Adventurer, to speak. Answer my question. Why is Enforcer Lisana so enamored with you, why does the Emperor find you so interesting? Speak *now*, and answer my question."

A pebble might not break under the endless waves of the ocean, but it *could* be swept away by the current, and as the governor unleashed a stronger compulsion, Edwin *felt* his concentration broken in an instant, snapped in half as a headache budded and flowered, flooding his mind with pain and scattering what meager defenses he had marshaled and restraining all his emotions. He was, in a sense, a prisoner in his own head.

. . . Wow, was it bad at imprisoning Edwin in his own head? Seriously, he did *way* worse than this to himself every time he had a depressive episode. The Skill did nothing to keep Edwin from *feeling* his emotions, just acting on them.

Huh.

Actually, this was kind of interesting. He mildly wondered if he could benefit from this sort of thing in his daily life. He didn't really care about the emotions *themselves*, after all, just how they made him act. But emotional suppression in this way had its own suite of problems, many of which were health-related . . .

In any case, if it was a Skill meant to keep Edwin calm and not, oh, plotting rebellion or whatever, it might work *superficially*, but there was no way this could function as a long-term solution. Now that was a thought. Was there a version of this Skill that would work in the long term?

Oh hey, getting distracted on tangents let him procrastinate speaking. Not for very long, perhaps, but it had been, oh, thirty seconds or so? Long enough to annoy the governor, at least. That he could distract himself from mind control . . . actually, that checked out, given the attempted mental control that he'd experienced when imprisoned by Clan Blackstone.

Okay, he still had a moment. What would he actually *say*? The question was why Tara and her superiors were so interested in him, and while he obviously couldn't tell the full story behind the latter, he *could* twist things so he wouldn't have to out himself. In that case, he had a perfect plan formulated.

He wanted to spit the words out to show his displeasure, but instead he found himself calmly nodding and speaking, "Certainly. I come from a far-off land, which Tara has informed me I ought to refer to as Fierisal. While there, I—"

"You come from Fierisal?" a new voice cut in, and Edwin spotted a scribe of some sort scribbling on a parchment off to the side, which he somehow hadn't noticed before. He blinked and briefly turned on Skillful Assessment, noticing some kind of Skill cocoon around the scribe that kept trying to divert his attention away. Curious. As he looked past it, he was able to get the vague impression of black-tipped fingers, as though stained with ink.

"That is what Tara told me when I informed her of my past. I have not returned so I cannot confirm that it is indeed my homeland, though I know not where else on Joriah I would have come from if not there." All technically true. Tara's cover story may not have been perfect, but he could use it just fine. "I was something akin to an alchemist-in-training, but found myself inexplicably teleported to the depths of the Verdant, waking up in the middle of the wilderness without so much as a single Skill on my Status."

That declaration brought around a round of murmurs and surprise from the watchers, particularly from the governor. "You *lost* your Skills?" she asked, incredulously.

"I don't know what happened. Er . . . Governor Shash'falara." Edwin may have been literally forced to be polite, but it didn't help him use perfect address. He needed to remember that sort of thing on his own.

"Hmm. So be it. Continue."

Edwin bit back another snappy response—he figured one would slip out eventually, but now was not the time—and nodded. "From there, I found my way to civilization, and Tara eventually came across me while she was on a mission. She heard my story and warned me against sharing it widely. She also agreed to keep some specifics of my Skills and past private, and she advised I do the same. While I have been unable to fully accomplish that task"—though his voice was calm and level, Edwin's mind *seethed* with rage—"thanks to the actions of some individuals in this room, I will still endeavor to fulfill it to the best of my ability. Tara, from my understanding, has kept those facts secret, and her report on me garnered the attention of her superiors, who decided it was worthwhile keeping a closer eye on me in the future."

There. The question was answered, and as the compulsion ended, it was like a bucket of cold water was poured over him, leaving him gasping and struggling to control his emotions before this became even *more* of a disaster.

He wasn't completely successful, but his hiss of "Is that what you wanted, *Governor*?" wasn't quite as aggressive as it might have been. He'd take the small victory.

"It was," she said with a sneer. "Was that truly so difficult?"

I bet I could have you killed slowly if I asked Inion to.

"I *said*, was that truly so difficult?" A hint of the pressure returned, and Edwin looked up with malice in his gaze as he wrestled his anger back into its box.

"Yes," he snapped back, "I'm certain that *was* rather difficult."

Edwin made a note that he really should try to learn avior body language; then again, he had enough problems with *human* body language. Trying to figure it out in a wholly unfamiliar body morphology was probably futile.

I wonder what you look like on the inside? Edwin mused. *I reckon I could get a ton of levels in Anatomy for cutting you open.*

He caught himself before *those* thoughts could go anywhere, shoving them into the box alongside his anger. He was not going there . . . yet. He *would* need to dissect an avior at *some* point, that was certain.

He hoped he could stomach it. There was a distinct disconnect between his learning brain and his squeamish brain.

"How are you useful to the Empire and to Rhothos?"

"I was under the impression that that was *Tara's* decision, not yours."

"*Tara Lisana* is not the governor of this province. She may be under the impression it is her duty to determine if someone is worthy of support from Rhothos, but her desire to spread unrest and Outlaws across this land is ultimately not her decision."

Edwin vaguely noticed the murmurs of their surroundings had quieted somewhat, and a glance at the court hangers-on revealed a thin Skill barrier between them. She didn't want people to hear her bad-mouthing Tara, then? It was a struggle to speak, but he had this. . . .

In any case, with his anger more or less under control, Edwin was swiftly losing interest in the conversation. For whatever reason, the governor had decided to try and antagonize him, and he wasn't interested in rising to the bait. That seemed like a good way to be thrown in the dungeons, and as much as he didn't particularly *care* about that—he figured it would last until either Tara returned or he just straight-up broke out—it would be marginally annoying and something he would generally prefer to avoid.

"So what then?"

"That *is* the pressing question. For now, I am deciding whether or not you are worthy of living."

Edwin cocked his head. "*Is* that your decision? I thought being an Adventurer, and *especially* an Ally, meant I had the same sorts of protections as Citizens."

"This is my province! My word *is* law. You are nobody! A foreigner from halfway across the world. You are here and you are alive at *my* discretion!"

Something Edwin had done seemed to make her *really* mad. He idly wondered what. He hadn't been getting that distracted, had he?

She realized it as well, it seemed, and started to regain her composure, loosening up somewhat and calming her tone, though it retained a sharp edge to it. "You are a foreigner and Outlaw, yet also treated as a Citizen of mine. I am fully within my rights as governor to imprison or execute any of those who fall within those groups at my leisure. Do not think you are some Outsider whose mere presence causes all who see you to fall over in worship. You're a mere human, no better than the rest of us. You come here, you show such utter disregard to my and my court's standards, you had best be on your knees begging for your life and praying I show leniency."

Edwin ached to speak up and correct her, but simple common sense combined with his inherent tendency to keep secrets close helped keep his mouth closed. Well, mostly.

"When did this become a trial for my life? Last I heard, I was simply here to satisfy your curiosity."

"This became such with your flagrant disrespect! I ought to strike you down where you stand!" She began to rise from her seat slightly, then everything *shifted*.

The first thing Edwin saw was the Skill. It filled up the entire room, illuminating everything in the same flat, monochrome light he was used to, but with an intensity he'd never seen before. If the governor's Skills were as bright as a flashlight, this was like the sun itself descended into the room, blinding Edwin for a brief moment before he disabled his Skill in panic.

Even unable to see it, though, he could still *feel* it. The overwhelming feeling of being a very, very small creature in front of a hungry predator wormed its way into his mind and triggered a primal fear response. His heart beat faster, his senses sharpened, and blood rushed to his extremities.

Hmm. I wonder if it's directly affecting the amygdala, or if it has some other trigger. Is it bypassing my brain altogether and directly increasing adrenaline production? Edwin mused. *I suppose it* can't *be bypassing my brain if I can get distracted from it, though. Some kind of forced attention, maybe? What kind of Skill would that be?*

Edwin's personal ability to get distracted from mind control notwithstanding, the governor seemed to be entirely paralyzed in fear, frozen to her seat from where she had fallen back onto it.

Around them, the air began to thin and Edwin felt his Ritual Intuition go wild as he felt the distinct impression of a hot summer's breeze envelop the room. Then the breeze strengthened, picking up speed more and more . . . it spilled over into the real world, a breeze from everywhere and nowhere, pushing him and blowing from halfway across the planet.

Then the wind stopped. The presence remained, though, and doubled down. Even Edwin's ability to distract himself failed under the direct attention of a very, *very* powerful being, and his mind scattered into incoherent mutterings despite his best efforts. If the governor was like a stream of water, this new presence was more akin to a *tidal wave*.

"Be mindful of your place, Soraia." The voice wasn't loud, but it filled the space as though spoken from right next to Edwin's ear and the end of the infinitely long chamber alike. Then, in the space between where Edwin stood and the governor sat frozen in fear, an avior appeared.

The newcomer had ashen gray plumage with a sheen that made it almost look silver and piercing eyes the color of the sky on a cloudless day. Clad in a simple yet golden outfit, a sleeveless and loose shirt with pants closed around the top of the talons variety that most avior seemed to prefer, he almost looked like a living statue of silver and gold.

"When one such as this comes to my attention, do not threaten them for spurious claims."

The governor stayed frozen in terror, though the overwhelming weight of fear began to subside in Edwin's mind, letting him focus on something *other* than the living god who stood in front of him. He took the opportunity to sneak an Identify in on the newcomer, trying to confirm to his mind that what he saw was real.

The High Sovereign of the Guiding Winds That Span the World

Yep, this was real all right. Though . . . was it? Edwin suddenly realized how drastically their surroundings had shifted in the past thirty seconds. No more was he in the garrison's throne room, but instead he was in a sort of featureless, gray expanse that reminded Edwin, and felt to his Ritual Intuition, vaguely like a rain cloud. How did he *get* here? He didn't feel a thing!

"Wha-what are you doing here?" the governor stuttered. "Why have you brought me? You can't do this to me, even you have laws to follow!" She sounded as though she was trying to convince herself as much as the newcomer, but her voice fell flat in the endless expanse, reaching no ears save the three of them, alone in this strange half-world.

Edwin got a distinct sense of disappointment or disapproval from the avior, the slightest shift in body posture conveying his meaning perfectly.

"Th-the boy disrespected me and your Enforcer alike! He must be punished! Those are the laws! We-we *have* laws!"

"Those are the laws of *your* Citizens, of which the boy is not one. You know this, yet you decide to ignore it. Why?"

"He-he's a nobody! If every random Adventurer was exempt from the laws used to govern my people, we would fall into complete anarchy!"

"Indeed. You are aware of my policy for those who would interrupt the proper order."

"Look at him! He's— He's an outlaw! A thug and a rejector of Your Majesty! Is he not out of order? I was merely doing your will!"

He shook his head sadly. **"And what, pray tell, are the young man's crimes? He was not born to the Empire, was missing our guidance. That he now seeks it is laudable, is it not?"**

"He disrespected me! And your Enforcer!"

"Oh, did he now? How did he insult her? Did he accuse her of attempting to spread unrest across the land? Frame her as an Ally of Outlaws?"

Even Edwin could see her shift nervously under that line of questioning. "Well . . . well, no. He disrespects her station and her nobility! Enforcer Tseyar would have thrown him by his ear for such actions!"

"Enforcer Tseyar was welcome to uphold his own code of address. As are you."

"So you agree! The boy glides in, outright ignores me, fails to address me properly, and refuses multiple commands of mine! By my capacity as governor, it is well within my rights to punish him as I see fit!"

Edwin frowned at the audacity of that claim. Sure, he'd not really known the proper methods of speaking to a ruler, but he'd also been yanked from the middle of his dinner and—

"Let us see what he has to say for himself, shall we?"

Edwin blanched at the suggestion, his thoughts scattered to the far winds at the interruption. He tried to marshal up the proper train of thought, tripping over his own tongue under the weight of presence still permeating every inch of space, "M-my apologies, G-Governor Shash'falara." Speaking felt like trying to do cartwheels underwater under 5 Gs. Slow, clunky, and he was barely able to manage to lift his tongue enough to say anything, let alone pronounce the mouthful of a name the governor had. "I was n-never informed of the proper forms."

As he spoke, it became easier for him *to* speak, though it also felt like some of the pressure was lifted in time.

"You see? Even now, he refuses to pronounce my ruling name correctly!"

"This does not seem unto me as though he is being disrespectful, does it truly to you? Merely incapable. Perhaps you would have been better suited to choosing a title more easily spoken by those whom you call forth."

"He— He still refused to answer my questions!"

"Did he, now?"

"Yes! I had to command him!"

"And what was this matter of grave import? Whether he was a spy? Whether he had committed a murder, or engaged in banditry? His allegiance to the Empire? Or was it a personal matter, in which privacy is reasonably expected?"

"Well . . . well. It was . . ."

"Enough. I've heard enough from you. Begone now, you have taken up far too much of my time already."

With a wave of his wing, he dismissed the protesting governor, and she vanished into a wisp of cloud, dissipating from this realm. With her gone, the pressure subsided until it was only just barely present. Edwin could still feel it, though it no longer restricted his ability to think, speak, or move—the latter of which he hadn't even realized was missing until it was suddenly restored—and he dropped into a bow. It wasn't entirely voluntary, even, so much as his legs refusing to cooperate any longer as the avior turned to face him.

"There's no need for that," the avior informed Edwin, and he found himself on his feet once again, staring into the sky-blue eyes of a predator.

"**Hello, Edwin,**" Emperor Xares greeted him, the emperor's voice calm and measured despite the sheer weight behind every syllable. As he spoke, though, it began to subside from the voice of a god into one of mortals. "**It is good to meet you in person at long last.** Let's talk, shall we?"

CHAPTER 4

Speaking with the Manager

Though the pressure may have subsided, Edwin was still *very* aware he was talking to quite possibly the most powerful person he had *ever* met. This merited his full attention.

Cough.

Hopefully his brain got the memo. He was hopeful, given the constant pressure he was feeling just from speaking to someone so powerful.

"What is there to speak of . . . Your Majesty?"

The Emperor didn't speak to correct Edwin, so he took that to mean he'd gotten it right. Instead, the Emperor gave a curt nod and spoke with an easy grace that warred inside Edwin's turbulent emotions, trying to put him at ease. "Peace, Edwin. You are far more interesting to me alive and unharmed. Do not give me cause to reconsider that position, and you will be released unscathed."

Edwin cautiously nodded. Fair enough.

"You have been within the Empire for scarcely a year, yet already have been quite the force for change. The new liquid stone beginning production in Farport was your doing, I believe?"

"Wait, they actually got it working?" Edwin blinked and hurriedly added, "Your Majesty." He'd screwed up methods of address badly enough for one day, he wasn't going to do it again.

"To a certain distinction of working, I believe. They possess not Skills for it, yet have a basic product functional already. It will perhaps be an interesting place for you to visit someday? I believe you intended to travel."

"Yes, Your Majesty. Particularly now, after . . ." Edwin trailed off, unsure what to say exactly.

He got a distinct sense of amusement from the avior, who gave a curt nod. "Understandable. Korizan is a lovely continent with many spectacular vistas. I frequently fly here when I wish to use my wings. As an alchemist, I believe you will find many of the herbs and creatures native to the Verdant, as well as the frozen lands to the north uniquely useful, though I believe you have some experience with the former?"

Edwin nodded. "Yes, Your Majesty."

"Befriended a fey, no less. Or, adopted by one, rather. You are quite fortunate, I must say."

"Oh?"

"Yes. You survived a year living with a fey? And you did not emerge from the arrangement as an eternal slave, mindless, nor missing several key emotions or sensations, and your name and personality are essentially intact. There is a reason they are usually confined to the Verdant—though impressive work bypassing the border, I must admit. That shows ingenuity, smuggling an Arcadian in through your very skin."

Edwin froze. "I'm not in trouble, am I?" He hadn't even considered the fact that he might be punished for bringing Inion into the Empire, but if fey were meant to be banned . . .

"Peace, Edwin. No, you are not in trouble for bringing your 'friend' from the Verdant. She is the agreeable sort of fey, which is to say she is likely to overlook minor slights and opportunities that others of her kind might utilize to wholly ruin a Citizen and instead focus her ire upon those who wrong her more directly."

"Thank you, Your Majesty. However . . . I don't imagine you merely came to discuss my social life?" Though Edwin was dealing well enough with the pressure the Emperor emitted, it was still more nerve-racking than any interview or even test he'd ever had, and he was eager to get it wrapped up.

"You would be correct in your assessment. It is nothing onerous; I must merely ensure my empire is not threatened by your presence."

"By me?" Edwin was confused. Surely . . . ah. It was the Outsider thing again, wasn't it? Some things never changed.

"Indeed," Xares confirmed. "Outsiders have always heralded great change and massive disruption to the world, and for the good of my Citizens, I must ensure they will be safe and secure."

"How . . . how will you do that, Your Majesty?"

"I merely have a few questions regarding your homeland, and of your first few days upon Joriah. If you could recount your experience from first waking up within the Verdant. Merely answer honestly and completely, and you shall return to Vinstead quickly."

Edwin idly wondered if . . . actually, he could just ask. What was the worst that could happen? "Does time pass more quickly here, Your Majesty? It's a long story."

"Very astute."

Edwin took that as a yes as he sat in silence, gathering his thoughts.

It was kind of amusing. He had literally just refused to tell the story to the governor not ten minutes ago and nearly gotten killed for it, and here he was, about to give the full story to another authority figure. It wasn't the same, he knew. Xares most likely already knew the entire thing, and he'd been quite reasonable this far. He deserved to know Edwin's tale at least as much as Tara did, if not more. However, this would be his last time telling anyone, he told himself. It was just too risky, required too much trust. Since he had left the dwarves, he had only told Tara and Inion, both of whom had been sworn to secrecy *and* had extenuating circumstances. Tara had him at swordpoint, and Inion already *knew*. Hopefully, Xares would keep quiet. Not that it really made a difference.

"I don't suppose . . . well, if you wanted to tell people who I was, Your Majesty, you would be capable of doing so already?" The avior didn't respond, but Edwin had already decided his course of action. "Well, I suppose even if time is less limited than it should normally be, it's still precious.

"The first thing I remember was waking up as I fell from the sky. I thought I was experiencing a nightmare, but . . ."

* * *

Edwin wasn't exactly *practiced* in telling people about his full history, but with a few expertly directed questions from the avior Emperor, who had conjured a pair of chairs for the two of them to rest in while they conversed—it didn't escape Edwin's notice that Xares's was taller and grander, but it also wasn't really a surprise, either—he managed to recount his experiences to an apparently satisfactory level of detail.

"*Was* that you, Your Majesty?" Edwin realized he could ask, when his story had reached his flight up the mountainside, fleeing from the immensely powerful beings fighting.

"It was indeed. I regret that it so nearly resulted in your death, but it is quite fortunate for us both that you survived."

"Would you be able to tell me what it was about, by any chance?"

"No."

Edwin waited for any further elaboration, but when none was forthcoming, he mentally shrugged and moved on. "Well, Your Majesty, from there I found myself caught in a snowstorm that . . ."

There was something about the presence of the avior that made recalling his past easier. Perhaps it was some report-getting Skill? Or perhaps a general Skill-enhancing aura that improved Memory? If Skillful Assessment was usable at the moment, Edwin might have been able to get some vague idea, but, alas, even flickering it nearly blinded him from the sheer *power* that Xares represented.

"Yes, that was last week, Your Majesty. I'm still familiarizing myself with my new Skills, and Refine I've yet to level even once."

"Interesting set of Skills. Such synergy and interconnectedness across such a diverse set of abilities is usually not seen until the fourth tier if not later. You've spoken to a Registrar about this?"

"Of course."

"Good. Now, some of those Paths, they are from your world? Physicist, Engineer, Biologist. What are these? You claimed you were a physicist?"

"Physics *student*, yes. Ah, Your Majesty," he hastily added, "I hadn't completed my education when I found myself transported here. Physics with a particular emphasis in material sciences."

"Science. That's what you called magic on your Earth?"

"No, it's more like . . . well, it kind of is. It's trying to understand the world and bend it to our will. It's not magic, that's more like an addition to the normal laws of physics from what I've learned so far. It's a way of skeptically interrogating the world for how it works. Specifically, it—"

"What are the sorts of things you can accomplish with it?"

"Well, from the time science was really 'invented,' Earth went from technology only slightly beyond what you have here on Joriah to mechanical flight, traveling to the moon, inventing and exploiting the *heck* out of electricity, making the internet, developing seriously advanced medicine . . ."

"Tell me of the wonders of your home. You clearly miss it."

"I . . . I suppose I do, Your Majesty." He hesitated in his response, slightly hopeful that Xares might pick up on it and inquire about it. Fortunately, he didn't, and Edwin breathed easy. He could talk about science all *day*. Few things helped him put off anxiety better than having something he could talk about with fluency. "So, where do I start? Let's see . . ."

"No, it's not magic. It's . . . well, it's about trying to discover new things that *other* people can then figure out how to use in inventions."

"Yet not anyone can discover this new knowledge?"

"I mean, yes? In theory, anyway, anyone with the right mentality and training could discover something new, but by my time, pretty much all those easy discoveries had been made. It would take *hundreds* of people to find anything new . . . maybe? We had this quote, back on Earth, which is attributed to this really famous scientist, to the point where practically half of all physics is named after him. 'If I have seen further, it is because I have stood on the shoulders of giants,' because no individual person can really push knowledge and development as far as everyone working together, even across time and space, can.

"Like, I won't say that science is better than magic. Or well, no, it kind of is? Or maybe not? They're different. Magic is a *thing*, science is a methodology. Well, in any case, magical science is the *best*, though . . ."

* * *

"This . . . 'internet' you speak of. You claim it is accessible to all?"

"Well, to most of the world, at least. It's not free, but it's not insanely expensive and anyone can connect over it in theory. Some people take it upon themselves to catalog knowledge on it, so there's these massive data banks of information that anyone can access. Sort of like your Skill database, but anyone can access basic information on pretty much any topic for free whenever they like. It lets people figure out what they might be good at, just by finding out that something they hadn't even considered as a skill they possessed is actually really valuable.

"If I might be so bold as to opine slightly over the setup of Liras?" Edwin let the Emperor nod before continuing, knowing he was on thin ice. His nerves returned in full force, but he'd already committed. "I do feel like that sort of approach may be superior to the Registrar system you currently have; let people figure out their own Classes based on what millions of people trying their own routes to success came up with. Then you don't need to worry about those who try to do their own thing, and you can learn better Skill combinations faster."

"We have tried similar concepts on a smaller scale a few times in the past," the Emperor countered. "Almost invariably, individuals took Skills that were utterly superfluous to their actual role in society, wasting their Skill allotment. Having access to this magnitude of knowledge, however, you say encouraged people to embetter themselves and learn of the world?"

"Well . . ." Edwin's mind brought up a slew of counterexamples. "Some people did?"

"Did the people of your world cast aside small-minded, foolish instincts when given access to facts that countered their views?"

". . . No," Edwin had to admit, his own experience betraying him. "But everyone was given the same opportunities to, and those who excelled did so spectacularly! Some people simply are hopeless, but that doesn't mean trying to bring those who are determined to waste their lives away up to a decent level of productivity should also involve dragging ambitious people *down* to that level too.

"Also, what about the people who just don't fit in?" Edwin started feeling himself get wound up, and he tried to pull himself back before he started insulting the System the godlike Emperor in front of him had set up.

He was . . . well, he didn't totally fail.

"I met one bandit who just had the bad luck of not being able to get the Walking Skill, but then because of the Management and intolerance for people who didn't fit it, he was forced into a life of being a murderer! How is that better?"

"Yes, that is the purpose of the Adventurer program." Xares was unflappable to the point where Edwin felt slightly ashamed of his actions, enough that he could wrestle his annoyance back into its box, leaving a stronger sense of embarrassment and sense of being out of place. "Many promising individuals were forced into ostracism through no fault of their own, and so the Adventurership system was established. If you would seek to use that as exemplary of the benefits of allowing individuals to control their own Skills, I would remind you that of those who leave my wings, fewer than one in ten survive to their thirtieth year, and the vast majority live in entirely preventable poverty. However, if you can present a solution for that problem, please do inform me."

"Ah, well . . ." Edwin didn't really have a response for that. He was sure there *was* one, but maybe if he'd had six months to prepare? "What else did you want to know about?" He sighed in resignation.

"Tell me of the government that can afford so many of its citizens wasting their lives."

"The US? Well, okay . . ."

"Okay, so yes, democracy has the issue of giving people the government they want, which might not always be good for them, but it's at least the people choosing that," Edwin insisted.

"Would it not be superior to simply provide a consistent government, which does not so readily bow to the idiocy of the crowd?"

"You know, Your Majesty, until maybe a year or so before I left Earth, I might have disagreed with you fairly vehemently. These days . . ."

"But, Your Majesty, Earth has the firm advantage technologically. So much of your manual work performed here is done instead by *mechanical* muscles on Earth. Hardly anyone needs to work with their bodies anymore, and as a result far larger and more complex projects can be undertaken."

"Is it not the case that you are simply incapable of performing the tasks, and so require these complicated machines you speak of? If you had the Skills that you feel impede progress, what need for such technological development would there be?"

"I think that's what I'm saying?"

"Yet you say it as though it is a hindrance for my Citizens, when it is in truth a strength."

"I mean, sure. If you have someone able to harvest an entire acre of wheat with two strokes of a scythe, then the combine harvester is pretty useless. But if you *didn't* have that Skill, then . . . Or, you know, what about if the harvester had a Skill for its use? Then you could have technology *enhanced* by technology, not so much a replacement."

"Why would you desire such a specific Skill, though? And what of the Skills required to create such an intricate piece of machinery?"

"Well, okay, I *guess*, but then you don't need to dedicate a Skill to it. It's a pretty big commitment, and with machinery, you don't need someone at the absolute peak of their career to continue working forever. What if the person with that Mass Harvest Skill died?"

"Then we have another take their place. It is one of the purposes of Class control, after all. We never need worry about losing a critical member of a project, for none have unique Skills upon which the entire project must rely upon."

"Well, I'm not convinced that that's a *good* thing. Why would you even *need* Mass Harvest, if you could replicate its effects with a machine? Wouldn't you prefer to have that be a Skill with an actually unique effect?"

"Well, fine. If you had Packing, then you wouldn't *need* to have massive cranes, but . . . well, no, you need trained operators to use them as well, I suppose."

Edwin stopped to think for a moment. "Well, it's not like those trained wouldn't also be able to do other things as well."

"Packing is likewise an immensely useful Skill. Surely that Skill is more valuable than any you might obtain as a 'crane user'?"

"I mean . . . I guess so, Your Majesty?" Edwin's stress had settled into a sort of meta-stable state where he felt moderately comfortable refuting the Emperor, even if he was still incredibly stressed. "But still, you don't need to be an expert crane driver to do the job. A few days of training is all, which means you don't need a dedicated person using the crane, but several who can all do the work."

"But what of the usefulness of Packing? Such a common and useful Skill is one that many would find useful fairly often. Is it not better that they are capable of improving? Furthermore, what of those who dedicated their lives to developing and building these cranes?"

"I mean, if you can have half a dozen people dedicating their lives to doing all the heavy lifting across the world, then sure. But that much work just isn't possible. It's just division of labor, but . . ."

"So am I the first one to come from Earth?"

"I do not know of the origin of most other Outsiders, though I believe you would be the only from your world, yes. Particularly with the Path you received saying as much. The System would know far better than I do in such matters."

"Is there any way back?"

"That I simply do not know. History is unclear on what happened to your predecessors toward their ends. At least one met their end facing down an entire army, though most simply fade from all records after a certain point."

"What have some of the others accomplished?" Edwin asked. He knew his forerunners had been impressive, but he didn't know *what* they did for that level of distinction.

"That is a tricky question, you understand?"

Edwin shrugged helplessly. "Why?"

"It is not always clear what an Outsider has actually accomplished or what is merely attributed to them. In addition, I am aware of at least one who later became conflated with, or perhaps *became*, a goddess."

"Oh! I know that one. Sal . . . Salverria, right?"

"Salverria, indeed." He assessed Edwin. "How did you know that?"

"Inion mentioned it, I think." Edwin shrugged. "Along with an Alchemy book I found."

"Ah, of course. I ought to have expected you would know of the founder of Alchemy. Yes, she brought knowledge of potions and magical materials to Joriah, overturning much of what was believed to be known about magic. Or would that be science?"

"Not . . . not sure, actually. Probably magic, though? Your Majesty."

"Hmm. It showed that external magics could be harnessed, even if personal spells and the like remain the dominion of birth. You claim to have not had mana previously?"

"No, Your Majesty. I do believe I obtained the ability to use magic after I arrived on Joriah. I *do* think that others should be able to learn it."

"Unlikely. Such things have been tried previously. It is most probable that the traveling imbued you with such magics."

"Well, I still think it was just being exposed to a lot of mana at once that let me get a magical Skill, and I just went from there?"

"Such things have been attempted in the past and have failed."

Hmm. He should ask to see the experiment logs at some point and find out if they made a fundamental error in their testing methodology. It wouldn't surprise him, but that wasn't what he needed to focus on right now.

"So, Salverria?"

"Of course. There was also Elthis, the creator of Vis'Daric and its Gozau, the unnamed Warrior of Koraith, the first druid Tasthen who is said to have created the weather itself, the enchanter Resslian, though it must be said it is unknown if Resslian is merely another name or title for Salverria, then further unnamed individuals responsible for the World Tear, the Destiny Weaver, and more besides. At some point, rumor, myth, and history all collide and it is impossible to tell reality from fiction."

"They all left pretty big marks, though, didn't they?"

"Every last one. This is why it was important enough that I personally assess that you are not a threat to Liras."

Edwin nodded silently, the eternal dread of *expectations* looming heavy over his head. How was he ever supposed to compare to those cultural giants? They might as well have been gods, though they had the benefit of exaggeration on their side. There was no *way* Tasthen managed to create the *weather*. That was just ludicrous. The others, though?

"What's Vis'Daric?"

"It is a wandering city-state that frequently flies over imperial lands and the rest of the world, populated by the Gozau, men of metal, wood, and glass no less intelligent for the fact. They are the premier location for newly created magical artifacts of any complexity."

"How old is this place?"

"Its age was already lost to time back when I first hatched."

Edwin let out a low whistle. A flying city-state founded in the mists of prehistory that still survived to this day, populated primarily by sapient automata? Vis'Daric *immediately* shot onto Edwin's list of places to visit, and he made a bunch of Almanac notes to look into how to reach the floating citadel once he had a chance.

"How many Outsiders do you think there have been?"

"I truly have no idea. At minimum, a dozen, with even more whose names are lost, blown by the breeze of time."

"They all accomplished so much, though."

"Much of which is still felt to this day, yes."

"So"—Xares finally asked the question Edwin had been dreading, and he wasn't sure if he had an adequate reply—"what will you do?"

"I want to change the world," he lamely admitted. "Not that that's an informative goal. I suppose . . . My world's strength wasn't in magic or in flying cities, or whatever else my predecessors had experience in.

"I don't have whatever they did. But what I *do* have is a Skill that lets me write down my knowledge and experience in a way that maybe one day anyone could access, and I want to share that knowledge with whoever it might help. I can bring science, I suppose. And science is big. It's really big. That saying I was talking about? 'If I have seen further, it is by standing on the shoulders of giants?'

"Yeah, I don't know that I can be the person standing atop the giants. There's just too much I don't know about the laws of this new world, too many enormous things to explore and figure out the fundamentals of. I won't be the seer, but hopefully I can at least be the giant, empowering those who come after me to see further and further than I ever could."

"An interestingly honest answer. Best of luck to you in that endeavor."

"Wait, just like that? You're not going to try to take me and use my knowledge to revolutionize your Empire, or drop me in a lab and try to learn things for you?"

"No. You are too much of an unknown, and as you admit yourself, you have no particular expertise I can utilize. Any funding I have toward Alchemy is better suited for high-tier alchemists already of the Empire. Their Skills are more useful than yours in any regard that matters.

"You may be an Outsider, and thus far more likely to *be* of use than another Adventurer, but you likewise remain an Outsider, and attempting to corral you or contain you will inevitably end poorly. Indeed, simply being near you is liable to be hazardous to any facilities you might utilize. Best to keep you far, far away from anything critical, which might suffer under the strain of a 'scientific revolution.'"

Ouch.

"Well, what about research? I have a unique take on things, I might find something totally new!"

"If you do, I am certain I will learn of it in time. You just told me your goal is to make everything you learn public knowledge, no?"

"But . . ." Edwin's newfound dreams of fabulous wealth working for the Empire vanished in an instant before they could even fully form. "I can ensure you'd learn about them sooner? And you don't have to worry about me dying?" he tried.

"Should you lose your life, is that not an indication that your ideals are less applicable here than you are used to? And should you survive and thrive, what care have I for such a discovery to come a decade earlier? It would still arrive in due time. And as I am certain you will not allow all your unique knowledge and training to die alongside you, even if you do not find all you might under sponsorship, your apprentices might, or the next generation of alchemists, taught the knowledge you have brought with you from Earth." The emperor forestalled Edwin's next rebuttal before he could even open his mouth.

"Could I at least get . . . oh, I don't know, a cart or a carriage or something? Just something that I can use in my travels as a bit of a portable lab and way to carry around my stuff somewhere other than on my back. I'd be willing to not hold that"—Edwin waved his hand in a vague indication of the mess with the governor—"against the Empire as a whole in exchange for something like that."

The Emperor gave a curt nod, scarcely even stopping to think before agreeing, "I will assign the cost of such as partial reparations for Soraia. You shall have your carriage."

Huh. He . . . hadn't actually expected that to work. Score! And so easily, too! The tight ball of stress wound up in Edwin's chest began to loosen, if Xares was so readily willing to help him out . . .

Then he promptly realized all the other possible things he might have been able to ask for: Adventurer status for Inion, maybe a house or something, some decent gear, or Alchemy ingredients, Skill training, access to the Grand Library . . .

Edwin silently sighed.

No wonder Xares had been so quick to agree. And if the governor would be the one to provide the cart, it probably wouldn't be that high quality as she tried to spite him or wiggle out of her obligations . . . he'd totally just screwed himself out of something potentially great, hadn't he?

Even as his stress rebounded, now strengthened by Edwin's own annoyance at himself and forming a tight knot in his stomach, Edwin forced himself to give a nod in thanks. "Thank you, Your Majesty." It wouldn't do to start bad-mouthing the source of his pressure just because he messed up. This was entirely his own fault, so he'd own it.

To be fair, it was still more than he had anticipated to get out of the meeting with the governor. He'd expected a boring hour or two of being prodded at, then being sent on his way. It may have ended up being far more stressful than he had initially anticipated, but he also got more out of it in turn, so . . . it broke even at worst.

He found it difficult to blame the Emperor for any of the recent revelations, honestly, though he suspected that was a Skill of some sort at play. Or maybe that was just sheer charisma and millennia of practice with diplomacy. Blinking Skillful Assessment on still just overwhelmed Edwin with a uniform, monolithic wave of Skill light, so he had no help from it in this case. Would there really even be a difference between supernaturally good diplomacy and centuries of experience?

His thoughts notwithstanding, their time was clearly coming to a close, and Edwin floated to his feet, giving another deep nod/shallow bow to the Emperor in farewell.

"Very good speaking with you, Edwin. Best of luck in your endeavors," the avior assured him, and Edwin almost felt like he was being pulled into a desire to prove himself worthy of the Emperor. He nodded wordlessly, doing his best to distract himself with something until the Skill effect faded.

He didn't *like* people messing with his mind with Skills, but some part of Edwin told him that it wasn't that different from just using words to try and convince him of something. Did that mean that he was . . . spiritually gullible or something? Skill-ly gullible didn't sound right. Emotionally gullible? Eh, spiritually gullible worked. In a world where emotion-altering effects were objectively commonplace, did that make them any less moral than simply being good with your words? Were kids taught as they grew up not only how to be skeptical of words being said, but also how to avoid acting out on unnatural emotions being shoved onto you?

It was . . . oh hey, the Skill had subsided. Edwin mentally reviewed what Memory told him the Emperor had said as the surroundings began to darken ever so slightly.

"I will return you to the gates of Rhothos's garrison such that you are hopefully able to avoid the attention of the full court. I will pass the instructions for you to receive a carriage to the governor, and you shall hopefully receive such within a reasonable amount of time.

"I expect I will be hearing much more of you in the next few decades, and I eagerly anticipate it."

Edwin gave out one last hasty thanks as the gray clouds around him thickened, enveloping him entirely and obscuring his vision as his surroundings blurred and faded away. For a brief moment, he felt utterly weightless and immaterial, like a cloud floating on a breeze, then reality returned and he crashed into the ground under the peak of the garrison's entry archway. Edwin barely caught himself with Flight, and even then he only had time to *soften* his landing, rather than blunt it completely.

There was some form of commotion going on inside the building, giving Edwin the perfect opportunity to slip away. This time, he didn't get lost on his way to the Golden Grain, no matter how nervous he may have been. As he walked, Edwin felt his emotions get rowdier and rowdier, trying to break free of their bindings and overwhelm him. He'd been on an emotional knife's edge for *hours*, and it was starting to wear on him.

Nope, not starting. The ball of stress he'd shoved to the side while talking to the Emperor was seriously unraveling. He quickened his pace, trying to get back to his room, where it was quiet and where it was safe. Most importantly, where there *weren't any other people*. Edwin's fingers grew jittery and he enabled Longstrider, nearly crashing into a few people and actually running into a few obstacles in his staggering gait. His breath grew ragged as he got back to the Golden Grain, and his hands were shaking as he opened the door.

The interior of the inn was busier now, as more patrons had come in for dinner, and the raucous laughter slammed into Edwin's skull like so many jackhammers. He rushed upstairs, only recognizing the inn-keeper's wave of greeting after it was too late to act upon it, and tried to open his room door.

Naturally, it didn't work, and Edwin fumbled for his key, withdrawing it from one of his pouches. He went to unlock the door and bit back a curse when he realized the lock jam from Apparatus was still active, for better and for worse.

It took him far too long, but he eventually managed to flip his head into the right space to cancel that manifestation of the Skill (and the ring he wore made of the same stuff at the same time), got the key in the lock, and burst inside.

He scarcely managed to close the door behind him, let alone lock it, and Edwin was a jittery, emotional wreck by the time he collapsed onto his bed. His hands were shaking to the point he couldn't even *tell* how bad his fingers were trembling, and he couldn't lift so much as his own pillow.

At least the noise from below was essentially gone. Though not gone enough. Faint echoes of yelling and singing still clawed their way through the sound-dampening Skill and to his ears, raking across his eardrums. His blanket was so itchy, tiny bits of wool digging into his skin and overwhelming him. Turning off Perception did nothing, and directing all his attention to his smell just made the stench of cedar splinter into his mind. Taste was little better, stale air and wet wool nearly causing him to gag as his mind searched for solace there.

Edwin sought any kind of escape. He needed to sink into unconsciousness, to get away from the suddenly so *loud* and *disturbing* world, which had finally abandoned all pretense and was now directly attempting to get him. No more was it trying to go through intermediaries; it had found out how to assault his senses and drive him mad directly. Adaptive Defense did nothing against this vicious attack, and he fruitlessly tried to escape his torment, scrabbling at his Skills but finding no purchase.

He needed to use Sleeping, but his mind refused to flex the mental muscles required to activate the Skill. He needed his sleeping potion, but even his own Memory was betraying him as it refused to tell him where the lifesaving medicine could be found.

Another burst of noise from below made him clench his hands over his ears even tighter, desperately trying something—*anything*—to escape the awful cacophony that defined his very existence.

When Edwin did eventually sleep, it was to the sound of his own whimpers.

CHAPTER 5

Daily Dallying

Sleeping was *wonderful*. Not just the action, but the Skill, too. Even though his dreams had been tumultuous and vaguely nightmarish, as Watchful Rest ensured that even unconsciousness wasn't enough to entirely disconnect from reality, by the time Edwin returned to full awareness, he just felt refreshed on a fundamental level.

His senses no longer warred against his mind, and the emotional load of the previous day felt so light, as though it had been weeks or months prior. He still generally dreaded seeing people after the previous day's utter *fiasco*, but it wasn't totally unpalatable either.

He rolled over in his bed, making a vague attempt to snag his blanket from wherever it may have landed, only to fail. Cracking his eyes open eventually had him see the cloth on the far side of the room, and he fell back, his eyes closing once more to try and shut out the brightness of the room.

Edwin's stomach rumbled, and he ignored it. He could skip food today and it wouldn't hurt. Today, he just wanted to do nothing and recover. When *was* the last time he genuinely just had a day off? he wondered. Not counting days of recovery after a fight, anyway. He genuinely didn't know. Then again, this probably didn't count as a nonrecovery day anyway. He may not have been physically injured, but that didn't mean he didn't need healing.

Mental health was important, after all!

Now shoo, loneliness. Get back in your box.

He idly wondered if he could develop an emotional healing potion. What he wouldn't give to dab some salve on his forehead or down an elixir and make the pain of last night vanish.

. . . That was just alcohol, wasn't it?

Except *not*, because alcohol was just a poison that targeted the brain above the body, inhibiting its functions. At *best* it was a painkiller. Except it was a painkiller that worked by damaging the nerves of the area being treated . . . how *did* painkillers work? *Wasn't* it by inhibiting nerve signals?

He should try some experiments with the pain-numbing sinbalyne now that he'd all but tiered up. What sort of interactions would it have with his new Skills?

He was just distracting himself now, and he wasn't sure if he wanted to. He'd check his notifications, that was the first step to being productive, right?

Level Up!

Skill Points 444→477

Adaptive Defense Level 11→24

Fey's Caress Level 35→36

Memory Level 57→59

Numeracy Level 14→15

Outsider's Almanac Level 127→128

Polyglot Level 59→60

Prototyping Level 12→13

Ritual Intuition Level 16→20

Skillful Assessment Level 19→29

Watchful Rest Level 9→10

Congratulations! For withstanding an overwhelming mental force, you have unlocked the Unbowed Path!

Congratulations! By experiencing your mental defenses being obliterated yet not losing yourself utterly to a mental Skill, you have unlocked the Canny Path!

Congratulations! For balancing your mind under the effects of multiple mental Skills simultaneously, you have unlocked the

Steady Mind Path!
Congratulations! For meeting in person the High Sovereign of
the Guiding Winds That Span the World, you have unlocked the
Brushed by Power Path!
Congratulations! For meeting the Emperor of the Lirasian
Empire, you have unlocked the Lirasian Citizen Path!
Congratulations! For reaching level 60 in a literary Skill, you
have unlocked the Scholar Path!
Congratulations! For explaining concepts to the High Sovereign
of the Guiding Winds That Span the World, you have unlocked
the Royal Adviser Path!
Congratulations! For improving the opinion the High Sovereign
of the Guiding Winds That Span the World has of you, you have
unlocked the Favored by Power Path!

That was a *lot* of Paths for one day, especially pertaining to Xares. Edwin decided he probably wasn't taking most of the Paths he got from the Emperor, although Royal Adviser did look kinda tempting.

Ah, of course. Adaptive Defense was leveling based on resisting mental effects, wasn't it? Well, it was nice to know he wouldn't be completely helpless against social Skills anymore. Fey's Caress was a bit confusing—he hadn't used the Skill any recently? Hmm. Maybe whatever thing the Emperor had used helped it somehow?

It was overall a pretty good spread for half a day of leveling, though given he had spent half of that time in direct and *terrifying* mortal peril, it wasn't an experience he was eager to repeat any time soon.

Edwin moved to get out of bed and hesitated. He might be due a cart soon, but he doubted it would come today. Or even tomorrow. The governor, if Edwin's assessment of the situation was right, would probably drag everything out as much as possible just to be petty. He didn't *really* need to do anything today, did he? Certainly nothing pressing, anyway.

He could stay in bed for now.

It was midafternoon when Edwin finally pulled himself off his mattress, stretching to try and inject some energy into his weary limbs. Stamina may ensure he was physically capable of the action, but he felt like he ought to get the Willpower Attribute for the effort, never mind that wasn't how the System worked.

In any case, time to kill or not, Edwin had spent the last year doing something every day, and it was hard to let that momentum go, and forcing himself to interact with people in a limited fashion would probably be good for him. He had some things he wanted to find out, after all. Like where he wanted to *go* once he left Vinstead. Perhaps he should look into finding out where Vis'Daric was?

Edwin chatted with the innkeeper while he ate his food—some thick stew and bread that tasted really good—and though the avior was clearly nervous about something, he didn't mention anything about it. Instead, Edwin asked a few questions about where he could get various supplies. Hopefully his annoyance at life didn't come across too strongly, or like it was aimed at the innkeeper. Maybe that was where the nervousness originated?

As the flood season was about to start, food was cheap and plentiful, which was fine by Edwin's reckoning. He still had loads of money from his talsanenris sale, and even in normal times, food tended to be costed in the order of ves per pound. It would be pretty simple for him to pick up even more food than what he already had on him, and with more variety too!

He subtly steered the conversation toward nearby places of interest he might be able to go, bringing up a few names that had caught themselves in his Memory and notes to investigate.

Vis'Daric, or the City of the Brass Sun as it was nicknamed, drifted around with no apparent pattern, and other than in specific situations, it was inaccessible from the ground. Not an issue for the avior-dominated Lirasians, of course, but Edwin would need to figure out some way up either on his own or by catching a ride with another flier.

That was rather annoying, though perhaps manageable once Flight leveled enough. The problem was the innkeeper didn't know where Vis'Daric was or where it frequently hung out. He said that it wasn't common knowledge this far out, and even he only knew about it from travelers who told stories about it, and he once in a while couldn't help but wonder if it was even *real*.

Apparently it gleamed like the sun, was larger than the Rhothos River itself, flew to the moon to make eclipses, could drop entire lakes from the sky, had a weapon that could obliterate mountains in a single blast—and may or may not have just been descending and squishing said mountain under the city itself—and more. Edwin figured at least half the stories had to be made up, but which half he wasn't sure. Any of them could be possible. Well, other than the one where they were secretly in league with tools the world over, who were alive and biding their time to strike. That last one *had* to be fake, right?

Of more actionable information was the town of Panastalis. It was also right on the border of the Verdant, though several weeks to the northwest away. One of the few towns actually located inside the Verdant, it was apparently the Lirasian Empire's primary source of medicines and potions on the continent. Of most interest to Edwin, though, was that it was in the next province over, Fellstrom, and thus *not* in the same territory as Governor . . . whatever her name was.

He figured it was probably a good place to check out, see if he couldn't learn anything for his Alchemy, and maybe pick up a few new ingredients fresh from the source. Edwin got vague directions from the innkeeper but was also told he didn't know the route entirely and he should ask at the courier's office, because they'd know better.

Edwin's food was long finished at that point, and so he bowed out of the conversation and took his leave.

Without his cart, and accordingly not knowing how much space he would have for his stuff, Edwin was fairly limited in how much he could buy at the moment. He didn't want to have to lug fifty pounds of flour to his room, for example, no matter how light it may have felt to him. It was just a matter of convenience.

It did leave him with some free time that he wasn't anticipating, though. He wasn't about to try and take the medicine class here in Vinstead, that was certain. He was sticking around no longer than would take him to get his cart and leave.

Edwin quietly cursed his luck that he *did* end up overpaying for his room, under the vague hope the cart wouldn't take too many days to "arrive." Ah well. Given the alternative was *staying* in Vinstead, leaving was still better than spending any more time in a city ruled by someone who clearly hated him.

Heh. And for once I know that's not just my brain playing tricks on me.

Maybe he could take the healing license class when he was in Panastalis? A more alchemy-focused medicine class would suit him better, anyway. He might even learn something from it!

So that still left him with the question of what he would do with his free time. For now he'd pay a visit to Inion. It didn't seem very likely he'd get her into the city this time around, and he ought to let her know as much.

Leaving the city was as simple as always; while the brief screening that he was always subjected to upon entering meant there was usually a line to get into Vinstead, they apparently didn't care who was *leaving* the city. Edwin idly kept his eye out for anyone he recognized, but other than a few random Almanac returns from people he'd walked by in the past, there wasn't anyone he'd interacted with to any appreciable degree—they didn't even have their names tagged.

Once he was out from the hustle and bustle of the city and its immediate surroundings, Edwin switched from practicing Flight to stretching his Longstrider, netting him a level in each and enabling him to rapidly close the distance to the Rhothos. This road was well maintained and well traveled, stone blocks tightly interlocking with one another and worn smooth from generations of use.

Edwin wasn't following the road the entire way, though. No, if he went on far enough it transitioned into a direct bridge over the Rhothos, the massive river passing through enormous stone blocks in a path that was presumably inaccessible during the massive floods that defined half of the year in this part of the world. Instead, he was following it to a few hundred feet from the banks, then turning off-road and switching back to Flight. Longstrider still wasn't quite at the level of mastery where Edwin could go on rough terrain with it . . . or anything that wasn't basically flat, level ground, unless he wanted to crash into things constantly.

It took a few minutes for Edwin to arrive at their preestablished meeting point, and he flipped a ves into the water. Apparently, Inion was hyperaware of any offerings made to her or the river in general, and so the copper coin was a great way to get her attention.

Sure enough, within a minute, the water coalesced into Inion's . . . very familiar shape.

"Please tell me you at least know *where* you left your tunic." Edwin sighed. "I don't want to have to get you another one."

"Who says you'd *have* to?" Inion teased him, and he shook his head.

"At least do that thing where you make your own clothes or whatever."

"Hmm . . . *nah!*"

"You know, you'll need to get dressed to enter Vinstead," he reminded her, hopeful that she wouldn't ask . . .

"*Ooh!* Did you figure out how to get me in, then?" Of course she'd ask. Fey practically *invented* misleading statements.

". . . No," he admitted, and responded to her beaming smile with a glare. "That doesn't mean you shouldn't put clothes on!"

She didn't acknowledge his admonishment, and Edwin sighed again. "Whatever. I *do* hope you kept your tunic, though."

"So? What happened? Tell me *all* the details."

"Why would I have anything that would require details?"

"You have that *look* on your face. Something *fuuun* happened, didn't it? Ooh! Did you find a girl last night?" she teased. Honestly, sometimes Edwin wasn't sure how much of her incomprehensibility came from being a fey and which parts she intentionally played up to annoy him.

Edwin responded with a baleful glance and rolled his eyes. "Ha. I would have taken that in a *heartbeat* instead of what actually happened."

Inion let out a low whistle as Edwin finally completed his story. "Wow. That's *quite* the eventful night."

"Tell me about it," Edwin muttered. "I thought I was dead at least three times over."

"I know! I wish *I* could have seen it!"

"Wait. . . . See it?"

"You mortals are so *adorable* when you do your little spats. I mean, I would have *killed* Miss Sassy-beak if she had lain so much as a feather on you."

No surprise there.

"But you *standing up* to her? Oh, so *great!* I . . . *don't* regret missing out on seeing the little Liras. He sounds like *quite* the force to reckon with. Maybe you'll get there someday, *eh?*" She elbowed Edwin in the side, and he shifted to avoid it.

"Please. He's got at least two millennia of experience on me and an entire empire of resources."

"You have *me!*"

". . . I don't think the power of friendship is going to help out here."

"No, no! I meant the—"

"Yeah, yeah. I was just messing with you. I *know* you mean the Muse Token." Edwin paused, confirming that it was what Inion meant before continuing, "But I still don't think that a slightly boosted leveling rate will make enough of a difference, unless it's *way* more powerful than you told me."

"You never know," Inion pushed, trying to be mysterious. "Maybe it *is* that strong."

"Is it?" he asked calmly.

"Well, *no*, but . . ." Inion fell silent at Edwin's skeptical glance. "Fine. You're hopeless and can never improve. Is that better?"

"Much," he teased, dodging a kick. He attempted to grab her foot, but Inion let the limb turn to water momentarily, letting it slip through his grasping fingers and sticking her tongue out at him as she did so.

After that, the conversation quieted down and the two of them spent a bit more time together, reclining next to the bank of the river and chatting. It was a . . . genuinely pleasant time. Inion felt substantially more approachable than before, and Edwin barely even noticed the time slipping away until the sun got so low in the sky it gleamed directly into his eyes.

"Whoops! I need to get back into the city before the gates close. Uhh . . . it was nice."

"It was," Inion agreed. "Go have fun."

Edwin waved awkwardly as he flew off.

* * *

The next day, Edwin was far more successful in pulling (well, floating) himself out of bed at a reasonable hour, and following a quick breakfast (a surprisingly good bowl of what looked like oatmeal but tasted like pudding), he set off into the city to do some shopping. With luck, he'd be done by lunch!

Edwin ended up missing lunch and nearly missing dinner by the time he had gotten the first few things on his list; namely, a decent satchel and new belt. His backpack and current belt were perfectly serviceable, yes, but Edwin had in his head what an alchemist "should" look like, and darn it, he was going to try and mimic that!

He'd never really gotten into cosplay or anything back on Earth, but that was more a limitation of his time and resources than an actual lack of desire. Now that he was on an actual fantasy planet, though? He could live out all his dreams of a belt full of glowing potions and a satchel full of bombs! Plus it would all be *practical*, not just decorative! This would be *amazing*.

The belt ended up being custom-made, which *did* make it more expensive, but he still only spent two ager on the whole thing, plus five ves on a maintenance kit. It was almost worth the price he paid just to watch the Experienced Currier make the entire getup in front of Edwin in about an hour. Now, he had dozens of (mostly empty) pouches in varying sizes, and several loops and leather strap ties that he could hold or insert vials and potions into. Said straps were mostly concentrated on Edwin's left, and pouches more on the right, so his new handbag could hang without running the risk of crushing any of his potions.

All his pouches and bags were bigger on the inside, naturally, but only—*heh, "only"*; who would have thought he'd already start taking something so fantastical for granted—three times bigger than their exterior would suggest. Improbable Arsenal already doubled the size of what it worked on, so he imagined the inherent amount of extra space in his packs would be swiftly overwhelmed by his own Skills.

Apparently the aging man had upgraded his Efficient Space when it was level 40 or so, trying to push to the Refolded Leather Skill instead of bringing Efficient Space to the nineties or even higher the truly dedicated pushed it to. It had served him well in his youth, apparently, but now that he was working as a malemaker (in the mailbag sense, apparently), he somewhat regretted the decision. After all, he had . . .

It was somewhat interesting, sure, but Edwin had only half paid attention as the man talked about his life's story, more interested in watching the incredible display of Skills he had been working with, something that had very much paid off.

Level Up!
Improbable Arsenal Level 16→19
Skillful Assessment Level 29→30

With the newest milestone in the Skill, Edwin was starting to ever so slightly be able to distinguish colors associated with different Skills being used. He needed to look really closely, yes, but it was still a massive improvement over what he'd had before.

Regardless, Edwin's biggest takeaway from the whole thing was still just how awesome he looked. Once he got back to his room, he filled in all the potion slots with Sapper's Arsenal rods shaped like potions, strapped his knives in place, and admired himself in the "mirror" that was Visualization.

If his imagination was accurate (it should be), he cut a pretty good figure, albeit one with haphazardly cut hair (Inion was *never* getting close to him with hair shears again). He did make an Almanac note to get a few more safety equipment/accessories, though. He might be able to get away without some PPE thanks to Fey's Caress and Fresh Air, but it never hurt to be overprotected. Goggles, a mask, and gloves were all must-haves, and he should visit the tailor to see about getting them made.

Tomorrow, he thought. Today, he'd finish packing up his outfit with alchemy stuff.

It was on the fourth day after the "incident" that Edwin was finally approached by a messenger to inform him he ought to report to the garrison—that word was becoming more and more inaccurate as he learned more and more about the building, but Polyglot kept translating the word the same way—for an unspecified reason at his first opportunity. He gave the Junior Skyling a ves for a tip, which the young avior seemed to be totally unprepared for, jetting off in happiness and bringing a touch of a smile to Edwin's face.

Well . . . he supposed he ought to head over now. After all, what could—

Nope, not thinking that. Not after last time.

Edwin didn't end up seeing the governor at all, an arrangement that he was *perfectly* content with, and was instead shuffled around until he met with a Lirasian Secretary, who in turn directed him to where his cart would be.

Much to Edwin's surprise, it was actually pretty nice! Small, yes, but it was everything he would realistically want *from* his cart. Well, it was more of a carriage in all honesty. Wooden walls and ceiling, tall enough to stand up in, and some, oh, ten feet long on the outside, more like fifteen on the inside? It had *loads* of shelves and some sort of Skill on them that would . . . that would . . .

Ah, forget it. He wasn't good enough with Skillful Assessment to tell *what* a Skill did, just whether or not it existed and what it affected.

Best of all, it came with a pack animal—specifically, a Mature Therassan Pony—to pull it! He barely came up to Edwin's shoulder, but he was more than strong enough to haul the carriage along the road without even a hint of strain. The secret was visible with a bit more examination: a Skill ran from his four hooves (which had their own ongoing Skill, presumably in place of the missing horseshoes) up through his body and into the cart. It vaguely reminded Edwin of Packing, though it had a number of distinct differences.

Edwin named the shaggy animal Bill.

After all, what *else* would he name a pony?

Everything was packed away nicely. Food had been bought, Edwin had all his new gear prepped—including a leather coat, which would apparently function as armor to some extent, but way stuffier than he'd like even after the Skills imbued into it for comfort—and some basic furniture bought and folded away under the carriage's bottom and fastened by many Apparatus conjurations. That process had brought him all the way up to level 29 in the Skill, and while the conjuration wasn't getting any faster, he was able to make significantly more intricate creations than before.

That didn't matter at the moment, though. Currently, he, Inion, and Bill were plodding down some fairly familiar roads. He wasn't going to lie; the idea of getting closer to the Blackstone Citadel made Edwin . . . nervous, but he knew he was being irrational. Sure, they had sent an assassin after him, but that had been taken care of, and Edwin was way stronger now anyway! Besides, he had Inion. That would surely be enough. He could take care of himself.

Bill performed his job admirably, trotting along at a moderate pace that Edwin would have once called a light jog. These days, it felt *painfully* slow, particularly at the start. Even a moderate walk with Longstrider would have let him run laps around his workhorse, but disabling the Skill would mean he'd fall behind unless he jogged every once in a while, which he didn't want to do.

Well, it wasn't like he was in any kind of rush, and this way he could practice his Flight. His top speed with the Skill was comparable to Bill's pace, though he was ever so slowly getting faster. He could also just tether himself to the carriage and stay "stationary" anyway. Of course, if he were to do that, he could also just sit inside, but where was the fun in that?

Besides, it was easier to direct Bill when he was outside, not that the pony needed all that much guidance. Edwin didn't have much experience with horses back on Earth, but Bill seemed particularly intelligent and focused, staying on course and at a steady pace the entire time. Edwin only needed to direct the horse when they encountered a fork in the road, or in one case, when they passed by a particularly luscious meadow.

The roads themselves were absurdly straight, even to Edwin's modern sensibilities. Only about once or twice a day did the road turn at all, with such incidents usually corresponding to another path splitting off from the main way. They were also *very* level. Other than a bit of slope from the center of the road out to the edges—Edwin had checked, with several Apparatus marbles—the road was absolutely level, with the foundation lifting it above the ground where it dipped at times, or cutting straight through hills in others, stone imposingly rising on each side for some of the larger hills present.

Even with the impressive construction inherent in ensuring the straightness of the road, the stones *still* had gaps between them that were *just* wide enough to produce some seriously impressive rattling in his carriage.

The roads were, simply put, clearly optimized for foot traffic, a fact proven by the occasional courier dashing by them, feet pounding against the stone and pushing up a massive cloud of dust in their wake as they rushed by. The one that Edwin managed to peek at with Numeracy gave him a velocity of about 175 m/s, which was *blisteringly* fast—over half the speed of sound.

Why the Empire didn't just use avior as their primary messengers was beyond him, given the flying humanoids wouldn't need roads at all to get around, but perhaps the relative abundance of humans pushed them to utilizing humans much of the time? Or perhaps Walking was more likely to give Skills that were useful for rapid overland movement. Something to ponder, and possibly ask Tara or Rizzali the next time he saw them.

There were other travelers on the road, naturally, and the sight lines of the roads (Maybe that was another reason for them?) ensured that Edwin could see them for miles before they actually passed each other and for miles after as well.

While neither the most interesting nor the most common, he did pass a few groups of merchants, with carts and wagons of their own, or with laden pack animals passing Edwin, usually saying nothing as they did so. He didn't spot anyone he recognized, either, despite keeping an eye out.

Three or four times, a group of heavily armored figures on horses rode past him, moving much faster than he and his solitary pony could manage. Usually, said sallies returned back in the direction of Vinstead within a day or two, but one time Edwin never caught the ride back.

There were even a couple of bards, dressed in distinctive and colorful clothing as they passed him. The first was a Wandering Herald-Minstrel, who seemed to be trying to compose a song as he plucked strings on an unfamiliar instrument, singing half-finished lyrics that hung in the air for minutes in the wake of his passing and echoed down the road for a good hour. A few days later, the second danced down the road to a beautiful melody, her eyes closed as her steps twirled her side to side, a flute producing notes that made even Inion close her eyes to appreciate the sound. The Seasonal Dancer of Whimsy barely even acknowledged them as she passed, but Edwin was happy to have encountered her.

The most plentiful group, though, was just locals using the roads for ease of travel. There were plenty of Lirasian Farmer variations, sometimes driving beasts of burden, sometimes carrying massive sacks of food, sometimes both simultaneously. Herds of sheep, kept in place by Shepherds or Farmers and a handful of dogs—Rhothosian Herders, according to Identify—monopolized massive sections of the road when they came through and stalled Edwin's progress until the fluffy tide continued onward.

There wasn't a lot of outgoing trade from Vinstead, all told. Apparently, other than the immediate surroundings for the city, most exports from the city were loaded up on barges and sailed downriver.

The scenery was *spectacular*. With the mountains to Edwin's left, and endless grasslands to his right, the sights were always worth seeing to say nothing of the *stars*.

And oh, the stars. Even back on Earth, Edwin had always loved looking up at the night sky. He'd managed to get far, far out into the country a few times, frequently with his time as a Scout, and beheld the full glory of Earth's starscape with such minimal light pollution as could be found in a modern world.

Here, though? With his newfound supernatural sight? And nary an electric light to be found this side of the universe? It was something else. The colors on display in a proper fantasy world were beyond spectacular, and the moon gleamed like a pink and blue crystal ball amid the green and orange nebulae-like shapes that swept across the sky.

Several nights had been spent lulling himself to sleep as he told Inion all about the incredible things that could be found in the infinite *nothingness* that was space. He spoke of galaxies and white dwarfs, of black holes and supernovae.

Every night, as he drifted off to sleep, Edwin wondered which of those might still exist, off in the eternal nothingness of space, and what further, exotic structures might exist when magic was added into the equation.

One day, he promised himself, *I'll see the stars.*

Maybe I'll feel at home out there.

Despite the interesting things he encountered, Edwin's days were frequently nothing spectacular. When he didn't want to practice Flight, he usually sat on the carriage and experimented with his other Skills. He found that Prototyping could either include or ignore the motion of the road beneath him depending on what he wanted, that Fresh Air leveled best when it had something to filter out, Health meant he never got blisters, and Adaptive Defense kept him from getting sunburns altogether.

Currently, he was seeing how fine of a chain he could make with his Sapper's Apparatus. Consistent use and practice had helped him lower the time required to summon his creations—the Skill leveling did nothing in that regard—but large or intricate creations made that shoot right back up. Chains, depending on how long he made them, met both criteria, and he was practicing summoning them one link at a time, which might well—

"Stop right there!" A voice broke Edwin out of his experimentation. His head jerked up to see a figure standing above him emerge from the surrounding light woods, seemingly melting away from the tree line. "Give me all your valuables!"

Well. It looked like he might have a bit of excitement today after all.

Level Up!

Skill Points 486→522 (Average Level: 33)

Adaptive Defense Level 24→25

Arcadian Elixir Level 8→11

Basic Thermokinesis Level 14→16

Flight Level 23→28

Fresh Air Level 8→11

Improbable Arsenal Level 19→20

Longstrider Level 22→27
Numeracy Level 15→19
Outsider's Almanac Level 128→129
Prototyping Level 13→16
Sapper's Apparatus Level 29→32
Watchful Rest Level 10→15

CHAPTER 6

Focus Is Key

Other than a spear, the man appeared to be unarmed, and he wasn't wearing any armor, just dirty Farmer's clothing. The bandit's eyes were fixed on Edwin, and he was shifting slightly, adjusting the spear to keep the tip pointed at him.

Edwin idly Identified the figure, seeing if . . .

Lirasian Reaper

Well, that Class name was only mildly terrifying, even if it didn't seem to match with the dirty-looking man in front of him.

"Are you dumb? I said, give me your money!"

Perhaps his judgment was *massively* out of tune, but Edwin didn't really feel like he was in that much danger from the bandit. "Why should I do that?"

"Because I'll skewer you if you don't! You got no guards, I'll gut you! I will! You won't be the first!" He paused. "And if you wanna think about fighting, don't! I got twenty more men in the woods, they'll swarm you the moment you make a bad move!"

"You're a terrible liar," Edwin muttered to himself, then reconsidered and said under his breath, "Or an absolute idiot. Maybe both."

He replied more loudly to the man, "Look, I don't really have any aggression to burn off at the moment—you would have needed to show up about two weeks ago for that—so I'm not really in the mood to fight at the moment. What about we make a deal? You turn around and go back to whatever hole you crawled from, and I'll just carry on my way. How does that sound?"

"You won't get away that easily! I'll stab you! I will!"

He was drawing closer to Edwin, the spearpoint getting just a touch close for comfort, and Edwin backed up to regain some distance. "Inion? Any help with this?"

His friend's vaguely sleepy voice sounded from atop the carriage, startling the Reaper, "You got it!" Edwin looked over to see Inion propping herself up on her elbows, looking down at the two of them.

Edwin sighed as the bandit jumped at Inion's voice and he swung to aim his spear at the fey. "Look, last chance to back out," Edwin offered. "There's nothing wrong with admitting you were wrong."

That seemed to be the wrong suggestion, as in response, the man just swung his spear around to aim at Edwin.

He mentally shrugged. Well, it might be fun to stretch his combat muscles. Intimidating Class or no, he didn't get the sense that the bandit was all that good with his weapon or that experienced. He *did* have the bigger weapon, though, so Edwin still needed to be careful.

If Edwin were just using his stick, he would be in serious trouble. The bandit's spear was easily twice as long and had a pointy bit on the end, meaning melee combat was not an option. Doubly so, given that Edwin belatedly realized that his walking stick was currently sitting in the driver's seat of his carriage, as his hands had been occupied with his Apparatus experiments.

Fortunately, Edwin was an *alchemist,* and what sort of alchemist would ever do something so crude as beat up people with a stick?

No, he had much more dignified weapons. Like a box of marbles.

Edwin dropped the chain he'd been working on and reached into one of his pouches, withdrawing a crystal box filled with tiny, marble-sized Apparatus spheres. He threw the container at the bandit's feet, who jumped back and off the ground to try and avoid it. It ended up being the exact wrong reaction, though, as the box broke against the ground, shattering into motes of Skill magic and covering the road with hundreds of the blue-crystal marbles.

The man landed directly atop the marbles, the tiny spheres jetting out every which way as the crystals refused to bear the bandit's weight. As he started to fall, the Reaper's frantically windmilling arms failed to keep him upright, forcing him to a foot down on the ground behind him. Instead of rolling off the hazard, though, the foot managed to *break* the marbles where it landed, giving the bandit the opportunity needed to retrieve his balance. Edwin narrowed his eyes. There had been a Skill involved in that action, he was sure, and flipping Skillful Assessment on confirmed his suspicions as faint brown motes of light dissipated from around the man's foot.

"Surrender now and I'll let you live!" The bandit seemed to have gotten a bit of confidence. "Don't make me call out my men!"

Edwin tsked annoyedly as the remaining marbles rolled off the road. He'd need to make his next batch more resistant to being crushed, and he idly wondered how strong they were. Something to test later, he supposed.

"You're still an awful liar," he responded, floating a few inches above the ground as he watched the rest of the marbles roll off the edge of the road. Hmm. He really ought to—

A flash of reddish Skill light appeared around the bandit, and pain suddenly blossomed in Edwin's side as the man somehow closed the distance between them in the blink of an eye, burying his spear into Edwin's torso.

"You stabbed me?" Edwin asked, more disbelieving than anything.

"He stabbed you?" Inion suddenly seemed to be paying a lot more attention to the fight. She didn't move yet, though.

"I warned you! But you didn't listen. Now look at what you've made me do! Now, . . ." The bandit kept talking, but Edwin wasn't listening, instead focusing on where he felt the spearhead buried in his muscle.

Fey's Caress.

The wound hadn't been too terribly deep—Health must have helped—but it was still deep enough to be lodged inside, and if it was yanked out or shoved in deeper, he'd potentially be in trouble. Before the bandit could do either, though, the area around the wound turned to steel.

It succeeded for a few seconds, as the triumphant grin on the Reaper's face turned to confusion, and Edwin felt some tugging on the transformed area as the man realized his weapon was stuck. Edwin reached up to try and grasp the spear haft, trying to burn it to cinders before . . .

He was too slow, as the bandit yanked on the spear, dragging Edwin forward. Flight ensured he wasn't pulled off-balance, but that was little compensation as the bandit raised his foot, pushed it against Edwin's torso, and activated the same Skill he'd used to crush Edwin's apparatus marbles. Edwin suddenly found himself shoved away, the part of his chest that he'd bonded to the spearhead ripped out.

Edwin gasped in pain, his mind blanking when he tried to focus on literally anything else. He desperately clutched his stomach, trying in some vain attempt to keep his insides where they were supposed to. The shock and burn also broke his concentration on Flight and sent him dropping to the ground. The bandit looked at the haphazard chunk of metal surrounding the spearhead as the Skill faded. As it returned to blood and meat, the bandit's casual interest turned to disgust, and he flicked the section of Edwin's torso away, where it splattered with a wet squelch against the ground.

Trying to accomplish anything through the pain and fumbling at his belt, Edwin's fingers closed around what he was looking for—a hexagonal prism with smooth sides. He drew the healing potion, the milky-white liquid swirling around in its vial, and tossed the entire thing into his mouth, dismissing the Apparatus construction holding it as he did so.

It was his most nonspecific healing potion, little more than a coagulant made from talsanenris, molai, and a tiny drop of sinbalyne, but it should keep him from bleeding out before he could more properly tend to his wounds later on. For good measure, he activated Fey's Caress again, this time binding the wound to the cloth near it. Fabric couldn't bleed, after all.

No longer in mortal danger, Edwin began feeling for the next vial he would need. Triangular with bumps . . . aha! His fingers deftly extracted the tiny vial from his belt, the faintly lavender-colored liquid barely even visible, and he was in the midst of getting it ready when Skillful Assessment warned Edwin of danger.

The bandit began using a Skill, a faintly red light building from around his feet and swirling up around his body and to his spear. It was the same Skill he'd used to dash forward and impale Edwin before, and given where he was looking . . .

Edwin tensed, ready to spring to the side as soon as . . . there!

The Skill reached a critical mass and began to explode toward Edwin. As he was ready for it, he was able to just barely bend out of the way, avoiding the attack and sending the bandit stumbling as he overextended on his strike, giving Edwin just enough room to grab the spear haft, his other hand grabbing the bandit's arm, squishing the vial against his sleeve.

While he may not have been stronger than the Lirasian Reaper, who immediately started pulling away, Edwin *was* strong enough to just lift the bandit wholly into the air like a misbehaving child. It wasn't even hard, at least until the bandit activated a brownish Skill and became really, *really* heavy. His feet were pulled to the ground like a powerful magnet, overpowering even Edwin's insane Packing level.

Once planted, the man became utterly immovable, and he began trying to pull Edwin's hand out from its grip around the spear. He let it go, and the brown Skill light around the bandit's feet flared, keeping the man balanced.

It was enough, though, and Edwin freed his left hand to smash the Apparatus vial against the bandit's face, causing sinbalyne gas to spill into the bandit's face. Edwin disengaged entirely, pushing on Longstrider to carry him away from the man and to the carriage while he let the drug begin to work.

It didn't take long. By the time Edwin had grabbed his stick, the man had already begun to sway unsteadily as the potion induced light-headedness. Edwin swooped in, the man's reactions slowed so much that Edwin was able to entirely circumvent the clumsy attempt to hold him at bay, twisting around the spearpoint and swinging his club at the Reaper's head.

It connected with a *crack*, and the bandit staggered back. Edwin grinned and twirled his stick in his hand, going in for another attack. Ignoring the gaping wound in his stomach, this was—

His thoughts were aborted as the spear came around, with two red Skills intertwined around its length, aimed directly at Edwin's head, looking to spear him right between his eyes. Edwin's mind turned in on itself, a cacophony of ideas bouncing around as he tried to figure out if he could dodge—he couldn't, and *ohshoothereitwas*. The next idea presented automatically won his internal debate, and Edwin slammed as much into his Skill as possible.

Overcharge.

The air turned crystal clear. The spear slowed enough to give Edwin reaction time, and his every muscle thrummed with power. Even with his newfound reaction time, there still wasn't much time to think, and he acted on instinct, turning to avoid the spear and swinging his stick as hard as he could.

The spearpoint didn't even miss entirely, cutting slightly into the back of his skull and letting blood cascade from the wound.

Edwin's retaliation was much more accurate, and Edwin turned his Perception away from tactile feedback as the shudder of his stick impacting the side of the bandit's skull traveled up the length of his weapon. Edwin heard the crunch and squish from the impact as the man's skull tried and failed to protect his brain.

The darkness that set in as Edwin's overworked body rebounded to and below the level of function it ought to have been at was a relief, as it meant he didn't have to see in perfect clarity as the bandit's bloody corpse sank to the ground. The details he could see were bad enough, and Edwin grimaced.

His body ached, burning with the strain of using Overcharge, and Anatomy helpfully informed him that while his intestines weren't punctured, it was a near thing, and that while bloody, the cut on his head wasn't life-threatening, thanks in large part to the antibleed potion he already had in his system.

Trying to use Flight resulted in a curious burning sensation in his chest, and Edwin decided not to push it. Instead, he put up with his protesting legs while he staggered over to the carriage. Bill had stopped walking when Edwin had, and as he sank onto the wooden driver's seat, Inion floated down next to him.

"What have we learned today?"

"That you're an awful guardian," Edwin mumbled. "Like, come on. 'You got this'? I feel offended."

"Mmm . . . not quite."

"I need to work on my marbles."

"Edwin . . ."

He groaned. "Fine. That I need to take better care of myself. Look, are you going to give me a hand with this or not? I'm going to need your help patching myself up, assuming my medicines are even up to the task."

Inion sighed as she ran her fingers through his bloody, matted hair. "Of course I will. Now, make up your mind if you'll hold still or help me while I get all this stuff off you."

Overcharge didn't completely knock Edwin out when used, but he almost wished it would. The persistent pain that racked his body was a constant annoyance, and his every limb felt like he'd Caressed lead. He flatly *couldn't* use any magical Skills, even Infusing Firestarting, so to boil water he needed to actually use his firevine oil for the first time.

He'd remembered to get clean cloths while in Vinstead, so he had bandages, and even tossed some healing potion ingredients into the boiling cauldron. With Inion's help, Edwin gingerly cleaned out his wound. He didn't have any stitches—not for lack of trying, he just fundamentally *did not trust* any of the linen threads available in Vinstead for anatomical work, to say nothing of the incredible lack of steadiness in his leaden arms. So instead, he applied touches of Fey's Caress to some wet clay he'd brought from Obairlann, made his skin nice and pliable, and stuck the two sides together, then let the Skill fade.

It didn't work perfectly, naturally. Beyond the distinct lack of precision he was able to accomplish with his shaking hands, when the Skill went away, skin did as it was wont to and pulled away, trying to return to its original state. However, just enough skin stuck that it created a sort of patchwork rough texture flesh-and-blood construct. A few more rounds of flesh-sculpting later, Edwin had something that should hold for the few days it would take for the primary wound to heal. Magic was great.

From there, he applied a poultice of crushed talsanenris berries, molai flowers, and a drop of firevine sap. The latter of the ingredients would help keep the wound sterilized while it healed over the next few days, with the alchemical fire functioning much like normal fire to creatures unfortunate enough to find themselves submerged in it.

The talsanenris would increase the heat, but thanks to the molai it wouldn't burn him. Instead, it would heat the area and further help combat infection, like the infection was swelling. Once the mixture was applied to the wound, he bandaged his stomach with his sterilized and medicinal bandages.

Edwin's head got a similar treatment, though without playing sculptor with his own skin. He just bandaged the wound after Inion washed out the wound and ensured no hair got into the cut.

One more downed general-purpose healing potion later, Edwin felt pretty decent about his odds about getting back into fighting shape within a decent amount of time. Before he tugged on Sleeping and First Aid to try and refresh him, though, he glanced at his notifications.

Level Up!
Skill Points 522→535
Adaptive Defense Level 25→26
Anatomy Level 26→28
Arcadian Elixir Level 11→14
Fey's Caress Level 35→36
Overcharge Level 3→8
Skillful Assessment Level 30→31

Not too bad. Fighting, or high-pressure situations in general, did a fantastic job of helping him level. He idly wondered which exactly it was, but it wasn't the primary thought in his mind as his tortured limbs were finally allowed to rest.

For the first time in quite a while, Edwin slept dreamlessly and with no awareness of the surrounding world—for the first half of the night, at least. Then he woke up to Watchful Rest helpfully informing him of his aching arms. He tried for a few minutes to get back to sleep naturally before triggering his Healing Rest Skill combination and falling back into pseudo-unconsciousness.

By the time he woke up again, the sun had already risen, and it was to the steady *trot-trot-trot* of Bill's hooves on the road. Despite some momentary panic about what was going on, Edwin swiftly adjusted and peered over the edge of the roof, seeing Inion in the driver's seat idly braiding her hair.

"Good morning?" he tried.

"Ah, you're awake! Good to see! How are you feeling?"

"Good." Edwin yawned, stretching to get the few kinks in his back out. "I think. I've got some phantom soreness, but that's about it." He peeked underneath his bandages. "Pretty much better, too," he noted. Other than a bit of a messy scab around his belly button, and a raised ridge on the back of his hand, there was no sign of the nasty wounds he'd gotten the day before. *Yep*, he thought once again, *magic is great.*

He floated down to sit beside his friend. "I'm surprised you got the day's travel started already."

She shrugged. "Well, *someone* had to do it, and you were lazy this morning," she teased, and Edwin rolled his eyes.

"What did you do with the body?" he asked. He wasn't complaining that he wouldn't have to deal with corpse removal, but he wouldn't have minded looking it over, to see if it had anything of note on it. You *always* searched the body, after all.

"Tossed it into the woods," she nonchalantly replied. "It was just attracting flies."

Fair enough. "I don't suppose you picked up any of my marbles?" He sighed when she shook her head. There was a few hours of work ahead of him, though maybe he could use this as a chance to experiment a bit. Perhaps he could stick caltrops inside of them or make them multilayered, so if the outside was broken, the entire thing wouldn't dissipate?

They passed through several smaller villages on their route, usually one just a bit over a day's travel from the prior. None were that spectacular, though, consisting of a few buildings and a tavern or inn (what was the difference?), usually with a marginally higher concentration of homes in its vicinity.

There were also *lots* of Curicnan way-shrines, and they passed one or two each day. Edwin was content with his current sleeping arrangement atop his carriage, though, and so didn't bother using them. Sometimes, Inion would join him atop the roof, and the two would stargaze for hours until Edwin fell asleep. About half the time, she was still there when he woke up. It was . . . it was nice to have her by his side.

If only *humans* could get along with him. Or, he supposed he'd accept other fey as friends, but there was no way he'd find another Inion.

Edwin kept himself busy, mainly experimenting with his Apparatus. Of all his new Skills, it was the one he was perhaps the most excited to really try out and experiment with. "Limits loosening" as the level increased implied that he'd get the most benefit of any of his Skills from leveling it, too. Maybe he could make the crystal flexible at some point.

For now, though, Edwin had a simple, if ambitious, goal, and one that could be fairly powerful if he could manage it. He wanted to get a comprehensive list of Sapper's Apparatus's physical specifications. Refractive index for fun with light, density and tensile strength for building things, heat conductivity and capacity for fun with fire and insulation, electrical conductivity in case *that* ever came up, and more. That would take him more time than even he had right now, so he decided to focus his efforts on the more immediately practical quantities.

Starting off with optics, Edwin quickly found that he only half remembered the required equations that he'd need to figure out the refractive index, so he had to re-derive most of them from scratch. In that whole process, Mathematics proved to be an utter *lifesaver*, and Numeracy helped a ton. But he still needed to use Almanac and Memory to avoid getting lost in the numbers. Matrix translations were no joke, even if the derivations themselves weren't too bad, though far, *far* from trivial.

His plan was to make a lens out of his Apparatus crystal, figure out what its focal length was, run some calculations based on the shape of the lenses and using the refractive index as the unknown, and solve from there. Normally, you knew the refractive index—glass was 1.5, water was 1.33, air was basically 1—and were trying to find the focal length, but the nice thing about math was it didn't matter what your unknown was, so long as there was only one.

Edwin had at first tried to use the thin-lens optics equations, but his results were wildly inconsistent until he stumbled upon his problem—namely, that his lenses weren't infinitely thin. Trying to measure the refractive index by making a prism didn't work—the light just exited a uniform bluish color that matched his crystal. That *implied* things, but he held his excitement until he could measure it more precisely.

He couldn't calculate the refraction index just from the pyramid's refraction either, sadly. The sorts of calculations needed required all sorts of tricky reference frame changes and angle calculations that Edwin wasn't sure he wanted to tangle with.

It was hard enough for him to re-derive the thick-lens matrix equations, he didn't want to do any more work than he needed to.

So Edwin now sat with an array of Apparatus crystal (he needed a better name for it than just that . . . he'd think of one eventually) rods, each as close to perfectly round and 1 centimeter in diameter as he could make them. Once he had numbers on the refractive index, he could do more work to figure out how precise he could make his Apparatus.

Thick-lens equations had been a colossal pain for Edwin once upon a time, but considering these days he could multiply two nine-by-nine matrices in his head thanks to Mathematics, it wasn't so bad. It just involved three basic components: a term to account for the initial refraction, when light passed from the air into the lens; a translation term for how thick the lens was; and a term to account for the refraction out of the lens and back into the air.

Things got more complicated when multiple lenses got involved, or when you started including reflection terms, but he was keeping things simple for now. And that meant figuring out the initial ray-matrix for his light source of the sun. If he assumed it was infinitely far away, all its light would be parallel, and by defining his axes properly he could . . .

Anyway.

Basically, he'd be running the calculation for a single ray of light with an angle of 0 radians at +0.5 centimeters, measure where it crossed the y-axis—namely, where the focal point of the rod was—and from there he could back-calculate what the refractive index was.

He cracked his knuckles and pulled up Almanac. This would be a lot of numbers.

Even *Edwin's* eyes were glazing over by the time he finally got his equation in a half-readable state. He triumphantly looked over all he had accomplished as he did the final calculations . . .

$$\begin{bmatrix} \dfrac{1}{n-n'} & \dfrac{L}{n} \\[2mm] \dfrac{}{Rn} & \dfrac{}{n'} \end{bmatrix}\begin{bmatrix} 1 & L \\ 0 & 1 \end{bmatrix}\begin{bmatrix} \dfrac{1}{n'-n} & \dfrac{L}{n'} \\[2mm] \dfrac{}{Rn'} & \dfrac{}{n} \end{bmatrix}\begin{bmatrix} y_0 \\ \alpha_0 \end{bmatrix} = \begin{bmatrix} y_f \\ \alpha_f \end{bmatrix}$$

$$\begin{bmatrix} 1 + 2L\dfrac{n'-n}{Rn'} & \left(1 + 2\dfrac{n'}{n}\right)L \\[4mm] \dfrac{n-n'}{Rn} + \dfrac{n'-n}{Rn'}\left(\dfrac{n-n'}{Rn}L + \dfrac{n}{n'}\right) & \dfrac{n^2 - n'^2}{Rn^2}L + 1 \end{bmatrix}\begin{bmatrix} y_0 \\ \alpha_0 \end{bmatrix} = \begin{bmatrix} y_f \\ \alpha_f \end{bmatrix}$$

$$\begin{bmatrix} y_0\left(1 + 2L\dfrac{n'-n}{Rn'}\right) + \alpha_0 L\left(1 + 2\dfrac{n'}{n}\right) \\[4mm] y_0\left(\dfrac{(nn'^2 - Rn'^3) + (Rn^2 + Lnn' - Ln'^2)(n'-n)}{R^2 nn'^2}\right) + \left(\dfrac{n^2 - n'^2}{Rn^2}L + 1\right)\alpha_0 \end{bmatrix} = \begin{bmatrix} y_f \\ \alpha_f \end{bmatrix}$$

$$y_0 + y_0 2L\frac{n'-n}{Rn'} + \alpha_0 L + \alpha_0 L2\frac{n'}{n} = y_f$$

Which we can then substitute our values of $y0 = .5$ cm, $L = 2$ cm, $n = 1$, $R = 1$, $yf = 0$ cm, $a0 = 0$ for:

$$.5\,cm + (.5\,cm) \cdot 2 \cdot 2\,cm \cdot \frac{n'-1}{1\,cm \cdot n'} = 0\,cm$$

Solving for n' gives:

$$n' = 1.25\,n'$$

$$1 = 1.25'$$

Wait, no. That didn't make sense.

Edwin groaned as he looked to try and figure out where his mistake was. He shouldn't have everything drop out so quickly. There was bound to be somewhere that the angle wasn't supposed to cancel quite yet. He was confident his equations were correct; he'd double-checked them a ton of times with various situations he knew the answer to.

"Stupid magical math Skills, don't even prevent me from making stupid mistakes. I swear, this was just like the *actual* class," he muttered.

It took him another *six hours* before he finally got all his equations lined up properly, and he had to use *another* set of formulae that would help him figure out the focal length from the matrix.

"And so then, the value of q is the distance from the closest point of the cylinder to where the focal point is—that's where all the light is concentrated into a single line, see? And q is A over C . . . no wait, that's not right. Ah, *minus* A over C, with A being the top left value of the matrix, and C is—"

"Okay, *okay!*" Inion cut him off. "*I get it!*"

"You do?" Edwin was surprised. "Because it seemed like you weren't a moment ago."

"No, *no*. I get that I'll *never* get this, and you can stop trying to explain what all this is about now."

"But it's so *easy!* Like, look, you don't have to understand that diagram. All that matters is that by substituting q for what we measured, five and a half centimeters, and assuming the air has a refractive index of exactly 1, and that the rod's diameter is two centimeters, we can figure out what *n prime* should be. See, like . . ."

"No! Nope!"

"It's *easy* though!"

"You take your blight-shunned numbers away from me! I still don't even understand what these decimal things are!"

"I thought you understood those? It's just a positional number system. So like . . ."

"No!"

"But . . ."

"Go talk to Bill if you have to tell somebody! He'll understand as much as I do!"

"Please?"

"No!"

* * *

So hopefully somebody *will eventually enjoy all these equations, after nobody now seems to appreciate the finer points of Physics. Anyway, check OpticsFormulae for the component equations, and if you really must, OpticsDerivationIndex has records of calculating all those equations from scratch. You're welcome, future person who will likely never be reading this because you'd need to be Identifying the crystal that Sapper's Apparatus creates. Or just looking at the page I make for it once I figure out what to call it, anyway.*

Now I'm just rambling. Here's the math.

$$q = -\frac{A}{C} = -\frac{1 + 2L\frac{n'-n}{Rn'}}{\frac{n-n'}{Rn} + \frac{n'-n}{Rn'}\left(\frac{n-n'}{Rn}L + \frac{n}{n'}\right)}$$

L=2 cm, R = 1 cm, n = 1, n' =?, q = 5.5 cm

$$-\frac{1 + 4\frac{n'-1}{n'}}{1 - n' + \frac{n'-1}{n'}\left(2(1-n') + \frac{1}{n'}\right)} = 5.5$$

$$4n' = -114n' + 66n'^2 + 23 + \frac{22}{n'}$$

$$n'(n'(118 - 66n') - 23) = 22$$

$$n' = 1.34$$

"Wait, isn't that the same as water? That doesn't seem right." Edwin sat back as he did the last bit of math. To confirm, he quickly conjured two spheres, one which he filled with water and the other as a solid crystal. Sure enough, they had different focus lengths.

"Hmm."

His math didn't seem to have any errors in it, after checking it several times over, which meant his measurements must have been off. He rechecked his measurement distances, finding his error quickly once Numeracy hit level 29. Focusing on it so much had raised it a *ton*, and it was already paying off.

"Ah. Not five and a half. Five point seven-five."

"I'm still not listening!" Inion yelled from the top of the carriage.

"I'm not talking to you!" he called back. "I'm just talking to myself!"

"Good! You found the only person on Joriah who *will* listen, then!"

"Oh, go jump in your pond!"

"*You* go jump in my pond! "

"Make me!" he yelled back.

Edwin patted Bill's head, the pony having stayed calm throughout their entire exchange. "You wouldn't get mad at me for talking, would you?"

His pack animal just flicked an ear in reply, and Edwin rolled back to stare at the sky, continuing to float in a fixed reference to the carriage. Okay, so he had the wrong focal length. How did fixing that change things . . .

Okay, so after rerunning the numbers, it looked like apparatite, as he had settled on, had a refractive index of 1.43. More than water, less than glass.

What was quite interesting, and quite frustrating, was that all light was bent equally by the crystal and didn't vary with wavelength. That meant he couldn't make a diffraction grating or prism out of apparatite, but did mean he could . . .

Honestly, he didn't know how he might be able to abuse that yet. But he'd figure it out at some point. Maybe there were some sort of fiber optic shenanigans he could get up to?

It wasn't too much of a limitation, anyway, as he could just shove a bunch of water into an apparatite container and use that instead. He could even modulate the water's refractive index slightly, by applying varying degrees of Improbable Arsenal to increase the density of the water inside, which he could probably use to figure out exactly how much of an increase Arsenal gave to the space it affected at some point, if there weren't already *much* easier ways to accomplish that same task.

Density was significantly easier to figure out. Though Numeracy didn't give him mass measurements, it *did* give him volume. Even still, copper coins weren't terribly easy to estimate the volume of, unless he set up a displacement measurement system, which Apparatus made trivial.

Honestly, Outsider's Almanac was having serious competition for the status of Edwin's favorite Skill these days. The ability to essentially 3-D print anything he could imagine *at will*, out of a type of crystal, was just *so darn amazing*. He didn't even have to worry about this one clogging or running out of filament!

Still, once Edwin knew the volume of a given ager, it was trivial to convert it to mass—copper had a density of 8.96 g/cm3—and use the coins as weights to compare against his apparatite.

By making a scale—it took him a few tries to get it appropriately balanced, but he managed it in the end—he was able to take a 1-cubic-centimeter block of apparatite and weigh it against his coins. It didn't take long, though it *did* require mutilation of a couple coins, to find the density was 2.44 g/cm3.

Once he had density, tensile strength was similarly trivial to determine. He fashioned a thin rod of apparatite, half a centimeter in diameter, and put a small loop on the end, from which he hung several known-volume blocks of apparatite.

At a whopping *318* kilograms, the stress on the apparatite finally was enough, and it all gave way, sending his ever-growing collection of crystal blocks cascading across the ground. With some quick math, Edwin figured that the tensile strength of the stuff was a respectable 149 Mpa, which was about half the compressive strength of *concrete*. It would hold up to a lot of stuff, that was certain.

Edwin sat back, content as he finished filling out his personal Almanac page on apparatite. He didn't have information on heat or electrical conductivity or capacitance yet, but those experiments could wait until he started exploring Basic Thermokinesis. His head hurt enough from the optics derivations he'd been doing for the past week, and he wanted a break.

"Okay, you can come out from hiding now." He told the top of his carriage. A few seconds later, the drifting hair of Inion came into view as she peered over the edge.

"Are you *actually* done this time, or are you just pretending again?"

"Look, I keep telling you it wasn't intentional! You just happened to say the perfect thing to get me unstuck from where I was at."

"Uh-huh. And that *won't* happen this time?"

"No! I'm done. For now, anyway. I have all the basic info I can think of for apparatite. Refractory index, density, tensile strength—"

"Okay, that's enough!"

"Wait, no! It was just . . ." Edwin trailed off as the fey fled back out of immediate earshot. ". . . those three."

He sighed. Well, he shouldn't be surprised that Inion couldn't stand him getting really involved in physics and material science stuff. Nobody *else* could, either, but he had vaguely hoped his "friend" would be able to at least *try* to act interested.

Well, he shouldn't have been surprised. Their interactions had been mainly on Inion's terms, and he hadn't had much of an opportunity to really show what his deep personality was like. No wonder she fled at the first opportunity when he started bringing it up.

Maybe he would be able to find someone in Panastalis who could appreciate the sort of work Edwin was doing with material science. A whole town of alchemists, or at least with a heavy alchemist focus. Surely someone there would be an aspiring chemist as well, right? Someone he could talk *science* with? He missed that sort of thing. Just being able to geek out with people . . . He hadn't found a replacement yet. He kept hoping, though.

Well, he'd find out soon enough. He directed Bill off the main road, and the tireless pony turned off onto the wide dirt path leading into the forest. About half an hour later, a giant grin crept across Edwin's face.

A massive tree dominated the area, its canopy hundreds of feet above them, casting the area in shadow. Beneath its leafy boughs ran a moderately sized river that quickly vanished into a moss-covered hole in the ground, surrounded by a slew of wooden and stone houses, mossy and ivy in some places. In a couple of instances, houses were built directly onto the massive tree, massive roots or branches serving as bridges from the buildings on the tree to the rest of the village.

It looked like it had been ripped straight from a fairy tale, and Edwin couldn't stop smiling.

Panastalis. He'd finally made it.

Level Up!
Skill Points 543→573
Arcadian Elixir Level 14→16
Flight Level 28→32
Fresh Air Level 11→14
Improbable Arsenal Level 20→23
Longstrider Level 27→29
Memory Level 59→60
Numeracy Level 27→32
Outsider's Almanac Level 129→130
Sapper's Apparatus Level 32→37
Skillful Assessment Level 31→32
Watchful Rest Level 15→18

Congratulations! For reaching level 60 in a Mental Skill, you have unlocked the Mentalist Path!

Congratulations! For exploring the utility of a new substance in the creation of new devices, you have unlocked the Engineer Path!

Congratulations! For deriving multiple optics equations from scratch, you have unlocked the Physicist Path!

Congratulations! For understanding and explaining complex mathematics, you have unlocked the Mathematician Path!

Congratulations! For thoroughly exploring the properties of a new material, you have unlocked the Material Scientist Path!

Congratulations! For pushing the boundaries of what you know about your Skills, you have unlocked the Skill Researcher Path!

CHAPTER 7

Recipe for Success

A few people naturally took note of Edwin rattling up to the entry of the town, but none paid him much attention. It made a certain amount of sense; they probably had loads of travelers and merchants coming in and out of the town on a regular basis.

In fact, he could even tell where the inn for the town was thanks to the row of wagons that had pulled up beside it, a few individuals milling around them. A few individuals caught his eye—one Skyguard and two Hired Guards already had Almanac tags on them from when he'd last traveled with a merchant caravan. He was vaguely hopeful he'd spot more familiar faces out and about, but it seemed that the trio had simply been hired by a different set of merchants. Even the wagons weren't the ones that he had seen before, and Edwin couldn't imagine they had an excessive number of those lying around.

As they pulled up to the inn, Edwin allowed Bill to loiter as he hopped down and drifted inside. The tireless pony lowered his head and started nibbling at a few tufts of hardy grass that had survived on a hard-packed dirt road.

Although Edwin's eyes didn't need to adjust too much as he entered the building, the massive leafy boughs of the tree Panastalis was built around already casting the entire city into shadow, his ears certainly did. Inside, a couple dozen individuals with a mix of travel-related

Classes and more typical Identify results sat around, eating, drinking, and enjoying a Melodic Wanderer's song as he sat, playing a stringed instrument that Edwin recognized from the road.

The innkeeper—a Canny High Merchant—looked at Edwin with a skeptical eye as he approached. "We don't serve your type here."

Edwin looked down at himself. "Look, I know most people don't like Adventurers," he started, confused, "but I assure you, I have dispensation for—"

"No, not *Adventurers*, you daft fool. *Alchemists*."

"Hold on, what?" Of all the things Edwin was expecting to potentially run into trouble for, being an alchemist in the alchemist town was *not* one of them.

"You're not guilded. I serve you, I'm inviting all kinds of trouble onto myself."

"Well, okay, but—"

"Out! Don't want your trouble."

"I was sent by the Emperor." It was perhaps a bit of a stretch, but not *that* much of one. Edwin would argue that the Emperor telling him to go and learn stuff on his own merit did include visiting Panastalis and learning about Alchemy. He might not have *specifically* said to do so, but . . .

That caught the innkeeper's attention. "You're lying."

"Nope! Talked to him just a month ago."

"You're either brazen or stupid."

Edwin gave a slight shrug and a smirk.

"Five ager a night."

Edwin scoffed. "That's robbery! Back in the city I got half a month for that price."

"This isn't the city," he shot back, and Edwin noticed a Skill interlacing the words. "It's a lot more expensive out here. Four."

"That's not how money works at *all*. Things are always pricier in a city because more people want the stuff."

"Yeah, well, look around. I'm not exactly hurting for business, and *they* won't get the place burned down by just existing. Nonguild alchemists are *not* welcome here, and I'm not taking that on my head."

"I'll look to join the guild? Actually, how do you know I'm not already part of it?"

"Well, if you were, you wouldn't be staying here."

"Any idea how I join the guild?"

"Nothin' specific."

"Anything general?"

"Well, I don't know where you come from, but it's usually considered bad business to give something away for free."

"Where I come from, helping out potential customers is a great way to get on their good side and make them want to choose your place."

"Ha! Where else would you go?"

"Well, apparently where— Ah. I see." Edwin sighed and grabbed a few ves from an internal pocket. "Will this do?" He slid the coins over.

"It's a start." The avior swept a wing over the counter, making the coins vanish with the hint of a Skill. "You can find the guildhouse on Stalis."

"The tree?" Edwin guessed.

The avior gave a quick nod. "You can't miss it."

"Sounds like I didn't get my money's worth," Edwin grumbled. "So a room?"

"If you join with the guild, then you won't need one."

"I have a traveling companion. Would she be really welcome in whatever guild-approved housing they have?"

"Two of you?"

"I *would* have asked for two rooms, but not at those prices. We'll settle for one."

"Hmm." The innkeeper tucked his head into his shoulder and preened some of the feathers there in thought. "I suppose there'd be no harm in renting to a passerby. She's not an alchemist, right?"

Edwin shook his head.

"Two ager a night for the two of you; you get the largest room I don't already have claimed."

"Please, I'm not a fool. I can sleep in my cart if nothing else. I did it on the road. One. Though I do have a pony that needs stabling, I could go up a bit for that."

"Three per two days, and we feed and stable your horse."

It wasn't *great*, but he'd take it.

"Deal."

It didn't take long for Edwin to get Bill and Inion properly situated in their respective places—though the latter immediately fled the inn, claiming she wanted to play in the river. Honestly, he felt like a parent at times, despite Inion being at least a hundred times older than he was.

He didn't waste any time once he was free and quickly made his way to Stalis. In some ways, Edwin felt that his sense of grandeur had perhaps shifted slightly since he had arrived in Joriah, in large part thanks to Vinstead's garrison and living in a literal fairy-tale home for a year. It was perhaps the primary reason the massive guild hall-complex built into a tree larger than a football field didn't amaze him, with its grand, sweeping roof and skylights spilling golden shafts of light across the floor.

The latter feature caught Edwin off guard, though it took him a moment to put his finger on *why*. Then it hit him. There wasn't any direct sunlight underneath Stalis; the apparent sunlight spilling into the room was artificial, mimicking the lighting away from the massive tree that was the town's namesake. That was . . . Well, Edwin didn't even know how to *begin* doing something like that.

Okay. That's not entirely true. The first step would be figuring out if they have some sort of light-storing or light-transmitting material that they could use to bring sunlight in. It might even use sunstalk. Perhaps by making some sort of transmission method or alchemical preparation to keep it active? Though that would just diffuse, not stick in cohesive sunbeams. Unless they had some kind of focusing effect. Maybe an alchemical crystal of some kind? Though that's basically just saying "magic." Just saying "A Wizard did it" is not *a real answer, darn it! How did the wizard do it, and how—*

"Can I help you, sir?" a mildly annoyed voice cut in, and Edwin sheepishly looked back at the receptionist. He looked human but had oddly purplish-gray skin and a dour expression. A quick Identify let him see the man was a Fastidious Alchemist, and Edwin nodded in apology.

"Sorry. Just admiring the architecture," he apologized. "I'd like to try and join the guild? What sort of thing does that require, what does it entail, that sort of thing."

"Yes, well. You need the Alchemy Skill—"

"I have that, yes," Edwin interrupted, then glanced away in apology when the man glared at him. "Sorry."

"The Alchemy Skill and Alchemist's Insight at level thirty, then you'll need to undergo a series of quality and knowledge tests before you can become a full member."

"Knowledge test? How does that work?"

"I was getting there," he replied, annoyed. Edwin avoided eye contact as the receptionist continued, "If you need additional tutelage in alchemy for the examination, the guild offers classes for aspiring alchemists for a mere seven ager per week."

"Mere?" Edwin was shocked. "That's half a grai per month! Why is everything so expensive in this tiny town?"

"If you cannot afford the prices, the guild offers loans for perfectly reasonable interest rates and may be paid off once a full member via commission work or general labor."

Edwin just glared at the receptionist.

I swear, it's student loans all over again.

"How long do most students take to learn everything?"

"Oh, usually a year or two if being trained from the Six"—Edwin recalled that the Basic Six were the Skills everyone had from childhood—"I don't know how long you would require, but likely a few months."

Edwin stewed for a few moments. "What about just taking the test? Can I prove that I'm a competent enough alchemist without having to take the classes for the specific terminology you all learn? I'm sure I can pick it up quickly enough anyway."

I hope.

"Hmm." The receptionist continued to sneer at Edwin. "Well, I'm not sure what we can do about that, but I suppose I can pass the message along to my superiors and see what they say."

"Thank you." Edwin nodded, though he internally wondered what the guy's problem was, not that he was really surprised that he was already annoyed with him.

He shuffled between his feet awkwardly. "So . . . what now?"

The receptionist looked up at Edwin. "Where can we find you?"

"I heard you guys had housing or something?" He doubted that it'd be open for him, but he didn't want to bring trouble on to the innkeeper if he could help it.

"Guild members only. If you're applying . . . see about getting a room at the inn. Tell the innkeeper you're a Prospective if he gives you any trouble."

Edwin nodded. "Thanks. You'll . . . find me there, I guess."

From there, it was rather simple to retreat, only slightly marveling at the massive displays of Skills that were omnipresent in the guildhall and faintly permeated the air. Inion was still gone when he got back to the inn, and so Edwin shut himself in his room and kept playing with his Skills.

Apparatus was as interesting as ever; as the Skill hit level 40, Edwin managed to create a fine chain reminiscent of a necklace string. In fact, he decided that was what he'd use it for, and he looped it around his neck, the crystal glittering in the light of his glowing potion bottles next to where Inion's Muse Token hung.

It was easy, if tedious, to layer instances of the Skill, and Edwin got his marble box about half restocked with recursive marbles—spheres stacked within one another—before giving up. He had made one marble of about twenty layers of Apparatus before deciding it was *way* too much work, and his future creations only had three nested spheres. Hopefully it would be enough, because he was already so very bored just making marble after marble.

He'd finish them up at a later point, and make his caltrop marbles at some point in the future as well. But for now . . .

Edwin swiped through his Status. He'd done well and he couldn't help but feel a bit proud. He'd gotten a lot in just the last few months. Sure, his pace was nowhere close to what he'd had in his dedicated year of training, but it was also so much less stressful—and he'd gotten so many new Paths, too!

Name

Edwin Maxlin

Age

1 year

Race

Extraplanar Human

Class

Alchemist-Errant

Attributes

Health 22

Impact 7

Mana 33

Perception 19

Stamina 30

Skills

Alchemical

Alchemy: 83, Alchemical Analysis: 15, Refine: 1, Alchemical Dismantling: 6, Sapper's Apparatus: 40

(Purify: 75)

Magical

Basic Thermokinesis: 16, Fey's Caress: 36, Ritual Intuition: 20, Mana Infusion: 85

Flight: 9, (Basic Mana Sense: 82), (Basic Mana Manipulation: 9)

Physical

Overcharge: 8, Longstrider: 29, Fresh Air: 14

(Athletics: 81), (Breathing: 76), (Flexibility: 74), (Nutrition: 73), (Packing: 92), (Seeing: 72), (Sleeping: 73), (Survival: 76), (Walking: 74)

Mental

Numeracy: 14, Prototyping: 16, Anatomy: 28, Polyglot: 60, Memory: 60

(Language: 36), (Mathematics: 74), (Research: 50), (Visualization: 80)

Combat

Bomb Throwing: 49, Adaptive Defense: 26

(Throwing Weapons: 48)

Utility

Outsider's Almanac: 130, Watchful Rest: 18, Skillful Assessment: 32, Arcadian Elixir: 16, Improbable Arsenal: 23 (Firestarting: 94), (Improvisation: 14), (Status: 22), (Identify: 80), (First Aid: 82), (Harvesting: 76), (Construction: 77)

Paths

Skill Points: 576

Combat

Assassin 0/60, Bomber 0/60, Giant Slayer 0/60, Heedless Hunter 0/60, Hunter 0/30, Killer 0/30, Titan Slayer 0/90, Warrior 0/60, Way of the Empty Hand 0/60, Trapper 0/60

Alchemy

Alchemical Medic 0/60, Demolitionist 0/60, Makeshift Alchemist 0/60, Potioneer 0/60

Science

Chemist 0/60, Experimenter 0/60, Researcher 0/60, Purifier 0/30, Scientific Revolutionary 0/90, Scientist 0/60, Engineer 0/60, Physicist 0/60, Mathematician 0/60, Material Scientist 0/60

Magic

Aerialist 0/60, Fey Friend 0/60, Feybound 0/60, Feycaller 0/60, Mage 0/60, Magical Gardener 0/60, Micro-Biomancer 0/90, Primal Constructor 0/90, Primal Ritualist 0/90, Realm Traveler 0/120, Skilled Arcanist 0/60, Fey Supplicant 0/60, Feykind 0/90

Mental

Dedicated Student 0/60, Lecturer 0/30, Scholar 0/60, Unbowed 0/90, Canny 0/60, Steady Mind 0/60, Mentalist 0/60

System

Almanac Administrator 0/60, Forerunner 0/60, Outsider's Almanac Specialist 0/90, Pioneer 0/60, Skill Researcher 0/60, System Scholar 0/60

Trophy

Blackstone Conqueror 0/60, Deepwoods Panther-Hunter 0/60, Stonehide Vanquisher 0/60

Career

Brickmaker 0/30, Butcher 0/30, Diver 0/30, Gardener 0/30,

Lumberjack 0/60, Merchant 0/30, Potter 0/30, Scribe 0/30,
Woodsman 0/30
Physical
Ascetic 0/60, Daredevil 0/60, Physical Alchemist 0/90, Survivor
0/60, Physical Laborer 0/30
Traveling
Escapee 0/30, Exile 0/30, Traveler 0/30, World Traveler 0/60
Medical
Field Medic 0/60, Medic 0/30, Steadfast Medic 0/60
Misc
Arsonist 0/60, Autopyromaniac 0/60, Burglar 0/60, Child 0/12,
Expert 0/60, Imperial Ally 0/60, Novice 0/12, Pyromaniac 0/30,
Razer of the Ruined Tower 0/60, Rebel 0/30, Slave 0/12, Trainee
0/60, Traitor 0/60, Brushed by Power 0/60, Lirasian Citizen 0/30,
Royal Adviser 0/60, Favored by Power 0/90
Completed Paths
CharLimitCanttalkmuchNocluewhathappenedDidmybestto-
helpyouli, Mage, Skilled Arcanist, Physical Alchemist, Bomber,
Linguist, Beginner, Warrior, Path Less Traveled, Athlete, Scout,
Unkillable, Superior Alchemist, Adventurer, Explorer, Out-
sider, Skill Researcher, Wanderer, Alchemical Warrior, Novice
Pyromancer, Novice Ritualist, Alchemist, Physicist, Engineer,
Physical Arcanist, Biologist, Practical Alchemist, Fey Scion,
Feytouched

Edwin idly toyed with the message, musing about what he wanted
to evolve Flight with. Aerialist was the boring option, no doubt. If he
were to hazard a guess . . . it might improve his maneuverability in-air?
Meh. What he really wanted was *telekinesis*, because that was perhaps
the single most awesome and broken superpower ever.

Plus, it would be great for sealed experiments and making volatile
stuff without risking his own life and limb.

But mainly it was just obscenely broken. Be able to flatly violate the
third law of motion? Yes please. He'd tried picking up a Tactile Telekinesis Skill by messing around with Packing and Mana Infusion again,
but to no avail. He just couldn't get it to "click" quite right. Maybe he'd

manage it one day, unless there was some sort of strange one-new-skill-per-combination rule to the System, which he didn't *think* was the case but he couldn't totally rule out either.

He didn't really know *what* he should try to use to get Telekinesis from Flight. None of his Paths particularly seemed to lean in that direction. Hmm . . .

Ah well, it wasn't like he was in any kind of rush. He didn't want to evolve Flight until it was at *least* level 60, and he had a pretty solid spread of abilities already. Tier 3 would bring with it a whole suite of awesome new powers, sure, but why rush it? Leveling all his current Skills to superhigh levels would help a lot too.

Satisfied, Edwin dismissed the notification and rose from his bed, looking outside. Hmm. It was starting to get dark. Inion had yet to return, but that was hardly a surprise. She'd be out playing in the water for a week if she could. They'd spent relatively little time traveling by rivers, so this was the first time in quite a while where she'd had extensive time submerged.

Well, maybe he'd hear from the guild tomorrow.

Bedtime for now.

"There was a message for you this morning."

The voice snapped Edwin out of his morning stupor slightly as he stared at the innkeeper. He'd just descended from his room. "Sorry, wha?" he blinked.

"A runner from the guild dropped this off for you. It is for you, right?"

The avior swept a wing across the counter, depositing a small black pebble on the wood. Edwin blinked at it uncomprehendingly. "Um. I may still be waking up, but that's a rock?"

Edwin was still awful at reading avior expressions, but it was clear even to him that the innkeeper was looking at Edwin like he was an idiot. Which wasn't really a *surprise*, but it didn't help him much here.

"Some problem?"

"Well . . . it's a rock."

"You have an issue with rocks? Where did you come from?"

"A very long way away, apparently," Edwin responded. "I still don't see how the rock plays into this."

"Have you never seen a message stone before? What did they use back for you?"

"Ink and paper, usually. So, what am I missing here?"

"The stone. Identify it." He was *really* done with Edwin, wasn't he? Sigh.

Edwin shrugged and triggered Identify on the pebble.

Itsa rock!
A very rocky rock. Rocking all over. It rocks. Not a very big rock, though. It might be stoned. Maybe it will roll?

Okay, that didn't work. Material?

I think this is granite?

Alchemical Analysis?

50–90% Quartz
50–90% Elemental Oxygen

He should update his Quartz tag to be silica, shouldn't he? It would also be nice if he was able to get actually pure substances so he could Almanac them properly and definitely . . . Eh, project for another day.

Edwin shook his head. "Not getting it. Not sure what you're trying to get me to do?"

"Didn't you Identify it?"

"I did. No messages, though."

"You don't even have *Common Knowledge*?"

"Look, I come from so far away, you wouldn't even believe it. I don't suppose you could read it for me?" he sheepishly asked.

"Fine," the innkeeper squacked. "But you'll pay."

"How much? I'll pay double for my breakfast."

"Hmm. That'll be ten ves, then, and you need to wait until I've got everyone else taken care of."

"Fine," Edwin acquiesced, mostly just not wanting to make any kind of scene—being seriously overcharged was fine when the payment was on the order of *ves*—and slid the copper coins to the avior, who swept them up off the counter with the same Skill.

"Thank you for your patronage."

"Food and message, please?" Edwin tapped his foot on the floor as he took a seat.

"Certainly, certainly." The innkeeper stepped into the next room over and returned a moment later with a small loaf of bread on a wooden platter. Edwin took it and tore off a chunk, chewing on the food while waiting for his answer.

"To the Alchemist-Errant, come to the Cope Hall at noon for an assessment of your capabilities."

"That's it?" Edwin was incredulous. "There's really nothing else?"

"You're welcome to look at it yourself. Or perhaps not?"

Edwin glared at the bird, snatched his pebble and loaf off the counter, and returned to his room.

Noon came around quickly enough and brought with it Edwin at "Cope Hall," a location he'd had to ask for directions in finding. It turned out to be a smaller building with doors surrounded by intricate carvings depicting some kind of story. Edwin was sure that it would be meaningful to somebody, but he couldn't make heads or tails out of the scenes depicted. Something about people and avior, along with children. Trees were involved somehow . . . ah! It was the history of Panastalis, wasn't it? Hmm. So that would probably be representative of alchemy somehow? What were they *doing*?

His slow piecing together of the decorations was cut short as Edwin realized he might run late if he spent too much longer on the task, and he cautiously crept inside. The interior wasn't particularly well-lit, with the only sources of illumination being torches burning in an eerie green color, casting a pallor upon every surface and making it all look . . . sickly. The walls were lined with skulls and bones, darkly bubbling vials and bottles that were either faintly glowing or just catching the light in an odd way.

It was, in short, an extremely theatrical re-creation of what a "potions lab" might be, sans a— Oh wait, no. There was the cauldron, though it wasn't bubbling and the presumed firepit it sat over remained unlit and stocked with white rods that Edwin couldn't Identify. There wasn't anyone that Edwin could see in the room, though.

"Hello?" he asked cautiously, looking around for whoever was supposed to be examining him. "I was told to come here?"

There was no response, so Edwin took a seat on a nearby stool and waited.

After five minutes, Edwin was starting to get a bit impatient. Was he supposed to do something? He was pretty sure this was Cope Hall, and it was noon. Was his examiner running late or seeing what Edwin was able to come up with entirely on his own part of the test?

Hmm. Well, he didn't know enough about any of the miscellaneous things in the room to do anything with them, so what did he have on him? He patted down his pockets, looking in his satchel. He mildly regretted off-loading pretty much all his ingredients into his cart, but it wasn't like he could do precision mixing on the fly when fighting. Besides, they were likely safer when secured under several layers of Apparatus and hidden on the underside of his shelf than they would be on his person.

Some of what Edwin did have was more appropriate for use in further experimentation, though. Concentrated firevine and sinbalyne oil, a few dried talsanenris berries, a flask of distilled water, and . . . not much else. Well, he could always make a healing potion. Maybe something to counteract hypothermia?

It was easy enough to make his tools—Sapper's Apparatus meant he was never without a mixing bowl or stirring rod—and he settled in, geared up, and got started.

The primary component was water, naturally. The substances he dealt with were all far too potent to be used undiluted. It was also the one ingredient he could be generous with; he could concentrate the potion later by boiling some off if need be, and it was the one ingredient he had a functionally unlimited supply of. His heatstone had been set on permanent duty in his carriage as a source of heat for his distillery, and by consistently filling the water feed tank, he had nearly a barrel of distilled water ready for use at all times. He also had set up a charcoal filter to try and purify fresh water and . . . well, he was getting distracted.

Edwin took a small measure of the water and, with a flex of Basic Thermokinesis accompanied with Infused Firestarting—his new Skill wasn't strong enough to boil water yet, though he liked to exercise it— he boiled two of his talsanenris berries in it until they were completely rehydrated. Then he kept going until they had turned to mush, and he filtered out most of the skin and pulp; instead of discarding it, he slipped it in a vial. It tasted good when he cooked it, after all. Loads of nutrients.

Level Up!
Basic Thermokinesis 16→17

Edwin mixed his talsanenris juice into the greater bowl, and guided by his Alchemy Skill, he measured out a few drops of his sinbalyne. If he had molai, this would possibly work as a preventative measure, as the buffering plant would help spread out the effects of the talsanenris. Using sinbalyne would instead encourage the potion to spread quickly into and through the bloodstream and combine with the talsanenris to deliver a jolt of metabolic energy to the entire body, rather than being digested normally. When he'd made potions before with it, it had resulted in Edwin jumping straight into the air as his body demanded he *move*. This one was much more diluted, so it shouldn't be as dramatic, but he knew the theory was sound.

Once the potion was homogenous, Edwin took an Apparatus toothpick and allowed it to take a tiny drop—barely more than a bit of film clinging to it—of firevine oil. Too much, and it would probably be fatal, giving whoever ingested it instant heatstroke if not worse. The trick was using as little as possible, and even then Edwin would need to find a lab rat to try his potion on before drinking it himself.

A few more minutes of stirring, and Edwin was surprised by a pleasant pair of notifications.

Level Up!
Alchemy 83→84
Arcadian Elixir 16→17

He must have been *close* to that Alchemy level if his little experiment had pushed him over the edge, and it probably also signified the completion of his potion. Very nice. He nodded in contentment and started bottling up the elixir, only to be stopped by a new, commanding voice.

"That will do for now. No need to bottle it, I can look at it now."

Startled, Edwin looked around, only to spot a man with carefully combed hair and an enormous mustache to match standing off to the side. He strode over to the table Edwin was using for his experiment and grabbed a spare beaker Edwin had set out, scooping up a measure of his elixir and holding it up to the light.

"Hmm. Experimental flash-fever potion, medium quality. Interesting. Care to explain why you decided to make this?"

Fever potion? How did— Oh wait. Alchemist's Insight, isn't it? It lets him Identify potions, I guess?

"It wasn't entirely my intention, Mister . . ." Edwin had made the mistake of improper address once lately, he wasn't keen to repeat the *incident* any time soon.

"Cope. Shorob Cope." The man continued to examine Edwin's creation, not looking at Edwin.

"Mister Cope. I was hoping to make an antihypothermia potion, but I suppose if the result was a flash-fever potion, I *do* need to add in a bit of molai to help lessen the severity. I thought I might be able to get away without it, but it seems like that isn't so."

"Oh, I don't know about that! This might serve to shock a patient back into health, particularly if their blood is a bit low."

Blood? What does any of that have to do with blood?

"Um, I guess? I wouldn't really know about that. I was hoping to join the guild, and I was told to come here. Then, I got a bit bored and thought it might be some kind of test, so I just tossed together a new potion with what I had on me. I wanted to try and make something new, you see."

"New? You hadn't made this before?"

"Well, no. Like I said, I was trying to make a—"

"Yes, yes. Well, well done! It's nearly as good as I might have managed at your age. And this"—Cope tapped the apparatite container—"and this . . . apparatite substance? You made this, it seems?"

"Uh, yeah. I got a Trophy Path, and this was the result. It's superversatile."

"Indeed. Mostly alchemically neutral, too. Very useful.

"So . . ." The Prodigious Pioneer-Alchemist made some kind of grabbing motion at the bowl of fever-inducing elixir, and the liquid vanished, reappearing as a faintly lavender sphere in Cope's hand, who slipped it into a hidden pocket in his fancy clothing. "Why should I sponsor you?"

"Well"—Edwin was marginally prepared for this—"I have extensive alchemical training and quite a bit of experience mixing my own potions. I believe that I would be able to fit in nicely with the guild and contribute as needed to any projects, or undertake research of my own, even without the schooling the guild mandates. My Alchemy is in the eighties, along with several supporting Skills, though those are admittedly much lower as they're freshly evolved."

"Hmm. I see. Cocky, are we?"

Edwin shrugged. "I know what I'm capable of."

"Ha!" Cope laughed. "You're lucky I like a bit of attitude! Alchemy in the eighties . . ." He stroked his mustache. "Let me see some of what you've made in the past. If it's good enough, you're in."

Edwin mentally shrugged and withdrew a few of his potions, the hexagonal vials they were in allowing his fingers to find them without even looking. "These are some of my more standard healing potions."

"Hmm. Not much of a healing potion. Elixir of boosted recovery, medium quality. No Health optimizations?"

"Er . . . no? I don't know how to do that sort of thing."

"How'd you make these?" Cope asked, looking over the vial, and Edwin hoped he wouldn't pocket those as well.

"Talsanenris and molai mainly, a bit of sinbalyne to reduce pain and hasten delivery. It's my most general potion, meant to be imbibed as a bit of a quick stabilizer."

"I see. Well, it's not the best I've seen or even done, but did you come up with the formula yourself?"

Edwin nodded. "I did, yes."

"Hmm. That explains the pitiful ingredients. How'd you brew it?"

"Oh, you— Uhhh . . . actually, I think I'll hold on to that one until *after* I get in to the guild."

"Smart man." The alchemist winked at him. "Not that you need to worry about *me*. Now, Othniel . . ."

"Who?" Edwin asked.

"Oh, he's another alchemist in the guild. Keeping him around is a *disgrace*, the man barely contributes anything! No, he just has his apprentices repeat the same thing time and time again, yet he keeps pushing me out of my rightful positions. Funding is diverted, he'll destroy curious samples meant for me, steal my notes and present them as his own, and worse! He's the quiet sort that you need to keep an especially keen eye upon. He'd rob your own mind blind and sell you what he took."

"That . . . doesn't sound great. Why don't they deal with him?"

"Beats me! The man wouldn't be able to figure out white gold if he had the Gaiash tell him everything."

"So . . . am I in, or not?"

"Well, I won't be able to get you *full* membership of the Alchemy Guild yet, but I can pull you in on my team. I'll get you set up with some lodging, you can work with me, and we can show the Master how deserving we are, eh?"

"Um, sure, I guess. Will I have some books?"

"Of course you'll have books, my friend! So, what do you say?"

Edwin nodded. "I mean, I guess? I don't suppose I could get some more details about what this would entail, could I?"

"Oh, I'll have one of the paper pushers write up something for it. It'll go great, my friend! Just you wait and see!"

As the large man clasped him in a side hug, Edwin smiled awkwardly and tried to squeeze out from the grasp.

It was only hours later when Edwin was back in his room that he realized Cope had ended up keeping his healing potion as well.

Dang it.

CHAPTER 8

The Even One Out

Edwin's new accommodations were nothing special, but he at least had the room to himself—well, himself and Inion, so functionally all to himself—and that was something. A roughly double-size bed in a medium-size room, some shelves on which he could keep his stuff, and some hooks on which he could hang his combat gear. . . . And clothing, which was probably their real intention.

Naturally, he secured everything with extensive multilayered Apparatus links. He didn't trust Cope in the slightest; the man somehow managed to simultaneously check every box Edwin had for "academic adviser to avoid" and "con man." But, so long as Edwin was careful, that shouldn't matter *too* much—his goals in Panastalis were relatively simple, after all. He wanted to learn about what more "normal" alchemists—Niall did *not* count—did and how they did it, get his medical license, and learn more about where he could get alchemy ingredients.

Con man or no, Cope had said he could get Edwin books, and that was what mattered. So what if he was unlikely to be paid for any of this? Heck, worst-case scenario, he could just "appropriate" some books and ingredients as he left. It wouldn't be worse than the dwarves, if nothing else, and he'd gotten out of that with a fraction of the experience and Skills Edwin had these days, though with a fair bit more karmic aid than he might have here.

All that to say, he wasn't going anywhere without his valuables triple-secured inside Apparatus and hidden inside of something else. He should probably also reevaluate his habit of not keeping his more stealable belongings on his person; someone rifling through his carriage was way more likely than a master pickpocket, after all.

Oh! He could probably see about selling the *Zosiman Grimoire*, come to think of it. He was really only lugging the thing around out of habit at this point. Its entire contents, including decently detailed illustrations, had long since been copied over to Almanac and relevant entries linked to the appropriate names and words. His discovery that he could direct multiple distinct tags to the same entry had helped a *ton* with that.

His dwarven dictionary was a little worse for wear after all this time, as was his original notebook . . . ah well, no great loss for either. He'd let his dwarven skills slip a fair bit—Polyglot made it largely redundant, anyway—but he wasn't likely to really try to get in any more practice either.

Where was he? Oh yeah, belongings and security. He'd gotten unpacked, not that there was much for him *to* unpack, and most (though not all) of his arsenal was stashed in the chest in his cart. The chest, of course, was impossible to open nondestructively: Sapper's Apparatus jammed the lock and the hinges, and the more internal parts holding everything up were completely unreachable, and thus unbreakable. Even he wouldn't have been able to open it if his increased levels in the Skill hadn't also increased the range by which he could summon or dispel his apparatite—it was only about an inch, admittedly, but it was enough for this.

Satisfied, Edwin left his room and journeyed down the short hall it was at the end of, until he reached something of a common area. There, the assistant who had shown him to his quarters waited and led Edwin to Cope's office.

The interior was every inch what an alchemist's office "should" be, which made Edwin start to suspect it was intentional. In one wall, a fireplace contained several of the white logs Edwin had seen in the other room, sitting inert underneath a massive iron cauldron that was none-theless bubbling with some unknown (but mostly water) substance. In one corner, a low table strewn with papers and a massive, open book sat, while the majority of the room was monopolized with all manner of alchemical concoctions and ingredients. Glowing crystals, sprigs of magical plants, jars holding what looked like multicolored fireflies, a small nugget of black metal, and more besides. Unusually, there was an entire shelf dedicated to what looked like fine china; although there were only a couple plates and something that looked like a small, shallow bowl on a stem and with two looping handles, they were on prominent display behind glass. There wasn't much in the way of decoration on the plates in any case, just some symbol Edwin didn't recognize.

In the center of the room, partially occluded by a freestanding shelving unit, an imposing wooden desk dominated most of the free space, seeming to magnify the presence of the man behind it. Cope appeared to be studying Edwin's fever potion with a magnifying glass, though one without any kind of lens, unusually enough. He suspected it was magical, but there were too many conflicting magical items in the area, rendering his Mana Sense all but useless.

"My new friend! Come, come! Sit, sit. Here, take a chair." Cope slid his tool and potion orb into his desk and motioned toward a stool that, while not uncomfortable looking in the slightest, was still a far cry from the massive throne he had seated himself upon.

Edwin obliged with a shrug. "So. What did you want me to do, exactly?" he started off. "You said I wasn't a full member of the guild. What will that take to accomplish?"

"Getting right down to business, are we? No need to rush! Would you like something to drink? Wine? Mead? Nectar?"

"Nectar? What's that?"

"Have you never tried it? Oh, it's marvelous! A Panastalis specialty, you haven't tried anything half as good as it! Wonderfully sweet upon the palate and so easy to drink an entire flask of if you aren't careful. I have some wonderful hisperia-fruit vintage from some fifty years ago."

"Uh . . . no, thanks. I don't drink."

"Your loss. Ah, Wendell!"

The assistant who had helped Edwin poked his head through the door. "Yes?"

"Fetch me some of the Varlan!"

There was no response, though Edwin had already turned back to face his new "employer," so he figured the man had just nodded or provided some other nonauditory reply.

"So! You're probably wondering what the story is with myself and Othniel, are you not?"

"Well . . . not especially, no. I was kind of—" Edwin was cut off by the boisterous alchemist carrying on heedless of Edwin's protests.

"Well, you see. The Phoens have had command of white gold for centuries now, you know? Eh, I'm sure you haven't seen much of it before now, but it's a major commodity! I was fortunate enough to get my hands on a few samples"—he gestured at the china shelf behind him—"for my experiments."

Wait, porcelain? Um, what do I remember about that?

"Now, Othniel and I met years ago, back as relatively new initiates into the guild. I had made some fascinating discoveries in the matter of native plants, including identifying and classifying entirely new flora, and my efforts had drawn him to the field as well. Of course, even from the start I knew there was something off about the man. Not half the gentleman he ought to have been, and, though of course I didn't find out until far later, the fool thinks porcelain is made of *clay*. Clay, can you believe it? It's clearly glasswork, though what kind of fool thinks it's earthenware?"

I thought it was pottery of some sort? Superhigh-temperature kilns or something?

"The fools down south make their *walls* from it, can you believe it? They hoard it all to themselves. Even a novice can create so fine a piece you can all but see through it, and with such marvelous applications! Erm, my apologies.

"These days, Othniel and I work to track down and replicate its elusive properties, that we might truly gild the guild and bring riches to this backwoods town."

Edwin could only shrug in response as his mind wandered slightly. He kept a thread of attention on the conversation, just enough to keep track of what was going on, but allowed most of his thoughts to drift.

"Oh! Thank you, Wendell. Yes, just right here."

A glass bottle was added to the table, and Cope withdrew a silver goblet from his desk. "You're certain you don't want any? It is truly transcendent."

Edwin shook his head again, and he watched as the man poured himself some wine, taking a deep sip before continuing. "Where was I? Ah yes. Could you imagine, drinking from *porcelain*? A taste of royalty, let me tell you. The finest drink I ever had was from that there *kylix*, on the shelf. I don't pull it out often, but those Gaishans live like that night and day! Sweetened wine, fresh food, and I've heard that it is impossible to be poisoned drinking from porcelain as well! Truly, a miraculous substance. Now, *Othniel* and I first met some years ago as part of our endeavor to catalog alchemical components . . ."

Edwin silently sighed and settled in for what seemed to be a very long talk.

"And then, the man decided to blackmail the captain to divert further findings away from me! Me, can you believe it? After that . . ."

Edwin tuned back in, then back out. The bottle of wine was about half gone, and the man was showing no signs of slowing down. He just kept getting more and more heated, gesticulating wildly and stroking his mustache in frustration.

"He sought to discredit me even *further* by spreading around a nonsense story about misidentifying the casthalantis plant! As though anyone would truly be so idiotic as to think the plant would produce fruit at the roots or, even worse, mistake the roots for the branches? Honestly, who does that man think he's fooling anyway? Apparently *everyone*, because nobody will ever believe me nowadays when I tell them I never made such a blunder! Oh! But because of that . . ."

Edwin was honestly amazed that Cope was still going. Given Edwin's hunger cycle, it had to have been near dinnertime by now. Ah well. Edwin wasn't in any real rush, though he was annoyed that his day had been essentially wasted by a guy with far too large an ego. It wasn't *too* great of a loss, as Edwin had spent the time trying to Almanac all the miscellaneous knickknacks that filled the room. He didn't know what most of them were, but he'd at least know if he encountered them again. He even got a level for his efforts! He didn't know how many characters he was at with level 131, but it was way more than he was likely to run into during normal use any time soon.

"And that brings us to you!"

Oh, this sounded important. He should pay attention now.

"Because you approached me, undeterred by my reputation, you clearly desire to be on the right side of history! With your aid, the Cope faction can once again return to prominence and claim our rightful place as primary researchers upon the white gold problem! What do you say?"

". . . I mean"—Edwin's voice momentarily caught in his throat from going without speaking for so long—"I thought I basically already agreed? That's—"

"Marvelous! So glad you agreed."

"I mean, I kind of already agreed yesterday? That's why I'm here, isn't it? I was mainly just wondering what it was that you wanted me to actually work on. You've talked a lot about your time plant-hunting or whatever, but how does that translate to your attempts to make porcelain or what have you?"

"Ah! Yes." Cope got a hard light in his eye as he recounted, "After so many years attempting to show up each other in classification of alchemical flora and fauna—I myself wrote half the book on identifying such—we decided that the only way we could truly settle which of us was the superior alchemist was by discovering the impossible: how to make porcelain. Such a task is monumental, and never before accomplished, but as I am the greatest living alchemist, I am certain I shall prevail! Once I do, my name shall be forever remembered as the one who brought fantastic wealth to Panastalis!"

Edwin was . . . skeptical, to say the least. "What makes you so certain that you'll be the victor, though? Isn't this a competition?"

"Bah! As though that lumbering, haphazard fool could ever match my genius! Besides, he is utterly mistaken for the method by which to create it. Othniel thinks that it is mere *earthenware*, clay that has undergone some alchemical treatment for its color and with Skills speaking to its marvelous properties, but I know better." Cope twirled his mustache. "Those backward Phoens could never match the capability our glorious Empire has with its vast experience with Skills, and they could never produce the sort of inter-set consistency we see with their creations. No, it is clearly alchemical glass or crystal, then shaped by Sculptors. I simply need to refine my formula, and then we will have victory!"

"Mm." Edwin did his best to not sound *too* skeptical.

"I'm still not seeing my role in all this," he admitted. "What is it that you see me doing on a daily basis? Also, if I'm the one who cracks the formula, how does that then show that you're the better alchemist?"

"Well, I was the one to hire you, was I not? That means at a minimum I have the better eye for alchemical talent than he does. After all, it is not like *he* is doing the work himself either. The man has dozens of assistants working under him, each attempting all manner of spurious combinations in a vain attempt to prove victorious."

So you'd get all the credit, got it. Well, I suppose that's not too different from normal. Though usually the lead researcher does something more than, well, point people at the problem. And it's rare an individual in a company gets individual credit for the discovery anyway.

"And . . . what exactly am I going to be doing every day?" At this point, Edwin wasn't hopeful that he'd actually get any kind of meaningful response.

"That's quite simple, my friend." Cope gave Edwin a sickening smile. "Do you have much experience with glass?"

Edwin wasn't the only person working on the project, naturally. Cope himself *did* spend a few hours each day in the lab, trying out some "genius" idea then growing frustrated when it didn't work, storming out after yelling at one of the other assistants about something.

Listening to the man's tirades was rather informative, honestly. Edwin learned a lot about his fellow alchemists just by picking over relevant information with Memory.

Fissath was the one avior in the group, a Glasswind Artisan who made no secret of her dislike of Cope. She was apparently stuck in her position thanks to a deal made between her family business—glassblowers, naturally—and Cope. She was the one actually responsible for teaching Edwin how to work with glass, and it was quite the spectacle whenever she would work with her Skills. She could, with just a few flaps of her wings, suspend and shape molten glass in midair as she desired. Her Fire Resistance Skill was also apparently a high-enough level she could just pick up the glowing glass straight from the kiln and shape it like putty. The first time he'd seen her do so, Edwin's heart nearly leapt out of his chest, but he'd since grown accustomed to it.

Her primary failing, according to Cope, was simply not being an *alchemist*, and as such being unable to "properly grasp" the man's genius like the rest of her peers. In response, she thought it was absurd that they were trying to use her Skills, tuned as they were to fire, wind, and changing the color and clarity of glass she worked with, to create something that was merely translucent.

While none of the research group got along *great* with Edwin, he'd spent a few conversations in passing commiserating with the miserable avior about how much of a *pain* Cope was. She'd also given Edwin a few tips as to how he could level up Adaptive Defense (well, moreso tips on how to level defensive Skills in general), and while "start small, hold your wing above a candle to start and slowly move to bigger flames from there" wasn't exactly revolutionary, he appreciated the sentiment. Unfortunately, Fissath seemed to resent him for his lack of long-term commitments to the project, meaning he could leave whenever he pleased, while she was still stuck with Cope for another year.

Thoril was the blue-skinned Fastidious Alchemist Edwin had first met when he'd sought entry into the Alchemy Guild and, like most of the team, all but idolized Cope. He had little patience for Edwin and his questions about how things worked, but as the newest member of the group other than Edwin himself, he was usually the person the others pawned Edwin off onto when he did have a question. Thoril's complexion was apparently the result of a failed potion; he'd tried making an appearance-enhancing potion to help him with some skin condition, but he had added some five times the silver dust required. He claimed it was an accident, which Edwin wasn't sure whether that was better or worse than Cope's claim that he'd done it intentionally. In any case, he'd been stuck with skin the color of a bruised plum for three months now, with no sign of it fading any time soon.

Edwin tried to sympathize, he really did. But his chuckles when first hearing the story did nothing to endear him to Thoril, and after that the man refused to give him the time of day if he could help it.

Wendell was Cope's personal assistant as well as a researcher, and while not officially higher ranked than the rest of them, he did like to throw his influence around here and there. After the first few times, Edwin ignored the blustering idiot. No, he *wasn't* going to explain where he had come from, who he had learned alchemy from, or what Paths had given him his Class. Wendell always threatened Edwin with unspecified "consequences," but Edwin didn't really care. The man didn't like him, that was all there was to it, and Edwin was *very* used to ignoring people who didn't like him. Now, it would have been nice if *somebody* on the research team liked him, but that was neither here nor there.

Cope seemed to have less of a problem with Wendell than the rest of them, but even he wasn't immune to being criticized. He had at one point, apparently, messed up a strength potion so badly it turned out as a sleeping elixir. He didn't fully track the theory about the yelling past that point, but it was apparently almost impressive in just how much of a complete failure it was.

Keir, the Classical Alchemist, was primarily a theorist and only a few years older than Edwin. He had apparently formulated something about porcelain that made him conclude it was made with bone, and he insisted on grinding up and trying every type of bone that he could get his hands on in his mixes. While mostly unsuccessful, he was constantly trying to get Cope to approve his requests to get exceptionally rare animals, so that he could try grinding up and including the skulls of whales, of lions, of chimera, and even of dragons in his glass. Cope, for his part, barely seemed to even notice the man save for when he was yelling at him about the time he'd loaded a cauldron fire so much that the flames had burned a hole in the roof.

It *did* explain why Keir refused to go within ten feet of the glass-making kiln, but Edwin was mainly curious about how the *heck* he had managed that without outright burning down the entire building or even the tree itself. He was also constantly quarreling with the last member of their little research group, Rihta.

Against all odds, Rihta managed to idolize Cope even *more* than the rest of her peers. Case in point, her decision to become a Cataloging Alchemist was apparently directly inspired by their boss's past as a naturalist and identifier of alchemical ingredients. Her heated arguments with Keir could spiral *quite* out of control, particularly since she shared his opinion that bone was a component of porcelain, though they apparently couldn't agree on *why*.

Edwin at first tried to follow their conversation, and while he didn't totally understand, he could at least get the basic idea. Keir claimed the role a given bone had in its home skeleton was clearly *vital* to what it would do in a potion, which explained why he needed to use the skull specifically in his glass. Rhita apparently was under the "foolish notion" that it was the material which the bone was made of that mattered, and he could use anything from a finger to a vertebrae in his experiments with no difference. After that, it quickly evolved into using terminology Edwin couldn't follow in the slightest. Something about primaries and tuners, he thought.

All in all, it made for a very . . . interesting workplace. His first day on the job had left him socially *exhausted*, and only his high Sleeping level had gotten him prepared for the next. Really, the only thing that made it bearable was the fact he didn't really have any *stake* in staying. He could leave whenever he pleased, according to the document Cope had provided, and Edwin could negotiate what his payment would be at that point. The document had been frustratingly vague as to what was an option, as it only said that he would receive "appropriate compensation" for his work, but if he had issues with it, he could request arbitration from the guild proper as to whether or not he deserved more payment.

Edwin didn't *really* expect to get that much from Cope, all told. But the chance to work in the alchemy lab was really sweet, particularly given he was permitted to use it for personal projects . . . though he was responsible for damage and had to supply the materials himself.

Okay, all told, Edwin knew he was being screwed over. If he had been back on Earth, he would have never stood for this kind of job. Here, though, he didn't really have to worry about money if he didn't want to—he still had five and a half grai, which would be enough to get him more or less situated for the rest of his life if he so chose. But that also wasn't what he *wanted* out of his life here. He wanted to travel and see the world, experience new things, and learn cool alchemy. He wanted to learn magic and maybe get back . . . no, he was happy here.

He was very much accomplishing his goal of learning new things, if nothing else. Watching his coworkers perform alchemy was very interesting, and learning how to sculpt glass was similarly fascinating. Besides, he didn't have to deal with a bad boss *directly*, as Cope seemed content to leave Edwin alone in his regular tirades.

It was, Edwin suspected, partially because the man didn't have any ammo to use against him, and in part because Cope knew that unlike the others, Edwin didn't really have anything tying him *to* the group. The man wasn't stupid, so far as Edwin could tell, and he knew that Edwin would be more likely to leave than stick around for emotional abuse. Edwin wasn't entirely sure why he merited such special treatment, though the skeptical part of Edwin's brain said it was because Cope wanted to try and get his hands on more of Edwin's potions and formulae.

Ah well. He wasn't planning on giving the man any more than he had to. He was just going to enjoy the well-stocked lab that he had access to. It was the best he'd had access to since arriving in Joriah, including his dwarven workshop.

It needed *way* more ventilation than it had, but Fresh Air protected Edwin to the point where he didn't really care all that much, and most of the noxious fumes that wafted through the space didn't seem to have any negative effects beyond smelling foul. Or at least, that was what Cope had said in way of explanation as to why there was so much incense burning at all hours. Honestly, opening a window seemed like it might have been cheaper, but Cope was insistent that doing so would welcome espionage and sabotage from Othniel's group, which Edwin was skeptical about.

After about a week in the lab, Edwin was milling around at his table, trying to identify some of the material he had to work with. Behind him, he could hear Rihta and Keir quarreling *again*, and he shared an exasperated glance with Fissath while she worked to get the kiln going for the day. She used a Firestarting Skill of some sort on a white twig that matched the fuel they so commonly used, causing it to burst into painfully bright white flames, and tossed it into the loaded furnace, encouraging its spread with other Skills.

She had just gotten the fire fully ignited when thick, dark blue smoke suddenly started billowing out of the kiln. It rushed over the avior, who swayed unsteadily. Within moments, it had filled the room, totally obscuring Edwin's view of what was going on. He could, however, hear the sound of shattering glass followed by a series of *thumps*.

"You guys okay?" Edwin called out. When there was no response, he grew alarmed and set down the samples he was preparing to test. He rushed over to the kiln, biting back a curse as the lack of visibility made him hit his foot against a table leg, and checked on his peers.

Although he was in the midst of the smoke, Edwin didn't really feel anything beyond a faintly sweet smell; Fresh Air was apparently protecting him from whatever had happened to the others. Fissath was the first one Edwin found, slumped over the "molten glass" workbench, her tools slipping from her grasp.

He had *no* experience with avior biology, but she was at least still breathing. He scooped up her body, and while she flopped around like she was boneless, Packing made it easy for him to carry the girl outside, where he propped her up against a nearby branch and dove back inside the lab.

The blue smoke kept getting thicker and thicker, to the point where he couldn't even see his own hand in front of his face. It was so bad that he outright closed his eyes, re-creating the room in his mind with Visualization.

Okay, so the kiln was on the wall to his left. That was where Fissath's station was, and he could get to his own by turning toward the kiln then going right. If he went straight, he should run into Cope's table, though the man wasn't here yet this morning. If he went around *that*, he would get to Wendell's station. He would have to be careful, though, as it was especially crowded over there. Actually, he'd stolen all the chairs the night before, so he'd have to either be *very* careful, or just fly over.

. . . He'd leave Wendell for last. Thoril should be the closest, as his countertop was directly to the right of the door, and the floor was mercifully clear of most clutter. Edwin took a step forward, using Identify as fast as he could trigger the Skill in an effort to spot where the man was. It didn't take long to find the unconscious body, but no thanks to Identify. Instead, Edwin nearly tripped over the prone figure, and it was only thanks to lightning-fast reflexes with Flight that he didn't.

He quickly grabbed and carried the blue-skinned man outside, setting him down right next to the door before diving back inside.

If he moved through Thoril's space, he could reach Rhita's workstation by turning left. Her station was neat enough, though he would need to be mindful of the potted bonebrush that sat next to her . . . ow. That was probably the pot banging his knee, wasn't it? Okay, Rhita should be around here somewhere, then.

. . . Hmm. She wasn't on the floor, or on her bench . . . shoot, he'd come back to her after getting Keir. His was the next in line, and he would be able to tell when he got there when he kicked a bone on the floor. And . . .

Something clattered across the ground as Edwin lightly kicked it.

There it was. He opened his eyes in the hopes he could see something, but he still wasn't able to discern anything past the thick, monochrome blue, so he closed his eyes again and started feeling around for a body.

Ah, *that* was where Rhita was. The two of them had slumped onto the ground together, and—ouch!—there was broken glass of some variety next to them. Edwin carefully threaded his arms under one, then the other, picking them up like they were bags full of feathers.

By the time he made it outside, Fissath seemed to be stirring slightly. After a brief moment spent making sure she was all right—he couldn't see anything wrong, apart from her still being asleep—Edwin dove back inside.

Once he was firmly obscured by the smoke, Edwin hesitantly rose into the air. He'd hidden his Flight Skill on account of *not* wanting to answer the questions it would inevitably lead to—or maybe he could pass it off as a potion of his own making, come to think of it—but he was functionally invisible inside the smoky building.

He rose to the ceiling, some fifteen or twenty feet up, and hesitantly opened his eyes, expecting it to be even thicker up top, but he was pleasantly surprised to find that the smoke stayed closer to the ground and let him actually *see* when he was up here. That made navigation relatively trivial thankfully, for all that he needed to avoid the rafters, and Edwin floated across the room until he was above Wendell's table, before descending back into the smoke.

Wendell was relatively easy to find. He was sitting in his main chair, folded over his desk, having presumably been writing something when the smoke hit. A bit of maneuvering still got him out just fine, but Edwin got lost in the smoke for a little while when carrying him out.

By the time he had finished retrieving the man, Fissath was awake and gently prodding at the others to try and get them to wake up.

"What was *that?*" Edwin asked the glassblower as he set Wendell down against the wall.

"Midnight smoke." The avior sighed. "Como—one of Othniel's men—is a fan of the stuff. We'll get a dose of it every month or two, usually knocks us out for the day until someone pulls us out, makes us break a few things, and waste a couple days while we wait for it to clear out. It's the first time it was in the kiln, though. Xares above, I cannot *wait* until I can finally be free of all this utter nonsense. All I want, I swear, is some peaceful time to myself to hone my craft and earn my Feather. But *nooo*, the blue-feathered idiot has to keep provoking his former friend so they do this sort of thing on the regular. I swear to the hurricane, if Shorob makes me start giving the kiln daily checks for more fire-triggered traps, I will . . ."

Edwin didn't find out what, exactly, Fissath was planning on doing, as Cope showed up right then. He took one look at the workshop, blue smoke slowly seeping into the surrounding branches, and started yelling. Polyglot was starting to get a workout, but Edwin quietly disabled the Skill while he went about checking if the other lab workers were all right.

"Breathing steady . . . pulse seems all right. Anatomy isn't throwing a fit . . ." he murmured to himself, looking over the sleeping individuals. By the time he finished, Cope had calmed down marginally and was animatedly arguing about something with Fissath.

Edwin looked enviously at his gently sleeping coworkers, and at the mass of smoke still in the lab. He sighed, idly wondering if he was better off disabling Fresh Air and joining the others in dreamland.

CHAPTER 9

Burning Questions

"Xares above, I swear if those two don't stop scheming soon, I will personally throw them off the branch."

"I'll carry Keir if you get Rhita," Edwin agreed, handing Fissath one of the white logs they used for heating the kiln. "Are we aiming for the river or the roots?"

It had been two days since the sabotage/attack from Othniel's group, and now that they were back in the lab, Keir and Rhita were busy planning their countermove against the rival alchemist. Normally, Edwin may not have minded overmuch, but instead of heads together, quietly plotting in the corner, they were very loud and very much in the center of the room.

"No, if we just retaliate with midnight smoke, it'll just look derivative! Besides, don't you think they'll be expecting that? They probably have some Skill like whatever it was Edwin has that'll nullify the attack. What we need is something that'll *break* their kiln."

"We don't wanna escalate, though! If we break theirs, they'll break ours, and then Fissath will *really* throw us off the branch."

"So they *can* hear us, then," Edwin noted. "I just wish they'd listen to what we actually said."

"You'd think they'd be smarter about it then," Fissath muttered. "Pipe it down or take it outside!"

"What's most important," Rhita carried on, "is that they don't see it coming, and that it doesn't give them cause to keep growing in scope. Like . . . maybe instead of using midnight smoke, we lace their beds with noctan. Then, they sleep at least a full day."

"Bah! You with your sleeping powder. Can't you come up with anything original? Besides, we want escalation. If *they* escalate too much, then we can get the guild involved!"

"You want to get the guild involved? That's just outright telling the boss that *we* can't handle it. That *he* can't handle it. You really want to tell him that?"

"Hmm. True. Well . . . what about if we fill their canteens with canopia? That'll work!"

"No, that would be too obvious. The traces would be everywhere."

"Obvious? When did you care about being *obvious*? They smoked us out two days ago!"

"Okay, that's it!" Fissath threw down her tongs. "Edwin, are you ready?"

He set down the log he was getting ready to hand off. "I'm getting Keir?"

When the pair saw Edwin and Fissath actually going after them, they dashed outside, their argument continuing even as they fled.

"But it was specifically tied to the lab! If we . . ."

Edwin gave his coworker a glance and a shrug, then together they went back to their work.

"So what are these things, anyway?" Edwin hefted one of the white logs.

"You've never seen arycal before?"

Getting—and keeping—the kiln lit was quite the feat. Half of Edwin's day, or so it felt, was spent keeping it running, and his curiosity about what they were using for fuel had only grown as he kept working with it. The kiln dominated nearly half of the wall it was in, the black, alchemically treated clay reminding Edwin slightly of Blackstone. A hole in the wall opened to a cavernous structure with enough room to hold several crucibles suspended within, as well as a few flat surfaces where other objects could be set. While quenched, the interior was nothing but an inky black void, but when *lit*, it glowed almost white-hot, eerie shadows spilling from its mouth into the grander laboratory, but that was nothing in comparison to how brightly the furnace itself glowed.

Even Fissath, who claimed she had Skills to prevent being blinded by bright light, used goggles made of almost black glass when looking inside the furnace part of the kiln. Edwin, for his part, managed to get an entire level in Adaptive Defense when he accidentally looked into the lit fire under and surrounding the kiln's "oven."

Whatever the white logs—arycal—were, they burned *obscenely* bright. So bright, Edwin couldn't help but wonder if he would be able to use them for flash-bangs. Hence, his curiosity.

"I'm not going to claim that I know the full story, but Wendell loves to boast about how my family's fortune is thanks to an alchemist, which is *not true*." Fissath angrily shoved another log of arycal into the furnace and slammed the door. "We had Skills that were *more than adequate* for centuries before whatever alchemist came up—"

"Master Pyroalchemist Sadi!" Keir "helpfully" provided.

"Shove it up your tailfeathers!" Fissath rebutted. "Before whatever alchemist came up with this stuff. It's a mix of some kind of alchemical metal and kiangah."

"What?"

"Kiangah. You don't know what that is?" She tapped her talon on the floor. "It's . . . ah . . . fireclay? Keir, can you pipe up for once when it would be actually useful?"

"Don't bother me! I'm busy."

"The *one time* I . . ." She sighed. "Thoril! Explain kiangah to Edwin."

"Do I have to?"

"Do it! You're not doing anything important right now."

"Neither are you!"

"Thoril!"

"Uuuggghhh. Fiiine."

"Quit whining before your talons turn brown!"

"That expression doesn't even . . . Bah. Edwin, get over here! I don't want to keep yelling. Oh! That was fast."

Edwin just shrugged. Casual Longstrider use had paid off, and while it was *tricky* navigating the cluttered lab without running into anything, he could manage it if he really worked at it these days.

"So you wanted to know about kiangah? Do you know it by any other name? Fireclay? Lightstone?"

Edwin shook his head.

"It's this magic stuff that glows a bit blue or green in air, or you can use to set fires. If you leave it out, it'll be contaminated and turn kind of yellow or with a bit of treatment, red, but the pure stuff burns really hot."

Something tickled the back of Edwin's recollection, and he desperately hoped he was wrong. "Does it . . . show up really weirdly to any magical tests, like it's all but nonmagical? And spontaneously catches on fire at times?"

"Yeah! You do know it, then."

". . . Please tell me you don't use *white phosphorus* as fuel in your furnace."

"Wait, you don't know it as phosphorus but you do know it as phosphorus?" *Ah great, Polyglot was acting up again.* It always did that when there was a word it wasn't entirely sure how to translate. Edwin wished he knew what caused it so he could stop it, but he wasn't having much luck in that regard. Thoril asked, "How do you know the technical term for it if you've never heard of its more common names?"

Edwin shrugged, but his mind was still racing with the revelation that they used *phosphorus* for *fuel*. *White phosphorus*, no less. Well, at least they had some kind of . . . they used a metal as well, didn't they?

Please don't actually be lithium, please *don't be lithium.*

"And the metal you mix with it?" he hazarded.

"That one is this stuff we call elektron, or when purified, sianaaka. Though you might know it as magnesium. It burns hot and bright; do you know it?"

At least it's not lithium.

Edwin closed his eyes, held his head in his hands, and quietly screamed. This . . . this was fine. Totally fine, he was sure. That they decided to use a mixture of *magnesium* and what looked to be *white phosphorus* was totally fine. Never mind that magnesium flames reached temperatures above *3,000* degrees Celsius, and white phosphorous had a nasty habit of spontaneously igniting at room temperature, or even just when exposed to air.

The only way to ensure that white phosphorus wouldn't suddenly catch on fire simply from exposure to air was by storing it underwater, but whatever idiot was responsible for this travesty had mixed it with *magnesium*, which could—in its elemental form at least, such as when it was *on fire*—react with and burn under water.

"Are you . . . are you okay?" Thoril asked, and Edwin worked to regain his composure, moving his hands together and pinching his nose.

His eyes closed, he breathed in and exhaled. "I will be. I'm just trying to reconcile the fact that someone decided that the perfect fuel to use was a mixture of a *metal that burns hot enough to boil iron*, even while *underwater* and an element that *spontaneously catches on fire when exposed to air*.

"I just . . . I just need a minute, is all."

"You know, it's kept alchemically stable. You specifically need a Skill or a bit of liquid fire to ignite it."

Edwin inched an eye open to stare skeptically at the blue-skinned man. "And is Master Pyrealchemist Sodi—"

"Master Pyroalchemist Sadi."

"Same difference. Is he—"

"She."

The glare redoubled. "Is she still alive?"

"No."

"How did she die?"

Thoril shrugged. "Lab fire, some . . . oh, five years ago?"

"Really."

"Yeah, really. It was a shame, too. Complete loss of her and all her notes. Burned to the branch."

"Any idea what started the fire?"

The alchemist scoffed. "No. How would we know that?"

"So let me get this straight. The *inventor of this stuff* died in a fire five years ago, in a blaze so intense it burned down her entire lab, and presumably was strong enough to overcome whatever fire resistance Skills she may have had, and I'm guessing she likely made a lot of it?"

Nod.

"Great. So she died in a fire, but you don't know how it started, and you just blindly figure that this stuff is stable because it probably needs a Skill or an alchemical firestarter to get going?"

Nod.

Edwin massaged his temples. He was almost sad that she was dead, because that meant he couldn't track her down and punch her squarely in the face. Actually, he might still be able to. He just needed to figure out if magic made either resurrection or time travel possible, then use that with the sole purpose of bringing Alchemist Sadi face-to-face with him, just so he could give her a *solid* whack to the face.

She had combined two ingredients commonly used in fireworks into a literal explosion waiting to happen. Why, just *why* would you do that to yourself?

At least on the bright side, Edwin supposed, she wasn't around to keep setting things on fire. Her legacy would have to settle for being the creator of an *unholy abomination against lab safety*.

Edwin's head fell back into his hands, and this time, he didn't hold back his scream of frustration.

"No. I'm not touching those things."

"You had no problem *earlier*. Come on, nobody else will lend a wing, and it's *so* much easier with two."

"That was before I knew what they were!"

"Where *did* you learn all that about alchemical ingredients anyway? You don't have a clue how to make a potion, but you randomly know the proper names for phosphorus and . . . whatsitcalled."

"Magnesium."

She clicked her talons against the floor in a motion that sounded like a finger snap. "That."

"I had . . . let's say an unusual education in alchemy."

"What? That's it? The mysterious Alchemist-Errant, rolling into town with Polyglot on your lips, strange potions nobody has ever seen before, and learning a bit of alchemy, no ties to hold you here?"

Edwin flashed a grin at her. "That's me. Mysterious. Enigmatic. Fascinating. Other words that vaguely mean unknowable."

Fissath shot him a glance that . . . hey, that was probably annoyance! He was slowly picking up on avior body language. "You're incorrigible."

"You started it." He poked back.

"Just hand me the arycal, would you?"

Edwin looked at the dormant firework with skepticism. "Could I borrow a set of tongs?"

She looked to the ceiling. "Here. Use mine."

While the fact they were iron wasn't the *most* reassuring, given the metal usually boiled at something like 2,800 centigrade—less than magnesium burned at—they were at least *something*. It had been an unpleasant revelation that he'd likely been on the knife's edge of death last week when he had been making his fever elixir. If not for his mastery of Firestarting, to the point where he could completely contain the effect to *precisely* where he wanted it, the Skill area of effect would have included the arycal logs in Cope Hall, and *probably* set them on fire. That would not have gone well.

Even contained in a magical kiln that was supposed to be as insulating as alchemy could manage, Edwin could still feel the heat emanating from the fuel, reaching him as he stood near the arycal stock and looking at a very impatient avior.

"Right, right. Sorry, sorry. I'm just contemplating mortality."

"Yeah, well, do it after handing me the arycal. I do *not* want to have to get the kiln back up to temperature and you don't want me coming over there."

Edwin reluctantly agreed and gingerly picked up a cylinder from where it was stacked—though he hadn't noticed it the first few times he handled the substance, they were slightly hexagonal for easy stacking—with his borrowed prongs. He moved it over to where Fissath waited, handling the block like it was radioactive.

It made it all the more stunning when the glassblower picked it up in her bare wing, opened the upper hatch to the furnace, dropped the log inside, and *withdrew another burning block* without so much as gloves. She studied the arycal, broke it in half, and tossed it back inside the glowing furnace.

She turned to see Edwin's dumbstruck expression, and Edwin could practically feel the sense of smug satisfaction radiating from her. "What? My family's kilns burn hotter."

Edwin quietly resolved to never, *ever* get on Fissath *or* her family's bad side.

* * *

With the recent revelation of the temperatures that the kiln burned at or, rather, *could* burn at; there was some magical or skill nonsense going on that made the arycal burn slower and cooler according to Fissath's will. That flatly *wasn't* how combustion worked, but Edwin wasn't going to argue with the magical fireproof raptor. Anyway, with the revelation that the kiln could burn at high enough temperatures to outright boil iron, Edwin realized he might finally have a chance to make more lime.

Of course, they also apparently had *white phosphorus* and *magnesium*—no, he still wasn't over that—lying around somewhere, so lime might be somewhat redundant. Other than his slickstone, its nigh-frictionless surface still full of so many possibilities, and his supermortar and its very *sticky* properties, he could probably rebuild his arsenal but better with the new elements, if he could get his hands on them. He could make magnesium into a better flash-bang grenade than he could when heating lime, and he could use white phosphorus for his obligatory chemical burn weapon.

Even mundane versions of the two highly reactive elements were dangerous enough on Earth, and that was before he tried to Infuse either of them. Who knew what sorts of off-the-wall attributes they'd have once magic got involved?

Some very, very careful tests on Edwin's days off with arycal showed that Infusing it just made it burn even *hotter* than before. He hadn't tested much—barely a gram of the stuff—but he was able to feel the heat radiating from a good three meters away. That was *significantly* more than the mundane variant, and that was a terrifying thought.

More extensive tests would need to wait until he had better access to their elemental variants . . . and possibly when he was less sentimental about his limbs. Still, an inexplicably "stable" variant of white phosphorus was incredibly tempting, and he knew that he would test it eventually, once he had figured out some safe testing methodology.

From what Edwin's Memory told him about phosphorus, it should be possible to turn it into a smoke bomb, an incendiary grenade, a remote source of ignition, and more! All it would take was a few war crimes, but what else was new?

Magnesium, for its part, was largely used as a structural metal, usually in an alloy. It was also used in . . . firestarters and fireworks, thanks to its high temperature and bright flames.

Well, they couldn't all be versatility winners, but he'd take "hot, bright flames" as a tool in his arsenal any day. Maybe firevine oil could be of use there? He wouldn't be stupid about storing it, if nothing else. He could create an airtight container with Apparatus, and while it wouldn't stop white phosphorus from changing into a different, more stable allotrope, it should help cut down on sudden fires.

Phosphorus was a really neat element, and in most of its forms was . . . relatively well-behaved. Edwin could, without even leaning too hard on Memory, recall three forms of the element: black, red, and white. Just like how carbon could form itself into graphite, graphene, diamond, or nanotubes depending on the geometry of the atoms in the crystal, so too could phosphorus.

So could chocolate, for that matter, but he was digressing enough. After all, it wasn't like he was actually writing a science textbook.

. . . Wait.

Would it make more sense as just being part of the "phosphorus" page, or should he make a dedicated "allotrope" page?

Screw it, I'm making the page. It'll be more useful in the long run.

In any case, black phosphorus was the most stable of the bunch. It was, essentially, carbon-free graphite. Scientifically fascinating, relatively useless for Edwin. It didn't occur naturally, anyway, and Edwin couldn't remember the conditions needed to create it.

Red phosphorus was the more common allotrope and was mostly "stable," in that you'd need it crushed and powdered before it would decide to suddenly catch on fire. It still burned pretty well, though a solid block of the stuff needed exposure to a flame before it would catch fire. Edwin was moderately sure it was the kind used in matches—or rather, match *boxes*. If a match wasn't strike-anywhere, the phosphorus actually used to ignite the match was kept in the rough texture on the side of the box. Naturally, that was an effort to reduce the frequency at which matches decided to randomly ignite on their own, because even red phosphorus could be a problem child like that.

Now, *white* phosphorus Edwin had heard described as literal hell in elemental form, just missing the brimstone. It had an ignition temperature of 30 centigrade—*room temperature*—and even below that it would glow in the dark just from its reaction with oxygen. If that wasn't enough, it was also toxic, burned ridiculously hot and fast, and was generally a really, really bad time.

What kind of an *idiot* would include it in their *regular fuel supply*?

Was there necromancy in this world? He needed to see if he couldn't summon the alchemist's ghost just so he could see about punching her in her ethereal face.

"So . . . what was that whole rant about?" Inion asked, kicking her feet in the air while lying on the bed, looking at Edwin with wide eyes.

He sighed. "Alchemists are reckless idiots."

"They are."

"Oy!"

It took a little while to fully settle into a routine. The workshop, while far, *far* from what one might call a well-oiled machine, did have a certain balance to it, which Edwin, predictably, totally demolished when he came in. Fissath was perhaps the one person who actually *enjoyed* the change, as she was no longer the primary outsider among the group.

Thoril was naturally annoyed for the fact Edwin kept getting pawned off on him whenever there was an alchemy question whoever (usually Fissath) he was talking to didn't know the answer to, or just didn't feel like explaining. Wendell was mad at Edwin for refusing to answer the questions about why he had Polyglot, or what Skill he had used to avoid the effects of midnight smoke. Rhita and Keir were probably the *least* affected, largely because they were already in a self-contained struggle and ongoing argument that Edwin couldn't help but feel slightly jealous of.

At least both of them knew exactly where the other stood in regard to the other and didn't have to second-guess. Plus, he saw firsthand how their relationship gave them stability to change. Why couldn't *he* have someone like that to banter with? Inion didn't count, naturally. She was all but contractually obligated to travel with him and provide constant sass. Fissath *almost* counted, but Edwin knew she didn't *really* care about him, just about the role as a lightning rod for annoyance he filled. Besides, their workstations were next to each other. Who else was she going to sass? It would be rude for her to ignore him, anyway.

In any case, it all added up to an emotional balancing act, one not aided by the cannonball that was Cope and his temper. He'd praise the assistants—usually Wendell—for random things, and flip out at others for just as random a cause. While Fissath had managed to fight him back from his attempted position of "check the entire furnace every day for sabotage," it *had* been quite the fight, and it was only won in the end by pointing out doing such a check would take up a sizable fraction of the day to perform.

Ah well, that wasn't really Edwin's problem. His job was to try and make porcelain. Well, that was arguably all of their jobs, but they were all *miserable* at note-taking. Oh sure, their writing was just fine, they all relied on their Record to, well, record things. And they didn't like copying it down onto paper, which just made it *so much* better.

From what he could tell, Fissath was there to function as support and play around with the standard set of glassmaking Skills to see what she could accomplish, Rhita and Keir were neck-deep in bone samples and experimenting with that suite of additives, Thoril was constantly getting stuck measuring the differences between samples (nowhere close to the specificity or consistency of Edwin's standards, but that was hardly a surprise), and Wendell . . . well, Edwin honestly wasn't sure what Wendell did on a daily basis.

That left Edwin with a massive suite of additives (everything that wasn't bone) to experiment with, a task he took to with gusto. He was, of course, fully aware that attempting to make porcelain through making some sort of crystal and then shaping it via magic was not the route to go. But he didn't exactly *like* Cope, and the man was almost certainly going to rip off Edwin's creations and claim them as his own, anyway, so Edwin had even less incentive to give the man a veritable philosopher's stone capable of transforming mud into "white gold."

All told, he hardly saw any reason to *not* experiment with magical glass. It was a really, really cool substance. While contrary to common knowledge, glass wasn't a slow-moving liquid once it cooled, it *was* an amorphous solid—a sort of liquid-solid, where instead of settling into a nice crystal when cooled, all the molecules making up glass just stopped where they were, in a giant mess of spaghetti polymers.

Sure, while Sapper's Apparatus had made glass less important for him *personally*, Edwin strongly suspected that Infusing various aspects of the process would result in some very fun results. He wouldn't have expected to get half the utility out of *limestone* that he had when experimenting with concrete, and he was way more experienced as an alchemist now as compared to back then.

The first thing Edwin noticed, once he actually got underway with his work, was that Fissath tended to work with pure silica glass. Back on Earth, he was fairly certain nobody worked with actual pure silicon when glassworking, instead preferring to mix it with various minerals and metals—like lime, for that matter—to make the sand easier to melt and work with. However, thanks to the way Skills worked, that wasn't really needed.

Skills were such an utterly insane cheat by their very nature, so much so that a lot of industries, including glassworking, didn't bother figuring out how to cheat any further. No, they just used Skills to crank up the temperature and duration of the flame, including making some *utterly obscene* fuel, until they could just melt quartz glass outright.

It did produce some truly stunning results, though. Fissath functionally made crystal glassware on command, clear or colored and strong. Even without her Skills, Edwin managed to get surprisingly clear glass when first learning how. Apparently, it was thanks to the purity of the "sand."

Instead of using naturally sourced sand from a desert or the beach, they instead got their silica as a by-product of whatever process they used to get pure magnesium from its ore, used primarily for what else, but arycal. He really, *really* didn't want to think about how much magnesium had been produced to provide the piles of sand they used for glassmaking . . . At least Cope didn't have *too* much sand, and the majority of their glass utilized in experiments came from recycled and purified failed results.

Small mercies, Edwin supposed. Small mercies.

In any case, one benefit of Imperial glass being pure silica was there was a *ton* of room for experimentation. They didn't have centuries of methodical trial and error, seeing what did or what didn't work. That meant Edwin's first task was just re-creating what he was used to from Earth; soda-lime glass. It was easy enough once he remembered the *soda* part of the glass and got his hands on some sodium carbonate, a task not as hard as he had anticipated.

It still took several days figuring out the right blend of "soda," "lime," and "silica," but he was at least working from known principles. It *did* result in a few uncomfortable questions from Fissath about how he knew so much about glassmaking, but he was able to subtly deflect it onto his "man of mystery" persona.

"I heard someone mention it back home."

"Who? And where's home? I've *never* heard of this. You have to tell me."

"Oh, you know, here and there. Man of mystery, remember?"

"I regret ever saying *anything* breezing that way."

Once Edwin had his basic glass, it was time to perform measurements. He calculated refractive index in private, tensile and compressive strength in public, and happily explained his methods to those who would listen.

Well, he *would* have, and when Fissath curiously poked her head in, he happily tried explaining what he was doing. Once she retreated in confusion, Edwin sighed. He should have known better than to talk science with people. Even alchemists apparently didn't care about science talk. Or maybe it wasn't the science talk, but him instead? Honestly, he didn't know which would be worse.

Edwin dutifully recorded all the results of his experiments in Almanac, naturally, and he left much more abbreviated notes, more in line with what Cope had provided him, in a notebook. How they were planning to read it once he left—did Polyglot affect his writings yet?—he had no clue, but that also wasn't *his* problem. It would probably be Thoril's problem, actually. Or maybe Wendell's.

With baseline measurements complete, it was time to get *fun*. Sparks and mirrors! Something like that.

It was time for magic.

Edwin made sure to sell the lie that he was adding a special ingredient to his glass that *wasn't* totally just "more sand," by once more hinting at his man of mystery past (to Fissath's mixed annoyance and amusement).

It turned out that even with the strange origin of the lab's sand supply, Mana Infusion resulted in the same strange superfluid-like behavior. Fortunately, it behaved as a *normal* superfluid, and not the sort of craziness that liquid helium got up to, and stayed in its crucible even as he melted it, quenched it, and pulled it out to start taking measurements.

Was it clearer than normal? Huh, it definitely looked almost invisible, but . . .

No. Bad Edwin. Wait for the results of the measurements.

Almanac Entry: Glass

Glass is primarily composed of silicon dioxide, or quartz, made by melting down some types of sand and then allowed to cool. Unless done by a high-level glassmaker, the melting temperature of glass is too high for practical uses, and it must be mixed with another substance to be workable. See GlassVariants for more information.

For a full technical breakdown on the properties of glass, see GlassStats. For a detailed description of what glass is, see GlassExplained.

When making Infused pure glass, the point at which the mana is Infused during the creation makes no difference (see GlassTestsA). While Infused sand (see Sand) has strange superfluid-like properties, once melted and cooled, there is no measurable difference between it and glass that was Infused while molten.

Glass made while Infused retains all measurable properties of glass (see GlassTestsB), including refractive index, despite becoming noticeably more transparent, to the point of near invisibility in some situations. As of now, the method by which these two facts work together is unknown.

Most interestingly, glass made while Infused is transparent to *mana*; Basic Thermokinesis will not work on it but will instead pass straight through as though it weren't there at all. This is in distinct contrast to normal glass, which will block or intercept magical effects. Flight will similarly refuse to latch on to it, with the tether instead passing straight through as though the glass didn't exist.

This property remains even if the mana is later somehow removed from the glass.

Glass that is Infused postcreation will gain the additional transparency to light, but does not gain the mana invisibility.

See also . . .

CHAPTER 10

Clearly Magical

Edwin didn't see much of Inion over the weeks he spent in Panastalis. She would drop in every so often to see how he was, but she was usually doing . . . something off in the Verdant. Whenever Edwin prodded her about it, she refused to elaborate, which was . . . well, it was *slightly* annoying. He wanted to know what was up with his best friend by default, but she was entitled to her privacy just as much as he was.

"Ahem."

"Whaaaat? I wanna know the *details*!"

"*Privacy*, Inion. I was *just* talking about that."

"Gah, privacy schmivacy. Tell me all about this! I can't believe you've been skipping out on all the fun stuff!"

"There's no details to tell! We don't even like each other! Besides, I am distinctly not interested in avior."

"Oh, so if she *wasn't* an avior, then you'd be interested?"

"No! That's not what . . ." Edwin buried his head in his hands. "There's no winning with you, is there?"

"Nope!"

"It wasn't anything even noteworthy! It had just been a really long day and she offered to fly me down as a way to stretch her wings is all. That's it!"

"Oh, you were in her grasp? Trusting her with your life? How *special*." Inion waggled her eyebrows at him, which Edwin responded to with a flat stare.

"If you count 'immensely uncomfortable and an experience I never want to repeat ever again' as 'special,' I *guess*. Avior talons are *pokey*. My arms will be sore for the rest of the night, I know already. Heck, I'd rather reveal my 'potion of flight' than get another ride up to or down from the workshop from her."

Inion patted his head, earning a half-hearted glare and swat from Edwin in response.

"Honestly!" he complained. "Who even started the trend of building workshops in the tree's branches anyway? You can't even see them from the ground, and they could probably set fire to the whole thing if they aren't careful. I mean, I get why so many buildings are built *into* it, the sap is superuseful or whatever, but *come on*. There's like five staircases that lead to the top, and if you can't fly it's *such* a pain. Why, just *why* would they do that to us?"

He fell back onto his bed and buried his face in Inion's arm. "Just . . . is basic convenience or an automated elevator too much to ask for?"

"So if you don't like *avior*, well, didn't you say there was a human girl in your group? Rhita, wasn't it? What's *she* like?"

Edwin raised his head to glare at the fey. "You are the absolute worst."

Well, Edwin noted, *at least Inion has a nice laugh.*

Joriah, or at least Panastalis, didn't really seem to have the concept of a dedicated "weekend." Oh sure, they had days of rest—even endurance-type Skills could only get you so far and were far from universal anyway—but there was no coordinated "five days working, then the same two days everyone gets off." Instead, it was much more variable depending on the Class (and thus occupation) of the individual in question. For alchemists, the typical cycle was two days off every twelve, but when those days were taken wasn't defined, being not quite *random*, but it usually didn't line up between Edwin's fellow teammates. Thoril took his in four-day blocks, using up nearly a month of weekends all at once. Wendell took his two together, in the middle of the cycle. Everyone else, Edwin included, took one day off after five days of work, though not all at the same time.

Granted, he didn't really *need* to take time off for general exhaustion. His time spent training with Inion, and college before then, didn't really give days off, and he was . . . okay, perhaps not exactly adapted to it, but at least accustomed to it. His Sleeping Skill helped a lot, but while it fought off exhaustion, and even mental fatigue to a certain level, it didn't help with being under constant pressure to perform.

Now, taking one day off work every once in a while didn't really fix that, *either*, but it was still nice to occasionally crash in his room and do nothing too productive. Heck, thanks to Survival, he didn't even need to *eat* on those days . . . not that he had much of a consistent food schedule. In his defense, *most* people tended to eat once a day at most, anyway, with Eating more than sufficient to keep them satisfied.

Mainly, though, it was just the break from being around people. His social fatigue was slowly setting in despite his best efforts, but taking breaks every so often certainly helped delay it. Mostly, though, a share of peace and quiet—along with a good book—was *just* what he needed.

Which was why Edwin was so annoyed to be pulled out of his reading—a volume on the history of the Empire, as he was still waiting for access to more alchemy-oriented texts—by a pounding on his door.

"Who is it?" he called out, grumpily sitting up and setting his book off to the side.

"The kiln went out!" a voice called out in response. It wasn't Cope, Rhita, or Fissath, that was sure, but he couldn't recognize it beyond that without . . .

Identify.

Alchemeister-Scrivener

Wendell (Panastalis Wendell)

He's the really annoying guy who's Cope's personal assistant.

Back in Panastalis. Was an Alchemeister-Scrivener last time.

Easily frustrated. Really nosy. Mostly toothless, though. Safe to

ignore.

"Go away, Wendell! It's my day off, and why can't Fissath help you?"

"She's gone too! Get out here, you slacker, or there'll be consequences, just you wait!"

"Wendell," Edwin yelled back, "I do not care one *iota* what troubles you have when I'm not there. It's my day off. I *thought* Fissath was in the lab, figure out the kiln on your own! It's not that hard, and not my problem anyway."

"You-you what? Get out here, you errant, or you'll regret it!"

Oh hey, pun. Probably wasn't his goal, though. Polyglot had resulted in a few awkward instances where he'd thought someone was making a joke, only to find out it was the result of an amusing translation instead of intentional wit.

"Do paperwork or something! I don't care if you can't figure out how to burn arycal! You should have more than just me and Fissath trained on how to run it anyway!"

The banging resumed and intensified. "Get out here this instant, you ungrateful *Adventurer*!"

Edwin started at the insult, then recovered from his surprise. Wendell didn't have even the slightest clue as to Edwin's status insofar as he knew, he was just trying to insult Edwin generically. He'd used it on others before, anyway, so he presumed that was what was going on.

He sighed and floated to his feet, approaching the door and dismissing the Apparatus blocks he used to keep other people out. Midknock, he unlatched and swung the door open. Wendell stumbled slightly as his knock felt no resistance, and he assessed Edwin.

"What kind of an alchemist's outfit is that?" he scoffed.

"One who has a day off," Edwin wryly replied. He was wearing his most comfortable and clean tunic over his cleanest pants—there was no noticeable difference in comfort there—and was barefoot on the wooden floor. "And who is *very annoyed* at suddenly *not* having one. Let me get this straight; if you make me step past this door, I am going up to the lab and getting the kiln started. Then"—he forestalled Wendell with a hand; the man ignored it, naturally, but Edwin just talked over him—"then I will be returning here, finishing my book, and *not* coming in to the lab tomorrow, because today was *not* my day off, and *you* get to explain to Cope why."

"Hmm. I knew you would see reason eventually. I hope you aren't planning on wearing *that* to the lab, though."

Edwin glared at the man hard enough he half expected to get a "death stare" Skill offered—he didn't, he checked—before finally spitting out, "I see. Well, I'll be up once I get into appropriate attire, then."

"Good! You can't keep showing up as such a slob, we have an—"

Edwin slammed the door in the man's face.

"Seriously?" Edwin complained. "You *really, actually* just needed me to light the kiln?"

"That *is* what I told you, yes. Why, were you expecting more?"

"Honestly? Kind of, yeah. Once I gave it more than a couple seconds of thought, I expected that I was in for some kind of surprise, be it Othniel's sabotage of the week, a kidnapping attempt, or just some kind of prank."

"Please. As though we would be so juvenile."

Edwin responded with a level glare. "Rhita and Keir are *right* over there."

". . . You have a point."

"'Course I do. Remember, you're responsible for explaining to Cope why I'm not in tomorrow."

"Please. As though—"

"Wendell?"

"What?"

"You're not an avior."

"And that is relevant for *what* reason?"

"We are *very high up* in this tree. The edge of the branch is right over there. You know I can lift you with a single hand. And I want to get back to my book, which *you* pulled me away from. Think *very carefully* before you finish that sentence."

"I'll tell the boss if he asks."

"Great! Was that *really* so hard? Don't answer that."

Most of Edwin's experiments with glass had been met with "failure," to no *real* surprise. He only had three real areas to experiment with: biological material other than bone, minerals and miscellaneous rocks, and metals.

Biological stuff almost invariably burned up in the intense heat of the kiln, leaving nothing but soot and ash. In some cases, that resulted in slight coloration changes, but usually just meant he had to deal with a brownish-black block of dirty glass he would need to Purify before reusing the silica.

They didn't have very many distinct metals, to Edwin's partial surprise. Oh sure, they had loads of different *kinds* of metals, but they were usually alloys of various kinds. He didn't *really* need to test five different types of bronze to officially determine it wasn't the right path to be taking with his porcelain research, after all.

Alchemists' analysis helped somewhat there, for sure. He could use it to make sure he wasn't doubling up *too* much, but at the same time it wasn't reliable enough to tell if he was dealing with similar but distinct mixtures of metal.

Generally, using metals just produced different colors of glass. Pretty, but not particularly earth-shattering given Fissath's Skills, which allowed her to do more or less exactly that already, but with way more precision and variety. Magnesium was an interesting additive, when he was able to sprinkle in a tiny amount of the stuff, as with each heating it underwent, the color it turned the glass changed.

The one that garnered the most attention, though, was when he added lead. The resulting glass was a heavy, brilliant crystal with a high refractive index. Cope had been thrilled by the finding and claimed it reminded him of true diamonds when he swooped in to grab it. Edwin tried to give a bit of a warning not to use the leaded glass in anything pertaining to food or with regular contact from people, but Cope seemed disinclined to listen or care, as typical.

The minerals were occasionally interesting, despite, like the metals, frequently being "glass coloring x" and little more, but given it included a couple of actually, genuinely magical materials for his experiments, it wasn't *completely* boring.

Edwin had found that even when he Infused his added materials— always done subtly, under the guise of him adding a special material of his own devising, which was close enough to the truth—the results were rarely *too* fascinating, Basic Mana-infused glass and its invisibility to mana notwithstanding.

Something Edwin did find interesting in his experiments, though, was that pure metals took an absolutely *staggering* amount of mana to fully Infuse. Using Numeracy, he found that it was at least a dozen and sometimes as much as a hundred times as much as something with comparable mass that wasn't made of metal. Even substances that Edwin knew had metal atoms in their molecular composition didn't take as much as a comparable amount of metal separate from their bonds. It must have been something to do with the metallic bonds, perhaps? It was the first clue he'd gotten as to how his Infusion worked on a physical level, and he was thrilled, if still stuck. It clearly had to have something to do with electrons, but the how or why eluded him.

While his attempts to make magical ingredients may not have turned out the most interesting, and indeed, most of the naturally magical substances he tested weren't that special, either, a couple had shocked him when he first made them.

His first discovery had been made when mixing some black-singed magical fulgurite into his batch of glass for the day. He had a whole slew of different samples in the kiln simultaneously, the enchanted lightning-made glass mixed in an array of concentrations from 10 percent to .1 percent, the smallest Edwin could reliably go with how small each individual mix was. He also tried out a single 5 percent with having Infused the regular glass, just to see what would happen.

The result was *immensely* cool, if admittedly a bit underwhelming for the scales he was working at. The fulglass had, as far as Edwin could tell, a constant static electricity buildup across its entire surface, which scaled in intensity depending on how much fulgurite was mixed in. The mana-glass acted the same, but instead of evenly mixing into the glass like the mundane varieties had done, the fulgurite coalesced into veins that reminded Edwin of a plasma ball, black tendrils stretching from the center outward.

While Edwin was initially hyped about the possibility of *infinite free electricity* as he constantly felt a tingle from the held crystals, the voltage was . . . low. Numeracy didn't give him any values, but he would have been surprised if even the 10 percent concentration was more than a single volt. Plus . . . Edwin wasn't really sure *how* to harness that electricity, if he was being honest. His classes hadn't really covered what you were supposed to do if you stumbled across an infinite electron generator, if that was truly what was going on. Maybe he could encase the marble in a copper shell and insulate it, then run wires from that shell . . . but what would function as "ground"? It would be like using a low-voltage Van de Graaff generator but without a grounding wire . . .

Well, that was a problem for future-Edwin to consider. He just wished he was able to make more now! Unfortunately, what he had used was the only sample of the stuff the lab had, and Cope wasn't willing to seek out additional samples just to make "strange tingly" glass. That was . . . fair enough, Edwin supposed. After all, it wasn't like he was about to explain to the man the literal infinite potential they represented. At the moment, the Alchemist simply took them as trinkets. Party tricks, like amber and fur had been on Earth.

Still, while he kept his notes on paper about the discovery sparse, Edwin gushed endlessly about the possibility the substance had in Almanac, which brought him into a whole divergence on electricity and subatomic particles.

It was a pity he didn't have any way to concentrate the fulgurite once he had mixed it in with the glass, but such was life. It wasn't like he'd had any indication beforehand that it would be interesting, as other than pinging his magic senses, the "pure" black glass had no unusual properties. It wasn't even the first magical substance he had tested, either, just the first with an actually noteworthy impact. He'd just have to figure out where he could get more of the stuff at some point, he supposed.

Once he realized his mistake in overdiluting the magical ingredient, though, Edwin was much more careful to not repeat his error in the future. That caution paid off a few days later when he tested "abysite," a dark blue gem found in seaside caves, and when Edwin made a mixture of fifty/fifty abysite powder and sand, the resulting product was . . . well, it was a liquid.

The glass had cooled as normal, and while the liquid was runnier than usual, that was nothing too strange. It was only when it lost its glow and turned transparent . . . without ever solidifying. Instead, it became a sort of liquid crystal that looked faintly blue-green. It was denser and with a higher refractive index than water, but despite an absolutely *insane* amount of surface tension, it flowed with very little viscosity across whatever surface it was on. It refused to pick up any contaminants, was just as dense as glass, and Edwin was sure he'd figure out more in time if not for Cope having scooped it up with a hearty congratulations on his finding.

Edwin hadn't even been able to properly study the full extent of its properties, sadly. He didn't know how much he could dilute the substance while retaining its liquid nature, and given the fact he barely had more than a large marble's worth of glass, would be quite valuable if he could go as low as 10 percent abysite or even lower before the properties began to fade.

He was only a little bitter about it, he told himself. It was totally fine, that he wasn't able to study this awesome and weird amorphous not-solid . . .

Yeah, he wasn't even fooling himself. But there wasn't much he could do about it, either, so he let it lie for the time being. He just knew where he'd be heading once he was done in Panastalis.

Actually, that was a lie. There were lots of places that he heard about, lots of alchemical substances that he tried adding to glass to no avail. Everice from the north, which stayed solid even in the ridiculously hot kiln; wyvern and hydra blood from the mainland jungles with strengthening and replenishing properties, respectively; powdered dragonscale; manticore venom (Edwin was warned it was incurable and so to be careful with it); magefruit juice; blazeflower blossoms; honeyvine honey; glass falcon feathers; glowstone; and more besides. All of them were amazing and Edwin sorely wished he was able to properly experiment with all of them. His Alchemy Skill practically *buzzed* with possibilities, but he restrained himself.

In total, he had a whole laundry list of places to visit and plants and animals to stock up on as he did so. There were hundreds of alchemical ingredients he could use, and hundreds of places where they were found.

In fact, the primary alchemical ingredient to be gotten around Panastalis was sap from the massive tree itself. It was used in an absolutely stunning amount of potions, where it served in every part of potions, from base to primary to secondary to aspect to tuner to . . . How did this all work exactly?

"No, *no*," Thoril insisted, "the base is just what you have as the fundamental aspect of the potion. It's not . . . your solver or whatever."

"But it's what you mix everything else in, right?" Edwin clarified, "Like . . . water, for a lot of potions, or I suppose glass for most of what we do here."

"Yeah. That's the base."

"Right. With my alchemy tradition, we call that the solvent. Then you have your solute, that's what's mixed in, and that makes your solution."

"Yeah, well, it's different. It's not your solvent."

"How so? That's what I don't get," Edwin pushed. "And that's why I'm asking."

"So, the base is what you put in the cauldron first. That could be blood, or water, or sap, or whatever you want, so long as it's a liquid. Unless you're making a dry potion, of course.

"If you stop right there, your potion is just whatever your base was. Then, you add your primary to give your potion whatever action it's supposed to have."

"I *think* we're talking about the same thing, Thoril. I genuinely don't see how it's different. Like, take water. If you dissolve salt in it, it's still water, but it also gets some properties of the salt, and some unique aspects to their mix. If you want to oversimplify things, anyway."

"It's . . . it's different."

"*How*, though?"

"It just is!"

Edwin rubbed his temples. "Okay, fine. Let's say they're different. So the . . . base has the biggest impact on what the potion is. Water has no particular leaning—"

"Unless you want something that's refreshing or healing or—"

"Except a whole bunch of exceptions, yes. Water is normal, and doesn't strongly impact the rest, though it can magnify certain traits. Blood makes . . . elixirs, or just things that only target living creatures. Glass, of course, makes items rather than potions. Oil is optimized for topological applications?" Thoril looked at him in incomprehension. "It's best used when you put it on top of something else," Edwin said with a sigh.

The alchemist nodded.

"Okay, great. And then *that* whole book talks about all the different bases, and their noted traits?" Edwin asked, pointing at the *Tome of the Foundation.*

Nod.

"Okay. So then the *primary* is whatever is the second-most abundant ingredient?"

"No! Not always! It could also be—"

"Could also just be the first thing you add, right."

"Or it's what has the greatest weight in the potion!"

"How is that determined?"

"Well, whatever is the primary is the greatest weight."

"Yeah. So how do you determine that."

"Well, importance, obviously."

Edwin's hands returned to his head. "And how do you designate importance?"

"By making sure that what you use has the greatest weight. Some stuff will always be the weightiest. Pretty much anything with dragons will be the primary weight."

"So it's an intrinsic property of the addition?" Edwin clarified.

"Sometimes."

"You do *not* make this easy, you know that?"

"It's a hard job. If *you* can't handle it, then maybe you shouldn't have been an alchemist."

Edwin closed his eyes and breathed out. He wasn't going to punch Thoril in his smug face, no matter how much everyone in the room would enjoy it. Fissath would *certainly* find it hilarious.

"You have," Edwin calmly replied, "*no* idea about how much work I've put in for this. And no"—he forestalled the inevitable question— "I'm not going to elaborate.

"So you have the base, which determines properties of the potion. The primary, which influences what the potion does. And then the secondary . . . is like the primary, but lesser?"

"Welllll . . . yeah." Thoril sounded so *defeated.* It was great.

"Same with the tertiary, quaternary, and so on? Each has less and less of an effect? They involve the 'weight' thing as well, right?"

Thoril seemed almost annoyed at the fact Edwin was catching on, which Edwin *probably* shouldn't have been enjoying as much as he was.

"But there's a difference between using saltwater as a base, and using water as a base and salt as a tertiary ingredient or whatever?"

Nod.

Edwin held back a groan. Why couldn't magic follow basic chemical principles? That wasn't how solutions worked. Well, most of the time anyway. Sometimes.

"And then you have . . . aspecters and tuners. Aspecters change *how* something is accomplished, and tuners are . . . okay, I don't understand that one. How is that not just an aspecter?"

"A tuning component is *utterly* different from an aspecting one. An aspecter is one that aspects the potion, meaning it has different methodologies of reaction, whereas a tuner tunes a potion so its reaction methodologies are distinct."

Edwin blinked at the man.

"Are you just messing with me now?"

"No! A tuner tunes, an aspecter aspects. They're completely different!"

"That's not . . . that . . . oh, forget it." Edwin took a deep breath. "I don't suppose there's a book that explains this? Perhaps with examples?"

Edwin was at least half sure whatever potion-making methodology Cope's team used was utter nonsense. Even reading through *three* different books on the subject somehow left him even *more* confused than when he started. His best guess at the moment was that tuners and aspecters were mostly interchangeable terms that alchemists liked to insist were different. Among the three books, he found no less than four definitions of what each of them were, and *none of them* agreed with one another. Even the three he had found in *Alchemie Primera* couldn't agree.

It all seemed . . . artificial at first, which had cast further skepticism on the entire concept. The System? Sure, that was one thing. But this potion-making seemed almost gamelike, especially at first. What had helped him was seeing the sheer variety of combinations that *didn't* produce a viable result. It made it seem more like a matter of notation than some strange minigame. After all, they *absolutely* got results, which helped convince Edwin that they *did* know, at least to some minor extent, what they were doing.

The best thing Edwin could liken it to was cooking. The base was what sort of meal you were making, be it a soup, a sauce, a sandwich, or a salad. Even if you used almost all the same ingredients, the resulting meal would be very different. The primary ingredient was then whatever contributed the "most" to the actual recipe. It didn't matter how many other things were in your salad, if it included chicken, it was a chicken salad. Secondary and further ingredients were then what defined the rest of the dish. Then tuners and aspecters were comparatively minor parts of the recipe, but with an outsize effect on the rest of the food. Even a tiny amount of ghost pepper sauce would make an entire meal spicy, after all.

Once Edwin figured that out, even if the details still didn't make sense to him, the overall shape started to unfold.

I swear, level 50 Research is useless. *Utterly useless.*

Now, his primary objection was with what their potion ingredients *were*. Midnight Smoke had a base of *sand*, a primary of octopus ink, a secondary of ground lavender flowers, an aspecter of the beak of a rooster beat into a powder, and a tuner of alderwood bark smoke, held in an iron skillet for the smoking process.

Oh yeah. Apparently the container the potion was made in could affect things. Because why not? To say nothing of the fact they were making a sleeping potion out of *sand*. That wasn't how biology, chemistry, *or* physics worked!

In any case, the result was a dark, dark purple crumbly powder that when blown into the air would billow beyond its apparent volume and create the midnight blue smoke so resistant to spreading out that had knocked out most of the lab back when he'd first arrived.

Even Alchemist's Analysis didn't show the substance as being made of sand once it was done, but instead wholly un-Almanaced ingredients. Clearly, *something* was going on, even if he couldn't figure out what exactly it was yet.

The *problem* was that when Edwin tried to make a relatively simple potion—an oil-based potion of fire resistance, made with oil as a base, fire elemental ember-ash as a primary, and giant spider's blood as an aspecter—it did nothing. Actually nothing. Well, the oil made the stick that it was tested on burn a bit faster, but the potion itself had no effect.

He had *no* clue what had caused that. He'd been giving it a good-faith effort, too, so there shouldn't have been some magical observer effect at play, where thinking it wouldn't work would mean it couldn't. Other attempts at other potions had no effect either.

He could watch people make potions, no problem. Most of the others did at least a few side projects in addition to the porcelain problem from time to time, and there was some really impressive stuff being made! Healing potions made from troll blood, fertilizers made from the sap of the giant tree Panastalis was built around, strength potions made from bear blood and bear claws.

Yet every time Edwin tried his hand at something, it failed. What made things *even stranger*, if it weren't bad enough already, was that if he followed the personal directions of someone overseeing his attempt, the potion would turn out fine. But if he read from a book, or tried to make a potion from memory? No luck.

He was starting to reconsider his certainty that it wasn't some kind of observer effect, but he *had* managed to make potions before. They'd just been from the *Zosiman Grimoire*, a book conspicuously absent from the limited libraries he had eventually been granted access to.

Making some vague, circumspect inquiries about the book only resulted in him finding out that it was apparently total nonsense and everything it said was wrong. He wasn't able to get any more information about it for whatever reason, but it seemed somewhat suspicious to him if nothing else. His personal experience told him that the *Grimoire* worked; he'd made two different kinds of potions—healing salve and dehydration oil—straight from its pages, and they had both worked out great. Plus, its herbology sections had been accurate insofar as Edwin had been able to tell . . . but he quietly went though and marked all his Almanac pages with information from the *Grimoire* as possibly suspect.

He was so, *so* glad that he figured out he could just edit pages about midway through his project, instead of having to wholly rewrite them. The discovery even got him another level in the Skill, which was *massive* these days, particularly given his leveling of it just a few weeks prior.

Even still, he was happier about discovering the edit functionality than the level.

Cope kept wanting Edwin to keep working on the porcelain problem, though. He kept thinking that it was just a matter of some combination of glasses of different colors, heated different times with additional additives each time, and he'd eventually get his porcelain.

Of course, Edwin still couldn't explain *why* it was a fool's errand, that Cope's approach was fundamentally incorrect, and that Othniel was the one with the right idea. It wouldn't go over well, that much was certain.

Most importantly, though, it would mean that Edwin would be pressured about *how* he knew that porcelain was a form of pottery, not glassmaking, to which he had *no* answer. A month of using Memory had let him remember there was something about a glaze with porcelain, but that the glaze was done at the same time as curing the pottery . . . he had never really *known* details, so Memory was of limited use there.

His "man of mystery" excuse would only go so far. He genuinely didn't know what each of his coworkers thought his history was, but he was pretty sure that revealing a secret jealously guarded by a city so powerful it could resist the Empire would result in them demanding answers, and he wasn't ready to leave quite yet.

Soon, perhaps. But not yet.

"Maxlin," Cope said as he approached Edwin one day while he was setting up his next trial, white-stained iron filings, "I've arranged for a medical license course for you. It starts tomorrow, I'll cover the cost."

Well. That was a pleasant surprise.

Level Up!
Skill Points 581→661 (Average level: 39)
Alchemical Analysis Level 15→26
Alchemical Dismantling Level 6→18
Alchemy Level 84→86
Arcadian Elixir Level 17→19
Basic Thermokinesis Level 17→20

Flight Level 32→37
Fresh Air Level 14→31
Improbable Arsenal Level 23→26
Longstrider Level 29→30
Mana Infusion Level 86→87
Memory Level 60→61
Numeracy Level 32→35
Outsider's Almanac Level 131→132
Polyglot Level 60→65
Prototyping Level 16→22
Ritual Intuition Level 20→25
Sapper's Apparatus Level 40→43
Skillful Assessment Level 32→33
Watchful Rest Level 18→26

CHAPTER 11

Cell Attributes

"Wait, you were actually working on that?" Edwin found himself taken aback slightly by Cope's declaration. He had mildly assumed that Cope wasn't actually keeping up any part of his deal, but apparently he was?

To his credit, the man looked slightly taken aback. "But of course! You've done a remarkable amount of work, it is only fair that I uphold my side of our bargain. Did you truly think so little of me?"

Edwin shrugged. "I mean, it's been some two months, and I still don't know how much I'm being paid. I was hanging around because I like the chance to learn more about alchemy."

Cope frowned. "You haven't been paid? I'll have to look into that."

Edwin gave him a vague look. "So . . . tomorrow morning, you said? Okay. I can do that. Where's it at?"

"Medicinal Workshop. I'll have Thoril show you where it is as you head out today."

The corners of Edwin's mouth twitched up slightly at Thoril's groan, as yet another task shepherding him was assigned to the unfortunate guy.

"So explain to me why this matters again?" Inion asked. "Don'tya already know how to heal people or whatever? Plus, it's not like you'll get any more First Aid levels."

"I want to get licensed," Edwin explained again as he reclined against his pillow. "And yes, I don't think I'll learn much on the *medical* side, though I am curious about the alchemical aspects of medicine, but that's not the main point anyway. I just want to be legally permitted to heal people."

"What is that for, anyway? Seems stupid."

Edwin closed his eyes as he leaned back. "I thought so, too, at first. But as I thought about it more, we had something similar back home. Of course, it was also way *harder* to heal people back there without magic to use as a cheat, but I can mostly understand why a culture that controls the distribution of Skills would want to be careful with who gets Skills pertaining to life and death, as well as ensure they actually know the basics of what they're doing."

"Mm. Well, I think it's stupid. You can heal people just fine, but they won't let you. What if you do it anyway?" She dropped onto the bed next to Edwin, causing the mattress to shift slightly.

"I'm . . . not sure, actually. Not that it really makes a difference. I wouldn't just let someone die if I could help it."

Shut up, brain. I don't need counterexamples right now.

"The license just means I'm playing the game, and I don't need to sneak around the law. Besides, Cope's paying for it. All I need to do is show up to the classes and lessons. How hard could it be?"

They were both silent for a moment, then spoke in unison.

"Shoot, I just screwed myself over, didn't I?"

"You realize you just jinxed it, right?"

Edwin sighed and groaned. "Great. Well . . . I mean, how bad—"

"You probably don't want to finish that, do you."

"You're . . . you're probably right, yeah."

The sights of Panastalis never *truly* got old. The utterly ridiculous size of the tree the town was built around made Edwin feel tiny no matter how many times he climbed it. If anything, the endless flights of stairs he'd had to climb oh so very many times had just *further* reinforced the scale of the titan in his mind. Meanwhile, the buildings built into its side did nothing to diminish the imposing scale, and really only served to remind him of the power of the Alchemy Guild locally.

From what he'd seen of Panastalis's layout, non-alchemy-related buildings were on the forest floor, away from the tree, then various offices and halls were built into the trunk of the tree, with more important individuals and subgroups of the guild near the base. Then, built into and atop the branches of the tree were all the workshops.

That the Medicinal Workshop, where Edwin's lessons were to be held, was at the very base of the tree was unusual to say the very least. Upon further reflection, it made sense that they might not want to have to cart people to the top of the tree for treatment, though that did raise the question of how they got people *down* from the top, if they were injured in the workshop. Surely, that had to be a semicommon occurrence? There hadn't been too many incidents in his work group, but they still had their fair share of cuts and burns that came alongside working with inadequate safety equipment.

Like everything else visible from the ground, the Medicinal Workshop was grandiose. Carved and stained wood elegantly framed the entry archway, and the door was covered with relief carvings, painted and glimmering. Even the animated, glowing, and colored depiction of a flickering flame only distracted him for a minute.

The interior was less grandiose yet no less impressive. There was a sizable waiting room of sorts, with a desk set to the side. Behind the desk, an entire wall of bottles, all shapes and sizes and organized in a manner that belied Edwin's momentary assessment, stood tall and imposing. You'd outright need a— Ah, there was the ladder, set on rails to allow for easy access to the medicines on every shelf. Off to one side, an open archway covered by hanging curtains led farther into the back, though there was nobody present.

"Hello?" Edwin asked the empty room. "I have an appointment?"

The walls didn't respond, unsurprisingly. It didn't take long for the curtains to part, though, and allow a new individual entry. A purple-haired, green-skinned gnome hopped onto some unseen ledge behind the counter and greeted Edwin.

"Heya! Sorry about the wait. What can I do forya?"

Experienced Managerial Shopkeep

"I'm one of Cope's assistants," Edwin explained, "and I was told to come here to get a healer's license?"

"Hmm? Ah yeah, the Alchemist-Errant." She pointed behind Edwin to one of the closed doors on the far wall. "Down that hall, first door on the right."

He nodded his thanks to the gnome and departed. "First door on the right" wasn't exactly tricky to find, so when he arrived, he knocked twice and waited for a "come in!" before entering.

Inside, Edwin found a relatively cozy office. In one corner, a blazing fire (thankfully burning wood, not arycal) raged, and all that defended the room from massively overheating was a massive yet solitary open window overlooking Panastalis's native river where it flowed below.

Most of the office space was, reminiscent of Cope's, lined with all manner of clutter. Unlike the arrogant alchemist, however, this room was filled predominantly with bottles, though bowls of herbs, berries, tree bark, and other natural-looking ingredients presented a strong front.

Presumably, Edwin thought, they were actually useful potions and potion ingredients, despite his not having any particular basis for that hypothesis. That said, the stock wasn't unanimously medicinal. In one corner, a taxidermied raven perched, surveying its domain as though all who came in were but more shiny trinkets to collect. Despite its apparent nature as a stuffed corpse, Edwin kept a wary eye on the bird as to ensure it wasn't some unusually still familiar or something.

His teacher, imposing in authority if not build, filled the desk with the outfit and hair that belonged to some mighty wizard or scholar. Long white hair and a sizable beard stretched beyond what Edwin could properly see, obscured by the desk at its tip. The man assessed Edwin with bright eyes, and his arms moved with the easy grace of youth as he worked to clear some papers from his desk.

Alchemist Vital

Oh, cool! Did that mean he'd gotten and completed the Alchemy Vitae Path? Had he created life of some sort? Edwin might want to ask about that at the end of this. He finished entering the room and—

"Close the door! You're disrupting the heat!" his teacher snapped, as Edwin was doing just that. While annoyed, he wasn't petty enough to abort his action just to spite the man.

. . . Okay, Edwin might be that petty on occasion, but he wasn't going to do so *this* time.

"And now who are . . . Ah, Alchemist-Errant? You would be Maxlin, then." The alchemist's voice wasn't too scratchy, but it still rubbed Edwin the wrong way.

"That's me," Edwin agreed as he took a seat opposite the man, "though you can call me Edwin. And you are?" he prompted.

"Alchemist Galen," the man snapped. "And don't you forget it, Maxlin!"

Edwin hadn't done anything to warrant that sort of hostility, had he? He figured he was probably just being overly sensitive, and he dialed back his threshold for "actively hostile" from the elderly alchemist in front of him.

"Certainly, Alchemist Galen."

"Hmm. Well, you learn quick, if nothing else. Good!"

He continued, "So . . . you're some fool who wants the First Aid Skill when you're at Tier 4 already? Or didya get a medical Skill from an upgrade. Why didn't your hometown medic get ya licensed, boy?"

"There were . . . extenuating circumstances. I didn't get my medical Skill until after I had left home, and once I did, I tried to apply for the license when I was in Vinstead, but that didn't go well. So, here I am."

"Hmm. It's a disgrace you were able to get the Skill prior to completion of the course. Though I must ask"—the man stood up—"what medical Skills do you possess?"

Edwin hesitated. He wasn't sure that he wanted to share. But then again, it had been fine when he had talked with Rizzali. Though that was extenuating circumstances. Would it be safe if he told Galen?

"Well, come on! We don't got all day for this!" the alchemist snapped, as he paced back and forth. Or was his hostility sensitivity too high still?

"Primarily First Aid and Anatomy."

"Eh? You got First Aid? Howzat work for ya?"

"That's a . . . long story, but one that I'd rather not go into at the moment."

"Bah! You youth and your secrets. I swear, you better not go Adventurer on me now." He waved a finger. "Far too lenient on those kids these days, I swear. Back in my day, I'll have you know, we didn't play into the 'oh I'm so special' mentality they allow these days. If you wanted to play with the Empire, you played by the Empire's rules, you contributed to society properly. None of this nonsense running around the woods."

Edwin very carefully stayed silent.

"Buncha blind fools, who think they know better than centuries of Imperial crafting. Makes me sick! I barely even recognize some of the kids these days, with their new classes and all . . ."

He continued his rant for a while, and Edwin steadily grew more and more impatient until he finally broke. Unlike previous times, he *did* have something he wanted to get done today, and he was worried he might give away something about his status *as* an Adventurer if he wasn't careful. "I don't suppose we could actually stay on topic?"

The man immediately stopped his rant. "I don't suppose we could stay on topic, *Alchemist Galen*," he corrected.

Edwin sighed. "I don't suppose we could stay on topic, Alchemist Galen?"

"Much better. Now, where were we?"

"My medicine Skills?" he prompted.

"Right! You had First Aid and . . ."

"Anatomy." Edwin sighed.

"Anatomy! Whazzat do?"

Edwin said, "So far as I can tell, it helps me figure out the internals of myself or of others. Mainly useful on humans, though I think that's just because that's where my primary experience with it is."

"Hmm. Doesn't seem too useful."

"Isn't it?"

"Well, it's not Vivification, Medicine, Vital Rebalance, or even Elixir Infusion! Now *those* are proper Skills for a Medic-Alchemist. Not that Anatomy nonsense. Did they really change up the Alchemy set so soon?"

"What is it with people not liking my Skills?" Edwin muttered. "They work just fine."

"Bah. Take it up with your Registrar. They clearly failed by not telling you what you coulda gotten. That's not what we're here for today, though, is it?"

Edwin sat up straight. He idly wondered what sorts of development they'd managed to accomplish with magical assistance, and what kinds of alchemical medicine they had. He still remembered how his healing potions Cope had only called "elixirs of rapid recovery," which were apparently different from normal healing potions. How did that work?

He realized his teacher was waiting for him with an expectant look on his face. "Uh, yes, Alchemist Galen. I want to get my healer's license."

He nodded. "Good. So, tell me. What are the Essential Attributes?"

"Wait, in a medical sense?" Edwin cast his mind back. Where had he . . . Ah! Right, the *Zosiman Grimoire*. He tapped his knee and quickly used a series of Identify to get to his "index" page, then jumped to the relevant part of his "digitized" tome. "The three Essential Attributes are Health, Stamina, and Mana. Health is—"

"Wrong."

"What? Wait, is that not what you wanted?"

"I want you to tell me reality! Not that archaic theory!"

"But you asked . . . Okay. So, the body works through a complex interaction of internal organs. It's organized by nerve clusters primarily originating from the brain, though the heart and intestines also have some nerve nets. The brain operates most bodily functions autonomously, feeding signals to the heart and lungs for—"

"What the ruddy stone are you prattling on about?"

"How the body works?" Edwin hazarded. "I was getting to the way Attributes interact, but I needed to establish some baseline."

"You couldn't be more wrong. I ought to track down whoever your teacher was and give them a firm scolding. You even had a Skill that helps you determine bodily function?"

Edwin hesitantly nodded.

"Bah! That you could be so led astray that even your own Skill tells you falsehoods!"

"That's . . . possible? I'd never heard of such a thing."

Then again, Edwin realized with a bit of consideration, *given I know my knowledge is right, they must have that sort of thing happen with their knowledge Skills. Huh. Can the System be outright wrong?*

"Neither had I, yet your Skill is worse than useless! What's your First Aid level, boy? If it's not at least fifty, this isn't worth my time."

"It's, ah . . . eighty-two."

"Eh?" Edwin felt a bit of satisfaction as the information caught the crotchety old man off guard. "It's what?"

"Eighty-two."

"How'd you go about managing that? Ah, no. You must have had it for years tryin to get it to compensate for such utter nonsense you fed it, didn't you?"

"Well . . . not exactly, but . . ."

"Exactly! Put it through the wringer, you did, boy. You'd best apologize to it!"

". . . Apologize? Also, aren't we getting off-track, Alchemist Galen?"

"Fine! Apologize on your own time then. Since you're clearly so lost, allow me to enlighten you on the *proper* methods of wound treatment. The body is made of three Attributes: Health, Stamina, and Perception.

"Health is the dominant Attribute, as it provides life and blood to the rest of the body. Blood, naturally, is heat and composed primarily of fire. It is how we digest and burn food, and gives us our body temperature. It, and the heart, are naturally responsible for intelligence, understanding and courage. This is why the heart is the most important organ in the body, as it is through it that blood is controlled and direction is given to the creature.

"Stamina is the supporting Attribute, and it is what grants motion to the heart itself. Thanks to it, we may move, blood reaches its destination, we breathe, and may utilize our limbs for the multitude of tasks we depend upon it. It is, naturally, made of the wind. This is why we must breathe, to restore our Stamina. It is released in the form of sweat when used, and subsequently returns to the world around us. However, it is treacherous and is similarly responsible for nervousness, stress, pain, and fear, among others.

"Lastly, there is Perception. Perception is the Attribute associated with water and connects us to the world around us, lets us see and lets us hear. It is in the subordinate brain, and why those without heads cannot sense, though they may still act and may yet live."

Edwin raised an eyebrow at the assertion that someone might "still live" while headless, but he'd held his tongue this far, he could keep quiet a bit longer.

"As it is the gateway between the self and the outside, it is thanks to it that we have compassion, grow tired, feel anger, and more besides. It likewise is responsible for digestion and speech."

"That's . . . How did you come to any of those conclusions?" Edwin couldn't help but ask.

"Indeed," Galen agreed, misunderstanding Edwin's reaction, "it required a true genius to determine such massive revelations. It was, in fact, a Panastalis native from nigh a thousand years ago, who made the *Alchemedical Manuscripts*. His name has been mostly lost to time, and is now known only as 'the Healer.' Truly inspiring, no?"

Edwin was speechless for a minute, though not for the reasons the alchemist seemed to think.

"So . . ." Edwin eventually said, sighing, "what about the other Attributes? The Attribute theory I was exposed to suggested Mana, not Perception, was the third Attribute."

"Bah! Zosiman knows not what he speaks of. Mana is far too rare to be an essential Attribute. Beyond the infinitesimal appearance of the Attribute itself, so few actually have mana of any amount. It is exactly as it seems, no more and no less. It is magic, not something that is an integral part of the body."

"And the other Attributes?"

"Much the same. Charisma is merely another form of Perception, hence the name, though one that pertains to the interaction of the self out into the world. Constitution is a rough, mocking combination of Stamina and Health, which separates the body from the ravages of the world. Dexterity is akin to Stamina, and more besides. Do you need me to continue?"

Edwin shook his head. He had a pretty decent sense of the sorts of stuff they believed. "So . . . how does this help when trying to give someone medical attention?"

"That depends on their ailment, naturally. In the purely physical, fever and chills are associated with Health, a cough or mobility issues with Stamina, digestive issues and pains with Perception. Similarly, more emotional ailments can be cured in similar manners, though with slight alterations. Once the required treatment is determined, it is merely a simple matter of returning the Attributes into their proper balance."

"And how do you do that?" Edwin asked, feeling defeated. He felt like he already knew the answer, but . . .

"Well, if one's Perception is overactive, they require far more sleep than usual, or ensuring they don't sleep if they are short upon the Attribute. If they are short upon Stamina, a potion restoring such is in order, whereas in the event they have too much, they are to stay as active as possible, or at the very least stay upright. Health is unusual in that it is more difficult in the event they do not *have* sufficient blood, as usually only alchemical means can regenerate it. In the event they have too much Health, the cure is simple."

"Bleeding?" Edwin guessed.

"You do know some medicine! I thought you were hopeless."

Edwin sighed, a long and exasperated thing. "Have you ever tested the effectiveness of bleeding people?"

"But of course! It is the standard response to any with a fever."

"And does bleeding dramatically improve recovery rates, Alchemist Galen?" he asked skeptically.

"Of course! Fever is nothing more than the excess of fire, and bleeding is the way to reduce the amount of blood within a person, obviously. Surely you can understand that?"

Edwin glared at the "medic." "Yes, I understand that bleeding a person reduces the amount of blood they have. That's obvious."

"Excellent! Now, the next thing—"

"Hang on, hang on. I wasn't finished. How do you know that removing blood from a person actually helps them recover?"

"Many who come to me or my apprentices recover admirably from their fevers."

"And some die?"

"That is simply the assurance of life."

Edwin groaned. He hadn't felt this frustrated in . . . well, about two months, when he found out what arycal was made of. "But how do you know they wouldn't have recovered just as good if not better without the bleeding? Have you ever tested the idea of whether or not bleeding a person actually helps them with a fever?"

"What, you would have me experiment upon my patients? Bah! I will only seek to provide the best medical care I am capable of. Why would I ever desire to not treat an individual when I would be capable of curing them?"

"Well . . . what about making sure that whatever cure you gave them *was* the best you could? Like, what if it turned out you were wrong? How would you find out?"

"Ah! I comprehend your reticence more now. Rest assured, we only use the knowledge passed down for us from generations ago, which has been in use for generations. We would never dare to countermand the wisdom of those who have put in the difficulty of realizing how the body works and how best to cure it."

"And what if they were wrong?"

The man looked at Edwin like he'd grown a second head. "You doubt the wisdom of your elders?"

Edwin resisted the urge to massage his temples. "Well, where I come from, bleeding *used* to be common practice, until someone actually took the time to compare how patients fared without being bled and with being bled, and bleeding them did *worse* than nothing. Centuries of people died at the hands of doctors who never questioned whether or not bleeding someone, reducing their *health*, would really be good when suffering from a fever."

"Nonsense. This is not a discussion, this is a lesson."

"No! You're killing people by bleeding them." Edwin started to lose his temper. "That's not how the body works!"

"Be quiet! I will not be gainsaid by the likes of you!"

"You've never even tried another method, though! You don't know the results of anything you do!"

"What, you would have me . . . experiment upon my patients, like they were some kind of test subject?"

"Yes! That's the only way to improve!"

"Then tell me, oh wise one. How *does* one go about treating a fever?"

Edwin was momentarily caught off guard. "Huh. I was expecting you to ask me how a fever came about. As for the fever, you don't treat *it*; it's just a symptom. You need to treat the base ailment rather than just trying to reduce the fever. In some cases, that can actually be harmful by itself."

"Very well. How do you propose reducing one's health if not by bleeding them? It's right in the name, after all."

"But . . . that's not what causes the problem. It has nothing to do with an 'overabundance of blood' or whatever. So far as I know, that's not even possible. Fevers are how the body tries to fight off infections, by raising the temperature past what most pathogens can readily withstand."

"Path . . . pathogen? Bah! If you wish to try and spout such nonsense, at least do not deign to making up words!"

"What? No. Pathogen isn't made up. Well, I suppose all words are made up, but that's besides the point. Let me think how to describe this . . . You know about parasites, I hope?"

"Naturally. They can be created when drinking tainted water."

"That's . . . I'll get back to that. Anyway, a pathogen is kind of like that, but instead of there being one big creature living in the host, there's thousands, millions, or even billions of *pathogens* that get in and start to divide, and the body trying to fight them off can raise the temperature to try and kill them."

"Divide? They kill themselves?"

"What? Oh, no. Think of them like . . . you have slimes, right?" Edwin had yet to see one in person, but Niall had mentioned them so they were likely real here. An Alchemist Vital, who had presumably created life in some form or another, probably had lots of experience with them.

"Yes, what of them?"

"Well, a pathogen—or bacteria, for the more general term—is kind of like a really, really small slime. So small and so simple that they can reproduce just by cutting themselves in half, more or less. There's more to it than that, but that's not relevant right now. Anyway, they're so small that they're basically invisible and live *everywhere*, but *pathogens* are some kinds that are harmful to humans—or other creatures—and the body tries to fight them off. That's what a fever comes from."

"So you claim that fever is caused by the body trying to fight off an attack by thousands of invisible slimes?"

"Ye— Well, kind of. They're really, really small, not invisible. You'd probably need a really powerful Skill to see them, or use a special tool."

"So thousands of tiny slimes cause fever? Bah! Utterly ludicrous. You seem so genuine, too. You poor fool, being filled with all these absurd lies. Worry not, I'll ensure you get a *proper* education by the time I'm through with you."

"Well, Alchemist Galen, if you don't believe me, how do diseases work?"

"Simple! Thanks to the elemental nature of Attributes, a misbalanced Attribute can disrupt the surroundings of the individual and cause a cascade of Attribute unbalance in their surroundings. When in an unbalanced situation, the body will mimic its surroundings, causing its own Attributes to unbalance and further spread the disease."

"That . . ." Edwin sighed. "Well, it's better than 'miasma.' Well, no. So what happens is that bacteria—the tiny slimes—will breed in their hosts, and then spread on contact, or when they cough, or go to the bathroom, or *somehow*. Fortunately, most diseases can't jump species, so . . . huh. How does the Attribute theory account for different species not crossing diseases?"

"Avior, humans, gnomes, and more all have different balances for their Attributes, naturally. What would affect one might be completely normal for another."

"So then, why doesn't proximity with someone possessing a different Attribute balance cause them to get sick?" Edwin prodded.

"For the same reason that merely being in proximity with another will not spread disease, despite every individual having a slightly unique balance of Attributes. Unless the body is ailing, it will not taint its surroundings. However, tainted surroundings can still exist separate from an ailing individual, and that is where the disease first comes from."

"That's . . . that's just not how it works, though. And by that logic, what about individuals with really high Attributes? Shouldn't someone with the Health Attribute but not Stamina or Perception then always have a fever?"

"It is the gift of the System that such bestowals strengthen, but do not disrupt, the balance of Attributes within us."

"So what, your explanation for how come the *one time* you can actually measure the supposed 'balance of Attributes' within someone doesn't correlate to the afflictions that supposedly come from those Attributes is just 'a wizard did it'? That's not how science works!"

"What do you mean by 'an adventurer-mage did it?' I do not understand the phrase."

"Adventurer-mage? Oh, right. Wizard. Basically, you just wave your hands and say it's magic when your theory doesn't hold up."

"The System would not irrevocably harm an individual. This is simply common knowledge."

Edwin rubbed the bridge of his nose. "Look, I know that you have tremendous respect for whoever came up with this theory, but can't you see it's complete nonsense?"

"I am the one speaking nonsense? Bah! You are the one who comes in and starts to speak of invisible slimes living within us. Indeed, what is your explanation for why not all diseases affect avior and humans alike, if not for the Attribute difference between them?"

"Simple. Not all bacteria—slimes—are equally harmful to all kinds of life. That's what I was saying, *pathogens* is the term for those types of bacteria."

"So what? These things simply live within us and do no harm?"

"Yeah, actually." Edwin shrugged.

"Preposterous! You're lucky I don't throw you out right here and now!"

"What for?" Edwin protested.

"For flagrantly disrespecting me, my predecessors, and my entire profession!"

"What, for daring to question it?"

"Yes!"

"But how else are you supposed to learn?"

"You ask questions, you do not question!"

"I'll pretend that made more sense pre-Polyglot," Edwin muttered. "Then how are you supposed to learn, if not by being asked questions you don't know the answer to?"

"I do know the answer! You simply refuse to accept it!"

"Yeah, because it's not the *right* answer!"

"Oh, so you know more than I and all of those who came before? A thousand years of knowledge?"

"Yes!" Edwin shouted, successfully shutting up the alchemist.

Then Galen shouted back over him, "I will not be spoken to in such a manner!"

Edwin paused to catch his breath and continued with a more sedate tone, "Besides, you don't have a thousand years of learning that you're falling back on. You just have one guy from a thousand years ago who came up with an idea and a thousand years of people then copying him. If anything, your healing is a thousand years *behind* where it should be."

"Get out of my room."

"What, because you refuse to listen?"

"Because *you* refuse to listen! Such impertinent youth. Know your place!"

"I do!"

"Yet you continue to challenge your elders!"

"That *is* my place!"

Both lapsed back into silence for a moment, staring the other down.

Edwin thought for a moment. "What if I prove it for you?"

"Prove what? The existence of these tiny slimes?"

Edwin's resolve set. "Yeah. I bet you that I can prove they exist."

"And how do you intend to do *that*? Are they not invisible?"

"Individually, sure. But I can either make something that would let you see that small, or get so many of them in one place you can see them yourself."

"And how," Galen scoffed, "do you intend to do that?"

"You'll see," Edwin replied, mind racing. "You'll see."

CHAPTER 12

Closed-Dish Cultivation

How did you prove germ theory to someone who didn't believe it? It was actually a surprisingly difficult question, given that technically speaking, even back on Earth it was, still just a theory. A *germ*— Ahem.

Granted, it was a highly tested and unanimously accepted theory, but because it was a matter of *biology*, it couldn't be a proper law. It just couldn't have the sorts of rigorous mathematical backing required.

All that was to say Edwin couldn't prove that germs caused disease directly. He could prove the existence of bacteria, yes, but without access to massive amounts of people who were sick with the same thing, he couldn't even show that the presence of a given bacterium was strongly associated with being sick.

Honestly, if he hadn't been so incredibly riled up by *Alchemist* Galen, Edwin probably would have been able to take a much more measured and reasonable approach. It was annoying, to lose control of his emotions at such an important time, but that was just life. He couldn't back down *now*, though. It would just be enabling the incredibly dangerous medical practices they'd been using.

Regardless of all that, Edwin still needed to figure out how to prove that what he was saying was true. His solution? Ignore the outright proof of germ theory for disease, just try to show that bacteria were real. There were two routes to get there. The first was to build a microscope and show Galen that bacteria were real; this would be tricky, but doable, potentially even with apparatite lenses instead of glass. The second was to grow a culture of bacteria in a petri dish.

Fortunately, Edwin didn't need to choose one route or the other. Both would work just fine for his purposes and mean there was less chance of being messed up in some way.

"Well?" Alchemist Galen prodded. Fair enough, Edwin had been silent for a minute while planning out his avenues of attack. "What shall I see?"

"I don't suppose you have any microscopes?" he asked. No point in reinventing the wheel if he didn't need to, after all.

"A . . . small-glass? What's that?"

"That's a no, then. It's a contraption that lets you see really small stuff. I didn't think you'd have it, but I wanted to check. I'll . . . make one, I guess. Just give me a few days and I'll have proof for bacteria's existence." Edwin nodded to himself. He'd head back to his carriage and try to get some kind of bacteria culture going, then build his microscope while it was developing.

"Hmm. Well, when you're willing to admit defeat, find me. Now run along. You've wasted enough of my morning already."

Edwin glared at the alchemist, but held his biting comments back. What he made would be far more convincing than anything he could say . . .

"I agree. Quite the wasted morning."

Dang it.

Petri dishes were actually quite easy to make. Well, it was that easy when Edwin had an instant "summon object" power and could simply create a glass dish by imagining the tool exactly as he wanted it to appear. It would have been *way* harder if he had to try and use actual glass in his experiments. Regardless, that was unfortunately where the easy part ended.

Awkwardly, this was the first time Edwin had actually tried cultivating bacteria. He'd been a physicist, not a biologist, and the closest he'd gotten to the squishy sciences since before college was when he took organic chemistry, which . . . well, it didn't cover bacteria cultures. Even back in high school, he didn't think he'd actually done anything like this. So he had to figure it out from scratch.

Memory told him that the substance used in a petri dish was called agar, but that came with precisely zero accompanying knowledge for what that was, why it was used, or even how *to* use it. Making an educated guess, he presumed it was food for the bacteria, which he hoped he could substitute with more readily available magical ingredients.

Talsanenris was the obvious option for magical food, given its utterly absurd caloric equivalent, though it might have been short in nutrients. Edwin *did* have a fair amount of talsanenris leaf, though, which he'd seen had *tremendous* nutrient density, so that should compensate well enough. All he'd need to do would be to crush some talsanenris leaves and berries together, then add water until it was a nutrient slurry, and he could use that as his base for his colonies.

. . . Probably, anyway. If this worked properly on his first try, it would be *amazing*. He'd had better luck with all his trials on Joriah than back in a lab for whatever reason (he suspected his Alchemy Skill helped), but he wasn't sure if that luck would hold over to biology. Well, fingers crossed.

He used a stagnant puddle near the stream for his bacteria source, scooping up a tiny measure of water and pouring it into his experimental dishes. Once they were prepped, Edwin found a warm but not hot corner of his lab and let them sit.

While waiting for his cultures to grow, Edwin started tracking down the materials he would need for his microscope. While he could make most of it out of pure apparatite, it wouldn't be suitable for the tube. The whole point, after all, was that only light from the sample could make it inside, and his transparent crystal wouldn't do a very good job at blocking out extra light.

He played with using paper and bark for his purposes, but paper was too translucent and bark was too inflexible. Ultimately, Edwin did go with a cylinder of beaten iron, purchased from the blacksmith for some twenty ager. Honestly, he should have checked there from the very beginning, but he was too accustomed to making everything himself. Magic could compensate for a lot of the supply chain, it turned out. At least it wasn't *too* expensive, though the speed at which he'd gotten his part made was bound to have upped the price some.

The rest of the build was . . . well, not exactly *easy*, but not too challenging either. Other than actually getting his lenses in focus, it was just a matter of playing around with methods of holding the iron tube up and at some kind of adjustable height.

It took time, sure, but it was just tinkering, and it was kind of fun. It still took Edwin the better part of a day to get the housing up, but he accomplished it nonetheless.

The next day was where things got tricky, and he ultimately decided he didn't want to have to deal with the math and instead resorted to trial and error. Granted, it was *educated* trial and error, but it still just amounted to trying different lenses until he found one with the focal length he wanted; namely, a bit shorter than the length of his microscope tube.

Once he started getting close, the rest of the work was straightforward, and within two days, he had a fully functional microscope. It still took a bit more tweaking to get it powerful enough to actually see bacteria and the like, along with more silver spent at the blacksmith's to get better caps on both ends of the tube, but he *did* manage it in the end.

While not all his petri dishes had grown any appreciable amount of bacteria culture, two had enough spots growing in the talsanenris slurry that Edwin felt confident in showing them to Galen.

And so, dishes in one hand and microscope in the other, he found himself knocking on the alchemist's door just three days after he'd last stormed out.

"Come in! Ah. *Maxlin*. Come to admit your failings, then?"

"Not at all, Alchemist Galen. I think I have some things you'll find particularly interesting, as it were."

He pulled out the dishes and set the microscope down. "So the first thing I want to show you are these bacteria cultures I grew over the past few days." He set the dish down and slid it over. "This is just from a sample of pond water and fed with some talsanenris. Each of these spots you see here? That's a colony of bacteria, grown from a single cell in the original sample. I started off with just a bit of water from the stream and food to grow, and here you are."

"Hmm, yes. Mold. I'm very familiar with this concept. You can create it from almost anything edible, with just a bit of water. So trivial the System doesn't even acknowledge it as creation. Is that truly the best you have to offer?"

"What? Create . . . Oh, you did mention that, didn't you." Edwin sighed. "You know, Alchemist Galen, other than magical shenanigans, life doesn't arise from nothing."

"Nonsense! We can see this happen all over the place! Just as rotting meat makes flies, mice from tall grass, spoiled potion waste water makes slimes . . . need I go on?"

"That's not . . . Okay, I don't know about that last one, but the former are definitely false. Hmm. Okay. So . . . I'll get back to that one, actually. For now, this is the microscope I was talking about."

Edwin fiddled around with his stuff for a minute, getting a slide ready. He made sure to show his process to the alchemist, taking a bit of seemingly clear water and dabbing it onto the slide. Once it was in place, he adjusted the microscope until the slide was in focus and he could . . . well, not exactly *clearly*, but still . . . see some larger bacteria.

"Right here. Just look down this and you'll see what I'm talking about."

"Bah. Kids these days, no respect for . . . Oh, now that's clever."

Edwin perked up. "You see it?" He looked over to see . . . Galen fiddling with the adjustment knob. Great.

"Quite the clever little setup you have here. So you turn this little knob-thingy and that raises or lowers the platform? Don't suppose you'd be able to share how it works?"

"Uh, I mean, I wasn't really planning to but I can think about it?" he replied, caught off guard.

"I don't see any of these invisible slimes!" Galen snapped, finally peering into the lens.

"What? Oh, you took the focus off."

"The what now?"

"I had it set up properly, but then you fiddled with the knob and . . . could I adjust it back, please? I'm going to need you to move."

"What? You're blaming me for it? You impertinent boy! I've been an alchemist since before your parents were eating dirt!"

"I mean"—Edwin found himself taken aback—"you also haven't used a microscope before today, so you wouldn't really be *able* to know how it works? . . . Just adjust that knob until the picture comes into focus."

Galen took that as an invitation to really start spinning the knob, far too fast to properly focus on any sample, prompting Edwin to say, "Um, that's not how you adjust it. You need to—"

"Shaddup, boy! I know what I'm doing!"

"Your . . . your, ah, actions speak otherwise, Alchemist Galen. Look, if you'd just let me, I can focus it and then we'll be on our way."

"No! I won't have you deluding me with whatever tricks of the light you're aiming to try and fool me, but I'm onto your tricks, you Adventurer." The man waved a warning finger at Edwin. "You need to have quite the updraft if you want to get one over on me."

"Okay, then just . . . go a bit slower, I guess? You'll never be able to find the right focus when you're twisting on it so much, and I'm kind of worried you'll . . ." Edwin found his warning cut off by a *crack* and glittering blue lights. ". . . break it," he lamely finished.

"Your damned doohickey broke," the man accused.

"Yeah. I see that," Edwin replied, unamused. "Can I see it now, Alchemist Galen? I think I can fix it."

"Bah. Fine, if you must."

Edwin gingerly accepted his creation and looked over, trying to figure out what had broken. There was no obvious external damage, but the adjusting knob spun freely and allowed the viewing apparatus to sink to the lowest point it could reach, almost touching the slide.

It didn't take too long for Edwin to figure out the problem. One of the internal gears had shattered, disconnecting the knob from the slider in charge of actually moving the contraption up and down. He could even see exactly where it should have gone, the transparent nature of apparatite a double-edged sword in this situation. After all, he could see through the outside just fine . . . but he could also see through the *inside* as well, and so had to try and figure out what tiny piece was missing by seeing which section of the interior was *slightly* less distorted.

Not fun and not easy to find, but certainly easy to fix. All it took was Apparatusing in a replacement part in the same position it should have been in, and he was good to go.

"Okay, there you go. Please try to not break it this time? Or, better yet, let me adjust it?" he tried.

"Bah. Fine. I shall allow you to present your best case, that your failings cannot be blamed on me," the alchemist reluctantly conceded. "Just make it quick."

Edwin successfully held back his grumblings as he set up the slide. Other than a brief hitch where he needed to replace his replacement part from the microscope—his initial fix hadn't interlocked with the further gears properly—it was accomplished without incident and he stepped back, motioning for the medic to take a look.

"So *what* am I supposed to be seeing? I don't see any of those tiny slimes you're talking about."

"What? There's lots of stuff. The cells, the green algae, the longer tubes . . ."

"Dirt? That's what you're going on about? Ha!" he barked. "No wonder you sounded so sure about yourself. Of course we well know that getting dirt in you's bad. You're not supposed to have earth in the body, just wind, water, and fire. That's basic!

"I will say, though, the idea that you could make more dirt in your body is a new one! Ha! Can't wait to tell the others about this."

"What?" Edwin finally composed himself. "How do you look at that and see *dirt*?"

He breathed in deeply. "Okay. You know what? I can *prove* that there's something alive that's that small, and that you can't just 'create' life by mixing sugars and water together. Though I have to ask, do you have any Skills that just encourage life to grow in any form? It'll speed things up."

Galen looked at him skeptically. "When this fails, you're going to leave me alone and quit wasting my time. But I do have Encourage Life, yes. What would you have me use it upon?"

Edwin clasped his hands together. "Okay, great. I'll be back in five minutes, I just need to grab a couple of things."

* * *

Edwin returned quickly, armed with his talsanenris agar-replacement and a vial of puddle water.

"So," he explained, "bacteria are like most living things. If you boil them, they'll die. Once they're dead, it doesn't matter how much food they have around them, they won't come back to life.

"Now," he admitted, "there *are* bacteria that can survive water-boiling temperatures and can even thrive in those environments, but they wouldn't live in the stream where I got this." He lifted the vials of water he'd grabbed. "But that being said, there *may* be tiny spots of bacteria growth on the dish. It just won't be anywhere near as prevalent as our control dish."

"Control dish?"

"Ah . . . comparing what will happen to doing literally nothing. Which is what you *should* be doing more often"—he glared—"particularly with medical treatments."

"Ah yes, the heartless act of experimenting upon your patients rather than treating them. Such a bastion of morality, are you not?"

Edwin took a deep breath, then figured it wasn't worth it and snapped at the alchemist, "Better that than killing people for a thousand years because of what somebody thought *sounded nice*. The world doesn't work how you think it 'ought' to. Science and alchemy is figuring out how the world *actually* functions, and no amount of so-so stories will change that. So yes, I would rather experiment on a patient than blindly trust that what I'm doing is the best. Now, I'd *ask* them first, but people who are desperate tend to be pretty open to trying out a new system that you think might work better than the existing treatment.

"The important thing is just that you *ask*. Don't force them to do something potentially dangerous just because you *think* it will help them."

"Ha! As though the fools could know what is best for them. They need a firm, guiding hand to avoid hurting themselves"—he looked at Edwin—"and others, with their dangerous ideas."

Right. Edwin recalled, *I'm still in the Empire, where "personal liberty" is choosing in what way the government controls your life.*

"Well . . . setting that aside . . ." Edwin moved on. "When doing an experiment, you need at least two groups. One is the control, where you do nothing, and the others are your experiments, where you can actually see what changes when you alter different variables.

"In this case," he explained, "we're comparing boiled water to non-boiled water. So when I take this vial and divide it in half, we can use that to compare what happens to basically the same water when either boiled or left alone.

"So with this half"—he lifted one of the two smaller vials he'd made—"we put it in this dish, and you can use your Skill on it. Then we can see what happens when we use your Skill on bacteria.

"Now, with this half, I'll take and boil the entire dish we put it in, just to try and sterilize any bacteria that might have gotten in from the food."

"Interesting methodology. Very well, continue."

"Okay, so here"—Ediwn mixed his control water into the dish—"use your Skill on this while I boil this."

The contraption he set up for boiling his petri dish was simple enough in theory, just a stand that he could set the apparatite onto, but in practice, making a platform out of his Skill that could withstand the temperatures of Galen's blazing fire—which he was using as a heat source in this instance—was a bit trickier.

Honestly, Edwin just hoped the crystal dish would survive the fire all right. It wouldn't be good if it broke and ruined everything, but there was only so much he could do in that regard. The stand was more vulnerable, anyway, because if he had it resting on the ground too close to the fire, it would be exposed to far more heat.

Eventually, he got a contraption hung from the top of the mantel, suspending the dish on what looked like crystal wires. Once Edwin made sure it was secure, he let it be and returned to Galen, whose Skill had already resulted in a few cultures popping up.

He nodded to himself and looked back at the dish, ensuring nothing was going wrong. A touch of Basic Thermokinesis helped it along, and it was boiling in no time. To be on the safe side, he let it go for several minutes, though he was constantly mindful of ensuring the water didn't boil away.

By the time he was satisfied with the boiling, Galen had finished up with the first dish and was looking at the circular cultures with detached interest. "This certainly is a fascinating demonstration of trivial life creation, I shall admit. Thank you for bringing it to my attention and not making this a complete waste of my time."

Edwin silently glared at the man, though the alchemist didn't look up to see his gaze.

"Now can you repeat the process? Here, this one is complete, though you may want to let it sit for a few minutes before touching it."

Edwin gently set the dish down on a premade stand, allowing the tongs he had been using to carry it dissipate back into magic. With a flourish, he directed the older alchemist to work his magic on the sample, and waited for vindication . . .

Wait, what?

"I . . . I don't understand." Edwin blinked. "This should have worked, what's going on?"

"As I told you, boy. You're seeing dirt and thinking it's alive, claiming to be able to show that life doesn't form under the right conditions—where else *would* it come from? You keep spouting nonsense, and by your own words, you're wrong."

Edwin looked at the dish in confusion. There were fewer cultures than the wholly untreated one, yes, but the ones that were there still blanketed most of the bottom. If he didn't know better, it would have looked like the heated mixture had just changed the type of "mold" that had grown. What was . . .

Hmm. Were bacteria magical here as well?

"Do you have anything you wish to say?"

"I can still prove this. I just need a better setup, I think. One that I thought about for more than ten minutes."

"Hmm, yes. I suppose that with sufficient changes and perhaps a new potion of sorts, you could indeed change the conditions enough that growth would no longer happen. But you outlined your . . . 'experiment' and it failed."

"But . . ."

"Get out of my office. You're wholly unsuitable for any form of medical license, clearly, and would simply use the permit for your uncouth 'experiments' upon your patients."

"I know what I'm doing, though!" Edwin protested.

"You clearly do not. Now get out or I'll report you to the Registrar."

Over the course of his research, Edwin had come to a realization about why exactly he found alchemists so frustrating. It was just a general pre-scientific mindset, actually. Basically, instead of looking around at the world, finding something interesting, figuring out what caused that, and then using that discovery to predict other parts of the world, they skipped the first step entirely. Alchemists looked at what they *thought* should be the case, and then fiddled around with all manner of variables until they either found something that more or less worked how they thought it "ought" to, or gave up.

He could see it even in his coworkers. Keir and Rhita both thought that porcelain was made with bone, and so they only ever worked with bone meal and other ingredients. In the unlikely event they somehow *made* porcelain, despite them not using any of the main components, they'd misattribute their success and focus on whatever bone they had finally tried alongside it as "the key."

That was probably how their potion-making worked, too, wasn't it? Someone had thought that a certain substance—say, sand—"should" be able to put people to sleep, and then played around with it until they found something that worked. Of course, there were still some kind of magical shenanigans going on that kept him from making potions . . . unless it was just the result of their standardized Skills? Maybe because he was missing—he checked his notes—Mixing, whatever magical oddities were at play refused to blend together because he didn't have the right equipment to make it work.

That would actually make sense, come to think of it. It could be any number of the fundamental "alchemist" Skills, really. Potion-Making, Mixing, Emulsify, Process . . . Heck, it might even be Colorimetry or Timing and his inability to tell with enough precision when he needed to perform certain steps that caused the entire procedure to fail. Or heck, they all had an absurd number of potency-boosting Skills. Maybe his potions *did* have an effect, it was just without multiplying said effect a hundredfold they were basically undetectable.

Whatever the reason, though, it made it *insanely* difficult to explain why his approach was different from the others'. After all, from what they could tell, Edwin was just basing his "bacteria are real" claim off exactly as much evidence as most of their propositions, and he was now just trying to brute-force his way into making it make sense.

He'd tried boiling—that hadn't worked. Cooling hadn't worked, either, though that one may have been more a result of not having any particularly effective way *to* cool, let alone freeze, his water. Ice was a luxury he didn't know how to make quite yet.

So Joriah had fire-immune, or at least fire-resistant bacteria that were way more common than on Earth. Perhaps it was just Panastalis, and some chemical in the water? It was a bit concerning that in the event he encountered a waterborne disease, boiling water wasn't an assured method of preventing its spread. Perhaps he should try to make an autoclave? Maybe he could use that to figure out what temperature these pyrophiles died at.

After all, if you can't burn something, you just haven't used a big enough fire.

Unfortunately, Edwin couldn't test any other ways that might kill bacteria. After all, it wasn't like he had any bleach or other common disinfectants to work with (not that he'd ever use it on drinking water) . . . he was pretty sure that filtering and distilling the water was successful at killing the bacteria, but his cultures still had growth even when he tried using only that, and he couldn't cultivate *anything* that never experienced any growth short of not including any food in the experiment, which was hardly a surprise.

That said, he expected it was due to the simple fact that he couldn't filter and distill, and thus properly sterilize, his talsanenris nutrient soup. If he had a powerful ultraviolet light, then he might be able to sterilize it that way, but he had literally *no clue* how to make a UV lamp.

Edwin had probed Memory to the best of his ability to no avail save a vague tickling sense it had been covered in a book he had read at some point. Maybe once he leveled it some more, he'd have better luck, but for now . . . he didn't quite have the recollection to piece together tiny fragments of what he'd learned and letting Research fill in the gaps.

The important thing was that Edwin knew he was right. He'd seen the evidence with his own eyes, knew exactly what the problem was, but nobody would listen! He wasn't crazy, he was *right*!

". . . That's what crazy people say, isn't it? 'I've seen the truth, you need to listen to me!'" he asked as his ranting to Inion drew to a close.

The fey nodded, and Edwin buried his head back into his pillow with a frustrated sigh.

After the . . . less than stellar outcome of his medical license attempt, and subsequent investigations into what went wrong, Edwin mostly just returned to his work on porcelain, though with much less enthusiasm. It had been a couple of months of *just* glassmaking, after all, and he was starting to get restless.

Plus, his coworkers had heard vaguely that *something* had happened and would not shut up about trying to figure out what was going on. Fortunately, whatever rumors were circulating didn't directly reach him, and those that he heard about indirectly were supercontradictory.

Sometimes, people seemed to think Edwin had made some sort of new healing potion slime, another time it was that he was secretly a healing mage pretending to be an alchemist despite what Identify said. Sometimes, he'd successfully gotten his license by revealing some brand-new treatment, other times he had been laughed out of the room by proposing that all dirt was alive and could be used to make golems.

Those were, thankfully, about as close as the rumors got. Other people said he'd shown some way to properly transmute blood into fire or fire into blood, or he'd introduced some fourth Attribute into the basic collection.

All told, Edwin's days of anonymity were long over. Previously, he could go basically unnoticed on his daily errands or when going up and down the tree, but these days simply walking around attracted stares and the occasional whisper. It was not the sort of attention that he wanted, not that he liked *any* all that much.

Finally, he couldn't take it anymore and told Fissath exactly what had happened with Galen. He categorically refused to tell Rhita and Keir because of how much they bugged him about it, not that Thoril or Wendell were too much better. Cope hadn't said anything, but Edwin could tell that the way the man looked at Edwin had changed, and he knew there would be some kind of confrontation with him at some point.

"Tiny, invisible slimes?" the avior asked incredulously.

"Well, not exactly. But sort of. You know how insects and that sort of thing can be really, really small until you can barely see them?"

"Yes."

"Well, life doesn't stop there, and it just keeps getting smaller and smaller."

"Makes sense."

"Bacteria are, to some extent, as small as life can get. While normally living things are made up of uncountable numbers of building blocks—cells—of all different sorts, bacteria are only made of one."

"Uh-huh. So what was the problem?"

"Well . . . I'm not entirely sure. My current theory is just that the native bacteria are way, *way* more resistant to temperatures than those I'm accustomed to. But I can't conclusively prove that, and that's the problem. Even—"

"Makes sense. Pass the arycal?"

"Right, sorry." He handed over the white, claylike disaster waiting to happen. Months of keeping the kiln running had reduced his fear of the substance a bit, though he was still quite skeptical of its supposed complete stability.

The formula for how it was kept stable was a guild secret, and he didn't qualify. Then again, given the normal sorts of potions the guild dealt with, Edwin wasn't sure that he'd feel reassured by finding out what nonsensical blending of substances prevented the two hyperreactive elements from doing anything.

"Even arycal fire, when I dared trying that, didn't quite get everything. So . . . yeah."

The avior shrugged. "It's interesting. I don't know enough about medicine to tell you if it seems reasonable though. The idea that tiny creatures that live inside of us and make us sick is hardly the strangest thing I've learned since I got to Panastalis, anyway. It's certainly more reasonable than some of the nonsense the Pair like to cook up, anyway."

"So then what would you say is the strangest thing you've heard?" he asked, their conversation naturally shifting along.

"Well, this one time Rhita tried to explain to me how . . ."

"Alchemist-Errant Maxlin," a voice called out as Edwin slunk down the road after a relatively boring day of work. It took a moment for him to process the statement, but once he did, he perked up and looked around.

The source of the voice was readily apparent, as a tall, dark-haired woman in fine, but clearly work-oriented, clothing approached him. He didn't *think* he'd met her before, but . . .

Eternal Master of Manifold Potions and Elixirs

Yeah, nope. Never met someone with that kind of Class before. Sheesh, how did you even *get* something like that?

"I am Master Kertoa"—her voice was firm but not harsh as she spoke to Edwin, and she looked him straight in the eye the entire time, his eyes unable to look anywhere else—"and you and I are due for a serious conversation."

CHAPTER 13

Local Cultures

The guildmaster's declaration didn't *overly* surprise Edwin; he had been half expecting something like this for a while now. However, he wasn't expecting to be approached on the street by the Master herself. Heck, he didn't even really know that the guildmaster *was* a she until just now.

. . . He needed to get better at preemptively looking up details about people, didn't he?

"Right now?" he asked.

"Preferably. Unless you have some activity that you find more important that you must attend to, which I find unlikely."

"Fair enough. Still, though . . . Anyway, right here?" Edwin figured she'd probably not want a conversation in the middle of the street, and he was vindicated when she turned away from him and motioned that he should follow.

"We shall speak in my office," she explained as they approached the primary guild hall, "There are fewer prying eyes and ears there."

Her tone wasn't harsh, though it was firm, and Edwin distinctly detected the edge of a social Skill at play, trying to worm its way inside his head and put him at ease. He squashed it before it could develop, Infusing his Adaptive Defense in an effort to get some Skill backing behind his efforts. While he still hadn't figured out exactly what Infused

Defense did—if anything at all—using the combination itself was still reassuring to him as a placebo if nothing else.

They didn't enter through the main entrance of the hall, but instead took a side door, tucked behind a root and almost invisible from any angle other than straight ahead. Once inside, it was a tight spiral staircase and a short hallway into what must have been inside the trunk of the tree itself. Or just absolutely massive spatial shenanigans, because that was also a possibility.

"Not that I question your decision," Edwin asked, "but surely you have more important things to do than just track me down and talk to me personally?"

"Understandable," she agreed, but she did not turn to face him. "While your concern for my time is commendable, it is misplaced and you need not worry about the manner in which I spend my time. I assure you, this meeting is not taking away from anything that might be deemed important."

Even with the reassurance, Edwin still felt a little awkward about taking the time of someone so influential—or just in general, really. He wasn't *that* important.

As the two of them entered what seemed to be Kertoa's office, an identical woman to the guildmaster next to him—tall, dark hair, slightly dark skin—stepped out past the two of them, making eye contact and nodding with her . . . no, not a twin. While that had been his first thought, it wouldn't explain why they also had a small, matching burn scar running along each of their chins.

Wait, what?

Eternal Master of Manifold Potions and Elixirs
"Master Kertoa" (PanastalisKertoa)
Guildmaster of Panastalis's Alchemy Guild

Yep, definitely the same person. He'd applied that Almanac note not five minutes ago, which meant there was either time travel or cloning going on. Probably the latter, given she was an alchemist, though just to check, he modified her *specific* Almanac label to denote her as "Master Kertoa 1."

When he checked the second now, he saw that her Almanac tag was unchanged, and with a nod, updated her to "Master Kertoa 2." Just to further check, he quickly checked them each out with Skillful Assessment. Sure enough, they were both fully suffused by an identical green-red Skill.

Kertoa looked at him with an impatient eyebrow raised, and Edwin realized she was holding the door open for him. He quickly muttered an apology and ducked through.

"Confused?" she asked, a tilt to her voice Edwin wasn't entirely sure how to parse. Amusement, perhaps?

"I mean, it seems like a really useful Skill. Would it be . . . Alchemical Cloning? Alchemical Simulacrum? How many can you have?"

She was taken aback. "Perfected Simulacrum, as the case may be." She blinked. "Were you forewarned by Alchemist Cope? It is generally assumed I have a twin upon first meeting one of my doubles."

Edwin shrugged, not really wanting to go too much into how Almanac worked. "Scar on your chin meant twins wouldn't work, not that twins usually look so similar into adulthood, and having the exact same really impressive Class name seemed unlikely. Since you have time to personally seek me out by standing on a street corner, that means you don't have too much pressure on your time, or alternatively have some way to be in two places at once. Combine all that with being a 'Manifold' Alchemist, and some sort of Skill-based biological duplicate made sense."

"I see," she replied as they took a seat at her desk.

Unlike most of the offices Edwin had seen during his time in Panastalis, the walls were mostly bare, other than a single massive bookshelf that dominated the back of the room. Even with Seeing, Edwin couldn't make out the titles of most of the books present, though the few he could see had impressive-sounding titles. *Secrets of the Vast Alchymical Arts, On the Homunculus, On the Nature of the Gozau,* and *The Vivinomicon* were all represented, none of which Edwin had ever seen before.

The rich wood of her desk—made of something Edwin hadn't Almanaced yet—was similarly visible, somehow free of the massive piles of paper Edwin normally associated with administration. Was this just a decorative office, then?

"I shall admit to being impressed by your awareness. Although I will not answer your question in its entirety, you are correct in your assessment that thanks to it I need not worry overmuch as to how I spend my time. I am fully capable of speaking with you and performing my numerous other duties simultaneously."

"That's . . . reassuring, I suppose, though also intimidating. Couldn't you just replace half the Alchemy Guild with that sort of Skill, though?"

"It does have limits," she responded. "However, I am certain you understand the desire for circumspection in your Skills, do you not?"

A paper appeared in her hand without so much as a flicker of a Skill. "Edwin Maxlin, Alchemist-Errant. Home registry, Vinstead. Adventurer *and* Ally of the Empire. Tier 2 Alchemist with mage Skills, and incredibly, Alchemy as the upgrade to *Improvisation* of all things, utilizing the Physical Alchemist Path. Special notes: a large variety of rather synergistic Skills, and a note-taking and expansion Skill whose details are unknown even to the *Registrar*. You are most unusual."

Edwin felt himself shrinking back in his chair. "How do you know so much about me?"

A smirk played across her face. "I *am* the guildmaster of the largest alchemy guild in the Empire. It is my duty to monitor the pulse of interesting developments, and a Tier 2 Alchemy Skill *certainly* qualifies. When your name came across my desk a few days past, it took me a little while to place where I had heard it before, but once I went looking . . ." She tapped the paper resting on her desk. ". . . I found quite the tale."

"Look, I don't want any trouble," he said defensively.

"Oh, I have no doubt you do not. Yet trouble has found you nonetheless. I have never seen Alchemist Galen in such a state before, and while the man can be irritable, you truly managed to push him to some spectacular lengths."

"So it is about that." Edwin sighed.

"But of course. Though we have more to speak about in addition. You are quite the curiosity, Alchemist-Errant Maxlin."

"You can call me Edwin . . ." he muttered. "But fine. What did you want to talk about?" he asked resignedly.

"We shall begin with your most recent incident, I do believe. Tell me of what happened between you and Alchemist Galen."

"Really? You don't already know?"

"I have heard what Alchemist Galen says about the incident. That is not the full story."

"Fair enough, I suppose," Edwin agreed. "So, part of my hope for coming here was to get a medical license—I have First Aid and want to be able to use it on other people if the situation requires it—so, anyway, part of my arrangement with Cope was that he'd figure out how I could get the license, and so about two weeks ago he told me he'd set up a meeting . . ."

"Interesting," Kertoa said once Edwin had finished. She didn't have any paper in her hand, but he had the distinct impression she had taken notes regardless. What kind of communication did she have between clones? he wondered. Was it full telepathy? Did she have another body scratching down everything he'd just said? Or did she have some other Skill that she was using, like how he utilized Almanac?

"So," she continued, oblivious to Edwin's internal musings, "in short, you challenged the Attribute model of anatomy and disease, you and Alchemist Galen got into an argument about medical ethics, and then you failed to provide sufficient examples that supported your argument? Does that summarize it appropriately?"

"Well, there was . . . no, actually I suppose that's about right," he agreed.

"Hmm. Well, hearing your side as well makes me tempted to grab Alchemist Galen and give him a hand throwing you into the river."

Edwin shrank back in fear and mentally started assembling potential escape routes.

"However, I recognize that is simply an impulse within myself brought about thanks to my disagreement with and general distaste for your blasé attitude toward human experimentation, neither of which are strictly forbidden within Panastalis. Therefore, I will master this impulse and discard it appropriately, so you need not fear for your well-being."

Edwin breathed a sigh of relief, though she continued before he could relax too much.

"Do not mistake my acceptance for agreement, Alchemist-Errant Maxlin. I still find your acceptance of human experimentation disgusting, although I can understand why you may hold your views. Similarly, though challenging belief is not *discouraged* per se, I still feel personal distaste for challenging such old and well-held beliefs in particular.

"Similarly in your defense is that you did not seek to further undermine Alchemist Galen's judgment. Had you been more belligerent in your efforts after he had dismissed you, this would be far harsher. We appreciate challenges, we do not tolerate baseless harassment."

She finally paused to take a larger breath. "Though I must inquire as to where you developed such an . . . unconventional theory as this 'invisible slime' postulate, or 'germ theory' as you call it. It is wholly unlike anything I had ever heard of."

Edwin scratched the back of his head. "It's common knowledge, back where I come from. That microscope I made? It's really, really weak in comparison to some of the ones back home, where you can actually see *inside* of cells and see how they work. Then, healers saw that some bacteria only appeared in the blood, in the saliva, and so on, of people who were sick with a certain disease, and it grew from there." He paused. "Actually, I'm not *sure* if that's how it happened, but I think it is."

"Fascinating." The note-taking vibe was back, though Edwin couldn't put his finger on why he thought that. "And you do not believe these are simply created by the body as a symptom of the disease why, exactly?"

"Well, because they can't be, not really. They're really, really different from what the body is and how it works. It's . . . well, we have a sort of Identify thing that lets us tell what is related to what, and bacteria are less related to us than trees."

"Hmm. Yet you could not prove this why?"

"Well, if I had more time and perhaps a more willing audience, I'm sure I could prove their existence—and disprove spontaneous generation while I was at it; life doesn't just suddenly appear—but proving they cause *disease* would be much harder. I don't really know how to do that without relying on *actually* unethical human experimentation. Even then that may not be proof exactly, but just strong evidence . . ."

Edwin realized he was prattling on a bit much, finished with, "So . . . yeah," and closed his mouth.

"You make a distinction about 'ethical' and 'unethical' human experimentation. Why is some experimentation ethical?"

"Well . . . I guess it's about intent for the person you're experimenting with? Sure, lots of horrible stuff can be done by trying to figure out if something is *bad* for a person, and that's unethical. But if you're trying something to help the *subject* out, then it's better. Say you hear about some new potion and you think it might help out people with a given problem. If you're trying to heal them, you'd obviously want to try and give it to them, yes? Because you're pretty sure it should help. But at the same time, you haven't really given it a full test yet, so you can't give it out too freely. Instead, you give it to some people with the problem and don't give it to others, preferably in line with what they want. Then, you can see how the new potion helped, harmed, or did nothing, and can make an informed decision from there."

"Yet you are still experimenting on people. Should you not ascertain whether or not something will help first?"

"Well, I mean obviously you should perform all due diligence and try to minimize the risk, which can incorporate all sorts of animal testing, or simulating tests . . . I don't even know what all you can use to try and simulate it without an actual person, but at some point you need to just go and try it on a human before you can know for certain if it'll help. The body is really, really complex after all. Sometimes, what works for one person may not work for another, and you just need to figure it out from there. What matters is you're always trying to help people to the best of your ability."

"Interesting philosophy. I find it reminiscent of the new Adventurer program in some ways, and although that has shown great promise, I still do not agree it ought to be extended to medicine. However, I shall admit that it is not as tasteless as you first made it sound, Alchemist-Errant Maxlin."

"Oops?" he tried. "I'm not . . . the best with words. I constantly annoy people with how much I talk about all sorts of random stuff, I know, but I also don't know how to do anything else, so I'm just sort of stuck in the middle," Edwin confessed.

"I concur."

Edwin frowned. Was that an insult or was that some kind of a . . .

"Now, we have spent an inordinate amount of time upon merely the first discussion point of several, and so it is time to move along.

"I hear you have interesting views on potions. Am I correct in understanding you are unable to brew most common elixirs, even under supervision?"

". . . Yes," he admitted. "I don't know what it might be, though I suspect it might be that my Skills aren't conducive to it. That, or there's some sort of magical shenanigans going on that are blocking me."

"Are you not a mage?"

"I'm not a very good one," Edwin defended. "I have . . . three Skills that relate to it? Maybe four. A sense, a way to make things magical, a heating Skill, and Flight. I don't know the first thing about how to use magic, and alchemy is *undeniably* magical."

"Interesting theory. I do not know of any mages who attempted to become alchemists, so I shall somewhat defer to your judgment there. What has brought you to that conclusion?"

"Because, well, a lot of the interesting stuff *is* magic. You use faintly magical ingredients a lot of the time, or there's magic involved in the process somehow . . . I don't know exactly, but alchemy doesn't work like it should."

"You have utilized that phrase multiple times now," the guildmaster said as she continued her interrogation. "What do you mean when you say something 'should' work a given way? I was under the impression, given your views upon experimentation, that how something did work was the ultimate authority of all else, regardless of how it 'ought' to function?"

"I . . ." Edwin hesitated. "I don't actually have an answer to that, I suppose. How things work without magic in play, I guess? Though there's no real way to isolate that . . . Huh."

"So in your view, because alchemy creates things that do not align with what you think would happen in the absence of magic, it is therefore magical in nature?"

"Yeah, I guess."

"Please elaborate on the manner by which you know how potion creation ought to work in the absence of magic. Insofar as I am capable of investigating, it appears more that it is the *introduction* of magic that interferes with the way potions 'should' be created, given you are the only mage we have, and you are unable to make potions."

"I . . . I don't think I can, really. It's related to one of my secret skills." Edwin was edging close to a lie—a risky proposition given he didn't know for *sure* that Master Kertoa didn't have a truth-telling Skill—but if he phrased things correctly he might be able to skate by on technicalities. "Which *definitely* ventures into some topics that I don't think I can really share, by Tara's advisement."

"Who?"

"Oh, Enforcer . . . Lisana. Based out of Vinstead," he explained after a quick check of Almanac, and the guildmaster nodded in understanding.

"I see. Interesting that you have imperial secrets. Most alchemists never discover something so important that it requires Enforcer involvement." There was that note-taking impression again, and Edwin had to fight the urge to correct her faulty assumption.

"So now we come to perhaps the most pertinent part of this conversation." She nodded. "Please, enlighten me on the nature of your relationship with Alchemist Cope?"

"My relationship with Cope? Why is that important?"

"Just answer the question, please. My comments and verdict will only be given at the conclusion of this discussion."

Well, that wasn't ominous at all.

"So . . . Cope, yeah. I mean, when I first entered the guild, I was met by Thoril, though I didn't know him at the time, and asked . . ."

"Thoril? Thoril Viskantal?"

"Um. Maybe? I don't actually know his last name. Actually, I might have assumed Thoril *was* his last name? Blue-skinned guy?"

"That is he, then. Do continue."

"So anyway, he told me . . ."

Edwin gave a brief overview of his experience attempting to join the Alchemy Guild and how he had ended up in Cope's research group, with the guildmaster occasionally stopping him to ask a clarifying question and prod him along his tale, until he'd explained essentially the entirety of his work to her.

"Most interesting indeed. Much obliged. Now, tell me what you know of Geoalchemist Hawizeh."

"Who?" Edwin genuinely had no . . . oh wait, it was probably—

"Talented Veteran Geoalchemist Othniel Hawizeh. You referred to him by name several times in your story, and as an assistant to Alchemist Cope, it is generally assumed you know Geoalchemist Hawizeh."

"Yeah, sorry. As soon as you said it, I realized who you must have been talking about," Edwin apologized. "Umm . . . I don't really know much about the guy at all. I also thought Othniel would have been his last name, but . . . anyway, that doesn't matter. I've never met him"—he shrugged—"just heard secondhand about him and his group. I never took part in any of the seriously over-the-top sabotages, just sort of rolled with them when I had to deal with them in turn.

"Actually, what is up with that? Is it just some sort of game to them? None of the sabotages were ever that severe, not like they were ever trying to do anything more than just mildly inconvenience one another. That's not how you do professional sabotage."

"I will answer questions to the best of my capabilities once you have."

It took Edwin a moment to parse her statement, but nodded in understanding. "Okay. So, what next?"

"I wish to know of your history prior to Vinstead. It is almost as though you appeared from thin air one day. Is that related to your unusual knowledge and secret Skills by any chance?"

"Yesss . . ." Edwin cautiously agreed. "Though Ta— Enforcer Lisana advised I not talk about it, I can say that she told me it was all right to explain I'm from Fierisal and that I ended up here . . . somehow. That's not me being coy, either, just genuinely not knowing how I landed in the Lirasian Empire, more or less. Technically I landed in the Verdant, but . . . that's not important. I can't really say much beyond that, sorry. My home was much more advanced in nonmagical science than here, I will say, though adding magic throws everything I knew into chaos. That's actually why I became an alchemist, really. I wanted to incorporate magic into my knowledge of the world."

"Interesting. A mage with little experience with magic."

"I did say I wasn't a very *good* mage," he defended himself.

"That you did. Very well." Kertoa paused for a moment and moved to clasp her hands together and rest them on her desk. "I believe I am prepared to render a verdict.

"Alchemist-Errant Edwin Maxlin, you have been found guilty of working with the guild while not having an approved Alchemist Class."

"Hey! I didn't—"

"Allow me to finish, Alchemist-Errant Maxlin."

"But I didn't know that . . ."

"*Allow me to finish*, Alchemist-Errant Maxlin."

"Sorry," he muttered.

"Alchemist-Errant Edwin Maxlin, you have been found guilty of working with the guild while not having an approved Alchemist Class. Now, as you did not ever attempt to impersonate a guild member, the onus was upon your employer to confirm that your Class was indeed viable. Given your employer was Alchemist Shorob Cope, I shall be investigating him once this incident has passed, and I will render due judgment upon him. Thus, while in violation of guild policy, you are deemed not culpable for this transgression and are thus free from monetary fines or further punitive actions."

"Thanks? I was kind of expecting that to go another direction, honestly. I was kind of worried I might have to run away from *another* unfair debt-based indentured alchemy tenure."

"You have had that happen before?"

"I . . . probably shouldn't have said that. But yes. Not in the bounds of the Empire, though."

"The Shandin Kingdoms or Quoena?" she barely paused before asking.

"Wait, what?"

"You 'landed' in the Verdant, and prior to that you were not an alchemist. Thus, your imprisonment by alchemy must have occurred in the time between your landing within the depths of the Verdant. Thus, the Shandin Kingdoms or Quoena."

"Um, the Highpeak Kingdoms? Is that the Shandin Kingdoms?" That was . . . impressively fast deduction.

She stilled for a moment. "Ah, of course. Polyglot. Yes, the . . ."—she paused for a moment in concentration—"Shandin and Highpeak Kingdoms are one and the same."

"So then what's Quoena?"

"The elven city. I did not believe that it would be them, but it is always prudent to cover one's base assumptions. But no, we do not place the fault or debt with those liable to be taken advantage of. You may thank Emperor Xares for implementing that ruling in the time of my predecessor. One of the few mandates he has given directly, as the case may be."

"Oh, that's nice. He did . . . actually, back up a moment. The elven city? In the Verdant? That's real?"

"Naturally. Now, while you are not to be fiscally responsible for this fiasco, you do remain responsible for your actions now that you have been informed of guild policy, and you must therefore cease your assistantship with Alchemist Cope or genuinely be found responsible for your actions."

"Is it an assistantship if I'm not actually paid? He kept saying he was going to, but I still haven't seen so much as a ves for my work. I don't care *that* much, I was much more interested in learning about alchemy—which I *certainly* managed—but . . ."

"I shall be speaking with Alchemist Cope on that subject, I see. If you remain in Panastalis by the time my investigations have concluded, you will be duly compensated."

"You don't mess around, do you?"

"It is my duty to ensure the tenets of the Alchemy Guild are upheld. Doing less would be a disgrace. Now, should you leave Panastalis for some cause prior to the investigation has come to a close, you are capable of retrieving the full amount owed unto you by returning to the city at some point within the next two years. After that point, you may retrieve half your owed amount, and that amount will be halved once more for every year that you do not take your payment. Should the owed amount ever pass under the sum of one ager, you will no longer be able to collect it. Do you understand?"

"I . . . I think so? I don't suppose I could get that in writing? Actually, no. I can just . . ." He quickly Almanaced himself a reminder. "Okay, I got it."

"Now, with that settled, I do believe you had some questions for me?"

"Yeah! I guess I did. Um, I don't want to take up too much of your time, so I'll try and keep them focused. But what's up with Cope and Othniel? I've heard Cope's side of the story, and he of course makes his rival sound like the devil incarnate, but I'm curious what is actually going on."

"Those two . . ." The guildmaster sighed in the largest expression of emotion Edwin had seen from the woman. "They used to be such great friends. A bit aggressive in their competitions, yes, but both quite promising in the field of alchemical classifications. Between the two of them, they had cataloged nigh a hundred and fifty new flora, fauna, and minerals. Then one day, Geoalchemist Hawizeh bribed a harvester to divert new findings to him in preference to Alchemist Cope, and the two never saw eye to eye again. Their reports began to devolve into bickering, and things only deteriorated from there.

"The two would send teams into the field to throw rocks at the other's group, to burn down interesting bushes or drive off native fauna. In their haste, they would frequently misidentify or both identify the same type of specimen as different. Alchemist Cope was particularly egregious in this regard and would scarcely stop short of direct coercion and slander in his . . . endeavors.

"Their current level of squabbling is the result of several injunctions toward the both of them. While undeniably brilliant, they were causing untold amounts of damage to the credibility of other Catalogers, many of whom petitioned me to put a cease to their open hostility. I do not know how they settled upon attempting to replicate porcelain to prove their respective superiority, but I and the rest of the guild are more than content to allow this state of events to continue, provided it does not escalate overmuch.

"I hope that helped ameliorate your curiosity?"

Edwin nodded. "Yeah. So . . . yeah. It makes sense. Interesting that they chose porcelain, though."

"It is quite a valuable material. Do you know of it?"

"Yeah, I *think* I remember how to make it, even. We had it back home."

"Truly? Do tell."

Edwin opened his mouth, then, thinking better of it, closed it and shook his head. "Nah, you know what? I think I'll keep that one quiet. You never know when knowing how to make something more valuable than gold would be useful."

Kertoa looked at him for a moment in thought. "Very well. Do you truly have knowledge of so many things?"

He shrugged. "Basically nothing about *magic*, and I haven't the faintest clue about half of the System, but this sort of thing? Science, materials science? I spent years learning all this before I came to the Empire."

"So do we, and yet you are so utterly certain in your knowledge, beyond even many experienced researchers." She tapped her fingers on the desk. "Perhaps we ought to look into this 'germ theory' of yours. Let it not be said that the Alchemy Guild guildmaster is scared of being proven wrong."

"Wait, what? I wasn't expecting that." Edwin was taken aback. "Just like that?"

"We will not take your claim at mere words, for they are indeed mere words. However, what harm might there be in investigating the claims of someone whose history and knowledge are of interest to the Emperor himself?"

"Wasted time, wasted resources?" Edwin suggested.

"I want for neither, Alchemist-Errant Maxlin. This is done for my personal curiosity, not because I believe you in preference to thousands of years of tradition."

"Well, regardless . . . thanks, I guess. For listening to me."

"Certainly, Alchemist-Errant. Now, was there anything else?"

"Not really, I guess. I know I'll have a thousand questions the moment I walk away, but that's it for now, I suppose?"

"Excellent. Recall your limitations."

Edwin nodded. "No more working with Cope, stick around if I want to be paid right away. Any idea how long that might take?"

"A few weeks, perhaps."

"Hmm. Yeah, I'll probably head out tomorrow or the day after, then. I wasn't planning on sticking around for too much longer, anyway, so this works out well, all told. I just need to wrap up a few things—not *alchemy* stuff, just personal stuff," he quickly clarified.

Edwin nodded his farewells and took his leave, going out the main door this time as he was directed. Right as he was nearly out, though, a thought struck him. "I don't suppose there's any way I might be able to buy some magnesium and phosphorus, is there?"

The guildmaster looked up at him with a quizzical expression. "I shall see what I can accomplish."

Overall, Edwin would rate his time in Panastalis a success. He may not have managed to get a medical license, but he had certainly learned a lot about alchemy and had a list of locales to visit. But most amazingly of all was the giant boxes of phosphorus and magnesium he'd managed to get. Kertoa had surprised him by pointing him toward the arycal manufacturer.

Sure, it had cost him an entire grai for the two (tightly sealed) containers, but he could make legitimate weapons now! Not just his cobbled-together stuff made from vaguely magical plants, but genuine—albeit still cobbled-together—smoke bombs, flash-bangs, and incendiary grenades!

His departure had been relatively smooth. Cope, of course, had been outraged that Edwin would leave, but when he mentioned Master Kertoa and her demand that he stop working for him, he made a pretty strong turn.

Edwin felt much less guilty about leaving when the man started blaming Edwin for not telling him that he wasn't an "Empire verified" alchemist, and mad at Thoril for directing Edwin at Cope instead of at Othniel when he was looking for a sponsorship.

Rhita and Keir nodded like they knew Edwin's secret all along, the dirty liars, and Wendell took Cope's side in berating Edwin or Thoril, whichever his mentor wasn't picking on at the time being. Fissath, for her part, shook her head in exasperation and glared at Edwin in envy that he got to leave the madhouse.

He had just smiled and said his farewells to the avior under the shouting and grabbed what few things could be genuinely considered his, as Wendell and Cope started yelling at each *other* over something Wendell had said that Cope disagreed on. . . .

Edwin was *so* glad to be gone. He hadn't really realized just how stressful he'd found the place until it was wholly behind him.

But Inion was with him! The sun was shining! He could see the blue sky! Inion was humming a tune atop the carriage, and Bill was trotting along after having been confined to a (spacious) pen for nigh on three months now, happy as he could be. The birds were singing, and there was a light breeze in Edwin's face carrying the scent of . . . Blood?

Edwin double-checked his arsenal, making sure everything was back in place after three months of being locked away. He even retrieved his stick from where it was resting in the wagon as he foraged ahead, waiting for whatever horrid thing awaited him down the road.

This time, he'd be ready.

Congratulations! For explaining the basics of how biological diseases work, you have obtained the Medical Lecturer Path!

Level Up!

Skill Points 661→692 (Average level: 40)

Adaptive Defense Level 26→27

Alchemical Analysis Level 26→27

Anatomy Level 28→32

Arcadian Elixir Level 19→24

Basic Thermokinesis Level 20→22

Memory Level 61→62

Polyglot Level 65→66

Prototyping Level 22→25

Sapper's Apparatus Level 40→46

Skillful Assessment Level 33→34

Watchful Rest Level 26→27

Name

Edwin Maxlin

Age

1 year

Race

Extraplanar Human

Class

Alchemist-Errant

Attributes
Health 25
Impact 7
Mana 33
Perception 19
Stamina 30
Skills
Alchemical
Alchemy 86, Alchemical Analysis 27, Refine 1, Alchemical
Dismantling 18, Sapper's Apparatus 46
(Purify: 75)
Magical
Basic Thermokinesis 22, Fey's Caress 36, Ritual Intuition 25,
Mana Infusion 86
Flight 37, (Basic Mana Sense: 82), (Basic Mana Manipulation: 9)
Physical
Overcharge 8, Longstrider 30, Fresh Air 31
(Athletics: 81), (Breathing: 76), (Flexibility: 74), (Nutrition:
73), (Packing: 92), (Seeing: 72), (Sleeping: 73), (Survival: 76),
(Walking: 74)
Mental
Numeracy 35, Prototyping 25, Anatomy 32, Polyglot: 66,
Memory 62
(Language: 36), (Mathematics: 74), (Research: 50), (Visualization:
80)
Combat
Bomb Throwing 49, Adaptive Defense 27
(Throwing Weapons: 48)
Utility
Outsider's Almanac 132, Watchful Rest 27, Skillful Assessment
34, Arcadian Elixir 24, Improbable Arsenal 26
(Firestarting: 94), (Improvisation: 14), (Status: 22), (Identify: 80),
(First Aid: 82), (Harvesting: 76), (Construction: 77)
Paths
Skill Points: 692
Combat

Assassin 0/60, Bomber 0/60, Giant Slayer 0/60, Heedless Hunter 0/60, Hunter 0/30, Killer 0/30, Titan Slayer 0/90, Warrior 0/60, Way of the Empty Hand 0/60, Trapper 0/60

Alchemy

Alchemical Medic 0/60, Demolitionist 0/60, Makeshift Alchemist 0/60, Potioneer 0/60

Science

Chemist 0/60, Experimenter 0/60, Researcher 0/60, Purifier 0/30, Scientific Revolutionary 0/90, Scientist 0/60, Engineer 0/60, Physicist 0/60, Mathematician 0/60, Material Scientist 0/60

Magic

Aerialist 0/60, Fey Friend 0/60, Feybound 0/60, Feycaller 0/60, Mage 0/60, Magical Gardener 0/60, Micro-Biomancer 0/90, Primal Constructor 0/90, Primal Ritualist 0/90, Realm Traveler 0/120, Skilled Arcanist 0/60, Fey Supplicant 0/60, Feykind 0/90

Mental

Dedicated Student 0/60, Lecturer 0/30, Scholar 0/60, Unbowed 0/90, Canny 0/60, Steady Mind 0/60, Mentalist 0/60

System

Almanac Administrator 0/60, Forerunner 0/60, Outsider's Almanac Specialist 0/90, Pioneer 0/60, Skill Researcher 0/60, System Scholar 0/60

Trophy

Blackstone Conqueror 0/60, Deepwoods Panther-Hunter 0/60, Stonehide Vanquisher 0/60

Career

Brickmaker 0/30, Butcher 0/30, Diver 0/30, Gardener 0/30, Lumberjack 0/60, Merchant 0/30, Potter 0/30, Scribe 0/30, Woodsman 0/30

Physical

Ascetic 0/60, Daredevil 0/60, Physical Alchemist 0/90, Survivor 0/60, Physical Laborer 0/30

Traveling

Escapee 0/30, Exile 0/30, Traveler 0/30, World Traveler 0/60

Medical

Field Medic 0/60, Medic 0/30, Steadfast Medic 0/60, Medical

Lecturer 0/60

Misc

Arsonist 0/60, Autopyromaniac 0/60, Burglar 0/60, Child 0/12, Expert 0/60, Imperial Ally 0/60, Novice 0/12, Pyromaniac 0/30, Razer of the Ruined Tower 0/60, Rebel 0/30, Slave 0/12, Trainee 0/60, Traitor 0/60, Brushed by Power 0/60, Lirasian Citizen 0/30, Royal Adviserr 0/60, Favored by Power 0/90

Completed Paths

CharLimitCanttalkmuchNocluewhathappenedDidmybesttohelp youli, Mage, Skilled Arcanist, Physical Alchemist, Bomber, Linguist, Beginner, Warrior, Path Less Traveled, Athlete, Scout, Unkillable, Superior Alchemist, Adventurer, Explorer, Outsider, Skill Researcher, Wanderer, Alchemical Warrior, Novice Pyromancer, Novice Ritualist, Alchemist, Physicist, Engineer, Physical Arcanist, Biologist, Practical Alchemist, Fey Scion, Feytouched

Eightfold Strategy

There was something thrilling about willingly going into a dangerous situation prepared for anything. It reminded Edwin vaguely of the buildup to a roller coaster, a hint of adrenaline spiking his bloodstream and shutting down extraneous bodily functions. If he turned his Perception inward, he could actually *feel* his body directing blood to his muscles and away from his digestive system.

"I want to try and do this on my own," he told Inion, who was poking her head over the side of the cart. "I'm not going to get sloppy like I did with that one bandit. I genuinely want to see how well I can handle myself."

She shrugged. "'Kay, but if you get badly hurt that's on you. Only so much I can do this far from water anyway."

"Do you need to do something about that?"

"Hmm? Nah, it's fine. Doesn't hurt too much, basically just itches."

While ostensibly still steering the cart, Edwin left his stick sitting next to his hand and an array of alchemical weapons inches from his other. All he needed to do was figure out what danger was present, and he'd be all set for a proper alchemist strike. His first instinct, his firevine cocktail, was no fireball . . . but it would do. He also made for himself a helmet out of solid apparatite, leaving only a tiny slit through which he could breathe.

Edwin's carriage rumbled along, and his eyes landed on the scene in front of him, immediately letting him know that he was right to be on guard. It wasn't quite a massacre, but there *was* a lot of blood. From the looks of it, a group of four had been traveling along the road, only to be set upon by . . . something. Bandits, maybe?

No . . . not quite. All their possessions seemed to be basically untouched, which wouldn't match if they'd been killed by robbers. An animal, then?

Edwin disembarked from the carriage and signaled for Bill to wait while he investigated the bodies. Even the birdsong faded away as he got closer, the somber mood extending even to the wildlife.

None of them—one halfling, two humans, and something that looked like a human but didn't register as one to Almanac—were slain by a weapon Edwin recognized. Or maybe, he realized, they were stabbed by needles and then allowed to bleed out. That was what Anatomy was telling him, anyway. What sort of creature killed like that?

Heck, what kind of creature killed its prey and then just let it sit out? They must have been killed some time ago unless they all died without a sound, which seemed . . . unlikely. . .

Edwin straightened as fast as he could, head whipping around as he prepared to confront . . .

Nothing.

Just the silence.

Was he being paranoid? He didn't think so, but he cast furtive glances at the surrounding woods while he rapped upon the stone path with his stick. If he was lucky . . .

Nope. Not lucky.

The stick struck the stone without so much as the faintest clack, as Edwin's suspicions were confirmed. Whatever was here, whatever was responsible for these deaths was still here, and it was dampening all sound to the point of near silence. He was literally deaf to whatever threat might be lurking nearby. What sort of creature was he dealing with, and what had he gotten himself into?

Edwin pulled out his firevine cocktail, ready to throw it at a moment's notice.

A blur of motion caught his eye, and Edwin leapt out of the way as a barrage of reddish-purple quills flew through the place he'd been standing just moments before. Tracking them back to their source, Edwin didn't see anything.

Until he unleashed a blast of Identifies, anyway. Then he at least found out what he was fighting, even if he couldn't see it quite yet.

Adult Titan Bear-Eater

That doesn't sound good, Edwin thought as he rushed to the side, Longstrider barely taking him out of the way from the next volley of missiles. He could see some sort of ripple in the air from where they originated, and he threw his prepared firebomb as hard and as accurately as possible at the spot.

There was an unholy screeching sound as the silence and invisibility effects broke simultaneously, unveiling a very large, very on-fire *spider*, covered with violet-red hair lurking just off the side of the road, barely ten feet from Edwin. Worse, it wasn't a full spider, either, but had legs that reminded him of a cat, long, lithe, and covered in thick violet fur. Its head wasn't the normal mandibles of a spider either, but instead had the head of a lion—no mane, though.

It reared back onto its back legs and *hissed*, the demonic noise screeching like so many metal rods being twisted and broken. Edwin recoiled on instinct and retreated even farther from the massive threat.

It dropped onto all eights, and Edwin's mana senses informed him of the colossal amount of magic the creature was holding the moment he activated them. It felt like. . . . It felt like a dark, dry desert littered with time-bleached bones. It wasn't hot, just expansive, dry, and *desolate*.

The magic flared and it was extinguished, the flames burning on the spider's back ceasing to exist without so much as a whimper. That . . . wasn't great and didn't bode well for the fight ahead. Still, Edwin reaffirmed his mind. He wanted to redeem himself. So far, every single fight he'd been in on Joriah had left him critically wounded in some way, or close to it, and it didn't matter how big the spider was, this time he *was* going for a clean takedown.

So . . . time for a plan. He was more mobile than the spider was thanks to Longstrider and Athletics, but it still could travel *way too fast*, as evidenced by the speed at which the monster leaped forward, its paws blurring into motion while it jumped at him.

It was only because he was ready for something that Edwin was able to get out of the way, and he pushed his physical Skills as much as possible to pull him off to the side, letting the spider jet past him and into the tree line on the other side.

Wait, what? It was way bigger than the space between the trees. How did it fit inside the forest?

It lunged back out at him, and Edwin caught a glimmer of the answer; a Skill surrounded its body, letting it squeeze between the trunks almost like it were made of liquid rather than legs. As it pulled itself into the opening of the road, the spider leaped at Edwin once more, and he had to pull on Longstrider to get him out of the way.

The process repeated a few more times, the spider not apparently learning that Edwin could easily dodge it, at least so long as he didn't have anything else to distract him. Edwin appreciated it, though, as it gave him time to properly formulate his plan.

So, should I focus on the legs? If I had slipstone, this would be way easier. . . Hmm. I have magnesium now, I should probably make more lime. But okay. Legs. Chop, slip, or trip.

The legs were muscular and enormous, so he probably couldn't cut them up. Slipping would be preferable, if he had something that might work for such. Also, Edwin was moderately sure that he had seen claws at the end of the catlike limbs, so that was a further complication. That left tripping, which suffered from the same problem as slipping, namely that he didn't have anything to trip it *with*, to say nothing of the troubles that came with attempting to trip something with eight legs.

Unfortunately, he didn't really have access to Sapper's Apparatus. Oh sure, he had the Skill. But even though he'd brought down the time it took for him to use it, anything that would be large enough to go under one of the spider's legs would take him a few minutes of concentration to make, let alone eight of them.

Okay, so its legs may not be as much of an exploitable weak point as Edwin had hoped. What about ways to kill a spider? It seemed more like a tarantula than a black widow, and Edwin hoped that similarity extended to any weak points it may possess. Which were . . .

He drew a blank. Tarantulas had never really interested Edwin, which meant Memory would have to do a lot more work to pull up any relevant bits of information than it might otherwise need to. Work that he couldn't *really* manage while focusing on evading the enormous arachnid. He wasn't going to have a repeat of his encounter with the Reaper, where he got so distracted he took a perfectly avoidable wound.

Well, spiders were arthropods. While it may have been half cat, the arthropod portions seemed to be basically the same. So what did he know about *arthropods*?

Still not much, honestly. But their exoskeleton was probably weak in the joints, and Edwin would do well to focus his efforts there. Maybe he could stab it with some kind of poison? Set it on fire from the inside?

Edwin's brain kept racing at a hundred miles an hour, and he realized that despite all his vague combat alchemy preparation, he'd never actually trained with or practiced actually *using* his Alchemy Skill in combat, and this was perhaps not the best time for a live run, but here he was and so he'd just make the best of it that he could. He'd make more definite plans after this fight.

He spared a glance at the carriage and noticed that Inion, Bill, and the wagon itself were encompassed by some strange bluish-green Skill bubble, sustained by the fey. Huh. Was that why the spider didn't seem to notice them? Still, Edwin was kind of glad that the spider was focusing on him rather than them, as he was much more capable of dodging than his hardworking pony and slacker friend.

The spider rushed at Edwin once more, and he finally got a chance to really study it. The bottom side of the spider's abdomen was free of the glowing violet hairs that shimmered across the rest of its body. Seemed a bit odd, given its size, but he wasn't going to complain. While no giant glowing eye, it was, hopefully, still a weak spot.

Now, what would he use to hit it? He doubted that poking it with a stick would do much, and most of his arsenal probably wouldn't be too effective . . . or he could try his firevine cocktail again and hope that it could only extinguish itself where the spider had hair? Or maybe it would recoil again and Edwin could throw a rock at it or something.

He did have some apparatite crystals premade for that exact purpose, after all.

Okay. So, grab a cocktail and set it off against the underside of the creature's abdomen. When it recoiled backward, he'd take one of his crystals and throw it at the section between its abdomen and . . . main body, whatever that was called. With luck, it would be enough to penetrate through its exoskeleton and he could go from there.

The monster lunged at Edwin again, and it landed with all eight legs skittering across the ground, trying to hit Edwin. Fortunately, he was outside the creature's (admittedly massive) reach and was able to easily dodge even farther away with just a tug on Longstrider.

With the creature's next lunge, Edwin led the beast farther away from the tree line and more onto the stone road. He didn't want to set the forest on fire, after all. As it approached close enough . . . there!

A solid underhand lob of his weapon brought it slightly off-center of the spider's body, breaking open perfectly and igniting the underside of the monster in a massive fireball. Edwin triumphantly waited for the spider to rear back again . . .

Instead of standing on its back legs, the spider hissed again, and the violet hairs seemed to vibrate. Within moments, the screeching had completely stopped, the sound vanishing alongside all other ambient noise in the area, just like the monster had been doing when Edwin had first approached the area. If that weren't bad enough, the light around the monster began to shimmer and become hazily obscured. Within a few seconds, the spider was a shadowy blob. Fortunately, it didn't become invisible, but it still made it hard for Edwin to properly track the creature.

Annoyingly, it extinguished his fire as well. Great. There went that plan, and that hypothesis. He couldn't even properly throw his apparatite rock because of how shadowy and murky the spider was! No way he could pull off a precision attack when it was like that.

Okay, so what was plan B? There had to be some other great weakness that he could exploit. It was just so *big*, there had to be *something*.

Hmm. Square-cube law?

It was commonly known that spiders and ants were *absurdly* stronger, proportionally speaking, than a human. Except, that wasn't actually a product of their biology, but rather the result of their size. Anything that small would be much stronger proportional to their anatomy than something of a larger size, and that was pretty much entirely based on the mathematical principle that was the square-cube law.

While magic may have messed with it somewhat, the basic premise should hold. Muscle, being functionally two-dimensional, squared in size as a creature became linearly larger—length and width of the tissue expanded. However, *volume* of both the creature and their surroundings were all *cubed*—height, length, and width all expanded.

Thus, it might be more accurate to say not so much that smaller creatures were *stronger* than it would be to say that everything around them was way, way lighter. Lifting ten times their body weight simply wasn't as impressive at those scales.

All that was to say, the massive spider in front of him was definitely on the wrong side of the square-cube law. The fact it could even exist was already something of a violation—the respiratory system of arachnids couldn't scale to those sizes—but Edwin wagered whatever magic allowed it to exist didn't extend too terribly far. Even from an evolutionary standpoint, why would an ambush predator that was already the size of an elephant *need* to be magically strong as well? No, much more likely that it couldn't take that much more weight.

So the update to the "make it fall" possibilities was "squish it." It was probably easier than the others, if nothing else, and had the benefit of reminding Edwin of squishing a spider with a newspaper. He could drop his carriage on it perhaps, but that was an awful idea for so many reasons.

A gleam caught Edwin's eye from where the fallen travelers lay. The one not-human of the group had a sword. It was still sheathed, and the hilt was somewhat obscured, but it might still work. He may not have any actual training with a sword, but he didn't exactly need it for a direct weapon, did he?

Two steps with Longstrider later and the blade was in his hand. It wasn't anything too special, but it looked well-made enough to serve Edwin's purposes. He dodged out of the way from the spider attacking him once again, and a half-hearted attempt of swiping at its legs later, he was by the tree line.

He'd never tried something *quite* like this before, but Edwin had made sure to pick a tree large enough around that he could feasibly pick it up, but not so large that its diameter was longer than the meter or so his sword was.

The spider lunged at him, but Edwin dodged out of the way and the monster vanished back into the undergrowth. He prepared for its return, but was surprised by, instead of a lunge, a volley of violet hairs being *shot* at him. There was a Skill involved, he could see, but it looked more like one for accuracy rather than a "give yourself the ability to shoot hairs as a projectile" Skill, and wasn't that something of a scary thought, that this was just something it could do naturally?

The hairs struck Edwin flat-footed, and while a lot of them stuck in Edwin's sturdy jacket without penetrating all the way, a few still hit him in his extremities, peppering his arms and legs with hairs. A couple hit Edwin in the head, but his helmet fortunately protected him well enough there.

Well, there goes my perfect battle, Edwin thought ruefully. Fortunately, none of the wounds he took were too severe, though they did go a fair ways into explaining the method by which the unfortunate victims of the spider had been killed. Perhaps the hairs disintegrated naturally after a short period of time? It wouldn't be the strangest thing Edwin had seen.

Still, it did put a slight damper on Edwin's plan, predominantly because the spider had yet to emerge back out into the opening. Hmm. He didn't actually *need* the spider out, did he? Not for the first part of his plan at least.

Edwin returned to his tree, hefting his sword into a two-handed grip and planting his feet on the ground and anchoring himself in place with Flight, pushing Harvesting and Athletics as much as possible as he swung the blade at its trunk.

It worked much better than Edwin had anticipated; while not quite as smooth as butter, Edwin's strike did pass through the entirety of the tree in a single stroke, though the reverberations traveled up the blade and into Edwin's arms, predominantly his right thanks to his grip. Surprised, he released the blade and watched his weapon fly into the woods.

Well . . . he didn't need that anyway.

Before the tree could fall to the ground, Edwin grabbed it, holding it with only a bit of difficulty thanks to Packing. The weight and inertia was a bit of a pain, and Packing didn't help with rotational momentum so he'd need to be careful, but he could manage.

The spider tried another salvo of violet hairs aimed at Edwin, but with his own personal tree to hide behind, he managed to stop pretty much the entire attack.

Unusually, the spider seemed to fairly quickly realize this tactic wasn't working and reemerged onto the road with a flex of its Spatial Skill. Unfortunately for it, it wasn't able to properly identify the trap waiting for it.

Edwin hefted the tree as much as he could, then dropped it right where the spider was due to arrive—thank you, Numeracy—allowing the full weight of the trunk to crash down onto the spider, pinning it against the ground and slowly crushing its abdomen. It screeched, trying to free itself, but the tree wasn't going to stop crushing the arachnid's body just because it complained . . .

Edwin's thought died as the tree *was* eaten through by the creature's destructive magic. He readied himself for round two, but he was unexpectedly relieved when the bottom half of the tree rolled off the side and onto the creature's right side. Three of the creature's legs burst immediately, revealing themselves as normal spider legs just disguised as those of a feline. The other was struck flat, and the monster splayed out, helpless and immoble as Edwin hefted the top of the tree and dropped it onto the monster's body.

Within thirty seconds, the horrible hissing had finally stopped as the spider finally died.

Edwin sighed and dropped onto the ground. That had been . . . quite the fight, and he was glad he was still in . . . *basically* one piece. It was nothing a potion and a night of sleep wouldn't fix, anyway, so he counted it as a win.

Congratulations! For slaying an Adult Titan Bear-Eater, you have unlocked the Titan Spider Hunter Path!
Level Up!

Skill Points 692→697 (Average level: 40)
Bomb Throwing Level 49→50
Flight Level 37→38
Longstrider Level 30→32
Numeracy Level 35→36
Ritual Intuition Level 25→26

Oh cool, another Trophy Path. Edwin idly wondered what sort of Skill it might grant as he fished out a general-purpose healing potion and downed it. The hairs stuck in his limbs had vanished at some point toward the end of the fight—he hadn't noticed when—leaving him bleeding at a steady rate. Once he took the potion, though, his bleeding began to slow and he could feel the itching of skin beginning to scab over at high speeds. The apparatite container he'd kept the potion in dissolved away with just a flex of his will, and the glittering motes of light drifted to the ground.

He looked at the battlefield with unwounded eyes, coldly wondering what to do now. He should bury or burn the spider's victims, of course—it was just the polite thing to do, if nothing else—but what about the spider itself?

The violet hairs still glowed slightly even in death, which suggested that it might have some kind of inherent magical properties. *That* meant alchemical ingredients! He really wanted to see if he could isolate whatever annihilation or desolation-type mana the spider was using to delete stuff like sound or light in the area.

Well, he had a Skill for it—two if Alchemical Dismantling and Harvesting counted as different—and he may as well put them to work!

Edwin's eyes caught the bodies of the spider's last victims. Fine, he'd take care of them first.

While all four of the travelers had a coin pouch at their belt, each was predominantly filled with ves and ager, not a single grai in sight. Still, it was money and Edwin didn't have any better alternatives to dealing with it, so he pocketed it all. The halfling wore a small, nonmagical silver pendant in the shape of an upside-down "V," and the not-human had an intricately carved wooden bracelet, filigreed with silver as well.

They were both probably a bit valuable, but they just weren't terribly helpful to Edwin personally, and he felt awkward about looting bodies for personal artifacts besides. Money was one thing, but he just wasn't comfortable with taking semivaluable trinkets to pawn off at a later point.

The rest of their belongings fell in a similar situation. None of the humans or the halfling had any weapons beyond a knife on them, not counting the lost not-human's sword. Beyond that, other than some food, which Edwin gladly took, they predominantly just had some miscellaneous travel gear and their clothes that wouldn't be that helpful to him. He just didn't need bloodstained clothing with holes in it. He'd be spending enough time repairing his *own* outfit after this fight, and he didn't want to take on even more.

The burials were easy enough. Inion didn't help, unsurprisingly. Instead, she spent the time poking at the spider, making inane comments about whatever flitted through her mind. Well, she also spent a bit of time supervising his digging efforts, but it was primarily spent disparaging the spider.

By leaning on an old trick of reframing his digging as "harvesting dirt," Edwin could get the Skill to engage with his task and make every single shovel cut through the ground and even tree roots with ease and help him quickly grow the size of the pile of dirt next to the hole. Stamina helped even *more* and meant he could continue at nearly full effort for the half hour it took to dig out enough dirt that his eyes were level with the ground.

Properly dug, he set each of the bodies inside gently, spending a moment of silence for each fallen, and filled the hole back in. Edwin was glad he'd done so first—they were already attracting flies.

Edwin made sure to be fully geared up when he finally approached the corpse of the spider, gloves, goggles, and hood covering every inch of exposed skin. It was basically inevitable that he'd poke himself with one of the spider's hairs at some point, but he still wanted to minimize the frequency of that occurring.

And so, armed with an apparatite knife and box, he began to slowly try and cut through the hairs.

At first, it was slow going, as he needed to angle his hand in an awkward angle to shave away the pokey quill-like protrusions, but as he kept at it, and felt his Dismantling Skill level up more and more, he fell into a bit of a rhythm.

The spider was large enough that Edwin would never manage to get all the hairs cut away, but it also meant he'd have more than enough for pretty much any purpose he could think of. In the end, he filled up a good-size box with them, and they found a nice corner of his carriage to live in, casting their faintly sinister glow through the crystal.

After the hairs came the venom, and while Edwin wasn't entirely sure if the spider *had* venom, given its lionlike mouth, he was glad that he had checked (and wasn't bitten). There were no less than six fangs that had channels for toxins to run along, and a corresponding venom gland hooked up to them. *Getting* to the venom gland was a bit of work, but Edwin managed it in the end via careful use of Flying to hover above the spider's body and cut into its carapace after it had been cleared of hairs (which he naturally added to his box). It actually required him to Infuse Dismantling to get it to work properly, much to his surprise.

The Infused Skill cut through the carapace like butter, and he seriously wished he had made the discovery *during* the fight, rather than afterward. Well, next time he fought an enormous magical creature he could try to use his Dismantling Skill as a weapon.

. . . That was probably why he'd gotten it from Alchemical Warrior, wasn't it? Seemed kind of obvious in retrospect, if he could use it as a weapon to pierce magical or alchemical defenses. Ah well, now he knew for the future.

Getting the venom out was . . . tricky. Normal tarantula venom wasn't particularly potent from what Edwin could recall, but he didn't trust that information in the slightest. Beyond the issues that might arise from him misremembering, it didn't necessarily apply to lion-headed ten-foot-tall monster spiders whose hairs could just straight-up destroy stuff, and he wasn't keen on experimenting on himself for this.

What he ended up doing was creating a bit of a closed syringe with Apparatus and using Improbable Arsenal to expand the interior of the container, pulling in the venom as the space expanded. Cool! He hadn't expected that to work.

He repeated the process another dozen times, until he had a respectable collection of the gray/purple liquid stored away, the syringe replaced with a more appropriate sealed container.

He also checked to see if the monster spider had any silk glands. Sadly, at least as far as Edwin was able to tell in his limited experience, it didn't. It was a shame, because if he *had* been able to get giant spider silk it would have been *amazing*.

The last thing to deal with was the carapace itself. It was fairly strong for its weight and thickness, after all. And while Edwin didn't have the space to deal with all of it, he did still take a few sections of the material just to try and do *something* with it at some point.

By the time he had completed everything, it was late afternoon and he was *tired*. The fight had left him running on pure adrenaline, to say nothing of how sore his arm was. Then, digging graves for the victims and now dismantling the spider? Sure, he could keep going for the rest of the day thanks to Stamina, and if he had some of his talsanenris rations, he'd be even better off, but those were more crutches than a true solution.

Edwin heard a clattering down the road, and he turned to see a wagon pass by him, pulled by a pair of horses and driven by an avior who looked around at the carnage—a downed tree, a massive spider, and Edwin standing in the middle of it all splattered with blood and spider detritus—before wordlessly looking at Edwin with horror, then wasting no time in snapping the horses' reins and encouraging the animals to pick up the pace.

Edwin couldn't help but chuckle a bit at the idea of the Gilded Feather trying to figure out what was going on, and he was kind of glad that nobody had seen him earlier while he was still . . . engrossed in harvesting the carcass.

He had totally missed a bunch, hadn't he? It wasn't like there were *that* many people on the road, but he still tended to encounter one or two each day going the opposite direction of him.

"Inion?" he asked, slightly dreading the answer. "How many people have passed by us while we've been here?"

"Hmm?" She yawned. "Oh, I don't know. Five or six? I was napping for a while, though, don't know if I missed any there."

Well, at least he wasn't embarrassed at the time, and now he could just take and bury that thought as deeply as possible. Memory only worked with active recall, after all. It wouldn't keep reminding him of the time he'd been so engrossed with dissecting a spider he outright missed a half-dozen people passing within twenty feet of him.

As tempting as it was to set up a temporary lab right there and start messing around with the spider venom and quills, Edwin knew it would objectively be better for him to work slightly closer to civilization. The massive spider carcass was bound to attract scavengers, and with the recent reminder that animals could be *massive* on Joriah, he didn't particularly care to meet any of them. He could have burned it, but that seemed like it could relatively easily result in a forest fire. He settled for carrying the body off the road fully and propped it up against the trees, its Skill allowing it to slip between the trunks no longer active in death.

So, Edwin carried on. Once he was out of the light forest, he could revisit the proposition. It had already been a couple days, and surely he'd leave the tree cover soon, right? He liked the forewarning that the vast, open plains afforded him when it came to people approaching. Sure, the road may have been straight as ever, but the shadows and moving foliage in the distance meant that it was still tricky to see people far away.

His thoughts were, ironically, broken by the sound of light pattering on the road behind him. He spun around, expecting another attack and his hand finding its way to a firebomb. Lack of concussive force or no, most creatures would still probably run away if set on fire.

What he wasn't expecting to find was a medium-sized brown-and-white dog running up toward him, short and clean fur gleaming even in the low light of the forest.

"Why, hello there, pup. What are you doing out here?" Edwin greeted the dog, extending a hand out for the canine to sniff.

Unexpectedly, it didn't approach, instead holding its distance and looking at Edwin with keen, curious eyes.

Stalwart Defender

. . . Hold on, was that a Class? Dogs could get Classes?

"Kyni! Kyni! Come on, boy! Where'd you go?" a young voice called out from a bit farther back, and Edwin looked up to see a boy running in his direction. He was still a ways back, just barely approaching earshot, but the dog didn't react immediately. Instead . . . "Kyni" stared at Edwin, not baring his teeth or growling, or even hiding his tail between his legs, just . . . looking at him, before turning around with a bark and, with a clatter of nails on stone, dashing back to the boy, nearly bowling the kid over.

Huh.

Edwin gently pulled Bill to a stop. The boy must have been barely ten at most, and Edwin wanted to make sure that he would be all right. Also, *dog*. He hadn't been able to spend nearly as much time with the objectively best kind of living creature since he'd been on Joriah, and the Stalwart Defender was a riddle wrapped in a mystery.

Looking again showed there was a cloaked figure a bit of distance behind the boy and his dog, the two now walking side by side.

Okay, so they did have an adult with them. That was good, at least. As the trio reached his Identify range, Edwin caught a brief glimpse of gold from the adult, and a quick Identify confirmed his fears. With a sigh, he rubbed his forehead in preparation of a future headache.

"Edwin! It is so very good to see you, my friend! It has truly been far too long!" Lefi exuberantly called out.

Level Up!
Skill Points 697→720 (Average level: 41)
Alchemical Dismantling Level 18→27
Anatomy Level 32→39
Improbable Arsenal Level 26→30
Sapper's Apparatus Level 46→47
Watchful Rest Level 27→28

CHAPTER 15

Petty Concerns

Guardian Mentor
Lefi Forolova—that guy that Tara stuck me with so I wouldn't
immediately die and as a punishment for him.

Wow, I forgot how basic my Almanac tags were way back when.

"Hi, Lefi," Edwin greeted the man. It had been over a year since he and the Adventurer parted ways, and Edwin could only hope that the man wasn't as annoyed with him as he once was. Then again, the guy was an extrovert. Holding grudges might not even be a thing they *could* do.

Tara had hoped that Lefi might keep him out of trouble, and vice versa, which . . . hadn't gone very well. Especially considering Edwin had convinced himself that Lefi hated him and ran off in the middle of the night straight into Niall's camp. *That* made Edwin suppress a shudder. It was a small miracle he hadn't killed himself trying to take down the serial-killing alchemist, but he had, and the man was long dead and buried by now. That entire debacle had been one bad decision after another barely held together by improbable luck, and Edwin could only hope that it didn't bear a repeat with Lefi's reappearance in his life.

"You are doing well for yourself, I see!" Oh yeah, the guy constantly shouted. Edwin mentally recalibrated Lefi's interpretation for a more accurate representation of what he was probably trying to say, "You've made it to Tier 2 with a truly *exceptional* set of Skills!"

Wait, could Lefi see Edwin's Skill list? Skillful Assessment showed he was using some sort of silver Skill, but it didn't *look* like a perception or Identify-type ability. In fact, Edwin couldn't tell *what* sort of Skill it was, just that he hadn't seen one like it before. Then again, Lefi was an absolute mess of constantly active Skills, so it was entirely possible Edwin was just missing it.

"Yeah . . . yeah," Edwin agreed. "Just carrying on, you know?"

Lefi nodded exuberantly, his golden firelike hair bobbing and flickering in perfect sync to the motion.

"Ah! Before I forget, I must introduce you to my latest wards. Meet Yathal." Lefi motioned to a young boy about eight or nine, with messy brown hair and curious, yet wary eyes. He stood next to the dog, hugging its neck like it was a giant stuffed animal.

Loyal Companion

"And Kynigos"; that was the dog, who continued to study Edwin with curious eyes. Other than the color—caramel and white instead of black and white—and the length of his shaggy fur, the pup reminded Edwin of a border collie. Kyni struck Edwin as far, far more intelligent than the smartest dog he'd met back on Earth, though.

As he watched, both of them had their eyes flicker with the white Skill construct Edwin had learned to associate with Identify, and he realized he should introduce himself.

"I see. Well, hello." Edwin awkwardly waved. "I'm Edwin. Lefi helped me get my feet a while ago, giving me some pointers for what I should do."

Yathal didn't say anything, shyly burying his face back in his dog's fur. With a surprising amount of care, Kyni turned his head to wrap around the boy as well.

Edwin turned a questioning eye at Lefi, who returned the look. After a moment, Edwin realized Lefi wasn't able to read his expressions like Inion was able to, and he elaborated, "Did you annoy Tara again? Are they the next 'me' by any chance?"

"Well, no and yes. After Yathal here broke free of Management, claiming his truest destiny, his parents didn't want anything to do with him. Fortunately, I was passing through at the time and so was able to take them along and show them the basics of Adventuring much as I did with you. Hopefully I won't chase them away this time, eh?" He winked at Edwin.

"Ah. . . . Yeah, sorry about that. I'm not really sure what came over me," Edwin guiltily said. "Really, I'm lucky I survived that whole mess after leaving you."

"Ah, you would have been *fine*." Lefi waved his hand dismissively. "I made sure of it. It was my fault, after all."

"I mean, it— Wait, what? What do you mean, it was your fault?"

A golden Skill bloomed in Lefi's chest, emanating outward. Edwin felt certainty descend onto him like a mantle, and he developed the unshakable feeling of being able to do *anything*. Climb a mountain, fight a dragon, brew the greatest potion ever.

Edwin shook his head, trying to clear it. He was way more used to dealing with mental Skills than he had been in the past, though getting rid of an ostensibly beneficial one was a new experience. He wasn't the only one affected, either, as Yathal stopped hiding in his dog's fur, standing straight and proud.

Edwin could tell Inion was stirring, too, but she stayed silent, hiding on the roof of the carriage. Then, Lefi released the Skill and the world finished returning to normal.

"So . . . you used that on me?"

Lefi nodded. "You were so shy and scared of everything, it was the least I could do! However . . ." He awkwardly trailed off for a moment. "I wasn't expecting you to think you could take care of everything on your own and run off. *That* was a new reaction, and I have since declined to utilize it in such excess for fear that it would cause others to jeopardize themselves as well! You managed to survive, but I would never forgive myself if my Inspired Courage caused another to die in their pursuit of glory, particularly if I was unable to guard them then!"

"Slow down, slow down. You followed me?"

"That is what you took from my statement? Indeed, I did, as I merely wished to ascertain that you would be all right. You mostly were, too!

There were very few times I found myself needing to intervene to save your life."

"So you watched me fight the bandits, too?"

"Helped as well! Now, you managed most of it on your own; I merely assisted your assault go easier than it might have otherwise. Did you not notice the ease at which your limbs responded with your every attack, the way your Skills responded at the blink of an eye? That was my doing. My mere presence brings out the most Exceptional Skills of my allies!"

Edwin found himself speechless. "I mean, I did, but . . . Why didn't you stop them, then? You must have known what they were doing."

"To speak honestly with you, I did not know it all. For the sake of Yathal, I shall not go into details," Lefi said, getting a . . . nod from Kyni. Okay then, ignore how weird it looks for a dog to be intelligently responding to prompting. "I did not know of their crimes prior to your own discovery. Much like you, I would have never found the place had I not been led there. I then observed you while you learned of alchemy—the time was as informative for my own Skills as it was yours—and when you moved to apprehend them, I assisted. Had you failed, I would have stepped in to save your life and apprehended the bandits myself."

"Well . . . okay then." Edwin still wasn't sure how to take this new information, but there weren't that many options. He quickly settled on accepting it and moving on. "So what have you been up to since then?" he tried. That was normal friendly conversation, right?

Gah. Human interaction was the worst.

"Well! Once I was certain you would be secure, or at the very least no longer in direct mortal peril beyond that which would typically be within the Verdant at least, I set out upon a glorious adventure!"

"Doesn't sound much like an adventure," Edwin couldn't help but note.

"Ah! But I am an Adventurer, therefore all I do is an adventure!"

"I . . . I don't think . . . actually, you know what? Sure. Carry on."

Lefi had barely even paused for Edwin's statement, barreling on as he was with his story. "Now, as I was venturing along, I encountered this cave, you see? It was strange, encountering a hill with such a large cave in it, let alone a hill *here*, but I, as one who would never back down from a curiosity, ventured within! And once I was inside the cave I realized that it split off into seven *more* caves . . ."

"Now, this giant was so massive that I could scarcely believe it! Now, you know we don't see many giants in these parts, but even compared to the giants you normally see, he was massive! They'd scarcely reach his knee! He invited . . ."

". . . Rigged the entire thing! Set his half of the lot *on fire*, which was why . . ."

Lefi really liked to talk, didn't he? Edwin was vaguely remembering why he'd gotten annoyed with the guy in the first place. However, the benefits he provided more than made up for the inconvenience, and he would stick with Lefi for as long as he could mentally manage to maximize his Exceptionalism or whatever. He could at least feel somewhat better about himself thanks to the knowledge that his decision to run off wasn't *completely* his own sound mind.

That's a lame excuse and you know it.

Shush, brain. It's important to pay attention to people while they're talking.

"So once I came across our fine young friend here and learned he needed help, I snatched him up and away before the Magistrate could have him exiled or worse!

"So now I am trying to meet up with Adventurer Rillah! She is far more experienced with this kind of trauma than I, far better with helping shy, but brave!"—he reassured Yathal, who kept popping his head up and shying away—"Such utterly brave! fellows learn how to claim the full world!

"Alas, she was . . . tied up in Sheraith and isn't able to come. Thus, we're off to see her and help her out!

"What of you, my fine friend? What was your time spent doing since you entered the Verdant to make a home for yourself? Where are you headed? Perhaps she could help you as well!" Lefi tried to elbow Edwin, but he easily dodged. It was in good nature, though, so he didn't mind that much.

"Well, I found a place for me to make a home, chopped down a few trees . . ."

It didn't take that long for Edwin to relay all that had happened over the past year or so. Lefi had roared in amusement at Inion's training antics, though he made a few murmured comments to himself that Edwin hadn't been able to catch.

By the time he had finished his story, however, the Adventurer was nodding along.

"So the question remains! Where are you off to now, and might we be blessed with the addition of yourself to our adventuring party?"

"I guess . . . basically in the same direction as you," Edwin admitted. "I have a whole list of places I want to visit and get some alchemy ingredients from, and there's at least something I want to get wherever." Edwin stroked his chin.

Hmm. I need to shave.

Edwin went on, "And even more alchemy ingredients from creatures that are *way* out of my league. I'd be . . . interested in traveling with you, if I could get some Skill instructions? I don't really know how to fight as an alchemist, and I guess . . . I guess I'm less disinclined to travel around with you if we can both get something out of the exchange. Or, I guess, if I can avoid being a drag. I'll happily provide some alchemical concoctions that I make as my part of the deal, plus you know, just another hand around. Not like I can really provide anything else, after all."

"Why, my friend! Of course I would love to travel with you! And you needn't worry about additional compensation. Your carriage alone makes for travel to be so much easier!

"However, if you *were* so inclined, all I might ask of you is that you might teach me just a bit of what you are doing! It makes learning Skills far simpler."

"Didn't . . . didn't Tara tell me explicitly *not* to teach you alchemy?"

"Bah! She doesn't come out this far, I'll have you know. We're outside of her province! And her worries are misplaced besides. I already have more Skills than I could possibly raise to Tier 3. What's a few more? Besides! I already have some levels in the Skill from watching you!"

"Okay, fine. But in exchange, I want your help learning how to *fight* with my alchemy. Inion helped me learn to survive, but I was just reminded that I don't really know how to finish a fight."

"You are asking me for aid? It would be my utmost delight to provide mentorship unto you, young Adventurer. Particularly given the apparently massive hole you have found in your training. Truly, this Inion was not the teacher you needed."

"Excuse me?" Oh hey. Inion finally decided to join in. Yathal seemed startled by the sudden addition of her into the conversation, but Kyni seemed relatively unsurprised by Inion popping her head over the side of the carriage—presumably, the dog had smelled her—and Lefi shot back without missing a beat.

"I do believe you managed to hear me just fine, my fair lady. It is far more important to *win* a fight than to merely not lose one. Not losing a fight simply delays the inevitable! Winning, however, sets you up for victory!

"At some point, you must face down your rivals. When you do so, the ability to dodge a punch will not allow you to overcome your obstacles, but merely seek to approach them. It is flawed both as a goal and as a tool. Finishing a fight is what matters."

"And *you* should know that it's more important to *survive* than it is to finish a fight!" she shot back. "You can always run away or just wait until I step in."

"Ah, but doing so produces a crutch for the learner! It then means that the mentor will inevitably be disposed of and drop the student in a situation for which they are wholly unprepared for. You make both yourself and Edwin vulnerable to the vagaries of fate by introducing such an obvious weakness into him."

"Well, better that he be in the situation where he's alive and has to run away rather than— Wait a minute. Joriah doesn't work like that!"

"And what would you, my dear lady, know of the manner by which tales are carried out?"

Edwin tuned the pair out as Inion floated down to the ground to argue with Lefi on his own level, walking to join Yathal and Kyni.

"So. You seem generally pretty nice. What's your story?" he asked the shy boy. "If you don't want to talk, that's fine. But I promise I'm not that scary." He gave what was hopefully a friendly smile.

Yathal didn't seem particularly impressed, hiding his face back in the fur of his dog, but Kyni nuzzled his master with his nose until the boy finally relented. "I'm . . . I'm from the town, and I really love Kyni and trust him too. So when I got the Path offered, I . . ." He trailed off, mumbling into the dog's fur.

"Sorry?" Edwin asked. "I didn't quite catch that."

"So Kyni helped me, but Mom got really mad and yelled at me and him about something. Oh, but Kyni's known me from when I was really little and he jumped . . . Well, he didn't like the new medic, you know? Got mad at Mister . . . Mister . . . but he was just trying to protect me, I know it! Don't like the guy. But Magistrate Tok— Magistrate Tokl . . . So Kyni just wanted to help, and I knew he did! And he did help! If he hadn't then . . ."

It took a while, as the kid kept jumping around between total non sequiturs and telling the actual story, but Edwin eventually felt like he pieced together what had happened. Once Lefi and Inion were done arguing for the time being, he talked to Lefi to fill in the last few pieces and felt vindicated that his guesses were actually accurate.

Essentially, Yathal was a shepherd boy from Valenasis, a town in the greater Rhothos area, and Kynigos his sheepdog. At some point, the boy managed to evolve his Animal Handling Skill into Companion, either as part of an unexpected upgrade or maybe an incorrect evolution? Edwin wasn't totally clear on the specifics there. Either way, the boy was no longer under Management and had a nontypical Skill set, and so fell under the "Outlaw" banner. While he might have still been able to function more or less all right in society, his parents had basically disowned their boy—who wasn't even ten!—for "disgracing them in such a manner."

It made Edwin *furious*, but there wasn't anything he could do about it. He was mostly just glad that Lefi had been able to step in when he had, getting the boy registered and trying to protect him while getting him to a place that he would thrive in. That said, Edwin was somewhat confused about what went wrong with the kid's Skill.

"So how does the Companion Skill work again and why is him get-ting it such a problem?" he asked as their group walked down the road. Well, Yathal rode on the cart, Kyni keeping the young boy company.

"Well, you see—"

"It's quite simple!"

Inion and Lefi glared at each other as they tried to answer Edwin at the same time. Inion opened her mouth to speak, but Lefi beat her to actually speaking. "The Animal Companion Skill enables one to fash-ion a bond with a creature that they have a very close connection with. It is fairly typical for shepherds to get it, by evolving Animal Handling with a "Friend of" Path. Now! The Animal Companion Skill functions akin to the Status for your companion, akin to the Management of the Empire. In this way, it is possible to complete Paths and accept or reject Skills, strengthening your companion."

"So it's just Status for a pet?"

"Not entirely inaccurate. Although there are additional benefits at higher levels."

"So . . . what was the problem?"

"The problem, you see, was that our good young friend did not get the Animal Companion Skill, but the Companion Skill."

"And that's bad . . . because why?"

"Because it goes the wrong way 'round! The bravest and smart-est dog that is Kynigos"—the Adventurer leaned over to where the duo were and scratched the pup's head—"was already classed! Now, instead of Yathal guiding and controlling Kynigos's Skills, Kynigos controls Yathal's! Fortunately, he's a good boy, aren't you, Kynigos? He knows he can do a lot of harm to Yathal and he doesn't want to! But who would teach Skill-lore to a dog? Other than myself, at least."

The dog barked in agreement, wagging his tail.

"So . . . you can understand me?" Edwin asked the dog, getting a nod in reply. "Huh. So that messed things up?"

"You're smarter than that, my friend! You can answer that question yourself surely."

"Yeah, yeah. So basically the dog adopted the boy, not the other way around?"

Lefi nodded. "Which is why I must teach them! I learned about Companions from the Beastmaster herself, back when she still lived on the continent. Now, who I give the advice to is different from normal, but it is nonetheless valid!"

"You don't have a Companion, though? How do you know your advice is good?"

"I do not have a Companion for personal reasons, not because I know not the method!"

"Are those personal reasons because you haven't found one that is exceptional enough for you?" Edwin teased.

"Personal reasons!"

"Yeah, Edwin, aren't you the one who's always talking about privacy and stuff?" Inion was double-teaming with Lefi now. That was just great.

"I think I liked it better when you two were arguing." Edwin muttered.

Being around people in a nonwork relationship was . . . tolerable, Edwin found.

He still wasn't the biggest fan of Lefi—the man was far too energetic and enthusiastic for him to really get along *well* with the guy—but he was at least, well, tolerable. Thanks to his supposed "Exceptional" Skill, he and everyone near him had their Skills level at a rapid rate, which on its own was already a fantastic benefit when paired with Inion's Muse Token. However, if that wasn't already enough, Lefi also had an absolutely absurd amount of experience with getting and using Skills. Thus, Edwin was able to try and get some pointers on his own Skills just by talking to the guy.

Lefi had some pretty startling insights into how Arcadian Elixir worked, for one. Somehow, he sussed out not only the Skill's existence but also deduced some basic functionality for it. It was like a cooking Skill, in that if he made something to eat the Skill would engage. That much didn't surprise Edwin. No, what caught him off guard was the fact that if he *grew* food, the same thing would happen.

He'd been . . . skeptical, to say the least. However, a brief experiment with a bean Edwin dug out and grew with his talsanenris confirmed the revelation. It made *sense* for a "fey food" Skill, but it still wasn't something he was expecting.

Oh, and what he made was also more nutritious. No surprise there. While Lefi wasn't able to figure out for certain whether or not it reduced the appeal, taste, and nutrition of food Edwin *didn't* make, he did confirm that the manner in which the Skill engaged was similar to Cooking, Hearty Meal, or Potent Concoctions. Thus, even if Edwin did leave some sort of lingering effect with his creations, he wasn't dooming people to a life of constantly pining after his food and his food alone.

At least not yet. And that was quite the relief. If he was the only supplier of food that was nourishing and didn't taste like dirt, and he could inflict the condition on whoever he wanted just by giving them a homegrown carrot . . . he wasn't really comfortable with the idea.

Would that make him some sort of not-drug dealer? Superaddictive, hand out apples to junkies?

Other vague drug-related concepts Edwin wasn't familiar with?

Moving on!

The primary area in which Edwin was hoping to get some pointers on was in using his magical Skills. Inion wasn't a good teacher in that regard (her normal tactics of "throw things" not working all that well for more complex tasks), so he was hopeful that Lefi would be able to fill in.

At least, Edwin was pretty sure that Lefi was a mage. His Mana Sense kept lighting up when the man did random tasks, even those that didn't seem to have any Skills associated with them. However, he couldn't figure out what *kind* of mage he was. Ritual Intuition provided exactly no information to that regard, to the point Edwin momentarily was unsure if he even had the Skill *working* (he did).

He'd ask the Adventurer about it at some point in the future, he decided. In the meantime, he'd work on not immediately chasing answers to every passing question he considered. Also, it would be rude to inquire about something Lefi was obviously trying to keep quiet. In the meantime, Edwin might slowly hint at the idea that he knew Lefi had magic, and once he did ask, it would be really circumspect.

"So . . ." Edwin hazarded, "you have magic?"

Hey, it had been a day! That was loads of time!

"Hmm? Magic?" Lefi was startled by the question. "What makes you say such a thing?"

"Well, I think you know I have a couple of magical Skills."

"Such as your Flight, yes. What of it?"

"Wait, how— Actually, I suppose that one is obvious, isn't it?" Edwin said. "Or did I just tell you? But yeah. Got it by combining Packing and Mana Infusion. Fun times. "

He shook his head. "Anyway, one of them is a magical sense, and it lights up all the time around you. But I can't tell what kind of magic you're using. It just feels like nothing and it's really weird."

"That is most curious! Though I fear I must disappoint you. I am no Mage, as amazing as such a status may be! I merely have hundreds of Skills, some of which are indeed slightly magical in nature. It is the inevitable conclusion to having so many evolved Skills—purely by random chance, you will eventually get a magical Skill, and once you have one, I'm certain you are aware, it is much easier to get another!"

Edwin frowned. "How does that make you different from a mage, though? I can only use magic in the context of Skills. Heck, I've *seen* you with a Mage Class, haven't I? But anyway, I have another Skill that lets me *see* Skills, though. And they don't always trigger in unison. So far as I can tell, you're using magic outside of the context of any Skills you have as well. How is *that* not a mage thing?"

"That is quite the conundrum," Lefi exuberantly agreed. "But perhaps it is more likely that you are simply unable to tell when I am using a Skill! I will confess to having some Skills that are indeed magic, though that is not terribly uncommon at higher tiers, you understand. However, they are just that—Skills."

"Why wouldn't I be able to sense the Skill?"

"Well, though your Skill Identify may be able to detect Skills I use, how sensitive is it? What do you sense? I am amazing at everything, after all," Lefi said with a grin. "It would be understandable if you weren't able to tell when one of my constant Skills begins using a magical effect."

"I don't fully follow. Are you saying you might have a passive Skill that you can push into being magical?"

"Ha! I knew you were smart. My Wind-Strider Skill is constantly in use, granting me fair winds everywhere I go, but if I push it, then I have the most magnificent ability to cause my cloak to flap!"

". . . what?"

"I believe you heard me! You are not deaf, no?" Lefi shouted.

"I mean, at this rate I might end up that way . . ."

"Ha! That's the spirit!"

"Are we sure *you're* not deaf?" Edwin muttered.

"Most certainly! I have Hearing at level seventy-one!"

"And your Listening Skill?"

"I . . . don't have that one."

"Explains a lot."

Lefi seemed genuinely confused for a moment before catching the joke and erupting into laughter.

"Let me guess?" Edwin winced. "You have Shouting?"

"I do indeed!"

"Okay, okay. I think we're getting off-track. So you have Skills that are always active, but if you push them you think I can feel them?"

"What else would it be?"

"Can we . . . test that?"

"Now, Edwin. How would you feel if I questioned you about *your* Skills?"

"But, like, you provided a perfect experiment for me! I want to test this hypothesis, *you don't know how important this is for me.*"

"What? It is important that you understand my Skills?"

"Yes! No! But you presented me with knowledge." Edwin's mind was racing with the sorts of experiments he could try. What exactly were the limits of his Skills? At what point did a Skill cross over into being a magical Skill instead of a "mundane" Skill?

"It's science. I can learn! You have to let me do this!" Even as he said the words, Edwin realized he was getting carried away, and he withdrew, his eyes falling. Lefi had pulled away while Edwin was animatedly pushing for experimenting, and it sank in just how much he'd messed up.

"Sorry."

"No harm done, my friend! None at all!" Lefi tried to reassure him, but Edwin shied away from the reassuring pat the man offered. He'd gotten carried away, he knew it, and wasn't particularly keen on empty platitudes to make him feel better.

He'd been doing so good in Joriah, too.

"Edwin!" A voice snapped him out of his musings. "Stop moping!" Inion had looked away from Yathal and made eye contact with him.

"I'm not moping!"

"Yes, you were!"

"How would you know?"

"You always get all mopey when you start moping," she offered in her typical nonanswer.

"That doesn't make any sense!"

"Should I leave you two alone?" Lefi teased, and Edwin turned to glare at the Adventurer. Inion just laughed, the traitor.

He wasn't entirely sure when she'd stopped teasing him about trying to seduce him, and while he was perhaps ostensibly happy—not that he'd ever *really* minded that a pretty girl wanted to flirt with him—there was the small, traitorous voice inside of him that said she wasn't interested in him because of how she'd gotten to know him better. He *tried* to squish the impulse of the social paranoia he knew it was, but it still stuck in the back of his mind as a niggling doubt.

After all, it made sense that she would travel with him and help him. She was Inion, after all. They were contractually bound together and had spent a year in close proximity. That sort of thing would always beget closeness. That didn't mean that she liked him for who he was, though.

Edwin mentally sighed. He wished that he had a friend who he could just . . . spend time with. Who wouldn't get bored and annoyed at him when he went on his diatribes about science, who would be able to talk to him about stuff *he* found interesting. No, Inion didn't count. He couldn't articulate why, but she didn't.

Lefi didn't count either. Beyond the fact he found the man slightly grating—though within the bounds of tolerance—he was clearly the sort of person who "liked everyone" and wanted to make them all feel included. Personally, Edwin suspected that kind of person just reveled in the feeling of marginally positive interactions with a lot of people. He couldn't *actually* care about Edwin on a personal level, after all. He didn't know Edwin well enough to make an informed decision about him. He didn't really care about *him*, just that he was a person. No, what Edwin wanted was . . .

"I said stop moping, Edwin! And I mean it!"

"Okay, okay! Fine!"

Did aggressively dragging him back from the verge of a depressive spiral count as care? He supposed it did, and he was glad that Inion could do that. But did she care about *him*, or just that he was the person to wake her up? Was there something about Edwin Maxlin in particular that—

"I warned you!"

Edwin looked up just in time to see Inion tackle him in a floating leap.

"Gaaahhh!"

"That . . . that . . . whoo." Edwin tried to catch his breath. "I didn't even *know* I was that ticklish. I think I might have gotten an Adaptive Defense level from that, actually."

He shook his head. "First off: where did that come from, and second, do you have a Skill for that?"

His former tormentor just grinned. "Well, when you get all mopey I need to do *something* to break you out of it unless I wanna see you not do anything for the next two days or more. Tickling was a last resort, but it did seem to be effective," Inion noted, stroking her chin.

"Wai-wai-wait. No."

"Oh, you didn't have fun?" she teased him.

"Well, okay, yes. But you can't just go grabbing me and tickling me for an hour to break me out from being mopey!"

"Well, why not?"

"It's not— It's not right!" Edwin lamely said, then tried to gather his thoughts. "I'm my own person, you can't just . . . tickle me for an hour just because you think I could benefit from it."

"But it worked so well!"

"That's not the point! Like . . . what if it were something more serious?"

"But it's not? It's tickling you and cheering you up!"

"But you're still doing stuff to me without my agreement."

"And?"

"That's bad."

"Why?"

"Because. . . " Edwin knew he was absolutely awful at debate, particularly when unprepared—his conversations with Xares and Galen had spoken to as much—but this was a new low. He also wasn't in the best mental state *to* debate, either. He was too exhausted from Inion's efforts to break him out of his spiral.

What made it more annoying was she wasn't *completely* wrong. His nihilistic "everyone hates me" urges *had* been pushed away for the time being, and while it wasn't a permanent solution, it worked, as much as he hated to admit it. He wasn't sure *why* it worked—barring Skill shenanigans anyway, which were entirely possible—but it had.

"It's still me and my body. It's a matter of principle. When I say not to do something, that's an absolute."

"Psshhh." Inion waved her hand. "You're not even a century old. What do you know about what you want?"

"I'm literally the *only* person who knows what I want! You certainly don't."

"Don't be ridiculous! I know exactly what you want."

"And what's that?"

She patted his cheek. "You want some friends your own age, and to learn about alchemy. You'll get there eventually, don't worry."

"Hey! You aren't my mother!"

Inion just chuckled and pulled him in for a hug. "Don't worry, I've got you. I'll take care of you just fine."

Edwin gave a half-hearted struggle more out of principle than anything. Human—or close enough, he supposed—contact was something he generally enjoyed. It wasn't a full substitute for having someone he was genuinely close to, but it *did* help fill the gap.

"I'm still mad at you," he muttered. "This doesn't change anything."

"Of course, Edwin. Of course."

. . . It was nice, he had to admit.

Very nice.

CHAPTER 16

On Tracks

"Okay, move it! Up and over it now!"

"I'm getting flashbacks," Edwin muttered, but still he complied. He barely brushed the side of the cart, his fingers passing within a few inches of its wall, before he yanked himself into the air, somersaulting over the entire carriage and landing on the other side.

He stumbled, not quite ready for the sudden change in motion that accompanied him landing perpendicular to the direction they were walking, but recovered quickly enough that he didn't face-plant into the cobblestones.

From behind him, he heard the cheering and enthusiastic barking of his spectators, and Edwin felt a grin glit across his face.

"That was—"

"Disgraceful!"

"Not what I would have said."

"But close enough, right?"

"No. *I* was going to say he's doing magnificently! It is you who has put the insatiable demands upon him."

"He's capable of so much, though!"

"He is also mortal! Good enough is good enough."

"My standards aren't insatiable, either! Edwin, tell Lefi my standards aren't unreasonable."

"Uh . . ." Edwin hesitated. "I decline to answer?"

Lefi and Inion carried on, descending into further bickering. Edwin genuinely couldn't tell if it was in good humor or not, but he decided that he would assume it was.

"I'm also not sure," he cut in, "how this is supposed to help me *fight?* Like, don't get me wrong, the tips you've given me on using my Flight for acrobatic stunts is cool and all, but it doesn't seem that different from what Inion would have had me do last year."

The two of them paused, and Lefi opened his mouth, then closed it again. "But of course I had a reason for you to perform such a stunt. What kind of mentor would I be if I merely had you perform random acrobatics for the sole purpose of watching you? No, of course not! Instead, I had the most marvelous of reasons. . . ."

Lefi functionally hemmed and hawed for a minute before conviction entered his eyes and he firmly nodded at Edwin. "My reasons of course are that it will be quite useful later on, but for now I needed to ascertain the level of mobility you were most comfortable with!"

". . . You just wanted to watch me flip over the carriage, didn't you?"

"*I* . . . decline to answer."

Inion just laughed.

They weren't making as good of time as when it was just the three of them (Edwin, Inion, and Bill) alone, but Edwin didn't really mind. It wasn't like he was in any sort of rush, after all. Only being on the move for only half of each day. It wasn't like he was really *wasting* the rest of the time, anyway, just that he wasn't continuing on in that time.

Now, the reasons that they stopped so early did vary slightly, but usually involved Yathal getting tired, them having some noteworthy place to check out, or Lefi wanting to give Edwin more training during the daytime hours.

Such as their current "exercise," which Edwin was mentally deeming Edwin-Pinata, but was perhaps more charitably described as "sparring."

Lefi was *wickedly* good with pretty much every type of weapon he had on him, and considering the sheer amount of weapons—ranging from small blades to entire polearms, though the latter were usually kept on the cart—he had, that was really saying something. Forty different proficiency Skills were nothing to scoff at, it seemed, particularly when they overlapped in effect.

Edwin was rapidly finding the limits of his 30 Stamina. While he'd thought it was essentially unlimited at first, he had learned the hard way that was only true when Walking was in play. Granted, thanks to his Breathing Skill he rarely had to catch his breath, but his muscles ached from raw exertion.

"What's your Stamina, anyway?" he accused Lefi, who seemed to still be at full energy.

The man just laughed. "Far more than you! I told you, Attributes are the greatest part of having hundreds of Skills!"

"Fine, don't answer my question then."

Lefi winked at him. "Now you're getting it."

"Getting *what*?"

"Come on, back up on your feet!" Lefi rapped Edwin's toes with his stick, and he unsteadily rose once again.

With a titanic expenditure of will, he retrieved a stamina potion—talsanenris-based again, naturally—and downed it. Immediately, Edwin felt relief flood through his limbs and he took his stance once more.

"This time, focus more on trying to hit me with your potions. Last time, you had a really horrendous showing. And don't forget your Skills! You shouldn't be able to be tripped, not with Flight."

Edwin didn't voice his response, just glared at the man. What was up with his teachers taking an inordinate amount of enjoyment from his pain? First Inion, now Lefi. Like Edwin had even the slimmest chance to use any of his Skills, let alone figure out which ones to call upon mid-fight. He had almost fifty, and if he didn't plan out ahead of time which ones he would use when exactly, there was no way that he'd be able to chain them together in the way Lefi wanted him to.

He shoved aside the part of his mind that said Lefi must have the same problem as him ten times over and nodded to Inion, who was serving as "referee."

Not that one was ever needed. That would imply he stood a *chance*. "And . . . Go!"

Edwin, even though he was waiting for it, had barely even processed the statement when Lefi was already on top of him. Edwin stepped back, trying to get space between him and the Adventurer. Longstrider flared, but before it could fully engage, Lefi had rapped his knee with the tip of his stick. The contact broke Edwin's concentration, and he lost control over his Longstrider, the Skill sending him sprawling across the ground.

. . . the exact same result as the last ten times.

"Back up on your feet, my friend! Remember—"

"To focus on my potions and not trip! I *know*!" Edwin snapped. "You just don't give me a chance!"

"Nonsense! You're already far better than when we started!"

That . . . Edwin had to admit, was—embarrassingly enough—true. Even earlier today, he hadn't yet managed to trigger so much as Longstrider before Lefi could knock him over and end the match.

"Can we do an attack round, at least?" Edwin pleaded. "I'm sick of landing on rocks. And I think we've well established you outspeed me by at least ten times."

From the side, Yathal gave an agreeing cheer. While Edwin didn't agree with *why* the little kid wanted Edwin to not worry about defense, he wouldn't complain about the results. Basically, the boy and his dog wanted a fight to last more than three seconds, and attack rounds *did* tend to last longer than that.

"Hmm. Very well, so be it." Lefi tossed his stick to the side, where it fell slightly obscured in the short grass of their campsite.

Attack rounds were simple. Edwin was free to use all his Skills and gear, move around as much as he wanted, attack from any angle, and his goal was to land a hit on Lefi's torso or head.

Lefi, in turn, couldn't move more than a half step, was completely unarmed, and couldn't press any attack, only follow up on openings Edwin gave him. He would win if he knocked Edwin on the ground, same as with any other bout.

It was exactly as one-sided as it sounded.

"And . . . Go!"

Edwin slung one of the water-filled apparatite spheres they were using in lieu of his actual potions at Lefi's torso, hoping to force at the very least a dodge while he closed the distance between them. Instead, Lefi intercepted the projectile—which had been moving at some seventy miles an hour if not more—perfectly, catching the ball and cradling it against his chest.

While not exactly the result he had been hoping for, Edwin still tried to press his opportunity, aiming the tip of his stick at the unarmored man's chest, bringing around a dagger with his other hand, beginning to throw it where he predicted that Lefi would dodge.

Once again, though, he didn't dodge. Instead, Lefi threw his held crystal sphere at Edwin's stick. The two collided with a *crack*, and the ball disintegrated, leaving only a spray of water dousing the wooden weapon, nearly reaching Edwin's hand. If it had been firevine or the like, the bout would have been functionally over as he'd need to extinguish his stick. But since it *was* just water and he was still standing, Edwin pressed on.

His knife flashed through the air, corrected at the last second to aim where Lefi was instead of where he had anticipated, and his stick thrust toward the man's side. Even though he knew better, he felt a bit triumphant seeing both attacks on their way to hitting him . . .

Lefi didn't even pretend it was hard and elbowed Edwin's stick out of the way. Edwin had learned, though, and didn't stumble from the interrupted attack. What he wasn't anticipating, though, was the sudden *clunk* and corresponding impact from the end of his weapon, as his *own thrown knife* was intercepted by his attack. Somehow, Lefi had used Edwin's second attack to block his first, and Edwin was equal parts frustrated and amazed at the action.

"How the *heck* did . . . never mind." He wrenched his mind back on track and stepped back out of Lefi's reach. He should have expected that going in fast wouldn't accomplish anything, not with Lefi having at least ten times more of whatever Attributes governed speed than Edwin did. Wasn't there a straight-up Speed Attribute? He remembered Inion mentioning something along those lines at some point. Maybe Lefi would know how to get it? He'd have to ask later, as Edwin didn't want to be rude and change the topic while they were sparring. Lefi deserved his full attention.

. . . Well, a good amount of his attention at least.

Hmm.

Edwin tapped his stick against the ground, thinking of how to attack his mentor. Off to the side, Yathal booed at his lack of attacking, yelling something about how boring it was getting; Edwin didn't pay much attention to the specifics. Well, fine then. He could step things up a bit while he formulated a plan. While he didn't really expect it to *work*, Edwin stepped forward and tried to strike at Lefi with his stick, stabbing and slicing with his training weapon as through it were a sword.

Meanwhile, Lefi casually leaned out of the way of every strike. He made it look easy, or maybe just made Edwin look incompetent. Probably both, honestly, given the man had just *closed his eyes*. Now that was just insulting.

Edwin leveled a wide sweep at the Adventurer. No way to dodge this unless he just jumped three feet in the air with his eyes closed and from a stationary position.

Even as Edwin made the attack he realized the mistake, and he felt more resigned as he watched Lefi do exactly that, giving an Olympic-level high jump over the stick, pulling himself two and a half meters (according to Numeracy) off the ground.

Edwin could use that! He refused to think about the possibility or impossibility of certain actions, but it was just the work of moments to figure out where Lefi would land, and he preemptively held his stick there.

True to the Adventurer's Skills, though, he managed to twist mid-air—his eyes finally opening—such that he was reaching out to grab Edwin's stick, trying to snatch it out of his grip.

Edwin pulled back his weapon before he could lose it, but consequently lost his perfect setup and Lefi managed to land back on the ground without incident, dodging a second "potion" attack in the same fluid motion.

Honestly, it was straight-up unfair. How was Edwin supposed to compete with a combat-trained gymnast?

Well, the obvious answer, he supposed, was to throw an attack that couldn't be dodged by the guy.

Edwin fished out another potion from his belt, and with narrowed eyes he threw it up in the air, swinging his stick to hit the apparatite like it was a baseball. They connected and the container cracked, disintegrating into Skill light and scattering the water inside.

Lefi's eyes widened and Edwin felt a moment of triumph as he felt like he had finally, *finally* managed to land a hit on . . .

The Adventurer thrust a Skill-laden hand out, palm-striking the air, and Edwin saw and felt the air warp under the light blue Skill, a ripple passing through the area and intercepting all of the droplets of water. Wherever they met, the droplets erupted into mist suspended in the air, forming a wall of fog that was swiftly ripped apart by the faint breeze in their campsite.

"Oh, come on!" Edwin complained. "How are you so good at *everything?* What even was that?"

"Do not despair! You forced me to enter my second group of Skills! That's progress!"

"Don't patronize me!" he yelled back, throwing a barrage of apparatite crystals at the man.

Even angry, Throwing Weapons assisted enough that they all went perfectly on-target. Of course, his annoyance at Lefi for so perfectly dodging every last one only continued to grow, until Lefi eventually decided enough was enough. He snagged one of the crystals out of midair and whipped it back at Edwin at even higher speeds than he was capable of.

Of course, dodging projectiles was child's play for Edwin, but he only noticed the second projectile coming his way too late, once his face had already perfectly positioned itself in its trajectory.

"So is there really a point to all this? Other than you demonstrating how utterly outmatched I am against people like you, both on an Attribute and Skill level," Edwin complained once his nose had finished healing. A broken nose was far from the *worst* injury he'd gotten lately, but it was still quite annoying and kept him from wanting to talk.

Worst of all, Adaptive Defense kicked in only *after* he'd taken the damage, meaning it was both harder and more painful to set it back in place than it had been to first break it. Next time, he'd know to disable the Skill first.

"But of course! It is valuable to learn one's own limits!"

"And it's fun to watch!" Yathal pitched in, Kyni barking his agreement.

Lefi chuckled. "And it's fun, yes."

"Glad *one* of us enjoyed themselves," Edwin grumbled, though his heart wasn't really in the complaint. "So . . . just so I can see how completely outclassed I am, I'm hearing? I could have told you that after a random solitary bandit managed to put a hole in my chest. I suppose technically the hole *was* kind of my fault, but that's besides the point."

Lefi glanced at Inion, who shrugged.

"Could you talk to *me* instead of her?" Edwin snapped. "Honestly. I'm the one being trained here! Inion doesn't know everything about me."

"Of course! It is simply that she is more aware of your level of strength on an objective scale."

"Her info literally predates the Empire! *I* know about as much as her when it comes to how strong I am compared to the average Adventurer or Citizen."

Lefi raised an eyebrow, and Edwin shrank away. "Fine." He grumbled, "I'll go sit with the other kids, then."

He slunk off to where Yathal and Kyni sat in the grass, floating down and giving Kyni a good scratch between his ears. As intelligent as a person or not, Kyni was still a dog and Edwin loved pets as much as any other canine.

He idly wondered if he could or should get a dog now that he was on Joriah. He'd always wanted one as a kid, but his family was gone from the house too much for it to be viable. *It wouldn't be fair to the dog*, he'd always been told, and while he *agreed* with the sentiment, both then and now . . . he still really wanted one. But he wasn't sure if he would really be able to adequately adopt and care for one. His personal goal of feeding himself daily failed a *long* time ago; how could he remember to do the same for an animal he adopted? Bill contented himself with whatever grass they found on the roadside, but a dog would be much more demanding.

It still would be nice, though. Yathal and Kyni were utterly inseparable. Other than when they passed another traveler on the road, or when some noise or scent would catch the dog's attention. He'd rush off to make sure whatever it was wasn't dangerous, maybe give a friendly bark or two to let them know everything was all right, then he'd be right back to Yathal's side, or serving as the boy's steed at times when he wasn't just riding on the carriage.

Sometimes, they'd work themselves into a puddle of boy and dog, each comforting and drawing comfort from the other. Other times, like right now, they would just be sitting next to each other. It was obvious that Kynigos loved his boy orders of magnitude more than anyone else, and he would do anything for the kid.

It was . . . really sweet, and Edwin wished he had that sort of dependability from someone. Or just someone who was willing to spend time in preference to that of anyone else. Even Inion clearly preferred the company of Lefi over him. It just . . .

Edwin sighed.

He couldn't fault people for preferring to spend time with certain people. Heck, he absolutely played favorites with the people he did like versus those he didn't. You could only have one person who you *most* liked spending time with, anyway, but was it too much to ask for *somebody* who would choose him over any other given person when given the chance?

He absently scratched Kyni's stomach—the dog's head was claimed by Yathal, of course—and looked around at the vivacious locale they'd chosen for their campsite.

They'd exited the forest about a day prior, and Edwin was happy for the change of scenery. Where they currently were camped was against a small hill a short distance from the road, the lush grass spilling out like an emerald carpet in all directions as far as he could see. The smells of the early-autumnal forest had also been exchanged for those of a wind-swept plain, the faint scent of late-summer wildflowers carried on the breeze and into Edwin's nose as he breathed in. As he lay back into the grass, he stared into the sky. Far overhead, a hawk circled in its never-ending hunt, and Edwin sighed in relief.

It was nice, he decided. While Lefi and Inion continued to talk about whatever—presumably him—and Yathal sat in silence watching them, Edwin picked a blade of grass and idly peeled it apart.

"What's that?" Yathal asked, and Edwin dragged his attention back to the wider world.

"What's what?" Edwin asked, looking around. He didn't see anything too unusual, what could the boy be wondering about?

"That . . . white thing. Over there!" the boy pointed to a part of the sky, but Edwin couldn't see anything of note that way. It was mostly clear blue sky, was whatever he saw obscured against the . . .

"Wait, the cloud?"

"That's not a cloud! It's waaaay too big and puffy! And too white!"

Edwin chuckled. "What, have you never seen a cumulus cloud before?" he asked, before catching himself and frowning. It had been a year and a half since he'd arrived on Joriah, and there had still only been a single time he'd seen it rain. Even that one time wasn't natural, so was it possible that . . .

"Have you ever experienced rain?" he asked Yathal.

"Oh, there was a couple of times! When I was a kid there was this one time that the Emperor himself brought rain and the sky turned really gray. It was all really wet for a long time and it was really annoying out in the field."

Huh. Well, okay then. Interesting that Rhothos had such a dramatically flourishing ecosystem if it basically never rained, but maybe the Rhothos River helped in that account? Along with the Verdant and whatever magical nonsense it provided, of course.

"Was that your only experience with clouds?" he asked, before immediately regretting his choices. The kid had just *said* that he had seen clouds before.

"Well, no. But clouds are really small and wispy, not like that," he said, and Kyni barked his agreement.

"Well, that there is what clouds are generally like, and what most parts of the world will experience. You just don't get rain because of the mountains, I guess."

"Why's that?"

"Well, you're in its rain shadow if I were to guess. Hey, Lefi!" he called out, getting the attention of the well-traveled Adventurer. "Have you ever been to the other side of the mountain range in the Verdant?"

"I have been much farther afield than that in my adventures! Why, one quest I undertook—"

"Great, great." Edwin cut him off before he could get carried away. "What was the weather like there? Was it as dry as here, or was it rainy?"

Lefi laughed. "I scarcely saw the sun! It was all mountains and valleys leading straight into the ocean itself, and there were nigh more rivers than dry ground! Now, I had an adventure there at one point where—"

"Okay, cool. Thanks." Edwin redirected his attention to Yathal. "Yeah, that's because of a rain shadow. Basically, water is picked up over the ocean and carried in the form of clouds until it can fall out as rain. However, because of the mountains, a lot of the water is kept from getting to this side of the Verdant and it all rains out either in the mountains or on the far side, where it just goes back into the ocean.

"If I were to guess, that cloud there means we're getting closer to the coast, and the mountains aren't blocking as much of the sky as they once were. We might even get some rain here soon!"

"I don't think that sounds fun. Can we not?"

Edwin chuckled. "I mean, we don't have much of a choice. Rain is a common occurrence *most* places, and a needed one when you don't have a huge magical forest and river making sure your home isn't a barren wasteland."

"Better that than havin' rain. Make the cloud go away!"

"Sorry, Yathal. Not much I can do in that regard."

"So! You have powers you are ignoring, my friend!"

"I mean, I haven't figured out how to *use* Refine, but that's not for lack of trying. I just don't dwell on my failures all that much."

"Eh? Refine? I meant your Overcharge! It's such a powerful Skill, yet you never utilize it!"

Edwin had given up on trying to figure out how Lefi knew so much about his Skill list. Inion was probably helping him or something. "I mean . . . it hurts a *ton* when I use it, and Inion cautioned me away from overuse. Something about black goop buildup or whatever?"

"I told you, Edwin. It'll be all right if you don't overuse it!"

"Yeah! That's what I've been doing!"

"How many times have you used it in the last four months you've had it?"

". . . Twice?" Edwin knew where this was going and he couldn't say he was happy about it, but what could he do?

"Ya! That's not overuse! That's neglect!"

"Fine," Edwin grumbled without any real weight behind the complaint. "I'll train my Skill. It just hurts, you know?"

Truth be told, he *had* been meaning to try and use it more often. His Adaptive Defense might have been at a high enough level to help offset some of the worse effects of the Skill's use at this point for all he knew, and it was too valuable a trump card to leave wholly unused. But complaining about it slightly when his trainers prodded him into working on it was his way of dealing with the soreness he knew he'd be dealing with.

"Okay, fine. Let's get this over with. Just . . . remind me to prioritize getting some unicorn derivatives, okay?"

The magical animals, true to their Earth mythological counterparts, were exceptionally pure—a property that extended to their horns, hooves, blood, and more. That made them useful in everything from antiplague treatments to antidotes, and they were on Edwin's list of substances to stock up on.

"You know, if you wanted unicorns, we're going in the wrong direction."

"Yeah, I know." Edwin sighed. *Unlike* their more mythological counterpoints, "real" unicorns (a thought Edwin still couldn't believe he seriously had) were more cervid than equine. That meant their natural habitat was sparse, warm woodland like that found in the southern reaches of the Verdant. They could live elsewhere, naturally, and there was apparently a family that lived in snow-covered lands where their white coats served as highly effective camouflage, but Edwin wasn't keeping his hopes up to encounter any "arctic unicorns" in his travels. He personally suspected that arctic unicorns might have been the original species, with the "normal" variety having migrated south. How else would an animal evolve a pure white coat if *not* part of a snowy environment?

"But we're also heading in the direction of one of the biggest trading hubs on the continent," he mused. "We might be able to find some horns there."

Unicorn horns weren't like rhino horns or elephant tusks, fortunately. Though he had no doubt they were still hunted for the rest of their body parts, unicorns in particular shed their horns every year like their deer cousins and so were more readily available than they might have been otherwise. Overall, it mildly pleased Edwin that unicorn horn could be sustainably harvested.

Granted, he didn't expect that they *were*, but that fact didn't particularly bother him. Unicorns were just another magical creature, with no particular degree of sapience in common members of their species greater than any other animal.

There was apparently an exception to all this in the form of the "Noble Unicorn," but Inion had refused to elaborate on that when Edwin had asked her to confirm what the book had said. Whatever. She said that there was no way the writers of the book had experience with it, and that their observations of the common unicorn's primary properties were close enough to accurate as to be useful for him.

"So! Do you intend to expand your repertoire by actually utilizing your Skills?"

Edwin sighed. "Fine. I don't suppose you have some sort of training-assist Skill or whatever? I don't mean Exceptional, but like a Skill that helps you utilize ones I have."

"My friend, I have Skills for *everything*."

"Awesome. So when we're done lighting my body on fire, maybe we can figure out how Refine works?"

Overcharge.

The strength rushed through Edwin's body once more, empowering his every twitch and thought as mana permeated the fabric of his body and imbued it with immense strength. This time, though, he was trying something different. This time, he was attempting to concentrate the effect in his right arm.

At minimum, it should help Edwin fight off the full-body pain and fatigue that he usually felt during these training routines. At best, it might improve the efficacy of the Skill itself, magnifying its strength by focusing its area of effect.

It was *hard*, though. Edwin's Mana of 33 was higher than any of his other Attributes, and his Basic Mana Manipulation was only *9*. Sure, Mana Infusion was one of his highest-level Skills, but that didn't help him all *that* much given it was already incorporated into Overcharge's effect.

Still, he tried. Inion was holding his hand, providing him with moral support as well as being literally on hand in case he needed immediate medical attention. Lefi was standing a bit farther back, blasting Edwin with a mix of beneficial Skills—including the dangerous Inspire Courage—imbuing him with the *certainty* that he would manage it this time.

Off in the corner of his awareness, Numeracy continued to tick up as he tried to fight the effect back to no real avail. Ten seconds, eleven, twelve, thirteen, fourteen . . . He tensed up in preparation for . . .

The high passed, and Edwin's entire body sagged with the unique sensation of electrocution and exhaustion combined with being set on fire from the inside out. It was getting better, though. Once Overcharge had passed the ten-second mark, Adaptive Defense had begun to have a noticeable difference on the intensity of the Skill's backlash.

The switch still wasn't instantaneous, though, and while Edwin had found that with repeated use of Overcharge he *could* bring the pain down to maybe a third, pain was hard to measure. So was "harm," for that matter, but that was what Adaptive Defense supposedly guarded against!

Pain notwithstanding, Edwin was learning a lot about his Skills. Adaptive Defense, for example, had a pool of resistance that was automatically applied to whatever was harming him most at any given time. The more he was harmed, the faster the switch. Once it was applied to a single source, it stayed tuned to that source until another form of damage began pulling the Skill toward it instead.

If he just let it go naturally, it would typically direct itself toward UV radiation and sunlight over the course of about six hours or so, protecting him from the heat of the day and sunburns. He could still tan, though, which was *awesome*. He had Skill-empowered sunscreen!

Its bias toward actual "harm" meant that he couldn't, in fact, level the Skill with or leverage its effects toward "tickling," much to Inion's chagrin. Well, really it was *his* chagrin, because she *wouldn't stop trying*. Gah. What happened to the days when she was perfectly content letting Edwin do whatever he wanted with himself? He missed those days. Yes, they had involved her throwing a lot of heavy and sharp things at him while he was blindfolded, but . . . no actually, now that he thought about it, he'd take the tickling.

"Edwin? How's it going? Did it work?" Inion brushed her fingers against Edwin's grimacing face, pulling him back to reality.

"Fine . . ." Edwin ground out. "I was successfully distracting myself there for a while, but it hasn't fully faded yet. And no, no luck. It's still my entire body."

"Very well! Let us go once more unto the breach! Onward!"

Edwin sighed. This couldn't *possibly* be healthy, could it? But Anatomy wasn't yelling at him yet about any strange fluid buildups, so . . .

Overcharge.

One, two, three . . .

Edwin lay limply in Inion's arms, looking up at the sky. For the first time in a long, long time, the stars were partially obscured by dark clouds drifting across the nightscape. It was an interesting shift in the weather, and while it hadn't rained yet, Edwin's intuition told him he should expect a drizzle the next day. His muscles *burned* to the point he could barely even flop around without using Flight—though calling on his mana was its own special kind of torture, and the day had objectively been a failure for his goals. Even now, he couldn't so much as spare a single fingertip from Overcharge's effects.

He was just glad it didn't require any effort beyond momentary thoughts to play with his Status, though, as it helped him remember why exactly he enjoyed traveling with Lefi so much. The past couple of weeks had been *fantastic* for his levels, he had to admit.

Level Up!
Skill Points 720→773 (Average level: 43)
Adaptive Defense Level 27→30
Alchemical Analysis Level 27→28
Anatomy Level 39→40

Arcadian Elixir Level 24→26
Basic Thermokinesis Level 22→26
Fey's Caress Level 36→38
Flight Level 38→40
Fresh Air Level 31→33
Longstrider Level 32→33
Mana Infusion Level 86→87
Memory Level 62→63
Numeracy Level 36→40
Outsider's Almanac Level 132→133
Overcharge Level 8→20
Polyglot Level 66→67
Prototyping Level 25→28
Ritual Intuition Level 26→28
Sapper's Apparatus Level 47→49
Skillful Assessment Level 34→40
Watchful Rest Level 28→30

CHAPTER 17

Proper Attribution

Edwin limply lay on the roof of the carriage, muscles slowly recovering. They'd pushed him so far with Overcharge that his sweat was slightly black in color, leaving him looking as though he was coated in a thin layer of ash. Worst of all, he *still* hadn't figured out how to concentrate the effect in one part of his body, and he was starting to suspect that brute force *might* not be the correct method to go about it.

Huge surprise, yeah. But in his defense, both Lefi and Inion had thought it stood a decent chance of working. That a week of using Overcharge at least every day and trying to direct the flow of mana hadn't accomplished so much as sparing his fingertips had passed meant he was finally trying the route of the Alchemist.

Namely, think about and theorize strategies without actually testing anything.

He'd test it like a *scientist* once his mouth no longer looked like he'd eaten charcoal for every meal in the last week.

In the meantime, his job was to lie around and think about himself. Literally. He'd turned as much of his Perception inward as was physically possible, pulling on Anatomy to try and help him explore his own form.

He'd found that Alchemy liked to prod him slightly as he did his examination, and while he had been left marginally skeptical as to the value of the Skill after his time in Panastalis, it hadn't led him astray so far. Granted, it had only really given him slight pokes about methodology in the past, giving him a bit of intuition about how much heat a potion needed and how long it should be left on the fire, but as the Skill approached level 90 it had begun to give him more underlying knowledge.

Such as, when combined with Anatomy, how his Attributes were interacting with his body. Now, the knowledge was basic. Really, really basic. But it was still there. Well, other than for Impact, but he wasn't clear what that Attribute *did* anyway, so . . .

Health he sensed concentrated in his heart like Galen had said, and for lack of a better word, it tried to maintain the status quo of his anatomy. It was a gross oversimplification, of course, but it seemed broadly accurate. It had a picture of what Edwin "should" be, and pseudo-intelligently either directed Edwin's natural self-repair mechanisms to restore him to that baseline or actively resisted attempts to pull him from that baseline. What was most interesting was how it prioritized what to repair.

Anything that was utterly critical for Edwin's life—namely his heart, brain, and lungs—was given an extremely high priority for repair, to the point where it outright made them more resistant to damage. Or maybe it had just cleansed and fixed those three organs so quickly Edwin hadn't noticed them be affected by his Overcharge overuse.

From there, it expanded its effects out to the rest of his internal organs, before finally moving on to his muscle, bone, and skin. It still had limits, of course. Because it utilized his own body's functions, Edwin didn't think it would enable him to regrow a lost arm or whatever.

That said, if he wasn't otherwise injured and had the entirety of his Health dedicated to protecting his limb, odds *were* good the Attribute might keep him from losing it in the first place. It was major enough that Edwin could tell so long as it wasn't busy trying to keep him from dying of blood loss or averted his death a couple of times, it would be able to keep his arm intact.

Overall, it was a curious process, and sensing his own body slowly scrub out the toxins—essentially charred cells if Edwin's theory was right—built up from raw mana overdosing was really fascinating.

Stamina helped, too, and was equally fascinating in its own way. That Attribute was all about motion. Namely, it provided energy to his body and carted waste away. Instead of nutrients randomly drifting through his bloodstream until they encountered his kidneys and were filtered away, Stamina seemed to guide the molecules to the place they were needed, be it through excretion in his sweat, being purified in his lungs (thanks to Fresh Air), or just his body's normal purification organs.

Because of how rarely he ate, he wasn't entirely sure where Stamina actually got the energy it used, and it remained a mystery until Edwin managed to activate Skillful Assessment looking inside his own body. Once he had, though, he was able to "watch" the process of Stamina taking energy straight from Survival and Nutrition, putting it directly into the cells that needed it.

Looking at his body and its Skills unlocked a wholly new dimension of analysis, too. He could see Nutrition working around his digestive system, Purify working double time in concert with Health, and the way that Flexibility and Athletics interacted with each other and Health and Stamina alike was really interesting, even if he couldn't fully grasp its intricacies.

None of his magical Skills, or even Mana, were obviously present in his physical body, which Edwin wasn't too surprised by in all honesty. They must have been associated with his soul or whatever. He'd go looking for the answer to *that* metaphysical question another day.

There was a faint flicker from his Mana Sense when he activated Flight, his skeletal system linking together into a single magical object and reaching a tendril out to his surroundings, but at that point, between splitting Perception between Anatomy, Basic Mana Sense, and Skillful Assessment, the clarity of his internal perception was . . . low. He'd revisit the proposition when he had a few more dozen points in Perception, perhaps.

It was tricky trying to figure out where Overcharge fit into the system. He wouldn't be able to fully tell until he actually used it *while* looking at himself in this manner, but he knew how it felt and he could speculate.

He *was* acting like an alchemist, after all.

So, random speculation time!

Overcharge was based on his Mana Infusion. Normally, he used Mana Infusion from his fingertips, but it obviously wasn't coming from there for Overcharge. Instead, it seemed to be coming directly from his mana reservoir. From his admittedly hazy memories of first unlocking the Attribute, that was located between his collarbones, at the top of his lungs. So, assuming that was accurate, the mana would flood out from there and fill his body. Perhaps it followed his blood, or maybe it was more closely associated with his breath?

I should test this, he traitorously thought before quashing the impulse with a reminder to stick to thought experiments only for this stage of the process.

Either way, he knew from experience that it was rather futile trying to keep an Overcharge originating from his chest from spilling out into his entire body. Perhaps he should try to change the source of his Overcharge, then? Like if he manually activated Overcharge via Mana Infusion, maybe that way he could get the effect to start from his fingertips? If it spread from the end of his arm, maybe he could keep it restricted to below his shoulder.

The only question was how he could do that. Maybe he could use his Health and Stamina for that? He *had* noted how his Health always fought to keep his body in place, and how Stamina was good at keeping contaminants contained . . .

Maybe he could leverage them in a combined manner where Health fought against the encroaching mana and Stamina worked to keep the mana contained? It might work, though he'd need some way to actually manipulate his Attributes. Maybe he could get Perception mixed in somewhere? It was the only one of his five Attributes he could *directly* manipulate, after all.

Oh! Maybe there were some sort of Health Manipulation and Stamina Manipulation Skills? Those would be very interesting, and hmm. Would he *want* them if he could get them? His initial reaction was no, just because that was his default response these days to new Skills, but if they could give him anywhere close to the sorts of benefits that he got from Basic Mana Manipulation, they would be *well* worth the extra effort. Maybe he could pick them up after he evolved Flight, if they did exist. He'd have to ask Lefi, he'd know.

Okay, back on track. How would he be able to fight off mana with his Health and Stamina? The former *was* higher than the latter two, though perhaps combined they'd be sufficient. Maybe he should try to alchemically boost his Attributes? He had what he referred to as his Health and Stamina potions, but that was just for convenience. They didn't *actually* affect the Attributes insofar as he knew. The former was essentially a blood clotting agent and the latter was practically just really sugared caffeine.

Something to look into, he supposed.

What might he include in them, though? He hadn't encountered anything that he'd felt had particular resonance or whatever with his Attributes, but maybe he just wasn't looking in the right way? Now that he could actually "see" his Attributes, maybe he could figure out if eating any of his ingredients provoked some kind of response from them? It wasn't a thought experiment, but he *was* getting kind of sick about just imagining stuff.

He popped open a new Almanac tab and felt around for his satchel. Test one, Talsanenris. . . .

Level Up!
Skill Points 773→778 (Average level: 43)
Anatomy Level 40→42
Flight Level 40→41
Overcharge Level 20→21
Sapper's Apparatus Level 49→50

Edwin woke up to the sensation of a drop of water landing on his face. He flailed around slightly, accidentally smacking Inion and waking up the fey in turn. She swatted Edwin in retribution, which was fair enough, but before she could fully understand what was going on, Edwin had already retreated from the roof of the carriage, carrying his sleeping pad to the vehicle's interior.

He needed to check on his potions, naturally. That was his excuse, and he was sticking to it.

When the sky pealed with a mighty thunderclap, unleashing a torrent of water, he remained quite dry inside of his little lab. And he would *stay* that way, which was why he shooed away Kyni when the wet dog tried to get inside the carriage.

There was a lot of stuff that water would mess up, after all. He couldn't have the pup shaking himself dry and getting all his stuff wet. He had spent a fair bit of time trying to sanitize everything, and getting dog-water over all of it would just contaminate his experiments.

He was just taking care of his potions, naturally. That was his excuse, and he was sticking to it.

Granted, it didn't hold up *quite* so well when Yathal tried to take shelter, but there was enough of an overhang above the driver's seat that he was still able to get the boy to sit there. As a bonus, Kyni could join him, so long as the dog didn't go *inside*.

Inion didn't care much about the rain, of course. She was still a water spirit, and it didn't matter where that water was. It was still her day to be on driving duty, but that position hardly required actually *being* in the driver's seat, ironically.

Lefi had some kind of Dryness Skill to keep himself in the clear. He, like the rest of them, kept most of his weapons and gear stashed in the carriage, but he retrieved his gray cloak and donned it once the rain started. Even hours into the thunderstorm, not even a drop of water had clung to or soaked into the woolen garment or the rest of Lefi's garb.

Amusingly, his fiery hair *had* calmed down somewhat, revealing black hair that smoldered with red light, like coal being kept down by the rain.

In any case, Edwin wasn't *totally* fibbing when he said that he needed his space in the interior to work on his potions. It was absolutely true. Now, he *had* been able to work in more cramped areas than the carriage in the past, but he still liked having the space to himself. And besides, who knew if one of his experiments might suddenly blow up? It *had* happened in the past after all. Never mind that he was unlikely to experience another coal dust explosion while working with talsanenris and sinbalyne.

His experiments had revealed something interesting. His talsanenris potions *did* in fact supplement his Health, but only slightly. It was more accurate to say that they relieved some of his Health load by providing basic preliminary healing throughout his body, freeing up more of the Attribute to act as it saw fit.

Sinbalyne was more interactive with his Attributes, but not in a good way. It interfered with Stamina as it attempted to go about its business, slowing down the delivery magic running within his body at all times.

It was that reaction he was attempting to replicate now. If he could somehow isolate whatever component of the sinbalyne allowed it to interfere with his Attributes, he might be able to plug talsanenris or other effects into there!

He wasn't having any luck at the moment, though. His initial trials didn't have any of the key attributes (heh) of what he was looking for, and it wasn't until he attempted functionally using Mana Infusion without using Mana Infusion that anything started to actually click. Essentially, the Skill liked to just insert mana directly into a substance with no regard for what was already there. While he was now able to Infuse some low-magic substances, his Infusion seemed to override whatever base magical abilities the substances had. Instead, what he was trying to do was use his Basic Mana Manipulation to manually add mana to the mixture, increasing the density without disrupting anything that was already present.

It took a fair bit of effort, but he eventually managed to pull out a metaphorical drop of mana to the tips of his fingers. However, it was repelled by the potion until he forced it into a slightly more concentrated form, making it feel like a tiny candle to his mana senses. Only then was it accepted into the potion, vanishing from his fingertip into the solution in the blink of an eye.

He jumped with the notification that accompanied it.

Level Up!
Refining Level 1→2

He'd left his notifications on free display in case he got an Alchemy level or something, but he had *not* been expecting that. Refining had been this strange, elusive target among his Skills, that every time he thought he might have a grasp on what would make it tick just hadn't triggered, but all of a sudden it was just leveling? What the heck did he do? Was it the attempt to concentrate his own mana? Including it in the potion?

He pulled up his Almanac entry on the Skill, to see If there were any hints there as to what he'd done differently.

Almanac Entry: The Refining Skill
   Description:
   Better. Faster. Stronger.
   Isolate and improve desirable qualities
   Strength of refinement improves with level.

   RefiningSources
   [Produced by the combination of the Practical Alchemist Path (PracticalAlchemistPath) and the Purify Skill.]
   RefiningLeveling
   [Absolutely no clue. Attempting to refine a minority component of a substance didn't level it, attempting to make a leaf more green didn't level it, and trying to make stone harder didn't either.]
   RefiningEvolutions
   []
   Refining is an interesting Skill in that I have no clue what it does. It seems to be alchemy-related, but so far it has yet to level despite numerous attempts to figure out what it affects. See Experiment Series A

   RefiningNotes
   [This Skill is my bane. I hate it so much.
   Oh hey, *that's* how you edit an entry. I'll leave this up for now.]
   RefiningCombinations
   []
   RefiningTestIndex
   [A-Series:
   Testing the parameters by which the Refining Skill will level, and accordingly, what it does
   RefiningTestA1
   RefiningTestA2
   . . .]

Hmm. No . . . nothing new or interesting there. Did he finally figure out what "desirable qualities" were, then? Did it help him connect his potions to the System, maybe? Did trying to boost his Attributes via potioneering mean that he'd finally hit upon what the Skill did?

He'd need to have a word with whoever called it "Refining" instead of . . . instead of . . . Attribution or whatever, if that were the case. Not Attribution, that was a terrible name. But he wasn't some strange quasi-omniscient System, *he* didn't have to come up with a better alternative to recognize that Refining was a terrible name if it did what he thought it did.

. . . he was probably wrong about what it did, wasn't he? He needed to figure out a series of tests to figure out what the Skill's limits were, but how would he do that?

Ah well, problem for future-Edwin. Now, he just needed to focus on this potion so he didn't screw it up.

Edwin fed a trickle of mana to the tip of his finger, pulling once more on the long-neglected Basic Mana Manipulation instead of the more streamlined Mana Infusion. After all, he wasn't trying to Infuse anything, just bring his mana to bear. With a final tug, he succeeded, and he looked on in satisfaction at the end of his index finger. There, the flavorless bead of magic hung, shining to his mana sense like a drop of water ready to fall off. But, he knew, it wouldn't fall. It wasn't going anywhere until he let it. And before then, he had a job to do.

Calling on Refining didn't do anything. No surprise there, though he'd been hopeful that now his Refining had actually leveled he might be able to contort it into being an active Skill, like what he'd done with Firestarting and Packing. Alas, it wouldn't be that easy. Refining still required he use the tools he had on hand, and that meant taking his drop of mana and compressing it as much as possible into a single bead of magic.

Basic Mana Manipulation was up to the task, if barely. It felt like trying to make a snowball with a teaspoon, but he had time. He could focus. He kept concentrating on the tiny pinpoint of mana, pushing it bit by bit smaller and smaller, trying to concentrate it into . . .

something. He was acting on instinct and hoping it was the System giving him a nudge, basically.

As he continued, it kept fighting him, and Edwin had to give it every last bit of strength he could muster behind his Skills. Perception was tuned to its max in Basic Mana Sense, and he just kept pushing, and pushing . . .

Edwin felt like a mad scientist and he *loved* it. Working in a small, cramped lab with a thunderstorm raging outside, surrounded by bubbling brews? This was the *best*. He was concentrating raw power at his literal fingertips, and all he needed now was a good maniacal laugh timed with a lightning strike and he'd be set.

Trying to accomplish that wasn't worth the distraction, though, so he pushed on. As he continued to push on the bead of energy, he began to feel imperfections of a sort. Or not really imperfections. Just . . . well, refinements he could make, by excluding aspects of his mana.

As he did so, the drop of mana brightened as it shrank, until eventually every last refinement he could make was complete, and a tiny star of mana shone at the tip of his finger.

Edwin grinned tiredly as he looked at his accomplishment. A tiny star of magic was at his fingertips, and it had clearly taken a lot out of him. He was actually *hungry*, for goodness' sake. He'd eaten barely a week ago, he shouldn't be feeling hungry yet. When was the last time he'd drank? That he was less sure about, but it should have still been at least a few days before his mouth was as dry as it currently felt.

Still, if regular food and drink was what it took to make this, it was worthwhile.

The tip of his finger descended into a beaker of sinbalyne extract, and the mote vanished into the solution, providing the lavender liquid an almost glittery quality. He grinned at the sight, but also the sensation that accompanied it.

He could still feel the pure mana connected to him, and he could feel the aspects present in the sinbalyne. He could still Refine the potion, use his Refined mana to direct how his creations turned out, even after releasing them. This was *great*.

Someone was saying something to him, but Edwin waved them off. He was really close to figuring this out, he could tell. And he didn't want to break his concentration and risk having the connection he felt to his potion be broken. No, that wouldn't do at all. He needed to keep working.

He pushed his Perception into the potion, feeling Alchemy come alongside him and point out the flaws in the mixture, the ways in which the unrefined plant made for a suboptimal elixir. He could fix it, though. He knew he could.

His mana swirled around like a swarm of distant stars, dancing at his command. He felt where there was a bit of pollutant in the sap, from a slight excess in the soil. Perhaps the pH was off or something. Whatever was the cause, it didn't matter. Edwin could fix it.

The stars swam back and forth, surrounding and attacking the imbalance. It broke into pieces, and then into mana. Edwin grinned. It seemed that not only did Refining reduce the number of impurities in a potion, but it turned those impurities into strength. No wonder it was an evolution of Purify.

Ah, there was the chemical responsible for sinbalyne's painkilling aspect. Edwin couldn't identify the molecule, but its purpose was clear thanks to Alchemy. In another potion, he would want to enhance that aspect of the potion, but not here. Right now, he wanted to distill everything into the plant's ability to interact with Stamina and other Attributes. Nothing else mattered. Heck, ideally he could even get rid of the fact the plant *interfered* with Stamina, maybe even spin it into an ability to boost the Attribute, but he was getting ahead of himself. For now, just try and isolate the part of the solution that interfaced with Stamina.

It was tricky to find, really. Not because it was hidden so much as because Edwin didn't realize what he was looking for until he'd found almost everything else. How long did it take? He had no clue. Probably hours, but he wasn't keeping track of the time. All external stimuli had been relegated to "deal with later" status. For all he knew, the thunderstorm might have ended by now. He wasn't looking and risking that it might break his concentration.

The fact the substance interfaced with Stamina wasn't so much an *aspect* of the potion, he'd found. Rather, it was what *he* was interacting with. The mana in the potion was capable of destroying and converting parts of the solution just fine, but what made it all so responsive was that the solution itself was helping him. He was controlling the entire solution with his mana, not just the energy itself. It was that interaction that allowed sinbalyne to interfere with Stamina. If he were to bet, it probably also interacted with Health as well. It was simply compatible with Attributes.

Did that mean he might be able to use Basic Mana Manipulation to control his Health?

No, bad Edwin. Think about that later.

Once he'd figured out that revelation, it was relatively simple, if a bit tedious, to drag the solution off to one side, pulling along all the potion that Health directly interacted with, and leave all the excess behind. At this point, he'd converted a lot of the sinbalyne into mana and so had a lot of substance to work with. Had he tried this before eliminating contaminants, he wouldn't be able to do nearly as clean of a separation, both because there would be a lot of additional things to try and pull free but because he'd have a lot less mana to work with. Sort of like trying to dig out the foundations for a house with a hand shovel.

He'd run through the process several times, separating the sinbalyne aspects that he wanted and discarding the rest. Now, he had a small thimbleful of pure mana-attracted solution, and several stages of waste. Okay, that stage was done. Now, he just needed to . . .

"Edwin!" The voice cut through his focus not because of its volume but because of the associated smack.

"Ow! What was that for?" He nearly dropped the precious Refined liquid in surprise, but after the heart-stopping moment, managed to save it without losing so much as a drop. "Actually, don't answer yet. Give me a minute."

He carefully set the container down on the counter and encapsulated the entire thing in a solid apparatite container. He wasn't going to risk *anything* with that. It was tricky, as the entire time he had to ignore whatever it was that Inion was trying to say. He'd get to her, this was more important. He gently set the solid block of apparatite down and turned around to see his friend.

"Yes, Inion?" he asked, "What is it?"

"Drink!"

"Oh come on," he complained. "You know I don't need to drink water every day. I could avoid drinking water for a month and a half without dying."

"Doesn't mean you should! You *know* you need to drink water every week."

"And?"

"It's been two!"

"Two . . . what, weeks? Please, I drank like . . . four days ago?"

"When you *came in here*, maybe. But after you were staring at your finger for a week and then poking at your potion for the last two days, it has been two weeks *exactly* since you had anything to drink." She shoved his water bottle in his hands. "Now drink."

Edwin leveled a glare at the fey. "Come on, I know it hasn't been that long." He did drink from the canteen, though. He was no more hydrated now than he had been after he finished initially Refining his mana, and his mouth was quite dry. "You don't need to pull my leg."

"I'm not," she said, gesturing outside. "Take a look for yourself if you want."

Edwin played along, humoring the girl, poking his head out to see . . .

Oh, huh. They were still in the midst of endless grasslands when he started. Now, though, there were some sparse trees scattered about. Not a forest by any reckoning, but endlessly more than what he had been accustomed to seeing. Never mind that there wasn't a cloud in the sky and that it was apparently *morning*, which meant Edwin had spent at least a full day in his lab.

"The dead awaken!" Lefi called out. "Well, not dead, but you certainly did not respond to anything we attempted to expose you to."

Edwin stretched as he dropped off the carriage. His muscles were unusually bunched up, which if it *had* been a week would make sense.

He yawned, more out of a sense of obligation than actual tiredness. "Was it *really* a week?"

"Give or take a day, yes. You seemed . . . focused." The man withdrew a cloth-wrapped package from one of his belt pouches, tossing it to Edwin. Hmm. He'd grown inured to the sight of seeing something be retrieved that was bigger than the container it came from, but this was perhaps the first time he saw something that was bigger than the *opening* of the container as well.

"Guess I was," Edwin admitted. He easily snagged the bundle from the air and unwrapped it, revealing a pastry that Almanac and Alchemical Analysis told him was filled with some kind of meat.

He took a bite and nodded in appreciation. It was actually *good*, which meant that none of his traveling companions could have made it. He, of course, was banned from cooking for Lefi, Yathal, and Kyni until they figured out if Arcadian Elixir was hazardous. Generally, he disliked what they made for much the same reasons, though he'd usually still make a bit of food for himself whenever Lefi or Kyni hunted something.

But that this meat pastry actually tasted *good* to him meant . . .

"We passed through a town?"

Lefi nodded. "A few days hence, there was a delicious town with a tiny little bakery."

Then Lefi frowned. "A tiny little *town* with a delicious *bakery*, and we all enjoyed what we got, and thus determined you might like some as well once you had finished!"

Edwin nodded appreciatively. Whatever Skill nonsense was going on meant that the pastry was *still warm*, and it was just what he needed to help take his hunger away at the moment. Whatever levels the baker had clearly were more than enough to surpass Arcadian Elixir's effects, and Edwin was grateful to have something that tasted so good that he didn't have to make himself.

"So," he asked around a mouthful of food, "what else did I miss?"

Lefi thought for a moment. "Nothing you might find relevant to your adventure. The thunderstorm persisted for some time; however, since that time we have experienced more overcast and sunny days. Yathal has been getting a bit bored without your training to watch, but that is all."

"Yeah! More hitting!" the bloodthirsty little scamp cheered from his position riding Kyni, and Edwin just barely managed to restrain himself from sticking his tongue out at the boy. *It wouldn't be proper*, he told himself.

. . . and his mouth was still full of meat pastry.

He finished scarfing down the food in a couple more minutes—the wonderful flavor leaving him far, far too soon—and took another deep drink from his canteen. He handed the cloth back to Lefi, who flashed a Skill and cleaned the rag in the blink of an eye before he tucked it back into his belt pouch.

"What magnificent creation have you come upon now, my friend? Surely after a week of work you must have something truly special, no?"

Edwin shrugged. "I'm not entirely sure, honestly. I was just following my gut and was trying to concentrate and include mana in a potion. I'd finally gotten Refine to level, see. So I wanted to follow that instinct as much as I could just to see what would happen."

"And? Surely, the great and mighty Edwin Maxlin, Alchemist-Errant extraordinaire, alchemical revolutionary must have some sort of magnificent result?"

"That's not how science works," Edwin sheepishly admitted. "If I did make anything, it would probably be really minor. All that it was was a proof of concept. Though admittedly Skill leveling makes it sort of a directed leveling . . . huh. What does make Skills level for knowledge-based abilities? If I do something right, does that level it? Does the universe automatically tell me when I'm doing something right? That doesn't seem like it's true given what was going on in Panastalis . . . anyway! I'm getting distracted. Basically, don't expect anything too special. But you might know better than I what it is, given your Common Knowledge Skill."

"Did you not obtain it?"

Edwin replied, "You were there when I tried. But no, my Identify upgrade just lets me see what things are made of. Useful in some situations . . . I really should use it more, but I just have so much stuff to do it can be pushed off to the back of my mind a lot. Anyway! I'm getting distracted again. Let me grab the result."

He ducked into his lab to Inion's vocal complaint, "Don't you go back in there before you sleep!"

"I'll be just a minute! I promise!"

"I will be *making* you fall asleep in a minute, young man!"

"You're not my mother!"

"Stop making me act like it, then!"

"I'm just going to show Lefi this and get him to Identify it. That's all, I promise!" Edwin protested.

He was really good at avoiding Inion's "attacks" at this point, which meant even with her interposed between him and his lab bench, he was able to sneak around and snag the crystal block containing his precious potion like she wasn't even there.

He pulled the potion back to Lefi, who took one look at the fluid— eyes flashing with Identify tinged with a sort of bluish-red, the color of Common Knowledge—and let out a low whistle.

"High-grade Stamina catalyst, according to this."

"What?"

"Not an alchemist, so I don't know much. But I'm pretty sure this is what you'd need to interact with Attributes such as Stamina. It is, of course, nothing less than I would expect from the brilliant Edwin!"

"Why do people keep saying I'm smart?" Edwin minorly complained. "But that doesn't explain why it would be 'high-grade,' not as a prototype. Unless maybe my Skills compensated for it, now that this interacts with the System in some way?" he wondered aloud. "Man, what does my Refining Skill look like now, I wonder?"

He started to turn his attention to his Status, but before he could even fully formulate the thought, his sleep-deprived brain not so much sluggish as unruly, a presence slammed into him.

"Minute's up!" Inion descended upon him like an avenging angel, a Skill forming in her throat. In a moment of panic, he recognized it as Restful Song, which would absolutely knock him out in no time flat. Unless maybe his Adaptive Defense was against sleeping? Would the Skill still affect him?

"Wait, wait! No!" he protested, "Just let me look at my notifications fir—"

Darkness.

CHAPTER 18

Moonlie

Edwin groggily groped his way into wakefulness, nearly smacking Inion in the face as he stretched. The fey was curled up next to him in her usual position. It was . . . it was nice, he decided. Physical contact, or really just proximity really, was a way he could feel connected to people even if the emotions he wanted weren't there.

He couldn't really describe it, either, or put his finger on why exactly it was so nice, so he could replicate it without people involved. Perhaps it was just the fact that touch implied the person preferred in some way his proximity over someone else's? No . . . that couldn't be it, he didn't think. Otherwise group hugs wouldn't have been appreciated.

Maybe because it reminds me of—

A faint tickle in the back of his head reared its head, but he squashed *that* particular emotion and associated train of thought before it could get anywhere. He wasn't . . . he wasn't going to think about that. Edwin blinked hard and rubbed his eyes *because they were sore*. Because he had just woken up and was trying to get the sleep out of them.

Apparently, not sleeping for a week then falling asleep for at least sixteen hours was a good way to build up a lot of crust in his eyes, and he found himself picking the accumulated stuff out of his eyelashes as he lightly touched down on the ground. Yathal and Kyni were curled up together on a blanket nest on the driver's seat, and the dog perked up to see what the disturbance was before giving Edwin a brief nod—that would never not be kind of weird—and tucking his head back in with his boy.

Bill had his legs folded underneath him, sleeping in the grass a short way off the road. It was kind of interesting, as Edwin had always vaguely thought that horses and ponies slept standing up, but it seemed that wasn't the case, or at least not always.

Off to one side, Lefi sat with his back to a tree, keeping watch. He had his sheathed sword resting on his knees, and Edwin sensed a few Skills flickering in and around the man indicating that he really was awake despite his closed eyes.

"Couldn't sleep?" Edwin asked, gently setting down in the grass next to Lefi. He kept Flight active, though; it provided the *best* back support.

"I rarely do." Lefi's voice was much more restrained at night, presumably as to not wake up any of the others.

"Really? So then all those nights when we were first traveling together and we bunkered down in the . . . whatsit shrines, you didn't actually need to sleep?"

"No," Lefi replied, "but you would feel bad if you felt like you were slowing me down, and it was valuable that you learned of a safe place to rest. There's not that many of us, we need to keep an eye out for one another."

There was a flicker of a Skill, and Lefi withdrew a pair of mugs and a flagon of . . . something Edwin hadn't Almanaced yet. Some kind of cider, it looked like? The Adventurer poured a steaming cup for each of them from the flagon.

"Is it alcoholic?" Edwin asked as he accepted the mug, to Lefi's shaken head. "Thanks."

It was good . . . but not great. Edwin silently cursed his Arcadian Elixir and tried to renew his reminder to figure out some kind of normally tasteless powder that he could add to food and drinks and allow him to properly enjoy food he hadn't made again.

"'S good," he thanked Lefi, and he received a nod in acknowledgment. Edwin, who finally got the chance to fully process what Lefi had said, frowned. "Hey . . . I wouldn't have felt bad about slowing you down."

Lefi didn't even have to say anything, even the low light provided by the pink and blue moon sufficient to display his clear look of skepticism.

"Okay, okay," Edwin backpedaled. "I might have felt a bit bad. But still!"

Lefi shrugged as he took a deep draft of his drink. "I didn't wish to burden you with anything else. It was clear you were unused to this world, and I wanted to make the transition as easy as possible."

"Oh come on," Edwin protested. "Does *everyone* know?"

Lefi grinned. "If you keep confirming it like that, then eventually."

Edwin shot a glare at the man, who hid his smile in his mug. "What gave it away?" he finally asked with a sigh.

"Your cover story about coming from Fieresal is all right, but Tara came up with it?"

Edwin nodded.

"She knows better, of course, but she hasn't internalized that the System exists outside of the Empire. She hasn't fully grasped what it means that it is *truly* worldwide and not only found in Liras, though they are admittedly the most advanced in its use. So, you coming in from the Unknown Lands to her would make perfect sense as to why you'd have no Skills, no Attributes. But you hadn't even taken the Beginner Path, didn't have the Child Path, and were missing so many Skills and Paths that someone like you would have naturally accumulated from your life. That meant you must have had either your entire System reset or come from somewhere without the System itself, making you an Outsider. Because of how little you knew of the nature of Paths and Skills, it probably wasn't the former. My little question just now confirmed the latter."

"I feel like there are other possibilities than just those two," Edwin said with a frown.

"Ah, but now I don't need to think of them. So thank you for that." Lefi flashed a grin that even in the poor lighting Edwin could see just fine.

He rolled his eyes and took a sip of his cider. "Well, good job I guess. Do they know?" he asked, nodding his head toward Yathal and Kyni.

Lefi shook his head. "You're doing a lot better nowadays. Instead of some strange figure with absurdly low-level Skills, you're a bit closer to either a slacker or a perfectionist with such high-level first-tier Skills and decent progress on your second. So long as you don't give anyone a complete list of your Skills and Paths, your secret should be safe so long as you remain somewhat circumspect when answering questions. Your Registrar probably knows, or at least suspects, but that's probably about it."

They sat in silence for a minute, and Edwin tried to remember what it was he wanted to do . . . eh, probably not important. Eventually, Lefi spoke back up, breaking the silence.

"Do you want to talk about your world?"

Edwin sighed. "Not . . . not right now, I think."

"So. . ." he transitioned to a different topic. "You don't sleep?"

"I don't need to. Naturally, I still benefit from it, but with the Power Nap Skill, I need but a few minutes per day. Otherwise, I use Meditate. It is quite relaxing and perfect for allowing time to pass, but I retain enough awareness of my surroundings to know when I need to break it. Very useful for keeping watch or noticing would-be sneaky Adventurers leaving a note for me and trying to leave."

"Touché," Edwin conceded. "I suppose Watchful Rest does something similar for me. Not that Inion would hear anything about setting up a night watch while she's traveling with me. Something about nothing on this side of the continent being able to threaten her."

"Hmm. Possibly true for wild and magical animals, though she is distinctly less powerful than a veteran soldier."

"I don't think I've actually met any. How would I know if I did?"

Lefi grinned. "You'd know. Veterans are the elites of the army, usually with hundreds of Skills all geared to fighting. When not upon a battlefield they may not be that particularly useful, but sometimes that doesn't really matter. I saw one drive off a dragon all on his own, now *that* was a glorious battle to witness."

"Dragons, eh? I've heard them mentioned a few times, but are they common?"

"I wouldn't say 'common' describes them. You'll always be in the territory of at least one dragon, but never close to any. To them, all this? The efforts of avior, humans, gnomes, all that? It's nothing. We have to strive and strive to reach the level of even a newly hatched wyrmling, and they only get stronger the longer they live. If you ever have to fight a dragon, my first advice is 'don't.' Run, as far and as fast as you can, and hope that's enough. If that doesn't work, find an army and hope you're the last one left standing."

"Have you ever fought a dragon?"

Lefi let out a low bark of laughter. "I'm still alive, aren't I?"

"Well, I don't know . . ."

"Nope. I've run from a dragon a few times, though. Stolen from a couple of hoards, too," he added with a grin. "Now *that* was a rush, and so far as I know Sennangraska is still looking for me to this day. If I ever get back there . . . ha. That won't go well. So much venom, but the Paths were so worth the price. Dragons are one of the very few creatures where nearly any interaction will award you with Paths, and the Dragonslayer Path is the *golden* standard for trophy Paths."

"Right!" Edwin realized, before quickly clamping down on his volume. He mouthed a *sorry* to Kynigos and waved his hand when Lefi motioned for him to continue.

"I just finally remembered what I was trying to do before Inion . . . put me to sleep." Edwin wasn't bitter, he wasn't. Inion . . . Inion just wanted what was best for him. She could be a bit pushy at times, but who couldn't? Sure, he might not agree with her all the time, but when did he ever? There was no lasting harm, he could let this slide this time.

"I wanted to see my Skill levels," he explained. "I figure I probably got *something* good from all that work, right?"

"Indeed. Let us see what your rewards for your endeavors are, shall we not?"

Implied familiarity aside, Edwin agreed with the sentiment and with bated breath, pulled up his System.

Notifications.

Congratulations! For going a full night without sleep you have unlocked the Insomniac Path!

Congratulations! For going a week without sleep in pursuit of a single goal you have unlocked the Sleepless Disciple Path!

Congratulations! For concentrating and altering your personal

mana you have unlocked the Attuner Path!
Congratulations! For magically distilling a potent alchemical
solution, you have unlocked the Mystic Alchemist Path!
Congratulations! For successfully creating an elixir based on
metaphysical concepts you have unlocked the Practical Alchemist
Path!
Level Up!
Skill Points 779→816 (Average level: 45)
Alchemical Analysis Level 28→31
Alchemical Dismantling Level 27→33
Alchemy Level 86→89
Arcadian Elixir Level 28→30
Prototyping Level 28→29
Refining Level 2→21
Ritual Intuition Level 28→30
Sapper's Apparatus Level 50→51

Edwin let out a low whistle. He'd gotten twenty levels in Refining from his work, which was impressive but still paled in comparison to the *three whole levels* he'd earned in Alchemy. He might actually hit his goal of reaching level 120 in the Skill and getting the Alchemy Specialist Path in a halfway reasonable time if he could recapture some fraction of that rate going forward.

It would still take *ages*, though. At least he didn't have to deal with Skill point debt anymore, that was nice. Maybe he *could* go for Health Manipulation or Stamina Manipulation if they existed . . .

"Hey, Lefi. Are there Skills like Basic Mana Manipulation for any of the other Attributes?"

"Whatfor do you mean?"

"Well, like in trying to manipulate Stamina or whatever. Perception is easy to control, but are there any Skills that would let me use Health-based Skills or Stamina-based Skills actively? Not like your passively magical Skills or whatever that just draw on your mana, but something more like my . . . mage nonsense."

The Adventurer stroked his chin. "I can't say that I do know of any that would fill that role, no."

Edwin sighed. "Pity, I suppose. It would be cool. Any chance it's still a Skill that you just don't know about?"

"That is always a chance! The System is as vast and incomprehensible as any other part of the world!"

"Hmm. You know, now that I think about it . . . did I already ask you? Ah, whatever. What's your take on the System? Why does it exist?"

"You do not have one where you are from, yes?"

Edwin nodded, and Lefi hummed in thought. "The System is said to be as old as the world itself. You may as well ask why the Verdant exists, or why the mountains are the places they are."

"I feel like it's a *bit* different than that, though," Edwin protested. "Also, I feel like those things do have explanations. They did on my world anyway. Not the Verdant part—we didn't have magical forests— but the mountain part."

Granted, he wasn't really expecting to get too much more from Lefi; his answer lined up well enough with everyone but Inion's reaction. The fey, of course, just said she couldn't tell him, but he was starting to suspect that might also have been her answer for when she didn't know something and didn't want to admit it.

"Like, come on, none of those are natural language-comprehending magical programs that give you supernatural abilities. Heck, why wouldn't you wonder about that? It's certainly more interesting than where *rain* comes from."

"Perhaps. But I am certain that greater minds than mine can accomplish such a magnificent task. I don't bother myself with it."

Was there something about the System that made people not question where it came from? Other than the ubiquitous answer that the System was created alongside the world, Edwin hadn't heard any myths about the creation of the world. Hmm . . .

"What about the world itself, then? Where did that come from?"

"It was . . . created alongside the System as the gods spoke it into being. From there, the System brought forth life and chose several animals from among its numerous herds, granting them the ability to see their Status. To this day, sometimes a new creature will be chosen, to see if their kin is worthy of access to the System"—he nodded at Kyni— "and though they rarely succeed past their own life and their immediate family upon occasion, it continues to try in the hopes more might see the world for how it is."

"Is . . . is that it?" Edwin asked. "No superlong, in-depth and really boring universally accepted creation story about hundreds of gods all doing really niche things in concert? Fantasy stories clearly lied to me." He said the last part as a mumble, and Lefi didn't appear to acknowledge it.

"Ah, do you wish to know the true story of creation that I came upon in my adventures, spoken to me by the gods themselves?"

Edwin skeptically raised an eyebrow.

"I do not have such knowledge," the Adventurer explained and prompted a chuckle from Edwin.

"No, but like actually. Is that it?"

"What use do we have for the gods? They have never asked much of us, merely made their presence known. Even those who receive their blessings are rarely brought from the realm of their faithful."

"But like . . . wouldn't people still be naturally attracted to that sort of thing in the hopes they might catch the attention of literal gods? Or, you know, avoid their wrath? Heck, isn't that what's up with the Curicnan waystations or whatever?"

"It is, yes. Naturally, people continue to say their prayers to whatever god they may wish to gain or avoid the attention of, but there is not much organization around the deities beyond minor group rituals. Who would care about a being so incomprehensibly beyond any of us as to make Emperor Xares look like a first tier? No, better to focus on attempting to grow, to advance."

"I . . . don't think that's how people work," Edwin said with a frown.

"Are you not the one who says it is important to look at what is, not what ought to be?"

"When did I— I mean, yes. But I don't think we ever had that conversation?"

"It was in your discussions with Niall, I do believe."

"Right." Edwin closed the discussion. He wasn't . . . he wasn't sure how he felt about that whole debacle. He *wanted* to blame Lefi for putting him in the situation to begin with, but he knew that was complete nonsense. It was still his conclusion to go after the bandits, even if it had been . . . impaired.

Did he blame Lefi for altering his mental state, like you were supposed to for people who tried to get other people drunk, or whatever? He'd never been *in* that position, but it seemed comparable. But did the fact he was genuinely trying to help him excuse him at all, like it did with Inion? Edwin . . . wasn't sure.

Lefi tried to say something else, but Edwin mumbled that he was glad for the talk, he was just going to go for a bit of a walk. Yes, he'd yell if he needed help. He just needed a bit of fresh air and a bit of space.

The moon was full once more. Had he ever seen it *not* be full, actually? Was this one of those things that was just different on Joriah? Maybe the moon actually glowed instead of just reflecting the sunlight? Eh, he'd keep an eye out for it now that he thought about it.

Edwin floated along on his back, gazing up at the sky in thought. Should he pass judgment on Lefi for trying to help him, albeit in a suboptimal way? He more or less excused Inion for a similar thing, but it wasn't as much of a blunder. She may not have respected his autonomy much, but at least it was only in minor ways.

Now, Lefi certainly had learned from his mistake, so that was a positive. But it was only thanks to his actions that Edwin had found himself in mortal peril to begin with at that point. But maybe it helped him realize he wasn't ready for mortal peril?

Yes, it was mortal peril of his own making, and he probably couldn't blame Lefi for his decision to stay and fight once he did know of Niall's crimes, but he stood by that decision as well. In retrospect, sure. Lefi would have killed all the bandits if Edwin hadn't, but he didn't know that at the time. He would have had to find an authority figure in a town two days walking away, then persuade them that he wasn't crazy and give them directions to a tower that was almost invisible until you were up close.

If he had failed at any of those steps, Niall would have been free to carry on chopping up people and putting them in potions. Edwin might not have even been able to find the Ruined Tower again for all he knew.

But he had still been in that situation because of Lefi. And worse, it was only because of the Adventurer's aid that he had won. It didn't sit right with Edwin, not in the slightest. Had he really never won a fight, completely on his own? He'd escaped the dwarves, but apparently he had almost literal plot armor in that fight because of karma or whatever Inion was talking about. He'd fought and beat Niall and his crew, but that apparently depended on Lefi's buffing Skills.

He'd . . . managed to kill a house-sized bear, that was something. Though that had just been running like mad and letting gravity do the work, so did that really count? He'd managed to kill a panther . . . but had set himself on fire and needed Inion to ensure he didn't die from his wounds.

He'd outright lost to the bugbear assassin the dwarves had sent after him, and only the last bit of karmic repayment and Inion saving him was the reason he was alive now. Once again, it had taken quite a bit of recovery afterward. He kept expecting the assassin to show up again with a metal arm and an eyepatch, ready for a rematch besides. You *always* confirmed the kill, after all. Whatever. That was getting off track from his brooding.

Then there had been that random bandit. He'd won, sure. But he also suffered quite the wound in the meantime. Sure, he was fine, but that was just a . . . random person with like one or two fighting Skills at most. If he had been a Lirasian Farmer initially, Lirasian Reaper was probably just one or two Paths away.

Edwin sighed. At least he had been able to beat a spider, though again he was injured. What if it was just a little bit worse? Were his claims to fame, when down to purely his own merits and skills, really running away from a bear, getting badly stabbed while fighting a farmer, and killing a spider?

He wanted to be *strong*, darn it. He didn't want to have to depend on the whims of other people to determine if he'd be safe. His training matches with Lefi might have progressed . . . adequately, but the man still seriously outclassed him, and Lefi himself said that he was far from the best direct fighter out there.

If Edwin came across someone who was actually good at what they did and wanted him dead, if he didn't have someone helping him either invisibly or obviously, was he just doomed? Probably, in all honesty. He might be able to run. Maybe. But that wasn't good enough.

Gah. He wanted to run off into the night and prove that he was capable of standing on his own two feet. But that would be really, really stupid. He couldn't, and he knew he couldn't. So . . . he was stuck with people. Ugh.

Edwin swatted at a branch, annoyed with himself as much as he was anyone else. Why did people have to be so complicated? He needed people but didn't like them . . .

Oh woe is me, he sarcastically mused. *Having really strong people who want to and* can *help me. How much better off I would be without them, probably lying dead on the side of the road or in the middle of the Verdant somewhere.*

He found another branch to swat at. Why did *he* have to be so complicated? He needed himself but didn't really like his own emotions at times. Things would be so much simpler without emotions.

He held back a scream of frustration. Even out in the middle of nowhere, he didn't want to let his frustration be that obvious. He didn't want to make Lefi think he was having emotional issues, after all.

Right, because the mumbled and sudden excuse trying to get away from Lefi totally didn't clue him in. Ugh. I would be lucky if he didn't think I hated him now. He doesn't seem to dislike me that *much, maybe I was just being paranoid last time? Or maybe it is the extrovert thing. I don't know, why is this so hard?*

Sure, he knew that everyone was an emotional wreck with their own unique concoction of problems, but really. Who wanted to get close to someone who was clearly having emotional problems that they couldn't deal with? Well, sure. Some people would. But they'd be primarily attracted *to* his emotional problems, either out of pity or some misguided attempt to try and help, and he didn't want to deal with either of those motives.

Now, emotional *vulnerability*. . . that was supposed to help, right? He was pretty sure it was supposed to. Not that it ever had for him in the past.

Ah, whatever. Maybe he'd find a friend at some point. A peer, rather. Not someone like Inion, for whom he was at best some kind of pet. She clearly didn't see Edwin as worthy of taking care of himself, or having his own opinions. But was that really so bad? She did care about him, he was pretty sure. She just had her own ways of showing it. And he *did* have trouble taking care of himself, clearly. That's why he was moping under the cotton candy–colored moon away from everyone instead of dealing with his emotions in a healthy manner . . . not that he knew what a healthy way to deal with his emotions *was*.

Wasn't it talking to people? He was pretty sure that talking to people was supposed to help. Maybe emotional vulnerability tied in there somewhere? He couldn't remember. So should he talk about his feelings with Inion?

Eh, going off past experience, Inion probably either wouldn't take him seriously or might even laugh at him if he tripped over his explanations at all. Granted, that one time he *had* been saying some pretty stupid stuff, so maybe he did deserve it?

No.

Edwin shook his head.

No.

He wasn't about to share with Inion. No way. That was just asking for problems there. Sharing stuff with Lefi might make the overeager Adventurer try to spend even *more* time with Edwin, but it would just be out of pity.

Actually, that was the problem overall, wasn't it, what it always came down to? He didn't want to be *pitied*. He didn't want people spending time with him because they felt *bad* for him. He didn't want a babysitter making sure he didn't kill himself, he didn't want sympathy from people to be the pillar of their relationship.

No. *No.*

That would *not* be him. He refused. If someone were to want to spend time with him, he wanted it because they chose it, not out of some sort of obligation. Nobody was obligated to do anything for him, any more than he was obligated to do things for other people. You didn't "owe" anyone *anything* inherently.

What did he even have to complain about? Oh no, he had it so hard on Earth. All basic needs he could ever want taken care of. Went to a decent school, had decent grades. Wasn't a complete hermit unless he wanted to be. He just didn't have anyone who *preferred* his time. So what if he couldn't just spontaneously do something with someone? He didn't *need* that anyway. He could just read, or work on homework.

He wasn't jealous of people who were always off with their friends, not in the slightest. Every picture posted of them going swimming in the summer just meant they didn't have an internship. All those times they watched a movie in a group meant they weren't studying for the next test. Who really lost out there? He certainly didn't. His life was great! He was just fretting over literally nothing.

He could make friends, sure! He already had . . . like six people who could stand his presence. Inion, Lefi, Yathal, Kyni, Fissath, Tara . . .

Eh, Tara probably didn't count. It was her job to put up with him, after all.

Rizzali, maybe? Hmm. Nah, it was his job as well and he cared more about Edwin's unique Skills than anything.

Actually, Kynigos didn't count, either. He was a dog, and dogs weren't exactly choosy about what humans they liked. Edwin wasn't counting "not hated by dogs" as an *accomplishment*.

Of course, that meant that *Yathal* probably didn't count, either. He was just a kid and Edwin was the cool older Adventurer who had potions and could fight with a stick and had magic. If he didn't come across as cool to a kid when he could do literal magic tricks, he was doing something terribly wrong.

Did Lefi count, then? The guy seemed to like everyone, but that just put his approval at about the same level as dogs and kids. He was basically an anime protagonist; you'd have to literally kick his face in to *maybe* get him to dislike you.

Edwin buried his face in his hands in shame. Did that make him the sulky supporting character who only existed to show how gosh-darn cheerful the hero was, because look at how mopey that person is and, wow, aren't you glad *he's* not the protagonist? How the hero would do something to win over his affection and then he'd be relegated to the back seat for the rest of the story?

Please, no. Just . . . no.

Okay . . . so, moving on from Lefi . . . Well, there was Inion. But did she *enjoy* being around him, or did she just like being away from the water? He wasn't sure, but given how much time she spent just loung-ing around every day . . . could she really like *him* that much?

Well, she at least tolerated him, that was all he was looking for anyway.

Yay.

Edwin kept floating around for a while, watching the moon slowly rise as he thought about all sorts of different stuff. He messed around with Prototyping some—*man,* the Skill was leveling at an insane rate lately; the double boost from Lefi and Inion apparently stacked with some Skills and was really great—and tried juggling apparatite from his back, and upside down.

The stars were very beautiful, and the sky was just as spectacular as always. Earth's sky had never gotten old to him, what with him liv-ing out in the middle of nowhere and with minimal light pollution to interfere. The infinite variety of the stars endlessly entranced him, and he always pitied the people who never saw the stars because they lived in cities.

Here, though? If he thought dark nights on Earth were spectacular, they had *nothing* on the astral tapestry above him now. Even the light of the moon couldn't wash out the sheer variety of colors on display, and he was endlessly entranced by the display above. He couldn't help but wonder how much of the detail was because of the complete lack of light pollution, and how much was just the result of his Seeing Skill. They both were bound to be contributing.

He really should stay awake more often. This time of night, every-thing was *phenomenal,* not that the earlier hours, when he was normally awake and admiring them, were any less brilliant. Night was so nice, and he was looking forward in some regards to Watchful Rest getting to the point where he could stargaze *while* sleeping, and just generally enjoy the night. After all, there were fewer people, less noise, less clutter, more stars . . . there were no downsides.

That was when Edwin noticed the eyes.

He'd always thought it was stupid, the idea of glowing eyes in the darkness, letting you know that some sort of dangerous predator was lurking in the dark. They were always bloodred and hungry. Sometimes slitted. Never friendly. And always hundreds, opening up one at a time to slowly reveal a pack of ravenous wolves.

But these eyes *probably* weren't glowing. No, they were just reflecting the moonlight from above, which made it *look* like they were glowing, right? They probably weren't red, either; that was just the pink light of the sky, surely. They weren't slitted, either. Just a vast array of red, luminescent orbs with a perfect circle of darkness taken out of the middle.

They *did* look hungry, though.

And there *were* a lot of them.

CHAPTER 19

Where There's Smoke

Edwin was torn. His first reaction was to run away, but *that* reaction was overridden by his desire to prove he could take care of himself by fighting off whatever pack of animals was next to him. *That* reaction was in turn subsequently vetoed in favor of yelling for help from Lefi, though.

Identify was no help. Whatever was attacking him, he couldn't get a proper read on them to get a response. That meant one of two—well, really three—things. Either Edwin couldn't properly focus on any of the eyes individually as to Identify *it* and not its neighbors, and the alternative was just that whatever it was didn't have an Identify tag, meaning it wasn't actually alive. He wasn't betting on that one. The third option was that it could hide from his Identify, which while possible was not something he'd encountered. To be on the safe side, he was once again assuming the first scenario was most likely.

It wasn't very flattering to his mental state, though.

"Lefi! Heeeellllpp!" he yelled into the silent night air, disturbing the gentle peace countless insects had so delicately established.

He scarcely looked back in his headlong flight, more interested in getting away than seeing how close whatever pack of predators had literally glowing red eyes was to catching up to him. He wasn't sure, but it looked like they continued to close in on him, judging solely from the terrified flashes of light his eyes caught on the edge of their vision.

By the time he slowed down, he'd left them far behind him, but he was still a bit jumpy that they might be right behind him. Fortunately though, Lefi had arrived, summoned by Edwin's yelling.

"Edwin! You are all right! When I heard your cries I feared the worst. What happened?"

"I'm fine, personally," Edwin explained, scarcely winded from his flight thanks to Breathing. "Just a bit of a scare. Some pack of creatures nearly pounced on me. Glowing eyes and all that, you know?"

"I'm afraid I do not, at least not especially. But there is a beast that needs vanquishing? Where might I find it? What do you know of the creatures?"

"They're magical predators of some kind. There was a big pack of glowing red eyes and they lit up on my magic sense—some kind of intense darkness. I managed to run away well enough," Edwin summarized. Those were probably the main points, right? Was there something he was forgetting? Oh yeah. "And I was having issues Identifying them. Not sure why exactly, but I don't know what they are."

Lefi perked up. "A pack of predators, you say? Is there to be a hunt tonight?" he eagerly asked.

"I mean . . . maybe?" Edwin tried. "If you . . . ah, who am I kidding? You'll be fine." He sighed. "You want me to come with you?"

Lefi patted Edwin's head, and he had to fight the instinct to shy away. "No, no. There is no need for such actions. I will be sufficient to deal with whatever attempted to prey upon you. You said it was back in that direction?"

"I . . . I think so. I wasn't paying that much attention, but I'm pretty sure it was basically a straight line that way."

Magical propulsion was much easier to ensure a consistent direction of travel than walking. After all, he didn't need to worry about obstacles other than just trees. He wouldn't be on a slight incline or need to slog through mud, after all. Hence, he felt moderately confident in saying his travel had been geometrically sound.

"Very well! If you'd just return unto the caravan, I shall return once this foe has been truly vanquished!"

The Adventurer vanished into the darkness, slipping away like a fleeting shadow. Within moments, Edwin had lost track of where the man was . . . which made sense; Lefi must have had a truly *astronomical* Stealth Skill to keep an eye on Edwin while he was with Niall for a few days while being wholly unnoticed. Vanishing into darkened woods must have been almost literal child's play for Lefi by comparison.

In any case, with Lefi off hunting the hunters meant that there was nobody at the camp, and Edwin flew off in that direction at a decent pace, not wanting to leave them all unguarded for too long when there were dangerous creatures about.

Everyone was still sleeping when he got back, and only Kynigos—did the dog *actually* sleep or not? Edwin was starting to suspect he didn't, and he just lay next to Yathal to keep the boy company—acknowledged his presence.

There was nothing else to do about it, so Edwin took a seat by the cart with a sigh and waited for Lefi to go and fight the monster for him, like he was a good little NPC.

Oy. Shut up, brain. As established, no complaining about friends being able to help out. That's how society works.

Lefi returned *very* quickly, all told, holding a dead, turkey-sized bird with black and green feathers by its talons, completely unharmed. "Edwin! I thought I was due for a fight!"

"So did I," Edwin muttered, looking at the fowl in Lefi's hand. "What's that?"

"This is a lybird! A powerful illusionist related to the peacock of the south! It summons the apparitions of glowing eyes to scare off predators! Fear not, they are mostly harmless but you are not the first to have fallen afoul of their defense!"

"Great, so I was scared away by an overgrown chicken? Wait, they're a cousin of peacocks?" he asked incredulously.

"Indeed!"

"I don't think that's how evolution works," Edwin replied. "Like . . . you wouldn't get an eagle that had a cousin with dragonfly wings. The end result may be similar, but the route taken was *drastically* different.

Also, I think peacocks don't actually use their plumage to scare off predators anyway."

"Perhaps, though it is not what Identify said!" Lefi shrugged. "But do such things truly matter?"

"Well . . . *Yes*, but I'm not a *Biologist*-Errant, and biology isn't a real science anyway so . . . no. I guess not."

Lefi looked at him oddly. "I did not comprehend your statement. Outworlder terminology?"

Edwin sighed. "Yeah, yeah. Just don't say it so loud, okay? The first time someone found out about it I ended up sort of enslaved."

"Do you want this?" the Adventurer asked, hefting the bird carcass. "I've never eaten lybird before and I want to see what it's like, but you're the alchemist."

"Oh, heck yes," Edwin hastily said. "Give me a minute to start the fire, but I can *feel* the illusion magic in its feathers from here and I just figured out what Refine does. I'll just grab everything we don't cook up. I've been meaning to make a proper smoke bomb and I think this is just what I need to take it to the next level."

Edwin was starting to get a hang of how Refine worked, he thought. He'd fiddled around with the Skill some in the intervening days (at least, when he wasn't busy driving the carriage, making up for the days he'd missed) since his all-week Alchemy session, preparing himself for the dissection of the lybird's feathers. The rest of the bird's meat—which turned out decent and didn't end up tasting like chicken—and other organs didn't show up as magical to Edwin's senses. While that didn't mean they had *no* worth to Edwin, he figured they probably weren't worth the hassle of trying to figure out what to do with them. Kynigos had eaten well that day.

For the time being, the feathers—which *did* still feel magical to Edwin's senses, reminding him of inky blackness with perhaps some other details drowned out by the void—were being kept alongside the rest of his alchemy ingredients while Edwin tried to suss out the details of his "new" Skill.

At first, he suspected it might brush alongside Alchemy Essentia. While his initial impressions had been that it had to do with System connections, it turned out to be much broader than that. His Stamina catalyst had certainly been interesting, all things considered. When he directly ingested a single drop, it lit up his Stamina across his body. It didn't seem to *do* anything directly, but it clearly interacted with it in some way. Trying to mix talsanenris in with the catalyst made his Stamina "glow," for lack of a better term, and it appeared to recover faster.

It wasn't very efficient, though, until he applied Refine to the talsanenris as well. With the higher Skill levels in Refine, and knowledge of how to use it in concert with Alchemical Dismantling, he was able to Refine a starting drop of mana in only an hour and had subsequently used that to Dismantle a handful of his dried berries into a greenish-white liquid over the course of an afternoon.

By the end, there was no trace of the berries, the magical ingredient wholly consumed by the process into a "distilled life energy" vial.

With Refining now in the 30s, and Alchemical Dismantling in the 40s, Edwin could render down a single berry in about two hours, two in two hours and ten minutes, eight with two and a half hours, and every subsequent doubling of berries required just ten minutes after that. Unfortunately, the longer he held it, the harder it was to maintain the effect, so he couldn't just continue the process arbitrarily long.

He could only Refine a single component at a time, though. If he tried to mix together a sinbalyne petal and a talsanenris berry, for example, the resulting creation would either be a Stamina catalyst or distilled life. Well, there could be other results, too, depending on what he focused on trying to Refine, but those were the primary things he was trying to create for the time being.

Then Alchemy hit level 90, and the whole world exploded into possibility.

The Skill had always provided little hints here and there, telling Edwin the rate at which he needed to mix two substances together and the like, though never the *why* before. He'd followed along with the nudges most of the time in part because the results were objectively superior to when he didn't, and in part because it was like muscle memory. Unless he *actively* tried to avoid following the Skill's guidance, he'd fall into the patterns without even thinking about it.

He still did his best to record everything with proper lab directions, of course, but he was starting to feel a bit jealous of the Empire's alchemists and their automatic transcript of everything they did.

Now, though, the Skill gave him more insight into how to make his potions turn out the way he wanted them, rather than his former blind experimentation. It didn't provide the knowledge directly, which he was grateful for, but if he provided it with a bit of Perception, he was able to . . . see the changes his potions underwent. He could tell how the color of his mixture changed in tune with his stirring rate, or the ways in which adding a bit more water would help to stabilize a volatile mixture by delaying the reaction slightly until he could add the next ingredient.

It gave him hints about temperature, quantity and timing for adding ingredients, and even what certain additions would do to a potion. Edwin made sure to ignore the Skill at times, in part out of stubbornness and in part to ensure it wasn't lying to him. It never was, but simply relying on the Alchemy Skill was what had gotten the Lirasian alchemists where they were today.

It was an additional factor to account for in his experiments, and a crutch to lean on when trying to make something new, but it was still just that: a crutch. He wouldn't get complacent with it.

Probably.

Hopefully.

He was trying to delay it as much as possible, anyway, and was still forcing himself to go through the normal hypothesis-test-results cycle that was so key to science . . . whenever he wasn't just messing around, anyway.

The Skill also confirmed his suspicions with Refining, that it was a basic form of Alchemy Essentia. He couldn't pull off some of the more impressive aspects of that particular discipline—he couldn't directly transfer the properties of one substance to another, for example—but he could use it to get effects that might not be possible with more "mundane" alchemy.

Edwin couldn't help but chuckle at the idea that *any* alchemy might be considered mundane, but that was just the nature of familiarity. No matter how impressive the subject, it would eventually become rote.

He was *really* looking forward to tearing into the lybird feathers now, though. He'd applied Refining to some of his Infused phosphorus, reducing it into powdered, chalky "fuminary essence" that consistently let off small amounts of heatless smoke and was now trying to do the same to his feathers.

Edwin breathed out. Calm helped, he'd found. If he was excited or nervous, his mana was harder to Refine. Fortunately, he had a *lot* of practice suppressing his emotions and so it only took a few minutes before he was ready to proceed.

He let his mana flow. He didn't know exactly what he was doing differently these days, but it felt so much smoother now. He would have suspected it was the result of Refining leveling, except he wasn't using it yet. He might have suspected he somehow got levels in Basic Mana Manipulation, but his Status showed that was as impossible as everyone said it was.

Or maybe I'm just getting better at this outside of the System's boosts.

He'd take some benchmarks with Flying later on. For now, he needed to focus.

Mana poured from his skin, invisible to all senses save one. Within seconds, his entire hand was sheathed in the mystical energy, but he kept at it. So long as he didn't try to control too much mana at once, he could hold on to a decent amount, but there were still limits. Thus, he was only able to spend about a minute gathering power before he activated Refining and began to feed his mana into it.

Forty minutes later, the tip of his index finger was blazing like a tiny star to his senses, and he was ready for the next stage. He lightly tapped the small stack of feathers he had at the ready, and the star vanished, spread out into the topmost feather and slowly seeping down.

Edwin mentally twisted his mana connection, designating it as his tool while he Infused his Alchemical Dismantling. Immediately, the strain present in maintaining the connection to the feather lessened. It didn't vanish, but it did become something he could use in a half-reasonable amount of time.

With his "mana knife," he slowly poked and prodded around the feather, using Alchemy to try and find the aspect of illusion—particularly one meant to hide things—that he was looking for. There was a lot here, and if he wanted to, Alchemical Dismantling would let him cut out what tiny amounts of fear-inducement, light-production, and illusion Essences that were present in the material. However, if he just used that, it wouldn't produce nearly enough for his purposes.

Instead, he needed to pull on Refining and Purify's abilities, which meant focusing on a single Essence and converting or destroying everything that didn't fit.

Eventually, he found what he wanted. Ritual Intuition, when threaded through Alchemy and Alchemical Dismantling, pointed toward the *particular* inky black cloud that would create a corresponding concealing mist in the real world, and Edwin knew what to tug on.

The aspect was ripped free, and Refining got to work. Wherever his knife passed, magical structures were torn apart like cobwebs. Some just dissipated, but others were cut in such a way that his Skill grabbed ahold of them and twisted them into matching the misty illusions.

There was a lot wasted, and the original "pattern" mana was destroyed quickly, replaced by the abundance of newly created misty mana. Overall, the process was highly inefficient. If he chose an Essence that didn't have enough base material, the process would possibly fizzle out. If he didn't use Purify to get rid of the destroyed and useless mana, it would have all clotted together and failed. If he didn't have the ability to cut the substance into raw mana with Alchemical Dismantling, or create more Essence with Refining, it would have fizzled out with no effect.

When all combined, though, the result . . . was most satisfying.

An hour and a half later, Edwin opened his eyes and looked upon his accomplishment. The feathers had been wholly replaced by a pile of what looked like powdered darkness to his Mana Sense, but in truth looked like a vaguely reflective, off-white pile of dust.

Edwin smiled.

Perfect.

A bit of testing found that the illusion dust—Obscuring False Cloud Powder, according to Common Knowledge but that was far too much of a mouthful—reflected light remarkably well, even when dispersed. If Edwin enclosed it in an apparatite ball and gave it a bit of a shake, the entire sphere turned semireflective white for the better part of an hour before the dust finally settled enough for anything to start to be visible. If it were a snow globe, it would either be the absolute best or the absolute worst, depending on what you felt the point of the decoration was.

For Edwin, it was exactly what he needed. A few tests showed that the dust wasn't flammable, making it just what he needed.

Perhaps he could have made an adequate smoke bomb with just that. He probably could, in all honesty. But why stop there? This wasn't an experiment, after all. He was just trying to make the best darn smoke bomb that he could. Later on, he'd start experimenting with different variables. This was just the prototype, and he was taking notes so it wasn't just screwing around.

The phosphorus Essence he chose to use for this had been optimized for smoke production when it burned at the expense of all else save its flammability and was appropriately named "elemental smoke." While he could try adding other types of Essence based on the element to it, Alchemy (and a bit of testing) informed him it would dilute the end result. Instead, he needed to find other ingredients and Refine *them* into ingredients that would enhance, not dilute, the effects of his potions. Thus, his current project.

Why that was the case, Edwin wasn't entirely sure. Well, beyond the magical explanation of them "polluting" each other. But that wasn't how it worked!

. . . Well, actually.

If he thought of his Essences as a sort of . . . magical allotrope of the elements he was using—and the elements were the same, he confirmed as much using Alchemical Analysis—then he knew that properties could change depending on the crystal structure of a molecule.

Was there something similar that happened with magical structures? Then, like how . . . well, that was where the analogy broke down some. Edwin didn't know of any allotropes that interfered with the properties of nearby substances, but perhaps it was like pH? Or maybe colors would be the better analogy. Shining green light and red light on the same spot didn't make "red-green," it made yellow. Whereas using a different substance might be more like changing the material the light was shone on, changing the color in that way?

"Further testing required," he promised himself. There was literally more stuff than he could focus on in a lifetime, which meant he either needed to figure out immortality, or not exhaustively delve into every topic he came across.

Probably both, in all honesty. And he'd still have deep dives into different substances. He wouldn't be able to *stop* himself. But maybe he shouldn't spend two months figuring out all the properties of a single element?

But that was how you figured out the coolest stuff! . . . and also where most research time was wasted, to be fair. And there was no way to predict what *would* be useful ahead of time. It wouldn't be research otherwise.

So what? Was he supposed to just leave potentially revolutionary ideas out to dry because he didn't have the time to explore them?

Yes, a traitorous part of him whispered, and Edwin had to admit he couldn't quite *disagree*. He just needed to get a team of alchemists also working on all this stuff, focus on the lowest-hanging fruit, *and* become immortal so he could reap the benefits of his apprentices' lifetimes of work as well.

So much to do, such few short decades to do it all in. Even though he could realistically expect to live into his triple digits. According to Lefi, having the Health Attribute tended to add at least a year to your life span per point you had in it, and that wasn't counting the massive benefits he got from Sleeping, First Aid, Purify, Breathing . . .

But that was a long, long time away. For the moment, he needed to cast aside everything that wasn't immediately useful to him. He had been picky with his Skills, he could be picky about this. He had to be, if he wanted to make any kind of headway on the *massive* project that was turning alchemy into magical chemistry.

. . . Did he *really*, though?

Edwin carefully heated his potion base, the Infused water to be kept warm but *definitely* not boiling. Yes, the extreme flammability of the phosphorus had been strongly tempered down, but he didn't want to take any risks. Well, not yet anyway. The end of the potion would definitely be risky, but there was no point in bringing that risk to bear already.

He measured out the phosphorus, which would serve as the potion's primary ingredient, gently stirring in the theoretically-not-volatile element into his beaker until Alchemy nudged at him to stop adding any more. Fortunately, Numeracy was able to record exactly how much powder that was, and so he was able to make a note for his future self fairly easily. It wasn't much, as he was only making a small batch, but he'd still need to know for when he upscaled production.

Next was just a pinch of the illusion dust, acting as more of a dye than anything. Edwin held his breath as he added the magical powder, watching as the two powders swirled around in the concoction. If he stopped stirring, the potion would settle and that wasn't something he wanted quite yet.

First, he needed to make sure it would actually burn. Normally, phosphorus *not* burning wasn't much of a concern, but he'd Refined room temperature flammability away from the element. He was still *somewhat* nervous about arycal's existence, sure. But firsthand experience had taught him that magical stabilizations should work adequately, so . . . maybe it wasn't as bad as he had first thought?

In any case, he needed to ensure his smoke bomb would ignite at the right time and not too soon or too late.

He hadn't managed to Refine molai yet—the mana-absorbing plant just gobbled up all the Refined mana he could bring to bear and cut off his connection from the magic. However, the plant's base properties should still be enough for him. Alchemy directed him in just the right way to cut and crush the flower's petals such that its mana capacity would be "fragile." In other words, the solution would accept a certain amount of mana, but once it reached capacity, the molai would release everything it had stored in one fell swoop.

When combined and primed to fire mana in the form of "alchemical fire catalyst"—Refined firevine—and assuming Alchemy was leading him properly, he would add just enough to fill the molai buffer to capacity, meaning that even a slight bit of flame or fire-based mana would ignite the entire canister.

If he did this in the future, he needed to figure out some way to keep the fire/molai mix separated from the actual smoke-making portion of his bomb until he was ready to use it. A secondary arming mechanism, basically. If only it weren't made complicated by the fact that if he didn't add the mixture prior to the concoction concluding its reaction, it wouldn't be part of the substance. Or maybe he could bypass the need for an ignition component if he used Firestarting? Something to try in future iterations.

Edwin carefully dribbled in the alchemical fire, the bright red liquid shining with some internal light. He took no chances, and each drop was taken by an apparatite stirring rod dipped into the warmed vial he kept the catalyst in, then carefully allowed to drip in. All the while, he made sure to regularly stir his beaker. If he stopped, the powders would begin to precipitate and finalize their composition, and it was much too early for that.

If he hadn't been so religiously ensuring the solution was continuously stirred, Edwin might have noticed when the concoction reached saturation. Then again, he might not have. His Ritual Intuition wasn't exactly the most *precise* sense after all, and the point of the molai was to absorb *all* the fire mana it came across. Maybe if he'd had the potion on a slightly lower temperature, he wouldn't have had the solution overload so quickly. Then again, perhaps not. By the time Edwin felt so much as a flicker of heat mana from the solution itself, it was undoubtedly too late.

Less than a heartbeat later, the overloaded molai released all the fire essence it had stored simultaneously. The infused water held it back for a second, but he could already feel the reaction kicking in. He didn't *think* it should be harmful, but he also didn't want to have to deal with any potentially burning smoke that resulted from excess fire being added to the mix.

So he grabbed the beaker and quickly poured it all into a freshly made waste container off to the side. As smoke began to billow out of the container, he realized his error and grabbed its lid to help seal in the concoction's by-product, slamming it down onto the flask.

That turned out to be a mistake, and Edwin's eyes widened as he saw another Skill step into the mix. Bomb Throwing was bringing its strength to bear, suffusing the sealed box with its effects as it prepared to blow.

"Oh—"

* * *

It had been a while since he'd caused a lab explosion, Edwin reminisced. At least this time there was no fireball involved, and he was completely unharmed. He . . . really should have seen that coming, in all honesty, and only had his eagerness to blame.

Still! At least he now had a decent idea as to how effective his smoke bombs would be. If such a small amount of that blend would produce so much smoke, what sorts of smoke screens would he be making once he really mastered the process and scaled up the payload? Now *that* was an image Edwin loved visualizing.

The container had blown its lid off the top almost immediately and instead of a puff of smoke and perhaps obscured vision for a few minutes before it all settled down, Edwin had found himself enveloped in a thick bank of fog that refused to vanish. Next time . . . he'd try using just Firestarting for ignition.

Once he realized nothing was going to come of trying to outwait the smoke while inside a poorly ventilated space, he felt his way out the door in an attempt to get some proper fresh air.

Unfortunately, the exterior wasn't much better. He had enveloped their entire caravan in white smoke, and while it blew away relatively quickly, wisps of smoke continued to cling to almost every surface, giving them all a ghostly quality.

Huh. Neat. How could he use that . . .

"You know, Edwin, you've been spending a lot of time in that carriage making potions. You haven't been dodging your training, have you?" Inion asked with a grin that suggested she already knew the answer.

"Would I be able to get away with it?"

"No."

"Well, there's your answer, I suppose."

"Well! Time for you to get out and get working, isn't it. We're three days out from Sheraith, and you still haven't figured out Overcharge."

"But what I'm doing is *important*," Edwin protested. "I'm an alchemist first and foremost. Making potions and new weapons are at the heart of what I do. I don't need to practice my Overcharge if I work instead on my primary stuff first. I'm almost done with my smoke bomb, I can feel it."

"Come on, Edwin. You've had that Stamina potion of yours for how long now?"

"Like two weeks? And it's not a Stamina *potion*, it's a catalyst."

"Precisely! In such time you might have reached a perfectly adequate level with your Skill, and possibly even wholesale mastery of its limited-area use had you been diligently practicing!"

"But I need my mana for Refining! If I use Overcharge, that knocks me down for at least the day when it comes to mana usage. All my struggling and pain is *way* worse when I actually try to purify my mana into its Refined form."

"Before you go to bed, then! Perfect. I'll get it ready for you, ya?"

Lefi chimed in, "You possess such magnificent power! I insist that you strengthen it."

Edwin glared at his trainers. "Both of you have no respect for pain, do you?"

"Pain is the body's way of letting you know you're doing something right!"

"That's . . . literally the opposite of what it does." Edwin sighed, but he knew there was no winning this discussion. "Fine, fine. I'll get to it soon. I just want to make a couple of potions to help me prepare first. It's not like I have a bunch of time for more trial and error, after all."

CHAPTER 20

Injecting Levity

Edwin picked himself up off the ground, hovering slightly. Flight was an unusual Skill in that it didn't really have a single functional axis of improvement. Well, it technically *did*—efficiency—but that was a very broad category. If he hadn't locked himself into such a low Basic Mana Manipulation level way back when, he could undoubtedly fly faster, higher, and with more power behind him like when Inion had been bound to him.

According to Lefi, it was pretty common—though not universal—that spells improved "mana efficiency" in some way, which cast further skepticism on the Adventurer's claimed status as "not a mage," but whatever. Edwin was just happy that with each level his speed, maximum height, and power behind his Flight all improved slightly. Sure, if he wanted to move at a normal jogging pace he had to be mere inches from the ground, and he was confined to a slow walk when more than a meter or so away from his support, but with every level he could go a bit faster a bit higher.

Really, it was all connected to his "tether." Activating the Skill brought the tether into existence, and it persisted until he either dismissed it or it broke. It wasn't terribly hard *to* break, all told. Just moving—or being moved—out of his maximum range was enough. Fortunately, it automatically attached to the closest valid target to him, specifically something that could support him without too much strain.

Packing didn't appear at first to work with Flight, but with some literal soul-searching thanks to Skillful Assessment, he *did* find that they were compatible . . . and already applied for his weight limits. Without Packing, he likely wouldn't even be able to lift *himself* with Flight at his current mana rate, which he decided to label as 1 arcan per second. Why arcan? Well . . . Edwin liked how it sounded.

He had tried using other people as an anchor, and he was really happy to find out that it *technically* worked, but they were still bound to the same limitations as anything else. Namely, that it had to be able to support him with very little strain. Inion while lying down? He could do that. Inion while standing up? . . . It worked, but it was very unsteady. Inion while she was floating around? Not a chance.

At least he didn't weigh *that* much. He'd always been on the scrawny side, after all, and his habits of not eating for a week or two at a time didn't help him *gain* weight, for all that it didn't harm him either.

In any case, at level 41—assuming he just had his normal gear on—and at the rate of one arcan per second, he had been able to hover just under a meter and a half off the ground while moving, or about two meters while stationary. It was a far cry from true, untethered flight, but it *did* make getting things off the top shelf utterly trivial, so there was that.

In any case, Edwin suspected that his practice with Alchemical Dismantling and his Refined Mana had improved his non-System control and throughput of mana, and he was determined to test it once again. He'd gotten sloppy with maintaining his notes on Flight benchmarks, but he had at least not missed any levels.

So, here he was once more, flexing Numeracy in an attempt to measure how far he was off the ground. Compared to his previous range of "about halfway between 1.35 and 1.62 meters," he was now at "just over 1.62 meters." Three decimeters higher with the same Flight level was . . . actually rather impressive. Certainly more than he had anticipated, at least.

He wasn't going to complain *that* much that his previously consistent mana flow was another factor to keep track of, but it *did* mean that all his future magical measurements were all but useless if it wasn't fixed at the System-provided rate.

Edwin's nonscientific part of his brain was unconditionally pleased to find out that it *was* possible to improve his mana power outside of the System's constraints. That was good to know, and while he didn't expect that he'd be throwing around lightning bolts anytime soon, he was happy to know he wasn't totally hopeless as a mage after all. He also felt like he might have been slightly more dexterous with his mana as well, that he was slightly more adept at manipulating the strands of magic . . . but that might have been his imagination.

He knew that brute force, trying to shove all nine levels of Basic Mana Manipulation he had against the inexorable tide of Overcharge mana wouldn't work. But he had real hopes for trying to tie it in knots with his newly developed proficiency in detailed mana manipulation.

Edwin found himself coughing up black phlegm by the time he called it quits on day one. Pushing himself to try and get a workable part-body Overcharge before they reached—was it Sherran? Shoroth? Ah, wherever they were going—was quite the feat, but one he definitely wanted to accomplish.

Man, *if only* he had some kind of alchemical ingredient that he already knew interacted with mana in a similar way as sinbalyne did with stamina. Maybe he could mix them, make a potion out of them that would enable his Attributes to war with and block one another?

Wouldn't *that* be nice?

Before bed, Edwin downed a new and improved Stamina/Health potion to try and help him get rid of the black sludge he was accumulating on account of his Overcharge abuse. Considering he woke up encrusted in a thin patina of what looked vaguely like charcoal . . . it probably worked? He still spent an extra ten minutes at the nearest creek trying to get it all off himself, though.

Molai.

As Edwin suspected, that turned out to be the key. Though he couldn't quite Refine it thanks to its unique, mana-absorbing properties, he was still able to incorporate it into a potion alongside sinbalyne for a sort of medium between Stamina and mana, allowing them to more directly interfere. The resulting potion even let him mess with his Stamina by using his Basic Mana Manipulation as a very rough appendage, enabling him to vaguely poke at the Attribute with the Skill.

It provided quite the nice surprise, too. Though perhaps he shouldn't have been *that* surprised?

Stamina Manipulation
Accept Skill? Y/N

He didn't take it quite yet, naturally. But unless he saw a convincing reason not to before then, he probably would after he evolved his Flight Skill. It probably wouldn't slow him that much, he tried to tell himself. Not if he was going to try and push Alchemy to level 120. That process would probably take years, and he could definitely raise another Skill or two to level 60 twice in that time frame, especially if it was likely to *assist* his alchemy. He just couldn't keep using that logic in the future was all.

The problem was, if he drank it like an elixir, it just prevented him from using Overcharge at all, the Skill not finding any purchase in his body. No, he needed to do something more . . . selective. Something that would only be in one specific part of his body for a specific amount of time and would be washed away by his metabolism.

Was this a stupid idea? Part of Edwin said it was. However, the other part of him—crucially, the part of him that had Anatomy and Alchemy on its side—said that he should be fine, just with perhaps some lingering side effects. Nothing as bad as using Overcharge *itself*, it was worth noting, but side effects nonetheless.

A few hesitant tests showed that yes, the potion worked just as good when injected directly into him as it did when he drank it, which meant the next phase of the test was a go.

He created a ring of tiny syringes. Perhaps more accurately, he created a bunch of syringe *needles*, just barely hollowed out and only open on the one side. To fill them, he just pushed the tip into his potion and activated Improbable Arsenal, the expanded space sucking in the liquid.

The initial prototype fit around his forearm, and he felt the prick of the needles push into his skin as Inion helped him equip the item.

Edwin winced, and the fey looked up in concern. "Are you all right?"

"It *pinches*," he answered. "And my Health is putting up a fit, which just makes it itch as well. Is it bad that I kind of want this to fail just so I don't have to put up with anything like this on a regular basis?"

"You'll live," Inion dismissed him—though not in an uncaring way, it seemed like? Gah, these emotion things were complicated.

"What is a bit of pain for the sake of glory, my dear friend? If you can strike a mountain in twain, surely a few pokes is a small price to pay?"

"Yeah! Punch it even harder!" Yathal piped in, and Edwin shot him a half-hearted glare. Honestly, the little scamp was so quiet he almost forgot the boy was there half the time, but when he *did* speak up it was always in the context of Edwin either being beaten up or Edwin beating someone else up.

Then again, would *he* have been any different when he was eight, and if he had the chance to see movie-level fights performed right in front of him? Probably not, if Edwin was being honest with himself. So he forced himself to not get annoyed at the kid.

"I *know* it's worthwhile, that's why I'm going through with this," he grumbled. "Doesn't mean I *like* it though. If this doesn't work, I'll have to keep looking for another way to control Overcharge. If I'm lucky, I'll find a method that doesn't hurt so much. But if this *does* work, I have better things to do with my time. Probably. Depends on how much it ends up hurting and if I figure out any alternatives."

"Mm. Okay, seems like it'll stay in place." Inion finished fussing over him, and Edwin pulled back his arm in annoyance, only to immediately regret his decisions.

"Sorry," he muttered, then spoke up more clearly. "Did you listen to anything I just said?" he asked with a sigh.

"Don't like the pain, kind of hope it won't work so you're forced to come up with a less painful version?"

"Guess you did," Edwin acquiesced.

He took a deep breath. "Well . . . it's not going to get any easier by waiting."

Edwin snaked his mana awareness to the tiny amount of magic keeping his needle syringes expanded in size. He steeled himself in preparation, and after a moment to calm himself down, yanked out all the magic and Skill structure that allowed the needles to hold more than half a literal drop of potion, forcing the liquid into his flesh and his veins.

He was already lying down, so he didn't need to worry about his balance as he turned all of his Perception inward.

It . . . seemed to be working all right. It wasn't a perfect ring of effect, obviously, as the potion diffused out into his bloodstream and beyond, but the cloud was very clearly affecting his Health and Stamina. They acted as though they were traveling through a pot of honey and quickly accumulated in the area.

Then, he activated Overcharge from the tip of his finger, and Edwin watched as the magic flooded down the length of his arm . . . and was held back by the ring of concentrated Attributes, just as he had hoped.

Some mana still leaked past, obviously, but that would be remedied with additional refinements to his setup and once he actually got a handle on how Overcharge worked exactly. Even now, it was probably within his Mana Manipulation capabilities to deal with.

Being able to confine it to just a certain part of his body was obviously huge, and beyond the obvious benefit of not making him feel like he'd been run over by a tank every time he used the Skill, the effect of the Skill seemed to be magnified. It made sense, really. The Skill still used the same amount of mana as it always did, but with it confined to such a small part of him . . .

Well, it was almost literally glowing with power. Awesome.

"Yay . . . but also dang it."

"Did your endeavor succeed?" Lefi eagerly asked. Honestly, did he have no patience or something?

"More or less," Edwin admitted. "Give me some of the rocks." He made a grabbing motion with his right hand while still reclined.

Either Lefi or Inion slipped a pebble into his awaiting palm, and Edwin easily cracked it with his increased strength. He couldn't *crush* it, no, but he could break it into pieces so long as he had a bit of leverage to use against it. So strength was working, good. Now . . . was the time Edwin wasn't looking forward to.

He nodded. "Okay. Stab me."

They didn't have long, of course, so the tests were kind of rushed and not to the standards that Edwin normally liked, but getting an approximation was better than nothing.

Of course, because he was getting *stabbed*, Edwin would have preferred it if he didn't need to test this at all, but it *was* better to be stabbed in a clinical trial than in the field. He just needed to know how capable he was of surviving a stab.

Lefi obliged him, holding down Edwin's wrist and trying to slice into his forearm.

While the initial stab used no Skills, Lefi quickly reactivated first all his truly *monstrous* number of passives one at a time, his body and wrist being flooded with a tapestry of colors, though definitely trending toward the yellow-brown and red end of the spectrum.

When none of them managed to break his skin—Edwin silently cheered behind gritted teeth of nervousness—Lefi started bringing more active Skills into play. These overlapped on the red Skills (maybe some were just active versions of his passive Skills?) but also had more black, silver, and white Skills in the mix, representing quite the array of Skill types.

Lefi kept adding low-powered Skills to the mix, and *just* before Overcharge ended, he finally broke through, the blade piercing Edwin's skin and drawing blood. Before it could get too deep, the Adventurer pulled back the blade in a truly phenomenal display of finesse.

After the Skill ended, of course, it felt like Edwin had dipped his arm in burning acid, but that was hardly new. The shallow cut was annoying, but similarly within tolerance. His pain tolerance was *significantly* higher than it had been before Joriah, after all, to say nothing of Adaptive Defense's work in that regard.

What was *more* annoying was the cut's stubborn refusal to heal. He should have expected it, but the serum designed to capture Health and Stamina did a great job of doing exactly that, and accordingly prevented his Attribute from healing the wound.

He sighed and applied a drop of healing salve to the cut. It wasn't as quick as it normally was, no doubt because Health wasn't there to guide it properly, but by the time his blocking potion wore off, the cut was already scabbed over, and he felt Health take over as he turned his attention more to Lefi.

"So? How did it go?"

"Marvelously! Your skin withstood hundreds of levels of passive Skills! And nearly a hundred active as well!"

"What does that translate to, though?"

Lefi's eyes flicked back and forth in thought. "Ah! Well, an active Skill—Piercing Cut was what finally broke through—could be thought of as being twice as potent as a passive, such as Steady Cut. As most will have but a single passive Skillset—that is, a single basic Skill and its evolution—for their weapon and a single active Skillset, or some average thereabouts, you should be fully capable of withstanding a blow from a third tier or fourth tier wholly unscratched!"

". . . What does that translate to, though?"

Lefi let out a short laugh. "You'll be able to withstand the attacks of most nondedicated Classes you come across. Few bandits will have the strength to pierce your defenses as they are rarely that strong in their combat Skills, and only the strongest beasts will be capable of scratching you. However, any who have a Combat Class will undoubtedly have little trouble wounding you assuming they bring their active Skills to bear."

Edwin nodded in thought. Honestly? The benefits were exactly what he wanted. A way to resist strong attacks and shrug off weaker ones? It might actually give him a fighting chance, the ability to defend himself!

If only the side effects weren't so painful. Heck, he'd settle for side effects that he could solve, that weren't just an inherent part of the potion doing exactly what it was supposed to. The most obvious of them was the method his very Attributes were ensnared. It wasn't instantaneous, which meant he would need to activate the potion full seconds before he actually used Overcharge.

Now, that might not have *sounded* that bad, but considering the situations in which he was likely to use the Skill tended to be superhigh-stress moments of *already* stressful fights, a few seconds was a lot. He could probably make it work, though. Once it was in place, it lasted for about a minute before the Health and Stamina it had collected overwhelmed the toxin and broke it down.

He didn't know what would happen to the mana powering Over-charge if it was still ongoing after that minute had passed, but he didn't need to worry about that! It still only lasted about twenty seconds, but that was quickly growing with every passing level.

It was a bit like applying a tourniquet, really. It completely cut off all Attribute circulation to and from his limb, and because his heart and head were where the majority of his Attributes were stored, there wasn't a whole lot of Health or Stamina in his arm to begin with. If anything somehow managed to injure him through Overcharge, or struck in the time between Overcharge ending and the potion fading away, he was in for a *very* rough time. He would be, well, fully human. No supernatural durability or endurance in the slightest. That . . . was slightly worrying, really, given how fragile humans were.

He'd just give a couple more tests to find out how it impacted repeated use of the same area, and maybe what happened if he used full-body Overcharge while his bracer was active. Now, he just needed to refill the delivery needles. . . .

"Okay . . ." Edwin panted. "That's enough for today. Thanks for not breaking the bracer off, Lefi."

His entire body ached as he worked on dismissing the apparatite pins that held the armband in place, and he sighed in sweet relief as the tight crystal released its grip. He flinched at the ring of holes in his arm reopening and watched as blood welled up and scabbed over the wounds in rapid succession. Having lots of Health in one place was great, even if the Attribute was more focused on putting him back together after so many uses of Overcharge.

"What *would* have happened if it did break off?" Lefi asked, curi-ous. Did he want something similar? There was no way the guy had Overcharge, though, so it wouldn't be any use to him.

"Well, with the combination of suppressed yet concentrated Health and Stamina, I suspect immediate-onset magical necrosis, which would rot my limb off in the matter of seconds to, or possibly even through, the bone. This would be while having twelve holes in my skin making veritable fountains of blood spurting out every second."

Both of his teachers leveled a glare at him.

"Okay, okay! Fine! It was just a joke, no need to be so touchy. I would be fine, I'd just need to make a new band, which I would anyway. Overcharging just my forearm wouldn't be enough most of the time anyway."

After all, his goals—discounting his ability to train Overcharge more effectively if his entire body didn't feel like burned meat after using the Skill; a single limb at a time would be far preferable—were to get a quick but not "final move"-level power-up that he could use to literally punch above his weight class.

Naturally, he wouldn't gain the full benefits of using the Skill in battle, but he would at least be able to continue to fight afterward. Or he could use his arm as a shield if needed, as even Lefi needed to strike at nearly full strength if he wanted to actually injure Edwin while Overcharge was active.

But all that meant he would be best served by Overcharging his entire arm, and that meant he needed to figure out a contraption that rested around his shoulder.

It ended up not being too terribly tricky, all told. A few hours of work and a level in Sapper's Apparatus later, Edwin had a ring that sat just past his shoulder, resting on his collarbone and encircling his entire shoulder. When he activated it, the potion would inject itself into the space just by his joint, empowering everything he would need to give an absolutely *massive* punch.

It did, unfortunately, leave his shoulder *particularly* vulnerable, as it wouldn't be reinforced by any of his Attributes, at least not yet. Any Health that went across that tiny sliver would be used to fight against the encroaching mana from Overcharge, and Stamina would be busy trying to get rid of the injection.

To protect his arm from being sliced off, Edwin devised a pauldron that would house the vials and also prevent someone from chopping his arm outright. For the time being, it was just made out of apparatite, but he hoped to get something stronger made for him once they made it to the city . . . whatever it was called. Sheraith?

Prototyping was especially useful in that process, and he even got a few levels in the Skill much to his delight. He just had so many Skills it was almost inevitable he was neglecting some of them as he progressed through his training.

It was frustrating, in some ways, that the exact same barriers that kept people from taking the Lefi route of getting *all* the Skills—there simply was a practical limit for which you started hitting diminishing returns for taking another Skill—had finally started coming into play. Edwin was either at or near that point, but at the same time all his Skills had their place and he wasn't sure which he would give up if presented with the opportunity.

Still, it annoyed him that even with two separate leveling boosters, he wasn't able to keep all his Skills in his training rotation. Well, that wasn't entirely true. He'd be *so happy* once he could pull Overcharge out of regular rotation . . . not that it was likely to actually happen, with this potion.

Edwin sighed. No rest for the weary.

It was kind of his fault, he supposed, for wanting to be so strong on his own two feet. If he just accepted that he was weak and would continue to be, then he would be fine . . .

But he didn't want to live at another person's mercy. Hmm. Maybe he could make a gun? If swords and arrows could be legitimate weapons here, then what amounted to an arrowhead traveling at supersonic speeds would *definitely* be an effective weapon.

He wasn't sure he trusted his ability to make pistols and pipe bombs, though. Not after the smoke bomb incident, at least.

Where was he? Oh, right. Safety at the whim of others.

It . . . it rubbed him the wrong way. After Tara had held him at swordpoint and forced him to explain his origins, he'd promised himself he'd never be in that situation again. And . . . friends might help, wouldn't they?

He looked over to where Inion and Lefi were walking, laughing as they talked about whatever it was they so dearly liked to chat about. Was it him? Probably not. He wasn't noteworthy enough for them to warrant speaking about him when he wasn't a part of the conversation.

Edwin tinkered with his pauldron prototype to try and distract himself. The needles already were separate objects from their holder, maybe he could insert them into a dedicated container that he could then expand with Improbable Arsenal? He might be able to arrange some sort of delivery contraption sort of like he had for the serum itself, where the needles popped out of their de-expanded container to jab him . . . it wasn't *ideal*, but it was better than running around with a bunch of needles constantly jabbing into him. If nothing else, it was a waste of Adaptive Defense, making it constantly be attuned to pain. It only was able to bring it down to a moderate itch anyway.

Yathal and Kyni were running around the carriage, moving fast enough they were sometimes only blurs out of the corner of Edwin's vision. He couldn't miss the laughing and barking that accompanied their play—it was the happiest they ever got outside of watching Edwin being violent—nor the occasional cry as Yathal tripped over something and skinned his knee or elbow.

Honestly, the kid was lucky the injuries weren't *worse*, and Edwin was sure it was only thanks to some Skill that Kynigos had—flaring golden every time the boy tripped—that Yathal didn't have actual road rash from such high-speed falls.

The first time it had happened, Edwin nearly sprang up with one of his healing potions, but he had been waved off by Lefi. Instead, Kynigos would always dutifully approach and nuzzle his fallen boy, before licking Yathal's injury, wiping away blood, dirt, and wounds alike.

Regardless, it meant that they could keep themselves busy and without needing to worry about what they had gotten up to. Eventually, Yathal would tire himself out and settle down into a walk or hop either onto his dog's back or the carriage itself for a ride.

Bill, of course, was completely unphased by everything going on around him. He was just a good, sturdy little pony who barely even flinched at the sound of explosions. Good pony.

Edwin hopped up onto the carriage. They were only two days out from the city, and he had more that he wanted to take care of. Sure, he was sore from overusing Overcharge, but what else was new? A quick sinbalyne-based painkiller knocked off the low-grade pain without also drugging him, meaning he was perfectly capable of doing low-grade alchemy work! He already had a bunch of stuff refined after all, and he didn't *really* know what the shelf life of his catalysts and other essences were. For all he knew, he needed to use them up quickly to ensure maximum efficacy!

Hmm . . . he'd start with his smoke bombs. Those should be quick, right? He'd almost gotten them to work last time, after all. All he'd need to do this time was exclude the ignition agent!

It wouldn't be *that* hard.

So he *did* manage to make his smoke bombs. It genuinely *wasn't* that hard, though he may or may not have gone without sleep one night to get them done before they reached the city. He was fine, though. If he could go a *week* without sleep and still be mostly cognizant by the end of it, he could do a single night and be fine.

Inion disagreed. But at least she didn't force him to sleep, just was moderately snarkier than usual at him after finding out. A small price to pay, all told.

After all, that was behind him! And his test bomb had filled a sphere more than *five meters* in radius, so Edwin was quite happy with the end result. It blew away after a few minutes, sure, but if he was outside that was plenty of time to get away, and if he were inside, the effect would last *way* longer.

He only had six at the moment and needed to Refine more illusion dust before he could make any more, but really. How likely was it that he'd need to perform more than a half-dozen "vanish into the smoke" moves while in a city, really? That couldn't *possibly* happen, right?

. . . Why did he always curse himself like that?

Anyway, they were just there to get . . . Rillah. Who was an Adventurer that was supposed to help out Yathal in some way. Edwin probably should ask at some point, or did Lefi already explain how they'd help?

In any case, Rillah hadn't been able to meet them because she was . . . held up, if Edwin remembered correctly. Held up doing what, he didn't know and he couldn't say he really cared either. He was still somewhat hesitant as to whether he would stick around with Lefi once their paths were no longer going in the same direction. Maybe he would . . . maybe he wouldn't. It would serve as a test as to whether or not Inion really *did* like him or not, or if she now preferred Lefi.

Did he want that question answered, though?

Edwin quickly quashed that train of thought before his entire afternoon was ruined productivity-wise. He was *fine* and would remain so.

He still had a few tasks to accomplish before they arrived in the city, after all. He couldn't spend hours moping again! He needed to . . . um . . .

Right! He needed to secure everything on the outside of the cart so it wouldn't be snatched away! Also, he should probably stow away some of his ongoing distillations so they weren't sitting out.

Edwin hopped out and looked at his carriage. Over the months, he'd started growing a few plants along the side—he left the roof clear, given that was where he usually slept—held in apparatite pots, just to try and keep some of his stocks full. He wasn't successful with *every* plant he tried to grow, but he had managed to get molai and firevine with some effort. Sinbalyne grew, but not well. He'd need to figure out what it needed at some point. Anyway, he needed to bring them inside for protection. Oh, he still needed to water them today, didn't he?

Oh! Of course, he should also make sure that . . .

Level Up!
Skill Points 837→885 (Average level: 48)
Adaptive Defense Level 30→32
Alchemical Analysis Level 31→34
Alchemical Dismantling Level 41→42
Alchemy Level 90→91
Anatomy Level 42→43
Arcadian Elixir Level 30→32
Basic Thermokinesis Level 26→28
Bomb Throwing Level 50→51
Flight Level 41→44
Fresh Air Level 33→34
Improbable Arsenal Level 30→33
Longstrider Level 33→35
Mana Infusion Level 87→88
Memory Level 63→64
Numeracy Level 40→42
Outsider's Almanac Level 133→134
Overcharge Level 22→26

Polyglot Level 67→68
Prototyping Level 29→34
Refining Level 32→35
Ritual Intuition Level 28→31
Sapper's Apparatus Level 51→54
Skillful Assessment Level 40→41
Watchful Rest Level 30→31

Name

Edwin Maxlin

Age

1 year

Race

Extraplanar Human

Class

Alchemist-Errant

Attributes

Health 25

Impact 7

Mana 33

Perception 19

Stamina 30

Skills

Alchemical

Alchemy 91, Alchemical Analysis 34, Refining 35, Alchemical
Dismantling 42, Sapper's Apparatus 54
(Purify: 75)

Magical

Basic Thermokinesis 28, Fey's Caress 36, Ritual Intuition 31,
Mana Infusion 88
Flight 44, (Basic Mana Sense: 82), (Basic Mana Manipulation: 9)

Physical

Overcharge 26, Longstrider 35, Fresh Air 34
(Athletics: 81), (Breathing: 76), (Flexibility: 74), (Nutrition:
73), (Packing: 92), (Seeing: 72), (Sleeping: 73), (Survival: 76),
(Walking: 74)

Mental

Numeracy 42, Prototyping 34, Anatomy 43, Polyglot: 68,
Memory 64
(Language: 36), (Mathematics: 74), (Research: 50), (Visualization:
80)

Combat

Bomb Throwing 51, Adaptive Defense 32
(Throwing Weapons: 48)

Utility

Outsider's Almanac 134, Watchful Rest 31, Skillful Assessment
41, Arcadian Elixir 32, Improbable Arsenal 33
(Firestarting: 94), (Improvisation: 14), (Status: 22), (Identify: 80),
(First Aid: 82), (Harvesting: 76), (Construction: 77)

Paths

Skill Points: 885

Combat

Assassin 0/60, Bomber 0/60, Giant Slayer 0/60, Heedless Hunter
0/60, Hunter 0/30, Killer 0/30, Titan Slayer 0/90, Warrior 0/60,
Way of the Empty Hand 0/60, Trapper 0/60

Alchemy

Alchemical Medic 0/60, Demolitionist 0/60, Makeshift Alchemist
0/60, Potioneer 0/60, Practical Alchemist 0/60, Mystic Alchemist
0/90

Science

Chemist 0/60, Experimenter 0/60, Researcher 0/60, Purifier 0/30,
Scientific Revolutionary 0/90, Scientist 0/60, Engineer 0/60,
Physicist 0/60, Mathematician 0/60, Material Scientist 0/60

Magic

Aerialist 0/60, Fey Friend 0/60, Feybound 0/60, Feycaller 0/60,
Mage 0/60, Magical Gardener 0/60, Micro-Biomancer 0/90,
Primal Constructor 0/90, Primal Ritualist 0/90, Realm Traveler
0/120, Skilled Arcanist 0/60, Fey Supplicant 0/60, Feykind 0/90,
Attuner 0/30

Mental

Dedicated Student 0/60, Lecturer 0/30, Scholar 0/60, Unbowed
0/90, Canny 0/60, Steady Mind 0/60, Mentalist 0/60

System

Almanac Administrator 0/60, Forerunner 0/60, Outsider's Almanac Specialist 0/90, Pioneer 0/60, Skill Researcher 0/60, System Scholar 0/60

Trophy

Blackstone Conqueror 0/60, Deepwoods Panther-Hunter 0/60, Stonehide Vanquisher 0/60, Titan Spider Hunter 0/60

Career

Brickmaker 0/30, Butcher 0/30, Diver 0/30, Gardener 0/30, Lumberjack 0/60, Merchant 0/30, Potter 0/30, Scribe 0/30, Woodsman 0/30

Physical

Ascetic 0/60, Daredevil 0/60, Physical Alchemist 0/90, Survivor 0/60, Physical Laborer 0/30

Traveling

Escapee 0/30, Exile 0/30, Traveler 0/30, World Traveler 0/60

Medical

Field Medic 0/60, Medic 0/30, Steadfast Medic 0/60, Medical Lecturer 0/60

Misc

Arsonist 0/60, Autopyromaniac 0/60, Burglar 0/60, Child 0/12, Expert 0/60, Imperial Ally 0/60, Novice 0/12, Pyromaniac 0/30, Razer of the Ruined Tower 0/60, Rebel 0/30, Slave 0/12, Trainee 0/60, Traitor 0/60, Brushed by Power 0/60, Lirasian Citizen 0/30, Royal Adviser 0/60, Favored by Power 0/90, Insomniac 0/30, Sleepless Disciple 0/60

Completed Paths

CharLimitCanttalkmuchNocluewhathappenedDidmybestto helpyouli, Mage, Skilled Arcanist, Physical Alchemist, Bomber, Linguist, Beginner, Warrior, Path Less Traveled, Athlete, Scout, Unkillable, Superior Alchemist, Adventurer, Explorer, Outsider, Skill Researcher, Wanderer, Alchemical Warrior, Novice Pyromancer, Novice Ritualist, Alchemist, Physicist, Engineer, Physical Arcanist, Biologist, Practical Alchemist, Fey Scion, Feytouched

Of Skill and Ink

Rizzali Skyshale could scarcely contain his excitement as Adventurer Edwin stepped out of his office and left his Conspiracy. Time snapped back to its normal pace, and he checked to ensure that none of his charges were waiting for his attention at present before he got too deep into the pile of utter, completely *ludicrous* wealth of information that he'd been provided.

The kid would keep him Bright for at *least* another century, he could tell. Still, it was little consolation when he had to deal with the bane of Registrars everywhere: *paperwork*. As a small measure of comfort, this was the best *kind* of paperwork and he was bound to note something fascinating in the Chronicles while he recorded Edwin's . . . what was it again? Ah yes, managing to take the common Skill of *Packing* and somehow leverage it into a Flight Skill.

Comprehensive Lirasian Registrar Records appeared before Rizzali, the massive sky-blue System list that had overwhelmed him so much back in his youth now so routine. Decades of service had fine-tuned both his skills *and* Skills with organization so what once might have been the work of hours took mere minutes.

He quickly navigated to the "Mage" section, simply checking to see . . .

Ah! It seemed as though Flight (Magical, Tether) *was* a known Skill!

Most curious. It was . . . Ah, of course. Mage Andrikan managed to earn that Skill instead of proper Flying as a fledgling, and he later used it to great effect as he upgraded it to Self Telekinesis, Force Armor, and Ablative Invincibility.

Most curious. Rizzali would have to mention it to Adventurer Edwin should he decide to employ his services as a Registrar and receive Skill advice.

Still, there was no record of the possibility of earning the Skill via Packing, and he added the due notes to both Skills. Given Adventurer Edwin's manner of speaking and odd knowledge regarding the nature of reality, he clearly was no random vagabond whom Lady Tara found. Perhaps he was from Vis'Daric? That did not adequately cover his low tier, however. Perhaps a hidden elf? It would not be the first time, though it would not explain his unusual comprehension of the System and ignorance to many of its foundational aspects.

Clearly, the boy must be an Outsider, he thought as he chuckled to himself.

Ah well, it was no great matter. He would likely piece together what he was missing at some point and determine the truth of the matter. There clearly was some *possible* explanation for the boy's quirks, he simply wasn't clever enough to piece it together from what he knew, and he had work to attend to.

The remainder of Adventurer Edwin's paperwork was noteworthy, but nothing *particularly* unusual once one's expectations were adjusted to a Mage and an Adventurer who preferred *Alchemy* of all things. It was almost a pity that the Adventurer was so prolific with his Paths; he would have loved to see what the "Alchemist-Errant" Path might grant, but similarly it was unlikely to be very long before the Adventurer reached a total of 2,400 Skill Points spent and unlocked it that way.

Come to think of it, he ought to speak with Registrar Seizan, to see if she had any insights from her experiences with mages. He'd visit her later, once he finished this filing. There was so much new information to be included within the Records, after all, and the Archivists required proper paperwork to include it.

Course set, Rizzali wetted his pen and began to write.

* * *

". . . of the night, see my blazing star. You shall see from the coasts of Vorian to the mountains of Tal Vaior those whom I call forth in service. I say unto you that the choices called upon today will be felt throughout history as the day which I placed my talon upon and bent the winds to my will."

"*Espethail*, truly? I was under the impression *Southern Hero* was still regarded as the superior option for Monologue training. Registrar Seizan, Trainee Istiel," Rizzali greeted the orange-haired Registrar and her protégé.

Registrar Seizan turned as Rizzali entered the room, bright green eyes widening as she registered his presence as she nodded. "Registrar Rizzali. Pleasure to see you in-wake. *Southern Hero* is indeed still in favor, but Registrar Sarlial believes that interspersing other performances into the training might yield better results, and Trainee Istiel has a penchant for *Espethail*."

"It's my favorite performance, Registrar," he confirmed.

Ah, the passion of youth. There were so few other gnomes out in Rhothos and those which were present were not assigned to him. The boy's emerald skin veritably glowed with enthusiasm.

"Most fascinating! Do let me know of your findings. What was your Plot?"

"Ah, well you see, one smith in the outer city I know has managed to use Greater Detailed Goldsmithing to make these *really tiny* steel stars . . ."

It was one of the great secrets of the Registrars, both the existence of and method of obtaining the Monologue and Conspiracy Skills. The former was particularly devious, as in order to earn the Scheming Vizier Path, one had to successfully plot the assassination of their governmental superior. Fortunately, one didn't have to *carry out* said plan, but the System was very particular in deciding what counted as successful enough to count. Conspire was relatively straightforward to earn in comparison, as Hidden Conspirator was earned simply as part of Registrar training. When precisely was variable, but it was apparently inevitable.

Of course, the two Skills were *immensely* valuable to the point of replacing the usually indispensable Polyglot. Monologue set the user in an odd state that slowed the passage of time, but it could only be used while speaking. Conspire then allowed one to include additional individuals in the effect, allowing even a full day in some cases to take mere minutes in reality and was one of the four pillars of the Registrar Class.

It also allowed Registrars to speak with one another for truly lengthy periods of time while simultaneously not wasting so much as a second, a fact they took hearty advantage of now that Trainee Istiel would be included.

"I cannot imagine this is purely a social visit?" Registrar Seizan eventually asked.

"It is not," Rizzali explained. "I had a visit from one of my charges this morning, a Mage Adventurer, and was hoping to discuss with you some of his options."

"Ah! Would this be Adventurer Edwin?"

"Indeed."

"What sorts of magic has he expressed?"

"That is part of what I wished to speak to you about. While he professes a desire to be more of an alchemist, he has magic ranging from the more pedestrian—he has a Heat Object variant, Basic Thermokinesis—to a Skill that empowers his body. He even managed to obtain Flight," Rizzali continued, explaining the peculiarities of Edwin's collection of magical Skills.

"I'm not sure how much help I will be," Seizan apologized. "The majority of my Mage experience is with Nature Mages, and they usually have if not *consistency*—"

Rizzali held back a laugh. Expecting consistency in a mage's build was pure folly. Much of the time, even theoretically replicable Skills reused to work for others following the same methodology.

"—They at least have similar expressions of their mana and I'm more familiar with that."

"I see. Well, I still have some questions that I hope to pass along."

"Go right ahead."

The visit to Registrar Seizan took scarcely a quarter of an hour in real time, and Rizzali returned to his office immediately after, which made it all the more surprising that he had someone awaiting his return.

"Ah! I apologize for the wait, Healer Firais. How might I be able to help you today?"

The avior inclined his head in respect as Rizzali took his seat. "Registrar. I would simply like to upgrade my Set Bone Skill, as it reached its threshold."

"Marvelous! Good job. I hope your patients were left healthy?"

"They were, Registrar."

"Excellent, excellent. Let me check . . . ah yes, just to confirm, you already have Greater Medicine upgraded?"

"It has been upgraded to Physician's Poultice, yes."

"Marvelous. And Set Bone is at least level thirty?"

"It is at level thirty-one, Registrar."

"Marvelous, marvelous. If you could put your points into Medic, we can get this dealt with."

Even most Registrars didn't have true access to the Status of others, so the questions were alas necessary. In theory one could lie about their Status, yes, but he and his peers were well versed in finding out such deception and quashing it ruthlessly.

Status Registration popped up off to the side of his vision.

**Lirasian Crashland Healer Firais Luftfugl would like to upgrade
Set Bone to Mend Wing.
Allow Upgrade? Y/N**

Rizzali mentally assented and felt the change manifest in his charge. "Congratulations, Healer Firais. I'm certain it comes just in time?"

"It does indeed."

"Marvelous. Was there anything else?"

"I would like to put in a request to earn the Dexterity Attribute, Registrar."

"Oh? And why would you like the Attribute?"

"I believe the Attribute would help me perform more delicate procedures. Deft Touch seems insufficient much of the time."

"Very well, one moment."

Rizzali sank deep into Comprehensive Lirasian Registrar Records, searching for potential conflicts the Attribute might have with other

Paths. It wasn't a terribly challenging search, and one type that he had extensive experience in, and so came back to himself within just a few minutes.

"I see no reason to deny your request, though you will have to wait to complete the Path until after you upgrade Healing Rest into Full Recovery. If you do not, there is a chance it would attempt to upgrade into Hospice Bed instead. Come with an extra sixty Skill Points after that point and I will approve the Artisan Path. I advise speaking with a Crafter you know for an appropriate project for you, but the things to make note of is that it ought to challenge your capabilities and be personal to you, something you truly enjoy and can delight in."

"Thank you, Registrar."

"You are welcome. Was that all for today?"

The avior nodded, and Rizzali gave him a smile. "Marvelous. I hope to see you again soon, yes?"

Healer Firais departed shortly thereafter, flapping his wings and taking off to the roof, and Rizzali returned to his paperwork. There was always paperwork to be done.

He was nearly done for the night, finishing up a draft for the ongoing Alchemist restructure now that he had a bit more information from Edwin, when a *presence* pressed down on the entire structure. Rizzali squeaked slightly. What was *Emperor Xares* doing here, and why was he upset? He could barely breathe under the intense pressure, but it left as quickly as it had arrived.

Rizzali picked himself off the ground where he had fallen, trying to catch his breath. That must have scared a good *year* off him, though he felt he'd sooner lose the year than experience that again.

Well, no matter, at least he was gone now, and Rizzali had a meeting to attend.

Outsiders to the Lirasian Empire were frequently surprised to learn that the heart of the entire Empire's success, Management, was attended to entirely by gnomish Registrars. They always expected it to be the avior themselves, fed lies by their enemies that Management was a method by which their "tyrannical emperor" kept his populace weak and harmless, forbidden from taking any Skills or Paths that might empower them. Those who promptly discovered that there were scarcely *any* avior Registrars frequently didn't know how to respond, and always made for the most *delightful* stories.

It still left a simple question, though. *Why gnomes?* Certainly, while frequently employed as paper workers, there was very little that Rizzali's kind had which obviously made them inherently good at administrative and guidance work. What was so special about them that *every single* Registrar from the last two and a half centuries had been brightskin?

The answer was simple. Gnomes could *dream*. Not the pitiful, inconsequential dreams of the feathered and dull-skinned, but true, *proper* Dreams.

Most importantly, they were the only species that could directly upgrade Dreaming into Dream Council, and they were accordingly able to keep in constant communication about their shared passion. The meetings rarely included *every single* Registrar in the Empire, but it was still an incredibly efficient way to communicate Registrar-only information faster than even the swiftest courier. It was the only way by which they could reliably keep the majority "in the know" for the latest developments and respond to new findings without needing to physically congregate in one location.

The Council which Rizzali joined that night was one he'd attended many, many times before. He was indirectly responsible for it, after all, and it was likely to continue many years into the future.

"No, we *cannot* remove Herbalism! We've been over this before!"

While finding a Tier 2 variant of Alchemy was potentially *revolutionary*, the fact that Edwin's method of obtaining the Skill was through Improvisation and Physical Alchemist, neither of which were a part of the current Alchemist Class, meant the Council would need to determine which of the six Alchemist Skills—Reading, Writing, Herbalism, Mixing, Measure, and Process—should be removed in favor of adding Improvisation, and then what should be done about the leftover Eating Skill.

"But look here! Farmer Xoracil, given provisional permission to upgrade Hardy Crop with Herbal Gardener. He *got Herbalism*. It's what we've been looking for!"

"No, it's *not*. Poultice and Potency are far too important."

"I still think we can replace Reading with Improvisation. I'm aware of the importance that Scribe plays in establishing the Class, but I believe there is untapped potential in 'Flavor Profile.'"

Unless the speaker made certain to show their identity, such information was indistinct at best given the number of participants and average level of Dream Council present. It wasn't especially important, however, not for this kind of discussion.

"No, Flavor Profile was a one-off incident, which we believe was influenced by the presence of Perception or the Exploratory Academic Class. We've found the more common result is Detailed Appetite. Besides, Mental Notebook is *far* too important for capturing all the procedural details of formulas that Mixing doesn't record."

Rizzali idly wondered what Adventurer Edwin's mysterious note-taking Skill was, and if it filled a similar role for him. Considering how expensive it had been, the results must surely have been impressive, if impractical for common usage.

"Yes, but I believe we can find a variant of Steady Hand that would function similarly if we exchange Marksman for. . . ."

"Attention, Alchemy Restructuring Council," a new voice spoke, this one *decidedly* identifiable as Administrator Fitzgilleth. "Point of order if you please. Tonight's search list includes a Sapphire-specialist Goldsmith near Kazath, an Elder-specialist Medic near Sheraith, and we're still looking for a Deepwater Diver for Taher Sirandar. There has also been a new development in the Human Lirasian Farmer of Plentiful Harvests, namely a reliable way to obtain its Class Path and use it to grant the Fertile Footsteps Skill. Details have already been added to the Records, and best of luck to you all."

Then Administrator Fitzgilleth was gone, off to the next Council to deliver the important news of tonight.

Conversations sprang up again immediately. A few had gotten slightly sidetracked about the Fertile Footsteps, but the majority returned to where they had been.

"Yes, but even with the loss of the steady-hand effect there, we can offset that by including Artisan just before the Artist Path, which shouldn't influence the Class overmuch and allow the additional Attribute Points to accumulate over a significant amount of time."

"You expect them to have an extra *sixty points* in the midst of Tier 1? When we're discussing adding in the Physical Alchemist Path? You're babbling."

"I do hate to intrude," Rizzali interjected, making his identity known, "but today I learned of another early access Skill, namely Alchemical Dismantling, from the combination of Harvesting and Alchemical Warrior."

"Alchemical Warrior? Hmm, that *would* significantly streamline the Alchemic Assistant Class if replicable."

"A *Warrior* Path? For Alchemical Dismantling? How is that considered Warrior-like?"

"Perhaps it is something of a Hunter Skill? Akin to how Harvesting upgrades to Dismantling with the Hunter Path?"

"Yes, but what of . . ."

They came to no conclusion that night, not that anyone expected them to.

ABOUT THE AUTHOR
=====

Kaleb England, also known as NorskDaedalus, is an author who loves to integrate magic and science to tell interesting stories. England holds a bachelor's degree in physics.

www.ingramcontent.com/pod-product-compliance
Lightning Source LLC
Chambersburg PA
CBHW021809110726

47902CB00006B/1713